Turning on one hip, I looked up at him through my voluptuous tangle of hair and smiled in outright invitation. At least I hoped I had. It had been a long time since I'd smiled invitingly at a man. Maybe I wasn't doing it right. A host of expressions chased across his face, but that was the extent of his reactions.

"Why are you wasting time, Nathaniel?" I murmured with all the come-hither I could recall.

"Damn!" he muttered, giving me a baffled look. His hand rambled through his hair. "Look, honey, maybe I'm dense about this, but why don't you spell it out for me?"

I bit my lip. None of my fantasies had contained that particular sentence. "Well, I'm trying to seduce you, but I must be doing it all wrong, because it doesn't appear to be working," I confessed wryly.

"Oh, it's working," he said with a dry laugh.

"Oh, good," I said, enormously relieved. Without thinking I reached up to touch his hair. He looked at me with a question in his eyes and amusement on his lips.

"Look, bear with me, will you? I mean, this is, ah, quite unusual."

"It's really quite simple," I said impatiently, for who knew how long this dream would last? "I want you to make love to me."

LOST IN MY DREAMS

FAYE ASHLEY

St. Martin's Paperbacks

LOST IN MY DREAMS

Copyright © 1996 by Faye Ashley.

ISBN: 0-312-95691-6

Printed in the United States of America

St. Martin's Paperbacks edition/January 1996.

10 9 8 7 6 5 4 3 2 1

To my critique group:

Rita Gallagher
Diane Levitt
Rita Clay Estrada

with loving appreciation for their help and support.

Chapter 1

Something touched me. Its presence invaded my sleep with a sweet familiarity that was totally alien to time and place. The strange, deep warmth that cocooned me was out of place, too. No one held me like this anymore. . . .

I came awake with a jolt, my eyes opening to confirm what I already knew. Nothing had touched me. I was alone in this big bed.

But *something* had roused me to goose-pimply wakefulness. Sitting up, I gazed around the bedroom, feeling groggy and confused and decidedly unfriendly toward whatever had disturbed my slumber. Sunlight and shadow, a ticking clock, the discreet sparkle of a silver unicorn and chain draped around the bedpost. All perfectly normal. Growing impatient, I stirred, then froze to the spot, half up, half down, listening. Tiny chills spidered across my shoulders as I realized what had nudged me awake.

It was that sound again.

A gossamer pulse of sound, the faintest *whisper* of a sound, like the soft sigh of a wind rippling through a distant meadow, or the gentle swish of waves breaking on a sugar-sand shore.

But Houston didn't have an ocean and I was nowhere near a meadow. I was huddled in bed clutching a goosedown comforter to my breasts while I tried to convince myself I'd heard nothing.

The wind's whispers grew more urgent with each

passing second. I could have sworn I heard a word in those kitten-soft murmurs. My name.

"Don't be ridiculous, Roseanna," I admonished myself, and immediately felt ridiculous. Furiously I kicked off the hampering covers and sat up. This was the third morning straight I had been awakened in this maddening way and I didn't much like being roused from sleep by a weird sound that refused to identify itself. Nevertheless, I found myself listening so intensely my ears popped.

And the sound responded, now rising, now falling, like a long exhalation, like a feathery coaxing.

Unnerved despite my anger, I got up to search the bedroom. I'd done this before, but in cursory manner. This time, I probed the entire area; behind the antique, full-length mirror in its beautiful rosewood frame, around the pale blue miniblinds and snowy muslin drapes, through the flower-bedecked sitting area, looking for a plugged duct, a half-opened air vent, anything that made noises. Even the dressing alcove came under scrutiny. Nothing. At least nothing that could be explained. The sound was nowhere and everywhere, soft, insinuating, here, but never *here.*

It could be imagination. Or it could be coming from outside my windows.

But it wasn't. The sound was coming from inside my bedroom, and there was nothing in my bedroom to make that sound.

Which left imagination.

Since I had a very active one, I decided to settle for that. But it was damned aggravating. It was also a little frightening, that the sound never came when my husband was here to hear it with me. Or not hear it with me, which, either way, would settle the taunting puzzle. David's pragmatic, attorney's mind would not permit otherwise.

"Imagination," I insisted, and drew on my robe as if to cinch the fact. I glanced in the mirror and wondered, momentarily, who that middle-aged matron was and what the mirror had done with that spritely young Roseanna it once reflected back at me. With a spritely but smelly oath I began searching for my slippers. They were under the pile of manuscript pages I'd been editing last night.

I walked from the bedroom with mind and spirit still entangled in the strangeness of my mood, which left my feet free to go where they pleased. Bypassing the staircase, they led me down the hall to the robin's-egg–blue door of what had once been a nursery.

We have a locked room in our house. That sounds melodramatic even to me, but in fact it's painful truth. David locked it right after the funeral of our infant son, locked it with a savagery I didn't dare question. Back then, sudden infant death syndrome was a tainted verdict, one that could crucify a mother with its brutal mystery; a beautiful, normal, perfectly healthy baby suddenly, causelessly dead.

If I try hard enough, I can still hear David's savage weeping coming from the closed nursery. I should have gone to him that day, tried to share our devastating grief. But the sounds he made were so shocking, I didn't know what to do. So I did nothing, just retreated into my own bitter anguish.

Even after ten years it still hurt to remember. I had been thirty-seven then, absolutely blissed out from having finally fulfilled my destiny and delivered a robust child, a son and heir for David and a grandson for Mother. . . .

"Well, so much for destiny," I said, shrugging. Now, as then, it's either wall it up, shrug it off, and get on with it, or fragment like bits of dried leaves ground underfoot. We Bently women don't fragment, we persevere, goddamnit!

I turned the doorknob and the door opened, as of course it would after all this time. The locked room now existed only in my mind. Several years ago David had combined the three rooms at this end of the hall into an office suite complete with bedroom and bath. He often slept here when he worked late. Or just felt like sleeping alone.

I have no surviving children. But David has a daughter from his first marriage. Alexis, or Lexi, as I call her, is twenty-nine now, a slim, lovely, feminine version of David. But she was only five when I first saw her, a thin, pigtailed, sober little girl with huge, needful dark eyes. I loved her from the moment she put her arms around my neck and asked, "Are you going to be my new mommy?" And I'd laughed and said, "Yes I am, but don't tell your daddy. He doesn't know it yet!"

Lexi has followed in her father's footsteps and is a brilliant young attorney. Both have fine, analytical minds that hum along on some rarefied plane well over my head.

An urge to relieve myself put an end to my reverie. I used his bathroom, then followed the luscious smell of coffee downstairs to the kitchen. David makes a pot every morning and leaves it hot for me. It's black and bitter and over-perked, but his coffee does grab you by the throat and shake you awake.

Topping off my cup, I wandered into the den, relishing the feel of plush carpet under my bare feet until my heel came down on a sticky, crunchy something. We'd had a twenty-bore party last night and I shuddered as I looked around the sleek, contemporary, black-gray-and-white room. It was David's decor, not mine; David's political friends, not mine. One had ground out a cigarette in the pretty china seashell that had held canapes. Another lipstick-smeared butt raped a bowl of clam dip. Topping off the litter were pages of the *Wall Street Journal* spilling around David's chair like giant confetti.

Grimacing at the mess, I made a half-assed attempt to begin the cleanup, but soon realized I wasn't up to it yet. After draining the coffeepot, I drooped my way through the dining room to the French doors that lead to the terrace, and stepped out into spring's gentle morning.

Lilting birdsong; melting-butter sunshine on the old red brick that floored the terrace. My every breath was sweetened by the perfume of a nearby jasmine vine. I felt a savage urge to grab a butcher knife and hack the damned thing down.

Tears welled up and suddenly I was crying, crying for something that had no name. I just felt raw with need, and what the hell did I need? I had everything in the world a woman could possibly want, didn't I? Husband, child, home, money, position, a fair chance of going to heaven when I died. Maître d's called me by name, I could read about myself in the society columns in case I forgot what affair I'd attended last, and there was a good possibility I would be mistress of the governor's mansion before I hit sixty.

"What else is there, Roseanna?" I hissed, frustrated by my lack of answers.

After sloshing coffee over a maliciously smiling pansy, I went back inside. Carasel, my miniature schnauzer, came yawning from her little wicker basket and greeted me with a high-pitched explosion of love, more sound than action since she's become a senior citizen. I ran to the kitchen for a tangerine and we sat on the carpet and ate it in companionable sharing.

Gathering up the peels, I drooped back through the kitchen. There was a green worm humping along my windowsill. I couldn't bear it. After doing my best to redirect its progress, I went upstairs to dress.

Absurdly wary, I hesitated at the bedroom door. My quickened breath was the only sound. Exhaling a rich mixture of relief and exasperation, I sauntered on to the bathroom.

The sink area was rich with David's smell and I lingered a moment. Even after twenty-five years of marriage, that dusky scent could still arouse me.

"Oh, Roseanna, a chocolate-chip cookie could arouse you," I sniffed, making a face at my big-eyed image.

A peculiarly horny wench, David once called me. Back in the good old days when we still engaged in such libidinous behavior, I thought with what even I recognized as valiant—if exceedingly wry—humor. It is my lifeline in all kinds of seas.

David is almost devoid of humor, which aids immensely in making us total opposites. He can be warm and charming; he can be so cold and forbidding he chills my blood. I'm whimsical, romantic, optimistic, and quick to forgive. He's methodical, organized, and so undeviating in a goal once decided that Gibraltar wobbles in comparison. And forgiveness is to be earned, absolutely.

He is also a bit of a snob, one who drinks Perrier with a twist and likes it. I love beer and cheap rum and find nothing wrong with screw-top wines. Only God knows what drew him to me; certainly David doesn't, I thought, sans humor.

But his attraction for me was obvious enough. To twenty-two-year-old Roseanna Bently, David Hadley Tait, Jr., was Prince Charming in the flesh. Tall, dark, and handsome, of course, but also intelligent. And an older man, to boot; a widower with a poor little waif-daughter who desperately needed a mother. If that weren't enough to enthrall me, he also oozed the kind of absolute self-confidence that acts like a magnet to someone who moves through life with all the control of a leaf in a high wind.

Depression clawed at me. I was hungry for something, and I didn't know what that something was. A trip to the moon, perhaps. Or maybe just a bouquet of tulips, a promise of passion, a simple "I love you" given with bursting-out-surprised spontaneity.

On the rare occasions David did utter those words, he would say it the way he'd shove back from the table and state, "That was a very good dinner, Roseanna. I commend you."

I would have been a lot more thrilled with: "That was a crummy dinner, Roseanna; let's go upstairs and fuck."

I laughed aloud at the thought of David actually saying something like that. David is not given to such impetuosity. He can't even say the word "passion" without a wry twist of mouth.

The novels I write twist his mouth, too. So I write under a pen name to spare him embarrassment.

Well, perhaps my literary spasms do merit concealment, I reflected, stepping into the shower's soft rain. They are erotic fantasies straight from the mind of a lichen-covered housewife, one whose own fires burn at fever pitch a lot of the time . . . most of the time, come to think of it.

Reminding myself that household chores took precedence over writing, I covered my short frame with a T-shirt, jeans, and Reeboks, and went downstairs to the grim job of cleaning the den.

I have always loathed housework. It's a total waste of time—houses just get dirty again. When, at three o'clock, Viveca Valante breezed in like a reprieve from Heaven, I greeted her with an exuberant hug. I love Viveca. We've been best friends for more years than either of us care to count.

Poppy-red nails waving a gay dismissal to my offer of freshly made coffee, Viveca veered toward the elegant little bar in our den and searched out a bottle of David's best brandy.

"So, how was last night's party?" she asked, dashing some liquor into a Waterford snifter.

"Interminable as cancer and about as jolly. Why brandy at three in the afternoon?"

"I've been screwing around with fourteen prima donnas this entire morning. I've earned this brandy." Looking so fresh and pretty that I experienced a sphincter spasm of envy, Viveca sank into a chair and took a lusty drink. She's forty-six, divorced, currently directing a community theater melodrama that will doubtless be a comical disaster. All her others have been.

I joined her at the table with my cup of black coffee. "Did you get anything settled?"

She gave me a marvelously disgusted look. "Are you kidding? Listen, let's talk about sex or clothes or miracle diets—anything but that friggin' play! How's your book coming? Still blocked?"

"Dead in the water. Damned thing just *sits* there, won't go forward or backward," I replied, both annoyed and wistful.

I stiffened as a man's face suddenly flashed through my mind. All I really caught was a pair of green eyes, green as new grass, sparkling with amusement, looking straight into mine!

I bolted upright. "My God, Viv!"

"What?" she asked, baffled by my screech.

What, indeed? "Oh, I was just-just visualizing my

hero's eyes. You know, they're green, and . . . well, they just seemed so *real* for a moment."

Ignoring my elaborate shrug, she turned those X-ray eyes upon my warming face and waited. Defeated, I burst out, "But they aren't real in the manuscript, they're cardboard, and so is he! So is she, for that matter. I'm already on Chapter 3 and my main characters won't even *talk* to each other! They just stand around like paper dolls, or, at best, like puppets waiting for their strings to be pulled—and it's driving me crazy!"

The lift of one perfectly arched brow acknowledged my vehemence. "Rosie, for heaven's sake, you've had blocks before. Why is this one so different?"

"Because . . . oh, it just is, that's why," I said snappishly. "God, I hate deadlines and multiple-book contracts! Why did I ever sign that thing, anyway?" My dramatic sigh foundered upon the reefs of her knowing smile. This book would fulfill my present contract, and I was already worrying about my next one.

"Let's talk about something else," I muttered, mauling my hair. "Let's talk about something else—anything but that damn book!"

Laughing, she agreed, and we spent the next hour or so discussing sex, clothes, and whether or not there was a snowball's chance in hell my husband would let me go on a month-long cruise with Viveca. At this point we ran out of topics and wound down to a companionable silence.

Viveca propped her chin on her hand and gazed at some inner vision. I considered telling her of the mysterious sounds in my bedroom but decided against it. Instead I pondered my strange mood some more. Though quiet and introspective at the moment, something simmered beneath the overlay of contentment like steam seeking a vent. When Viveca rose to pour another brandy, I snapped, "Viv, you're drinking too much."

"Oh, now, Rosie. If David starts bitching about his cognac I'll buy him a bottle, okay?"

"That isn't what I meant and you know it."

"Well, I agree, but this is all until tonight. Can I get you something while I'm up?"

"Yeah. Kevin Costner. I'll share with you."

"Honey, we're far too old for ole Kevin," she drawled. Viveca is that rarity of rarities, a native Texan. Her soft, melodic voice and that easy drawl combine to produce delightful sounds.

"Too old for Kevin, too young for Medicare," I muttered.

She chuckled. "Yeah, just like being thirteen again." Ignoring my expressive look, she sat down and defiantly took a sip of brandy. "I hate to tell you this, but there's a green worm on your windowsill."

"Oh, hell, I know it. But I don't know what to do about it. I put down some paper, but it refused to use it."

"You're trying to housebreak a worm?"

"Oh, don't be silly, Viv! I wanted the worm to crawl onto the paper, then I could put it outside where it belongs. Little bastard just turns around and goes the other way," I accused.

Viveca didn't comment. We sat watching it for awhile. Two grown women, enrapt in a green worm that moved along by grotesque humping. It seemed discomfittingly symbolic of something.

But hazy afternoons in April are such insidious things. They strip away protective cynicism, dissolve layer after layer of painfully acquired shellac, and leave you as vulnerable as a soft-shelled crab. The breeze blowing in the open French doors came straight off a sun-drenched tropical isle, soft, erotic, tawny-skinned, reaching deep down and triggering unfamiliar memories.

In actual fact, that breeze is probably blowing straight off the Houston ship channel, but my life is structured on interlocking fantasies, and my mind readily supplied the missing ingredients. I crossed my legs in a tight squeeze. All the misty yearnings my island breeze evoked had funneled directly into the furry triangle between my thighs, which had not had any other kind of funneling lately. That could be why I'm so restless my skin feels too tight.

Or perhaps I'm just run-down, I thought limply.

Maybe I need a spring tonic, something like that ghastly concoction Mother forced down my defenseless throat when I was a pale, weedy child. Maybe my inner malaise has nothing to do with the fact that David never grabs my ass anymore and forgets for weeks at a time that I have other uses besides hostessing his parties.

Carasel was lying under my feet. I dug my toes into her silky fur and gave a long sigh.

"I should be going," Viveca said without conviction.

"Why? What do you have to do that's so important?"

She shook her head with a rueful smile. "Not a bloody thing. By the way, I have a haha message for you."

"A haha message?"

"Yes, you know, when someone says something dead serious, but they don't want you to take them seriously, so they end it with a haha. It's from Colin the Hunk. The message is, quote: He thinks you're a smoldering volcano. His exact words," she said, frowning at my choked laugh.

"A smoldering volcano?"

"Yes, well, remember this is Colin," she reminded. "And if you ever get the urge to screw around, he wouldn't mind trying to light your fires, so to speak."

"You're kidding!" I said, coming alive with a snap.

"Did you hear a haha?"

"But why would Colin want to sleep with me?" I asked more or less sincerely.

"Well, hell, why does Colin want to sleep with me?" she retorted, not at all happy with her question.

It was a good one, as good as mine, even. Colin is a six-foot chunk of stunningly sexy man, golden hair, golden body, a male fashion model, and randy as a billy goat. On a scale of one to ten, he's a solid eight, possibly a nine, if you don't mind arrested mental development.

Viveca minds, but she does what most women do: takes the best you can get of what's available and makes do with it. Colin is twenty-some years younger than she, which makes for some snide comments.

"You didn't answer my question," she reminded me dryly.

I looked at her appraisingly. Viveca is class with a capital C. She has lustrous auburn hair and the long, willowy body that dress designers have in mind when they sit down at the drawing board. Her face is lovely, with patrician features. She even has cheekbones. I suppose the tiny brown spots on the backs of her slender hands could pass as freckles. But the lines around her eyes and mouth betray her age.

My silence was overlong, perhaps. "Thanks a lot," she muttered.

"Oh, Viv, stop it! You know you're gorgeous. Anyone can see what Colin wants. But what makes you think he wasn't joking—about me, I mean?"

"He wasn't joking," she said flatly.

I wished to hell it didn't feel so good. "Oh, Viv, really!" I laughed.

"What's so blasted funny, Roseanna? You're not exactly a dried up old bag, you know."

"No, just a well-worn Goldie Hawn," I murmured.

Viv peered at me. "Not so worn. Besides, Colin prefers older women. We're so sensual, you know, so eager to please. I think the sweet little beast has a mother complex," she said flippantly.

The amber eyes watching me were so vulnerable that I was forced to swallow before speaking. "I very much doubt that Colin is attracted to your motherly qualities," I said lightly.

"Jack says it's my money," she agreed, only half joking. Jack was her ex-husband.

"Oh shit, Viv. You don't have that kind of money, and, besides, Jack has already proven himself a menopausal idiot. Why listen to what he says?"

"Force of habit, I guess, and the fact that I'm not exactly stupid," she said very softly.

I got up and went to the coffeepot, stalling for time to assimilate and respond. Viveca was wearing her abandoned-waif look again, and I find it terribly hard on my heart. For twenty-some years she'd been married to a chubby little ass who, notwithstanding his Pillsbury Doughboy look, had managed to get himself a piece of young fluff and rubbed Viveca's face in it.

Incensed at such injustice (she had never, ever,
screwed around during those interminable twenty-some
years), Viveca had hired a razor-edged lawyer and
stripped the bastard of a helluva lot—including his manhood, apparently. Whenever he was in his cups, Jack
referred to his ex-wife as "that castrating bitch."

Viveca was secretly devastated by her altered lifestyle.
A year spent on an analyst's couch had helped. But she
had only come out of her tailspin when Colin what's-his-
name latched onto her and offered his shoulder to cry
on.

When he offered her something besides his shoulder,
she took it. It went against all her middle-class mores,
but at least she knew she was still a woman, and God
bless Colin for that.

I blew a sigh into the silence. In a couple of hours
David would be coming in the door, calling my name as
he always does, rushing through his shower and urging
me to hurry up for God's sake and get ready or we'd be
late for that goddamned banquet.

Personally I hate goddamn banquets, but we went to
an awful lot of them. Tonight our table would host the
senior members of the Jacobs, Tait, Rogers and Rogers
law firm, which should enshroud our group with all the
fun and hilarity of the morgue.

As I glanced at Viveca, I noted the sag of chin and
jowls when she lowered her head. Her hand flew defen-
sively to her neck. "I'm thinking of getting a face lift,"
she blurted.

I was stunned. I get stunned, shocked, appalled, dismayed, all quite easily. Of course I knew about face lifts,
but people in our set did not go in for such, just like we
didn't go in for wife swapping or overt bed-hopping. I've
always had a yen to, if not actually participate in an
orgy, at least witness one. But David would hyperventi-
late at the thought. I get my excitement vicariously, and
most of it from Viv's hissing new sex life.

"So have a face-lift," I snapped, deeply desirous of
her happiness. Envious, too. She didn't have to attend a
banquet tonight. Or sleep alone, either.

The telephone rang. It was my stepdaughter, Lexi.

David comes from an enviously solid background. His family is jelled into the very rocks of Connecticut, old, stainless-steel–spined, Yankee Clipper–ship-type people whose terse speech and piercing gaze strips a person right down to bedrock. After my initiation into the barnacle-covered lap of his family, I came home with my quivering bedrock hanging in tatters. And Lexi, I reflected as I listened to her questions, has a helluva lot of her paternal grandmother in her.

While I described my attire tonight—my black Chanel and the family pearls—Viveca finished her drink and stood up.

"Must go, honey," she whispered, mouthing a kiss.

Gucci handbag in place, she shook back her chin-length hair and glided out of my kitchen. Such a smooth, oily glide, I thought resentfully, watching her svelte hips undulating out the door. Viveca is a very feminine woman. You'd never catch her in a pair of ass-splaying jeans like I have on. And she's never in her life had to diet. Sometimes that does tax a friendship.

"Lexi, darlin', I promise not to do anything scandalous tonight. In fact, I promise to do your daddy proud—if you'll just stop haranguing me and let me get started," I caroled.

I heard her sweet, husky laugh. "Sorry. Guess I'm just naturally pushy. Genetics, no doubt!"

"No doubt. See you tonight, love." I rang off and raced upstairs to bathe and dress.

While the tub filled, I studied my nude image. The mirror confirmed my suspicions. I was small, reasonably slim, a little saggy in the ass, the breasts, the chin. A poochy tummy, but otherwise well preserved. Attractive, I thought sadly. Beautiful would have been nice. Wildly, gloriously, ravishingly sexy would have been even better. I unpinned my hair and watched it slither down my shoulders. It was the same soft, red-gold color I'd been born with and would continue to have until the day I died. David had said he loved my hair, so I kept it long, though now, scrutinizing myself in the mirror, I was keenly aware that this tawny lioness mane did not go with a subtly aging face.

David is tall and distinguished-looking, courtesy of a rigid athletic program and the fact that men age so damn beautifully. The lines on his face bespoke maturity. Mine bespoke woman getting on up in years.

Suddenly outraged at this injustice, I flung myself into the hot and steamy water. I finished my bath with a quick, icy spray from the shower massage and tried to ignore the fact that I was decidedly horny. David says only men get horny. David knows about as much about women as a hen knows about eggs. Respectively speaking, they both lay them, but they don't know exactly how.

That's not to say that David is ignorant in the woman-pleasing department. He can be a delectable lover when he wants. Frequency is the problem, at least for me. Because for me sex is right up there at the top of the list of deliciously fun things to do, second only to a full box of Godiva chocolates.

The cold shower had revived me somewhat. Deciding to air-dry myself, I went to the huge, walk-in closet that is mine alone.

As I reached for the light switch, a faint breeze brushed my damp body. I stood stock-still for an instant while another spidery shiver crawled over me. "Oh, for God's sake, Roseanna!" I muttered aloud. This was going from the absurd to the asinine.

Willfully disdaining the sensation of moving air, I took down the simple black frock and placed it on the bed. The telephone rang. It was David.

"Hi, hon," I chirped. "I'm getting ready."

"Well, I just thought I'd remind you," he said testily. "I'm running late, so you be out of the way when I get home."

"I will, I promise." I pictured him sitting at his big mahogany desk, crisply pleated gray trousers molding his firm thighs and the tantalizing lump between them, ice-blue shirt with the sleeves rolled up, that fine, silky dark hair rumpled by a strong and restless hand. "Ah darlin', I wish you were here right now," I added with cheerful lust. "I'm sitting on the bed naked." My inviting pause went unanswered. "And there's a humping green worm on the kitchen windowsill."

"Christ, Roseanna, I'm strung out over seven counties and you're prattling about humping green worms!"

I shot to my feet, ready to fight. "Well, it's there, dammit! And I'm not about to touch it—it's slimy!"

"All *right*, Roseanna, I'll take care of your worm when I get home. Just don't make us late." He hung up.

My throat knotted as I slammed down the receiver. A soft despair engulfed me, giving rise to a sudden desperate need to be held. Since there were no other arms available, I hugged myself. Questions seeped in like water through a widening breach. Was I, as Viveca once gently suggested, trying too hard to convince myself I was happy? How long could I continue shoveling sand into this deepening void in my heart and soul?

And why did I always have to get so damned *weepy!* I blew my nose and reminded myself that my period was due at any time, a dandy excuse for my emotional confusion. Just feminine weakness, I told myself with bitter-tinged humor, something easily sluffed off if one just *applied* oneself.

Carasel was scratching at the door. When I let her in, she leaped upon me with hysterical cries of joy. At least I was perfect in someone's eyes. After hugging her, I walked back to my dressing table and misted myself with perfume, sprayed my armpits with deodorant, and went to my jewelry cabinet to accessorize the vaunted Tait pearls. My bath had mellowed me. Impulsively I took a long, heavy gold chain and fastened it around my waist. Not bad, I thought, admiring the whimsical effect in the mirror. I left it there and returned to the closet for an evening bag. The one I wanted, a simple black clutch, was missing from the shelf.

"Oh, shoot!" I said aloud, which brought Carasel on the run. Fending her off, I ran a hand along the top. Nothing but dust. The tall, narrow set of shelves had been built into the far corner of the closet. For some reason never explained to me, the carpenter had left a space between it and the adjoining wall.

This space was just big enough for me to slide into if I

chose. Meanwhile it held two plastic garment bags containing evening wraps. Thinking the purse had fallen to the floor, I knelt to search the carpet. Nothing but more dust. Maybe it was caught between the wall and the back corner. Rising, I pulled aside the garment bags and tried to get in there, but they were too bulky. I took the smallest one off the rod and tucked it under my arm, then inched into the space.

Carasel promptly wedged herself between my ankles and tugged at the garment bag. Laughing at her antics, I stepped back a little more. My foot caught in the slippery plastic and I tripped over my other one.

And lurched backwards.

And kept on going.

There was no time to react; it was instantaneous, and yet it took forever. I was in freefall, tangled up with Carasel and the garment bag, fully expecting the wall to slam up against my back and stop me. Startled, aware of a wrongness—and *still falling backwards.*

My elbow struck the shelf. The resulting pain was a split second of normalcy. But it was lost in whirling confusion.

There was no wall behind me.

I was falling through space. Black space, shot through with laser streaks of light. Light seen not by my eyes but with some inner part of me.

I heard Carasel's cry. I heard my own. The flimsy garment bag was still in my arms and I clutched it desperately, falling . . . falling . . . thinking, *Oh God, God!*

And then I landed—somewhere.

Chapter 2

$\mathcal{I}$ was lying on my back at the edge of a meadow.

Naked, breathless from it all, a green plastic garment bag billowing up in little hills and valleys on my belly.

At the edge of a meadow under a deep blue sky studded with snowy puffs of cloud. "Jesus!" I whispered, awe-stricken.

Convulsively I gulped air. It was clean and fresh and honeysuckle-sweet. Grass tickled my bare skin and a pebble dug into my left buttock. I heard before I saw the bumblebee that settled fussily on a nearby daisy.

Everything *felt* very real.

I closed my eyes and opened them again. Everything certainly *looked* real.

One more thing appeared to be terribly real—I was stark, raving mad.

Should I be scared? I wondered. Terrified, even? I thought so. But I wasn't.

When a wet nose nudged into the hollow of my neck and shoulder, I did scream. Carasel's liquid black eyes were round with amazement, both at the scream and at our current situation.

"Where the hell are we?" those eyes asked.

"God, I don't know, Carasel," I whispered.

I bit back the hysterical laughter that battered my teeth. Not only had I gone crazy, I'd taken my little dog with me.

The garment bag was sweaty on my skin. It was warm

here, wherever *here* was. Setting the bag aside, I rolled onto one hip and looked around.

The vista stretching before me was too lovely to be real. Which it wasn't, of course, I reminded my mad self. The meadow flowed gently downhill, its lush grasses strewn with daisies and primroses. Off to the left was a little copse of trees with round, silvery leaves rippling in the wind. Beeches?

Although I could not see it, I heard the soft babble of running water. As I twisted to look uphill, the breath whistled through my teeth. In the distance, towering mountains, their snow-covered peaks glistening in the sunlight, reached up to touch an indigo sky.

Tall, dark pine trees stood like ancient sentinels on a far hill. The gleam of a lake was barely discernible through the fringe of trees beyond my feet. I felt I was in the middle of the huge landscape that once graced Mother's den.

Something had escaped me. My mind had caught it, though my eyes had not. Carasel nudged it through just because she was so solidly real. Yes, now I saw it; like the familiar electric towers of Earth, steel giants strode across the low hills just above the meadow.

I was on Earth? Well, of course I was! Where else would I be?

Carasel gave a quick, shrill bark. Her head left the sanctuary of my shoulder and her tail wagged in that way that says, Something approaches and I may or may not attack. Although I tensed, I wasn't really alarmed. She reacts like this to anything—a worm, a leaf, the postman. But I did take a swift look around.

Seeing nothing untoward, I relaxed and continued my visual exploration. Just to my left was an enormous gray boulder, a beautiful thing with glints of crystal glittering like diamonds in the sun. In a deep cleft grew a wild blue columbine with one lovely blossom and many tight buds.

Carasel gave another warning bark, then pranced off to investigate the tantalizing holes at its base. What had she barked at, a vicious butterfly? I could see nothing that should not be here. Except me.

It was so quiet. I heard birdsong of course, and the wind blowing through the daisies. But no cars, no people, no airplanes growling overhead. I did see what looked to be a disintegrating jet streak, but it could have been just a cloud.

This was such a pretty place I'd dropped into. It was far too peaceful to pose a danger to me.

Carefully, rather curiously, I examined myself, first physically—not a single bruise—and then emotionally. It was amazing how I felt, unafraid, undisturbed; quite good, actually, considering that I had merely stepped into my closet to find a purse and fell into a flowery field in the wilds of God-only-knew-where. What now? I wondered. Surely whatever had brought me here had a reason for doing so. I waited expectantly, feeling a sense of childish anticipation.

After a few uneventful moments, I propped up on an elbow and watched Carasel's enthusiastic digging. I simply could not think of anything else to do. I wasn't about to get up and investigate the boundaries of my madness. To move from this spot seemed pure folly.

Dirt sprayed my arm. Scowling at my energetic little dog, I scooted out of range and resumed my lack of constructive thinking. Idly I scratched an itch on one rosy-nippled breast. Ah, Lord, I sighed, David would be home at any minute, rushing in the door and calling for his wife. And where was the little wifey? Lying naked in the grass marveling at how good she felt. Crazy as a loon. Why didn't I feel more dismayed?

"Carasel, we have to do something," I said, just to show I was aware of the oddity of my present state of existence. Where was I? How did I get here? And why *wasn't* I scared? What I felt was akin to that euphoric state reached only after consuming half a dozen Margaritas. Or good sex.

I stretched with voluptuous, sun-warmed pleasure. My body felt wonderful, lithe and taut, muscles supple as velvet. When the glint of gold caught my eye, I realized I still wore the chain now twined around my hips. Thinking back to when I'd placed it there, I heaved another sigh. It seemed ages ago.

Drifting on this time-out-of-time, I picked a daisy and stuck it behind my ear. The primroses smelled faintly sweet. I tucked one in my pubic hair and another between my breasts. "Crazy, Roseanna," I reminded, and felt a twinge of sorrow that I was.

Carasel's head shot out of the hole. Stiff-legged, she began barking. An ant attack? A sweeping glance around the immediate vicinity revealed nothing to warrant her excitement. I lay back and closed my eyes. The riotous wag of tail indicated that she had liked whatever the hell it was, thus I was safe. Then again, I thought dreamily, she would probably love bears.

"Well, hello there," a warm, husky male voice said.

My eyes flew open in incredulous wonder. Merciful heaven, I *had* gone mad, but what a madness it was! The man towering over me was absolutely fabulous, a bacchanal of masculinity. Six-foot-two, I estimated. Lean of hip and broad of shoulder. His green eyes were framed by indecently long, thick lashes. Deep, tongue-teasing dimples adorned each side of that amused, lusty, be-still-my-heart grin. He had an arrogant, high-bridged nose, a sexy mouth that looked chiseled by a sculptor's blade, as well as an unruly thatch of chestnut brown hair with a sly lock falling over his brow.

Search though I did, I could find no flaw in his strong features. He was, I decided, the secret male fantasy who lives in our eternally virginal hearts. Dangerous. Virile. Laughing, teasing, tender, passionate—perfection.

Of course he was. I had created him. He sprang full-fleshed from page six of the book I was working on.

It was astonishing—*I* was astonished, but I felt no anxiety or unease. This didn't seem quite right. Forcing myself to face facts, I outlined them in rapid sequence. I had fallen in my closet and landed in a meadow; I was nude, with a primrose stuck in my pubic hair and a gold chain draped across my middle; a character from my book had come to life and was standing over me, real, animated, speaking. Carasel had her head buried in a hole again, digging with lunatic enthusiasm. And I felt wonderful.

Incredible!

Not only that, but all of this seemed sublimely natural. I had felt more discomfort meeting that humping green worm on my windowsill this morning.

My hero's hair was slightly damp, and beads of sweat glistened on the springy curls nuzzling through his open collar. The faded jeans and blue chambray shirt he wore might have come from Sears. His brown leather sandals looked expensively comfortable on his feet—which were clean, I noted approvingly. I would never create a hero with dirty feet.

Pushing back that lock of hair, he eyed me with a quizzical grin and one arched eyebrow. "Sorry, I didn't mean to startle you," he said when it became obvious that I had been rendered mute.

Still wide-eyed and mouth agape, I stared at him. How on earth did he arch just one eyebrow? I had read of it but never seen it. And what was I to do about this new complication to an already complicated day?

The answer came swiftly, and it was so simple I laughed aloud. I was dreaming. Yes, I was caught in the middle of one of my fantasies, asleep, in bed right now, with David beside me. Any minute I'd hear him start snoring, which he does whenever he turns onto his back.

For just a second more, I grappled with my irrational logic. What if it wasn't a dream?

Oh, of course it was a dream! What else could it be? Blissfully relieved, I smiled at this dream man. Lying back slowly, I felt my hair spreading over the grass like molten gold. "Hello," I said, low, throaty, and rather belatedly.

As his gaze flickered over me, I felt no modesty, no prudish urge to cover myself. Until I remembered my stretch marks. You can't go through three pregnancies and not have stretch marks. They were ugly things, little spiderwebby white lines that crisscrossed my belly and thighs. Raising my head, I glanced down to see what he was seeing. An instant later I sat up and stared at myself in rapturous disbelief. Smooth ivory skin, kissed with gold and only slightly rounded: my twenty-year-old belly! Bewildered, but in the best way possible, I examined my legs. No cellulite, no marring lines, just slender, silky-skinned thighs.

Of course! I of-coursed again. Did I think my marvelous mind would send me into a fantasy all wrinkled and flabby? I looked up at him. He was plainly baffled by my presence. That made two of us, I thought with a lilting little laugh. That eyebrow slanted again.

"You want to tell me your name? And just why you're lying here in my meadow?" he asked in a lazy drawl.

"Am I not welcome in your meadow?"

He threw back his head and laughed just the way I liked it, rich and dark and husky. "Well, hell yes, you're welcome in my meadow! But it isn't every day a man finds a lovely little nymph naked in the grass . . . makes a man wonder, you know?"

"I know," I said. "It makes me wonder, too."

That induced another virtuoso performance from that frisky eyebrow. "I see. Are you from around here, or have you just dropped from the sky?"

"Yes," I answered the latter part of his question.

"Uh huh. Do you have a name, pretty lady?"

"Woman, thy name is Vanity," I murmured, deliciously buoyed by his flattery. When he just stood there giving me a perturbed look, I frowned. My fantasies are always swift and to the point. I wanted sex—and he was certainly ready, I thought, glancing at the front of his jeans.

His gaze followed mine and another grin curved his mouth.

"A dead giveaway, every time," he cheerfully acknowledged.

He was certainly blasé about this. Not at all abashed by his erection, either. "Um hum, man's insurmountable problem. What do you have in there?" I asked, eyeing the big orange thermos he carried.

"Lemonade. Would you like some?"

"I'd love some! Thank you!"

"My pleasure, ma'am."

I felt the most incredible thrill as I watched his big, capable hands unscrew the cap. He filled the cup and handed it to me, studiously keeping his eyes on my face.

As the tart, icy liquid laved my throat, it occurred to me I had now done something decidedly physical for a dream.

The tiny sliver of doubt was instantly vanquished. Greedily I emptied the cup. "Thank you, that was very good. But it needs more sugar."

"I'll try to remember that next time." He stood up and recapped the thermos. "You do this often, do you?"

"Do what often?"

"Lie around in the grass without any clothes on." With remarkable sangfroid, he sat down beside me.

"Oh. Well, no, not often," I said faintly. I plucked at the chain. "Anyway, I'm not exactly nude. This counts for something, doesn't it?"

"Very little." Superbly at ease, he plucked a grass blade and nibbled it. "You didn't tell me your name."

Carasel exploded into our midst, dashing back and forth, ecstatically licking his face, then mine, in lavish love.

"Hello, what's this?" he exclaimed. "Hey there, little one, where'd *you* come from?" Laughing, he ducked her kisses while gathering up the delighted little dog.

Well, damn, Carasel!

"This is Carasel," I said. "Carasel, meet Nathaniel."

He stared at me, eyes narrowing. "How do you know my name?"

Oops! "I'm a nymph, dropped from the sky, remember?"

He put Carasel down and she headed back to her crater at the base of the boulder. "How do you know my name?" he repeated quietly.

"I-I've heard of you. My name is Roseanna," I offered.

"Roseanna. That's beautiful. It fits you. But no one calls me Nathaniel. Around here I'm known as Nate."

"You will always be Nathaniel to me," I said dreamily. "I know all about you, Nathaniel Knight. You're twenty-nine and you have a big ranch nearby. You keep a dusky-skinned mistress in town and you have a kid sister named Tara—"

"Wrong!" he said, chuckling.

"I am? What part am I wrong about?"

"Everything. I don't have a ranch or a kid sister. Or even a dusky-skinned mistress, for that matter."

"Well, darn, you're supposed to." Confusion nibbled at my pretty dream. Those green eyes riveted me to the spot. "Uh, I guess my crystal ball got cloudy," I said lamely.

"I guess it did." His dry response made me wiggle. He grinned a mischievous grin. "I do like your flower vase. A decided improvement over a jelly jar . . . or even fine crystal."

I blushed all over as I followed his gaze to the primrose decorating my mons. "Oh well, that."

"Uh huh, that," he murmured.

Twinkling green eyes danced with mine. "It wilts quickly, though," I said, and gave him the limp flower as evidence. As I glanced down the long expanse of lean, hard male, I was suddenly reminded of what I wanted from this dream.

Turning on one hip, I looked up at him through my voluptuous tangle of hair and smiled in outright invitation. At least I hoped I had. It had been a long time since I'd smiled invitingly at a man. Maybe I wasn't doing it right. A host of expressions chased across his face, but that was the extent of his reaction.

"Why are you wasting time, Nathaniel?" I murmured with all the come-hither I could recall.

"Damn!" he muttered, giving me another baffled look. His hand rambled through his hair. "Look, honey, maybe I'm dense about this, but why don't you spell it out for me?"

I bit my lip. None of my fantasies had contained that particular sentence. "Well, I'm trying to seduce you, but I must be doing it all wrong, because it doesn't appear to be working," I confessed wryly.

"Oh, it's working," he said with a dry laugh.

"Oh, good," I said, enormously relieved. Without thinking I reached up to touch his hair. He looked at me with a question in his eyes and amusement on his lips.

"Look, bear with me, will you? I mean, this is, ah, quite unusual."

"It's really quite simple," I said impatiently, for who knew how long this dream would last? "I want you to make love to me."

"Just like that?"

"Just like that." I nibbled my lip some more. "Unless I don't appeal to you?"

"You're very lovely and very appealing," he said huskily.

"Really? I am?"

"Yes, really. But I . . ."

"Don't want to make love." I stated. I felt wretched all of a sudden. My heart actually hurt at his rejection.

"Roseanna, it's not a question of wanting, it's . . ." His hands rose in a charmingly helpless gesture. "Don't you think we ought to get to know each other first?" His tone went dust-dry as I shook my head. "Nothing profound, just full names and perhaps dates of birth."

"No, there isn't time. It's now or never, Nathaniel," I warned him. "Why does it bother you, anyway?"

"Blast if I know," he admitted. Those marvelous green eyes looked at Carasel, scanned the meadow, and finally came to rest on the chain laying saucily around my hips. "Are you all alone?" he asked abruptly.

"All alone."

"And you want me to make love to you."

"If you would," I said with genuine diffidence. This certainly wasn't one of my more romantic fantasies.

He laughed, but I caught the subtle edge to it. "Glad to oblige, ma'am."

I was chewing on my lip again, a sure sign of mass confusion and doubt, but he didn't notice. His gaze was moving boldly down my body. A hardness had invaded his features. Methodically he took off his shirt and tossed it aside, removed his watch, laid it on the shirt. "Not only a naked nymph but a horny nymph," he murmured.

I blinked. The men in my books never describe their women as horny.

Noting my reaction, Nathaniel's face softened, and the faint gleam of disdain vanished from his eyes.

"Sorry, honey." He touched my nipple with a fingertip. "So pretty! For God's sake, who are you?"

Who was I, anyway? A middle-aged hausfrau, I thought hazily. No, I corrected, a young, lovely, ready to be, about to be, well-loved nymph. That sounded so much better. "I am Roseanna," I whispered. Without further ado, I slid my hands into his hair and drew his mouth to mine.

Lovely. Purely lovely. His mouth grew hungry as my fingers roamed his smooth back. Smooth as satin, I thought. I kissed him and kept on kissing him. He was delicious.

With a groan, he drew away. "Let me take off my pants."

I was all for that. Watching as he stripped off his jeans, I felt my throat tighten unmercifully. He was magnificent.

"You don't wear underwear?" I asked.

"Ordinarily, yes, but I've been swimming in the lake." His eyes crinkled. "Do you? Wear underwear, I mean."

"Well, certainly I do!" I said so indignantly—and so incongruously given my present state of dress—that even I had to laugh. "Do you like to make love?"

"I admit it ranks among my greatest pleasures."

"Do you do it often?"

He just grinned and knelt beside me again. I had to touch him. His quick breath was honeyed pleasure. I pressed my lips to the dimple in his cheek. "That's a lovely place to kiss." I sighed.

"Mmmm." His dark head leaned to my breasts and I shivered all over. Strange things were happening to me. Inside, I mean. Heartstrings I didn't know I had were pulling me to him in a wild, sweet rage of yearning. He kissed me and I was filled with all the delirious confusion of first love.

He touched and stroked and caressed and tasted. I clung to him with abandon, adrift and rudderless on a gorgeously rough sea.

Pleasure swiftly turned to single-minded passion. His long body covered mine exactly as it should. He was so excited that I feared he would quickly end it. But he pushed into me, slow and easy. Then he lowered his face in my hair and lay very still.

I could feel him throbbing inside me, filling empty spaces I didn't know were empty. It was a glorious sensation, and surprisingly new to me, given my age and experience. But surely I had never felt like this before! Delighted and a little awed, I whispered, "This is wonderful! Thank you."

"Oh, God," he said, and buried his face in my hair. His shoulders shook. I just held him until it passed. "You smell so good," he muttered.

"So do you. Oh, I do like this!" I exulted.

He raised his face and laughed softly. "Do you!" He took quick, sipping kisses that peeled several more years off my psyche. I was drowning in the emerald depths of his eyes. "I am in imminent danger of drowning in your eyes," I warned.

"And I am in imminent danger of going off like a rocket."

"Yes, one little wiggle and I'm lost." I sighed.

"Oh, yes."

He traced the outline of my mouth with his tongue, an inexpressibly tender caress. Shocked, I realized that we were making love with the sweet intimacy of lovers rather than total strangers. But we weren't strangers, I thought dazedly. We had known each other since the dawn of time . . . loved like this before . . . kissed and whispered and touched like this before. . . .

"My darling Nathaniel," I whispered, and meant it.

Nathaniel groaned and began moving in a way that spun my head. I was so intensely aroused that the thought of being left unfulfilled was unbearable.

"Please, don't leave me behind when you come," I half moaned.

"Ah, no. No, little one, I won't leave you wanting." He kissed my neck, then sank his teeth into it. I was absolutely compelled to arch my hips and drive him deep inside me. He groaned again. I laughed with sheer exultance.

And then he took me.

Filling me, splitting me, plunging, withdrawing, plung-

ing in again. He was killing me with rapture, kissing me
with his mouth locked on mine and it was good—oh,
goodness gracious, it was good! A frothy, tumultuous,
expanding coil of excitement hit my loins, spreading out
and rolling in undulating waves, ricocheting from vaginal peak to vaginal peak and ravishing the valleys. He
convulsed against me and the world turned inside out.

A luminous eternity later, I turned my face to the one
nuzzled into my neck. He smelled so good, sweaty,
musky, spicy, grassy, a combination any cosmetic firm
would pay a fortune for. His cheek was salty under my
lips. I licked it like a kitten lapping cream. I kissed his
hair, analyzing: crisp, silky, clean. I kissed his shoulders
with ferocious pleasure, absolutely glorying in the taste
and smell of the man.

Wrapping him in my arms, I closed my eyes. I now
had three options, I mused. Insanity, slumber, or Paradise.

He raised his head and smiled at me. "My little
nymph, you are very good loving," he murmured. I wriggled like a puppy who's been patted on the head.

"Do you think I'm crazy?" I asked languidly.

"I think we're both a little crazy," he replied ruefully.

He kissed me. It went on and on in a soft frenzy of
affection, and I was starved for it. "Again?" I said on his
mouth.

"Yes, again," he whispered.

His eyes were brilliant, a succulent apple green, with
little flashes of gold flaring in the depths. I wondered
how many other women had been laid by the power of
those eyes.

His mouth pressed hard on mine, and I forgot to wonder.

"Roseanna. Who are you? Where do you come from?"

The low, half-whisper stirred my hair. We were still
entwined, our heartbeats calming and our breaths easing, welded together by a thin film of perspiration. I
glanced over his shoulder and saw Carasel snug in her
freshly dug hole. Beside me lay the garment bag, a
plastic shroud blowing in the wind.

That wind sounded familiar. But I was feeling too blissful to bestir myself. There was a worm crawling up the stem of a daisy and I remembered the one that had been on my windowsill this morning. . . .

"Roseanna?"

"Oh! Oh, Nathaniel, who knows who I am? Perhaps I'm Venus, come down from—from wherever the gods dwell these days. Then again, I may be an angel. Do angels make love?" I asked seriously. The possibility was there. Who knows what happens when you die? Especially someone who has lived as virtuous a life as I have.

He laughed. "I doubt you're an angel, honey. This is much too substantial." Turning onto his side, he tipped up my chin. He has beautiful hands, does my Nathaniel.

"Now, tell me who you are and why you're here in my meadow."

"I—I live—that is, I'm staying with friends," I floundered.

"What friends? I haven't seen you around here. Believe me, I would have noticed."

"Just down the hill a ways," I said nervously.

"Where down the hill . . . the lake? Are you part of that artist colony by the lake?" he asked, frowning.

"Yes! Yes I am! But I'm not an artist, I'm a writer."

He was getting angry at my evasiveness. I chomped down on my bottom lip.

"That explains why you lie around naked in the grass and screw whoever comes along, hum?" Nathaniel drawled.

It hurt. And it made me mad. "I do not screw whoever—you're the second man I've ever made love with," I sputtered.

"Who was the first?"

"I—my lover—we were in love . . ." Oh Lord, I was getting in deeper and deeper.

"Then why did you make love with me?" he asked quietly, his eyes intense.

"Because I—because . . ." I shut my eyes.

"Yes, because?"

"Dammit, Nathaniel, what are you, a member of the

Spanish Inquisition?" I exploded. "Why is this so important?"

"I don't know why it's important, but it is. Why did you make love with me, a total stranger?"

"But you're not a total stranger," I rebutted with what seemed like logic.

"Yes, I am. Now why?"

I smiled. "Because it was so very right," I said softly.

Giving me a peculiar look, he picked up my hand to kiss my fingertips. It was my left hand, a decided jolt. The third finger was bare, however. I had taken off my rings before creaming my face and had not put them on again.

"Nathaniel, let's not talk anymore right now? Just lay your head here and let me hold you for awhile."

Acquiescing, for which I was immensely grateful, he nestled his cheek into my breasts. I put my arms around him and permitted myself another small increment of bliss.

I lost track of time. Through half-closed eyes I watched a lavender butterfly settling on a primrose. It seemed so fitting. This pastoral scene; man, woman, meadow, flowers, butterfly—the garden of Eden.

The original Garden, I suddenly remembered, had a serpent.

"Nathaniel, are there any snakes around here?"

"Lord, I hope not," he growled. "I'm too weak to swat a fly."

The hand on my hip stilled and we drifted into a soft drowse. Time unrolled so slowly that I could almost see the seconds falling into minutes, like drops of rain on the surface of a pond. Somewhere, I thought drowsily, there is another garden in the backyard of a big two-story house in a place called Houston. A Roseanna dwells there, too, but in another time, another world. . . .

"What are you thinking about?" he asked idly.

"About nothing. About everything. Now hush, you're breaking the mood," I chided. A soft laugh was my reward.

We floated along on currents of rekindling excitement. At first we did nothing too intense, just nibbled and kissed and touched a bit. My nipples were arousing to heated buds under his ministrations, and warmth furrowed downward from those two points. Playfully amorous, we just kind of tumbled into the most bewitching fun possible.

Enchanted, I bent my head and kissed his hair. How well I knew this man I held so sweetly. Perhaps that was the key, I *knew* him. Had he been a stranger, I would never have behaved so shamelessly. In fact, had a strange man happened upon me in my present state of being, I would have scrambled to my feet and tried to spread my two hands over three strategic spots, shrieking like an outraged virgin.

But this man had lived with me for weeks now. Like all my characters, he had slowly gained substance until at last I'd formed a real person, one so familiar that I knew how he would react in any situation.

Yet it was different with this one, I remembered, chilling as I recalled the inexplicable writer's block that had stalled my progress.

Well, he's come alive, I exulted. I tightened my embrace and floated on my velvety cloud. There was no past, no future. All I cared about right now was this infinitely sweet present. . . .

When I opened my eyes again, I was totally disoriented for a frightening instant. A twist of my head brought me into contact with emerald green eyes and I realized that I had fallen asleep! This was another finger pointing at lunacy; how could any sane woman fall asleep under such extraordinary circumstances? And yet, it seemed the most natural thing in the world for Nathaniel to be here beside me and Carasel asleep at the foot of an ancient gray boulder. Natural and wonderful, I thought serenely.

Then I noticed the long shadows striping my meadow. The mountain peaks were no longer pink, but a deep, hazy purple, steaked with hot orange. Suddenly gripped with unease, I wondered what time it was.

Nathaniel was watching me. I formed a smile. "Hello," I said. "I guess I fell asleep."

"I guess you did." He kissed me, and nuzzled my neck. Carasel got up and shook herself, then wandered over and flopped down in the crook of my arm.

"Nathaniel, I have to be going, it's so late. . . ." I trailed off. How was I going? How did one get out of a dream? I should have awakened from this one hours ago. Hours ago? How long had I been here—and *where*, my Creator, was *here*?

"What time is it?" I asked worriedly.

He picked up his watch. "Five-thirty."

Well, that was helpful, I thought irritably. It was five-thirty here, but what time was it at home? Oh, this is silly, Roseanna, I chided silently. You are at home, in bed. . . . Wasn't I asleep in bed? Unease became anxiety.

"I've got to get home! Really I do, Nathaniel! Ouch, Carasel! You scratched me! Nathaniel. . . ."

"Relax, honey, it's only fifteen minutes to the lake."

That did nothing to reassure me. I was struck with a dreadful suspicion that things were going to get sticky in a very short time.

Nathaniel had a small scar high on his cheekbone. Had I written a scar there? I touched my lips to it and he hugged me.

"Hey, I have a marvelous idea!" he said. "Why don't we go to my place and find something to eat? Or if you want, there's a barbecue and dance in town." He wrapped a strand of hair around his fingers and ran it slowly across his mouth. "You've got lovely hair, Roseanna. Well, what do say, pretty lady? You don't really have to go home, do you?"

That smile lit his face as he coaxed. My heart did an odd little flip and settled into a new rhythm. I wished I could go to that dance with him, but of course I couldn't. Not even a Roseanna fantasy lasted that long.

"Yes, I do have to go home. But thank you for the invitation. It sounds like such fun," I said as wistfully as I felt.

"Ah, honey, it would be fun. If you don't feel in the

mood for dancing, I'll fix some steaks. I'm a damn fine cook, if I do say so myself." He grinned wickedly. "You could even come as you are. I wouldn't mind!"

I would only give one of my fingers to go with him. "Now stop that. I'm a terribly weak woman and you're tempting me beyond endurance. I absolutely must go home now."

"All right, get dressed and I'll walk you home then," he replied with flattering reluctance.

Getting to his feet, he pulled on his jeans, while I lay there bedeviled by searing questions. Get dressed? In what? Walk me home? How could he walk me home? "Oh God," I beseeched. Nathaniel was the most solid-looking figment of imagination I'd ever seen.

He was reaching for his shirt when the garment bag billowed up on a puff of wind. As he straightened, I could actually see the question form in his mind.

"Where are your clothes?"

"I—uh, in that bag."

"In that bag," he repeated slowly.

I chewed my lip.

He shrugged on his shirt, then reached for the bag. When he ripped off the plastic and took out a thigh-length evening cape, it was all I could do to keep from giggling at his expression. The garment was burgundy velvet, lined with hot pink satin, with two black frog closings at the throat. My giggles were insistent. Defeated, I flopped onto my belly, buried my face in my arms, and gave in to a mad outburst of laughter.

"Roseanna," he began, but seemed incapable of continuing.

My laughter increased in pitch. This crazy dream was turning into a situation comedy. I moaned. Carasel moaned. Nathaniel sort of grunted.

"Roseanna, what the hell is this?"

"I—look, Nathaniel, just . . . just go on home, huh? I'll be all right, truly I will."

"No, dammit, I said I'd walk you home and I will. The lake's a good half mile from here."

"Nathaniel, you can't walk me home!" I burbled.

"Roseanna. . . ." His voice cracked right down the middle. "Did you come here like this?"

Oh God! I burrowed deeper into my arms and moaned again. Carasel frolicked around my head, her little red tongue seeking my face. "Carasel!" I groaned.

"Roseanna, get up. This is foolish," Nathaniel said sternly.

I nearly died. He pulled me up and held me erect despite the fact that my legs kept dissolving.

"Oh, Nathaniel!" I chortled. I knew I could not awaken until he left me. How did I know this? "Beats me," I mumbled.

Nathaniel pronounced my name again, shaking me a little.

Wiping my eyes, I said, "Listen, my beautiful man, I do not want you to walk me home. I came here by myself and I shall leave by myself. Now please, just go. Truly, I'll be okay. No, go on now. I want you to."

"Roseanna, I'm not about to walk off and leave you here alone, naked except for this—what is this, anyway?"

"It's an evening wrap," I had difficulty saying. His eyes were so incredulous, I moaned again. I looked up at my tall, green-eyed man, so handsome, so baffled. "Nathaniel, I want you to go," I said absurdly. Why on earth did I want to end this dream? But I knew I did. I was a little afraid of it now. It was too real and he was too wonderful. Already my heart was aching. I would never see him again . . . or would I? Dreams do recur —hadn't I dreamed about that lusty plumber three nights in a row before I stuck him in my last book?

"Don't be ridiculous!" Nathaniel snapped.

For a wild second I thought he was referring to my plumber and I protested, "It's not ridiculous, he was very attract—Oh! Well, I—I'm not being ridiculous, I simply want you to go. In fact, I insist on it." I drew myself up and tried to look imperious as I picked a leaf off my butt. "Now, will you kindly oblige me?"

"Hell, no, I won't oblige you." His voice cracked again. "I can't just walk off and leave you here!"

"You have no choice in the matter," I half-wailed. "Now go! Right now, Nathaniel!"

He stared at me long and hard, then shrugged. "If this isn't the damnedest thing I ever got mixed up in. . . ." He wrapped the cape around my shoulders. "All right, I'll go. I sure as hell don't like it, but if that's what you want, you've got it. But I want to see you again."

"Ohmigod!"

"Tomorrow night? I'll come for you. What cabin?"

"Oh, good grief!"

"Roseanna!"

"Okay, okay!" I cried wildly. "Meet me here—no, in that little grove of trees, tomorrow night at—at seven!"

"In the grove," he repeated to himself. "Roseanna . . . well, you're calling the shots."

His level voice both annoyed and wounded me. "Yes, I am," I said evenly. But then, impetuously, I took the gold chain from my hips and pulled it over his head. That was twelve hundred bucks' worth of chain, but, Cinderella style, I wanted to leave something behind.

"I want to give you this, something to remember me by," I said, admiring the glint of gold against his bronzed chest. "In case I do not pass this way again," I ended simply.

His face was unreadable. I stood on tiptoe and kissed his hard mouth. He did not participate in the kiss, but accepted it with his hands clenching my arms.

"We have a date for tomorrow night, remember?"

"Yes, I remember," I replied gently. At that moment, it was exceedingly difficult to hold tight to the awareness of illusion.

After a little more grumbling, still shaking his head and wearing his mystified look, my Nathaniel left me.

Standing there with my little dog, filled with utterly indescribable feelings, I watched the tall figure striding down the hill. He turned and looked back, and I could see the concern on his face. When he took a step toward me, I shook my head. Mockingly he raised his hand, then disappeared into the trees.

I shivered in the strong breeze. Dusk was coming to

my meadow. The mountains were entirely purple now, their tops hidden by clouds. Birds twittered softly in the grove, and the air was blue perfume. I felt saddened to the point of tears.

But it was only a dream, I reminded myself. A dream such as I had never dreamed before. The flattened patch of grass caught my eye, testimonial to love on a summer afternoon.

I swept this beautiful place a slow, encompassing look, then stepped backwards, still holding onto the wriggling Carasel.

It was not a conscious decision, for my eyes were on the trees that sheltered Nathaniel. I could just see their silvery tops over the boulder.

Blackness suddenly enveloped me. I wasn't expecting it, and yet I *knew* it was coming. Although I was standing up, holding my dog tightly, I was falling again, falling through a star-streaked void.

Then, gently, my bare feet touched the softness of carpet.

Chapter 3

$\mathscr{I}$ was in darkness except for the luminated outline of a door a few feet away. I had left a light on. Why was it dark?

Taking several deep breaths to calm my fluttery anxiety, I released my struggling pet. Carasel promptly began scratching on the door. Encouraged, I opened it, and stumbled from the closet just as my husband walked out of the bathroom.

A green velour towel wrapped David's hips, and he was drying his hair with a blue one. When he looked up and saw me standing there in my cape, his hands froze in midair.

My problems immediately took on a wild, new slant.

"Uh, hi, David," I said.

When I took a step in his direction, my thighs squished so lustily, I was sure he could hear it, and I stopped.

"Roseanna?! What in *hell* . . . where have you been?"

I bristled. How did I know where I'd been? And even if I did know, could I tell him? "Not bloody likely," I muttered, borrowing Viveca's favorite new phrase.

"What? Christ, Roseanna!"

David's voice rose, making me jump. He was angry, and I hate his anger. Ordinarily my insides curl up when he gets angry. But at the moment my insides were remarkably loose. Slipping a hand to each hip, I pointed out, "You're shouting."

"I am not shouting, I'm just . . . I got home half an hour ago and looked all over for you. Goddamn it, you know there's a banquet and it's important!" He stopped to inhale, deeply. "Why are you standing there wearing that ridiculous cape? And your hair . . . all that wild, loose hair. . . ."

He inhaled again and his dark gaze transfixed me like a wide-eyed doe caught in the glare of headlights.

"Roseanna, would you mind telling me where you've been and what you've been doing?" he asked through his teeth.

I quivered. My world was shredding all around me. Was there a remote possibility that I was yet dreaming? David's eyes were dark as night, and that smarted. After all, I was totally innocent. I hadn't asked to get into this delicious mess. I had been thrown into it, literally pitched headlong into the hot middle of it. It wasn't my fault. What was I to do, turn up my saintly nose and say no to that fabulous fun?

"I am waiting," David said.

So am I, I said to me. David's hair is black and fine and well behaved. His face, I noticed, was getting redder. "Oh, David." I sort of sighed, clutching the cape tighter.

"Will you take off that idiotic cape? You look like a mad bullfighter! And where were you? I've asked twice now. Is it necessary to repeat it? All right then, where were you, Roseanna? Why are you naked? And why is Carasel so dirty? Look at my legs!" he exclaimed as the dog rubbed against him.

I looked. His muscular calves had little dabs of soil clinging to the hairs. He brushed at them, and shot an incredulous look at his fingertips before his gaze impaled me again.

"Well, obviously she's been digging," I said.

I was beginning to get incensed—what kind of fantasy was this, anyway? Since when did husbands get in on the tail end and demand explanations? There stood David glaring at me. Do I deserve to be glared at? Hell no, I don't! I am *innocent*, dammit! Suddenly furious, I ripped off my cape and flung it to the floor.

Whatever I meant to do or say next was wiped from my mind by David's lustful expression. He was coming toward me and as he moved aside, I saw myself in the mirror. I gaped, incredulous, utterly bewildered and positively delighted, all at the same time. I was gorgeous! Even during my very young years I had never been this gorgeous. My hair was a riotous tousle, cascading over my shoulders in golden disarray, the sort of effect models strive for, and here I had it naturally! My skin was young, dewy, radiant; my eyes were glowing like blue stars, my lips like crushed cherries. My goodness!

His face intense, his eyes gleaming, David grabbed me and I was shot right back to crazy again. When his penis stabbed my belly, I was rendered incoherent, both in word and thought.

"David, the banquet—we can't!"

We couldn't! I was still wet from Nathaniel, which I absolutely could not be since Nathaniel was only a phantom—oh, help!

"David, listen—"

"Hush, Roseanna," he grated, bringing me against him.

With the movement my thighs squished again in blunt, impossible reminder. Would he realize? Would he be able to tell that I'd been with another man? But there was no other man, I would never betray David!

"Wait, I have to—to go to the bathroom," I said frantically.

"All right, but hurry. We really do have to get to that banquet sometime tonight," he muttered.

Totally overwhelmed, drowning in a mudslide of confusion, I pulled free and lurched to the bathroom. I threw up. Why not? It fit! After cleansing myself as best I could, I flushed the toilet and went to see what awaited me on the other side of the door. Relief swept through me with unsettling force when I saw him clad in boxer shorts and a shirt.

"Get a move on, Roseanna," he said, buttoning his shirt with steady fingers.

"Well, I'm glad to see your momentary weakness has

passed or been conquered or whatever, without trou-
bling you overmuch," I said wryly. "After all, we
wouldn't want to be late for the banquet, would we?"

"No, we wouldn't. You wearing this dress? Good
choice. Now, where were you when I came in?"

"Oh, David," I sighed.

"Oh, Roseanna," he mocked. "So?"

"I was in my closet."

"In your *closet*?"

"Yes, I . . . I was looking for something and I fell
asleep on the carpet," I said, hoping it didn't sound as
stupid to him as it did to me.

"That has to be the most absurd thing I've ever
heard."

True.

"But it's the truth," I said softly, and most sincerely.

It had to be the truth. I wasn't in bed innocently
asleep and dreaming, so obviously I must have fallen
asleep in my closet, because obviously Nathaniel was a
dream, a fantasy, a character in my book.

"Jesus, Rosie, are you getting senile?" David grunted.
He sniffed me. "I do hope you plan on bathing? You
smell like you've been working in the garden all day," he
continued dryly.

David has a fastidious streak in him. He doesn't like
ripe smells. I probably shouldn't, but I do.

"Yes, a quick shower, and I'll get dressed."

"And a shave, too. There's hair under your arms."

"Odorless, and hairless, too," I muttered. "I'd give up
chocolate to see you get a bikini wax, David."

"Very funny, Roseanna." His frown slowly edged into
puzzlement as he stared at me. He came closer, squint-
ing a little. "What *have* you done to yourself? You look
so . . . different."

I scampered for the bathroom.

"Carasel, will you get down?" I heard his exasperated
voice through the door. He chuckled. "Filthy little
beast! How'd you get so dirty, anyway, hmm?"

Limp with relief, I leaned against the door. That he
had accepted my explanation without further conflict

amazed me. Saved by the banquet, I thought with a buzz of hysteria.

And why *was* Carasel so filthy? Because she had been digging herself a hole in some never-neverland and wallowing in the dirt, that's why. "Lord, Lord," I whimpered. At that moment I was the most confused person on the face of this earth or any other that might or might not exist.

I took a sponge bath, scraped off offending hairs, draped my body in silky black Chanel, stuck my feet into Ferragamos, and tamed my wild mane. My skin still glowed. My eyes sparkled. A bit of powder and lipstick, and we were off to the banquet.

As I expected, and hoped otherwise, our guests included David's two senior partners, two colorless, twitchy little men smelling vaguely of musty closet and virulent Brut. Privately I called them Tweedledum and Tweedledee, Dum being the bald one and Dee the one with a frizzy halo. The banquet was in honor of the mayor for some reason or another. David was a familiar of both the mayor and the city's movers and shakers; he fully intended to occupy that office himself in the next election.

I glanced around the room, spotted Lexi and blew her a kiss before returning my attention to my own table. Beside David sat an odd-looking female with black-and-white–striped hair, and perfectly square shoulders. Vanessa, Tweedledum's wife. Or maybe Tweedledee's, who knew?

She toasted David's assured political future.

I proposed a toast to love. David looked startled and embarrassed. Withdrawing from him, a very large part of my mind went off to delve through the hours I'd spent with Nathaniel. Such a fabulous fantasy, too delicious and yummy for real life. It had felt so good. . . .

When the odd-looking female asked how I was enjoying the banquet, I shoved my wayward thoughts back down, but they just popped up on the other side of my mind. Nathaniel's chest was so beautiful, I thought dreamily. My fingers tingled as they, too, remembered that chest. Dark hair curling crisply at his throat, an uneven sward down the center of his chest, tapering to a thin line down his belly, blossoming out again into a tantalizing jungle in which grew one, magnificent tree. I shivered.

"It's a lovely banquet," I told what's-her-name.

I felt absolutely marvelous. Sort of floaty, like I had been dipped in rapture and now glowed fluorescent from head to toe, I thought, wishing I could indulge in a lissome cat-stretch. David's pleasing laugh suddenly struck a peculiar chord inside me. I turned to look at him, *really* look at him, as if forming my first impression of a stranger. It was a good first impression, and I gave him a flirtatious little smile that only reaped another startled frown. So I had another peach brandy.

Exhaustion set in to further blur my perception. Still, I must have gone through the evening without too many gaffes; David wasn't jumping down my throat.

When we arrived home, I stumbled upstairs, let my dress fall to the floor and crawled into bed.

Instant oblivion. Thank God.

The next morning, sounds drifting up the stairwell roused me to fuzzy awareness. Stretching, I looked around the spacious room with its filmy draperies, ivory blinds and carpet. The walls were delft blue because that's my favorite color. I had always adored this private haven, but now, lying in bed watching lemony streaks of sunshine striping the floor, I felt alien to my surroundings.

I turned on my side and hooked my fingers onto the golden bamboo headboard. We had lived in this house for twenty years. We had reared a child, fought, loved, laughed, and cried within these hallowed walls. Why, then, was I filled with faint foreboding?

Because my mind was leaking cold little streams of dismay.

Because of what waits in my closet.

Nothing waits in that closet, I told myself firmly. But my mind still leaked its tarry streams.

I found myself listening with electric intensity. Nothing. No wind, no mysterious sounds. Releasing the breath I'd been holding, I sealed the leaks and refused to think with that area of my mind.

Denial was vitally important. Without it, I'd fly apart.

At least I felt as though I would. Actually, I have no idea how strong I am. But neither do I care to find out.

It was Mims the maid I heard downstairs. David had left for work hours ago. Mims is our weekly, a frightening woman who intimidates me. It was she who decided whether or not I would hire her. Sighing, I got my nude self up and plodded to the bathroom.

The mirror both shocked and reassured me. The face looking back at me was every bit its true age. Sleep-wrinkled and droopy, with little canals carved into its cheeks by the pillow, fine lines very in evidence. Raccoon eyes and smeared lipstick. My hair was a ragmop mess that would be a bitch to comb.

Slathering on cleansing cream, I began my familiar morning routine. My mind, I discovered, resembled an overflowing trash can, littered with thoughts and likely an unsightly mess, if one could but see it. As soon as an empty space occurred, I thrust another thought into it, because I did not dare permit the dangerous ones to surface.

Brushing my teeth, I thought of a dozen different things, yet that one shining spot at the back of my mind glowed like a speck of stardust fallen to earth. I flossed absentmindedly, then wandered back to the bed and sat down and gave a long sigh.

The wall directly opposite me was a collage of family portraits and pictures. David's, I thought, was faintly accusing this morning. Had I never noticed before that he has on his stern counselor's face? He gazed at me with an arrogant lift of chin, prideful, all of a piece. The truth is, David could function perfectly well without me, while I've always feared that I'd be utterly lost without him. This was very wounding when I first became aware of it. But after all these years, the intolerable had become acceptable.

I meant it when I told him I loved him. I did, and always would, love the beautiful young Adonis I had met by running my car into his in the Safeway parking lot. He had looked, as he always does, solid, superbly groomed, and dignified. I looked, as I always do, fragile, innocent, and coming apart at the seams.

We sorted it out, though I've forgotten just how. Very likely David ended up paying for damages to both vehicles. But by then we were hearing wedding bells everytime we kissed.

He did love me then, I *know* he did, I insisted fiercely. As for me, that young, tender lover was my first and only love. I could never forget that, regardless of how much he changed.

Perhaps who and what I loved no longer exists, I thought with the caution of one who is sticking a toe in an icy sea. But I had known no other man but David.

Until Nathaniel.

No, no, no, no, no! I could not afford the luxury of this trip, I had things to do today. Pulling on a robe, I scurried downstairs, nearly tripping over Carasel on the second landing.

Carasel, whose fur was dingy, whose thin film of soil wiped off on my hands! I scooped up the little dog and hastily bathed her, while Mims watched, stolidly accepting this use of the kitchen sink.

"Filthy!" I heard her mutter.

God, now I'm filthy.

Sensing my lack of attention, Carasel gave a mighty leap and nearly escaped. "Oh, shit, Carasel!" I shrieked.

"Filthy!" Mims repeated almost under her breath. She had brown and gray hair pulled back so tight her eyebrows were permanently atilt. I gave her a mollifying smile.

"Dogs!" I said like an equal.

She sniffed.

The telephone rang. It was my turn to man the gift shop at our local hospital, not because I wanted to, but because it was de rigueur for middle-aged housewives in our social strata to volunteer their idle time for this or that good cause. Everytime I turned around lately I was harpooned by a Good Cause. Promising to be there in fifteen minutes, I handed Carasel into Mims's capable hands and raced upstairs.

After a quick shower, I hurried to my closet, only to find myself unable to open the door. "Oh shoot!" I swore. I willed my hand to turn that damn knob and it did, but it sure didn't want to.

I stepped inside and fearfully looked around . . . a very large but otherwise ordinary closet. What had I expected? Phantoms drifting through the air? A yawning chasm opening at my feet? Both my feet were standing on white carpet badly in need of vacuuming. I made a mental note to point that out to Mims. I don't vacuum closets.

The space beside the shelf was empty. I tiptoed up to it and forced myself to look. The way it's constructed keeps this gap in near darkness, which is why I'm forever losing things in it. The wall glimmered dimly, but it did glimmer. That wall was solidly *there*. I would trust my eyes, I decided, since my fingers refused to reach back there and prove it.

Should the wall prove unsubstantial, should my hand go right through it . . . I shivered deep down inside, where ice forms.

Ohmigod, the garment bag! It still lay . . . where? On the grass in some distant meadow. I was a litterbug of the worst sort. My hands clamped around my ears as I imagined the wind blowing through that little grove of beeches. Panic rose up in a smothering flood, and for an awful moment I thought I would suffocate.

Responsive only to my growing dread, I grabbed another garment bag and shoved it into the empty space. It helped. But what if Carasel fell into that nonexistent chasm? Tugging down a suitcase from the overhead ledge, I stuck it into the space. The case tipped over and fell against the wall. At least I think it did. Certainly it was standing on edge, and it had to be leaning against something to do that.

What a blessed relief! Just the same, I decided not to test this assumption. Righting the luggage, I grabbed my pale blue uniform and slammed the closet door, then leaned weakly against it. I felt as though a pride of lions lurked behind that fragile wood shell.

Really, this is ridiculous, I told myself. My heart was

hitting against my ribcage like a trapped animal. I was still trembling and damp with the perspiration of panic. I don't think I have ever felt so frightened in my life.

I had trouble snapping my bra, and pantyhose were a laugh. It was stupid to make such an onerous task of simply getting dressed. A sudden image of a hill crowned with tall, silvery-leaved trees nearly dissolved what calm I had achieved. If this kept up, I wouldn't be worth a damn today. Taking myself in hand, I shook Roseanna until all the pieces settled into place, with hardly any left over.

I squinted at the mirror. With my hair knotted at the back of my head and my plain white shoes conforming to the uniform, I looked exactly like a little volunteer trotting off to do good. So comforting. How could anyone who looked like this go screwing around in alien meadows?

When David came home at six, I was in the kitchen trying to figure out my bank statement. He picked up the mail, asked if I'd gotten his suit from the cleaners, all perfectly normal things. Then he said, "Don't forget I'm playing tennis at seven, so let's eat something light," and normalcy flew out the window. I sat frozen, watching the stack of carefully sorted checks falling from my hands in a blizzard of blue-inked snow. A tennis date at seven. I had forgotten. And I had told Nathaniel that I would meet him in the meadow at seven.

I hadn't exactly forgotten. I'd just shoved it down, way down, deep enough to ignore. Kneeling, I gathered up my checks.

"Did you hear me?" David called from the den.

"Yes, I—I heard you. We'll eat in ten minutes. Just soup and salad, okay with you?" My voice was a marvel. I crammed the checks back into the envelope and put it away.

By rote, I prepared our supper. We ate. David left, looking fit and trim and attractive in his white tennis rig. I suddenly wanted desperately to call out to him. *Oh David, come back and scoop me up, carry me upstairs and love me, keep me safe!*

" 'Bye," I called.

I considered attacking my bank statement again, but I was too itchy to concentrate on figures. I paced the den and roamed the living room. My grandfather clock chimed seven in slow, ponderous, slightly ominous strokes. *Was Nathaniel waiting by the rock?*

"Of course he isn't because he doesn't exist, Roseanna, except in your book," I said loudly.

My book. I could work on it for awhile—oh God, no, not that book!

The telephone obligingly rang just then and I leaped for it with unbridled relief.

"Rosie? You want to run up to the hospital and see Julie with me? I forgot to tell you she went in yesterday."

"Yes, oh yes, Viv!" I cried.

"Hey, Rosie, she's not dying, she just had her appendix removed," Viveca said dryly.

Thursday morning I awoke to a soft wind blowing on my face. It took several wild seconds to remember that I'd turned on the ceiling fan last night. The faint whirr of the lazily rotating blades masked any unwanted sounds, had there been any.

Thank heaven there hadn't been, for I was, to put it mildly, nervous. I got through the day by immersing myself in frantic activity, but by evening I had a tropical disturbance in my stomach. When David told me he'd be out of town tomorrow night, my storm increased to a full-fledged hurricane. I could not stay alone in our house, not with that closet right there in my bedroom! Calm down, Roseanna, I commanded. There is nothing in that closet except things that belong in closets.

The hell there's not! Roseanna hissed back at me.

Suddenly icy-hot and breathless, I shot to my feet. "David? I think I'll go spend the night with Viveca, then. It's been ages since I've done that . . . yes, that's what I'll do, I'll just go spend the night with Viveca. I haven't done that in *ages!*"

"Why don't you go spend the night with Viveca?" David mocked.

I glared at him. What the hell did he know about it? I can and do go around proclaiming my imminent descent into madness, but when it comes right down to the naked id, I don't want to be mad. Not really. And if I stayed alone in this house at night, when David returned from his trip he would find his wife huddled in a corner sucking her toes.

Because, quite simply, I was terrified. It was a deep-down-in-your-bones fear, ancient and primitive, the kind you can't catch hold of and question. The kind that just *is*.

"Okay, then, I'll spend the night with Viveca," I decided.

Saturday morning, David called to remind me that we were having dinner guests that night, and he would appreciate it if I didn't screw up. I said a few appropriate words after I'd hung up but, faithful as an old plow horse, accepted my yoke and got with it.

In the supermarket I grabbed a cart with four wheels going in opposite directions, and hurried down an aisle.

Fresh veggies, I decided. Perhaps these really beautiful baby carrots, glazed in orange sauce. . . .

Did Nathaniel ever get to that dance?

But so many people did not like carrots. . . .

Who did he take if he did?

David loathed them, in fact. Grabbing up two bunches of carrots, I moved on to the meat counter and rang the bell for the butcher.

On the wall behind the counter hung a calendar with a woodland scene. Absently I gave my order to the butcher who faintly resembled the side of beef visible through the window. The calendar scene was really a pleasant alpine meadow in Switzerland, but as I concentrated on it, the mountains scaled down and the scattered trees regrouped into an enticing little grove. I mentally painted a huge gray boulder in the foreground, just at the corner of the picture, and strewed daisies with gay abandon. There, almost perfect. . . .

I took my prime rib roast and stopped at the deli for

flaked crab and a luscious-looking pâté. I was exhausted already and I hadn't even hit the liquor store.

By the time David came home that evening, the house sparkled, the table glittered, the prime rib roast was perfectly cooked, and I'd even remembered to fill the antique silver ice bucket that David's Aunt Leona had sent us for Christmas.

Our guests arrived shortly afterward and dived into my hors d'oeuvres like bears fresh out of hibernation. To my distracted relief, dinner was declared a triumph. Afterward we went into the impeccably clean living room for liqueurs and long, rambling tales related by David's esteemed new client, a jolly, portly man with cold, fog-gray eyes. His wife was pale, fluttery, and given to startled looks whenever anyone focused attention on her. He called her Mother. She called him Norris, but in a tentative way. Our neighbors—frail but rich Lucas, and Doris, a militant, outspoken woman who reminded me of Maude of television fame—had joined us to enliven the evening. Every time Norris called his wife Mother, Doris half sprang out of her chair.

And so it went.

When David and I were finally, at long *last,* in our bedroom, I asked somewhat anxiously, "Well, how do you think it went?"

He sat down on the bed and took off his shoes. "Very well. Dinner was great and you even managed to conceal your yawns."

"Oh, David, come on, now, that was the most boring, utterly killing evening I've ever lived through. Now admit it, it was." I slipped out of my dress and rolled down my pantyhose.

Smiling, he patted my bare bottom. "Yeah, it was. And you deserve credit for a job well done. You charmed the pants off him. But I've had to listen to that crap for a week now."

"You deserve credit, too, then." In sudden but obscure desperation, I put my arms around him and drew his face to my naked stomach. "David, let's take a vacation! You know we haven't had one in years. Some romantic tropical isle, perhaps! Slow dancing and soft breezes, and the two of us all alone on a moonlit beach. Why, I could make reservations tomorrow and we'd be out of here by Sunday at the latest!"

"Oh, Roseanna, I'm up to my ears in work and you're prattling about tropical-isle vacations? I'm much too busy for—"

"Oh, David, you're always busy, you will always *be* busy because that's the way you like it!" He tried to move, but I fashioned my hands into a vise. "But I need this, honey, I need it very much. It's time—maybe past time, I don't know, but I do know we'd better take time for us," I said with a touch of grimness. "Your work is fine. But we're not. So let's—"

"We're fine, too," he said firmly. "I simply cannot leave right now, Roseanna. But maybe later. . . ."

"You always say that! Why can't you take a few days off? Why do you have to run this rat race, anyway? We have everything now that most people strive for all their lives—money, success, social position! Why do you always need more?"

He didn't answer; he didn't need to. He was the grandson of a Supreme Court judge, the son of an ex-governor, the brother of a senator. And David was merely an attorney, albeit a partner in one of Houston's most prestigious firms, but still. . . .

"Well, I have needs, too, David. Please, take me away from . . . just take me away?" My voice cracked, my hands clenched as I felt the rawness in my plea.

His mouth twisted. Swiftly I changed tactics. "Okay, we'll postpone the vacation for now and just fire up the hot tub tonight, drink the rest of that splendid wine and mellow out," I suggested, kissing his hair. My voice lowered enticingly. "We can pretend it's our second date, and I'm being bold as brass inviting you into my little hot spot! Naturally you can't resist such an invitation, because who knows where it could lead?"

"Umm, sounds good, but I'm really beat tonight." He yawned. "Give me a raincheck, okay?"

I stepped away from him, my smile small and wry and fleeting. "I would, but it would probably expire before you ever got around to using it."

"Oh, for Christ's sake, Roseanna." Badly strained patience tinged with annoyance shading into exasperation.

I always feel about an inch high when he does that.

Fingers trembling with anger and hurt, I pulled on the jumpsuit I'd worn earlier in the day. He stood up, his frown deepening as I put on my sneakers.

"Where are you going?" he demanded.

"For a walk."

"At this time of night? You can't be serious."

"I'm dead serious. It's either that or get shit-faced."

"Oh, Roseanna," he said with a sigh, elevating my blood pressure dangerously. "If you want to make love this much . . . come on, let's go to bed."

I felt the most astonishing flare of outrage and hurt. Turning, I stared at him, my mouth twisting with wry, bitter humor. "Well, now," I drawled, "a woman who's spent half her life trying to get her husband into bed ought to jump on that invitation like a chicken on a june bug! But silly old me, I just feel insulted. Go figure."

"Oh, hell, I didn't mean—" He threw up his hands. "Look, I may have been a little insensitive just now, but I *am* tired—"

"Yeah, so am I." I headed for the door. "Good night, David."

His quick laugh sounded hollow. He caught me at the door, swung me into his arms, and kissed me. Ordinarily I'd have been thrilled by this he-man display of passion. But this felt more like manipulation than passion. Outrage escalated into fury. I wrenched away.

"You're a dickhead, you know that, David? An ignorant, flea-brained *dickhead*!"

Stunned by my outburst, we stared at each other. His mouth opened. But he had nothing to say that I wanted to hear right then. Wheeling, I ran downstairs to put Carasel on leash for our walk.

The next afternoon the florist delivered a dozen red roses. This was totally out of character, and for a moment I reacted as any wife does when flowers arrive for no official reason—suspicious and wary. But I told myself that David had realized he'd really hurt me. These roses were his apology.

Later he called and I thanked him for the flowers. He laughed, dismissing my thanks.

"Just a little compensation for that bit of silliness last night. Roseanna, just bear with me, hmm? You won't be sorry, I promise," he said with a tantalizing touch of huskiness.

It had struck me as more than a "bit of silliness." But at least I knew he cared, I reminded myself, like taking an aspirin for my stubbornly persistent heartache.

Monday. Exactly one week from the day I had fallen down in my closet and dreamed a dream. The screwiest week of my life, I reflected drowsily. Nothing had changed. I had packed down all thoughts of Nathaniel, the meadow, our fevered lovemaking. With each day's dawning I had relaxed a little more, until I was finally beginning to accept it for what it had to be, an illusion created by an extremely fertile mind.

On the heels of this rational conclusion came an irrational confession. I was scared spitless by the hole in my closet wall that didn't exist because I was scared spitless that it did.

Sleeping alone was unrestful, for I was bedeviled by anxiety. What if I started sleepwalking? What if that beckoning darkness drew me to the closet? What if my subconscious then took over and propelled me down the rabbit hole again? Such wild night-thoughts heightened my prospects of having an ulcer before my next birthday. Although I've always believed in unicorns and magic, being considered abnormal, an oddity, a *freak*, for God's sake, was not something I wanted to experience.

I had done no further work on my book. The one time I'd tried, Nathaniel was suddenly *there*, as full-fleshed and realistic as the computer keys under my fingertips. I had been struck by a fiery yearning to see him, alive and so very real to my heart, just once more. Hastily I'd put the manuscript away. I was only on page sixty. The Nathaniel in my book had just met the tempestu-

ous, impossibly beautiful Alicia. They hadn't even gone
to bed yet.

I did not want Nathaniel in bed with that brazen Alicia. . . .

I roamed around our den, straightening pillows, picking up the newspapers I had scattered with abandon,
wanting something to do besides pick up newspapers.
David was out of town, another overnight trip, and I felt
so itchy my skin curled. But damned if I was going to
run to Viveca's again.

I could clean the refrigerator. It certainly needed
cleaning, as David had taken pains to point out. When I
opened the door of this appliance with a half-hearted
notion of actually doing some cleaning, I was appalled
by the many little containers sitting on the shelves.
Their contents were not readily identifiable. Little dabs
of this and that, all sprouting weird, gray, fungus-type
growths. Probably some new antibiotic was in the making right now in my refrigerator.

I did not feel like cleaning a damn refrigerator.

I took a tangerine and wandered outside to a lawn
chair. What did I feel like doing? Like making love.
Like taking off for the North woods for two solid weeks
of living in a cabin with a handsome, green-eyed man.
Like letting down my hair and flinging my pagan self
into the arms and mouth and body of that good-lovin'
man. If women were permitted this therapeutic privilege
even once a year, there would be fewer neurotic females
huddled on analytic couches.

Carasel snuggled down at my feet and went to sleep.
Filled with longing, I sat lost in thought, releasing, inch
by inch, little dabs of Nathaniel.

My wistful melancholy was interrupted by Viveca. I
had to smile, for it was a pleasure to see her strolling
toward me. That auburn hair glowed in the sunlight, and
her long, easy stride was beautiful.

Up close, she looked a little tense, I thought. "Viv, is
everything all right?"

She drifted down into a chair like a graceful feather
and crossed her elegant legs. "I'm making it. How about

you? You've been looking a little nervy lately yourself,
love."

"Oh, nonsense," I said crisply.

Viveca frowned. "I am a trifle miffed at being put
down to 'oh, nonsense.' You're being inhumanly stoical
about something and I want to know what it is. It's my
right. You're not ill or something—some dreadful dis-
ease you're keeping from me?"

Responsive to her concerned voice, I felt a sudden
wild urge to throw myself into her arms and pour out
my heart's unease. Viveca is tart-tongued and sometimes brittle, but loyal to the core. I trust her implicitly.
But even her compassion extended only so far. She
would, quite correctly, think my mind overtaxed, and
she would, incorrectly, blame it on David.

"No, sweetie, no dreadful diseases. I'm fine," I said.

She was skeptical and I couldn't blame her. When she
left, loneliness wrapped around me like a coarse blanket. Nathaniel filled my mind and quite a bit of my heart
as I sat listening to the wind sigh through the tops of tall
pines. The evocative sound seemed to infiltrate my being until it touched my very soul.

I simply could not bear it any longer. Racing upstairs
with Carasel in huffing pursuit, I went straight to my
closet and snapped on the light.

My heart pounded. Wonder and fear quickened my
breath as I stared at the shadowed nook between shelf
and wall. Could I return to that lovely fantasyland?

There was only one way to find out.

Chapter 4

The meadow was buttery with sunlight, and that little wind rippled through the daisies. Mountain peaks gleamed pink and white, the boulder glittered, and beech trees fluttered silvery leaves in welcome.

"Well, God, here I am again, wherever that might be," I said with a joyous little laugh.

I wasn't lying on my back this time. When I stepped into the space beside my shelf, I held Carasel tightly and moved backwards one cautious step at a time. The shelf rubbed my hip and I fully expected the wall to touch my back and halt my progress. One more step—and I was falling again, through a whirling, light-shot tunnel. Not really falling, I realized belatedly. It was more like floating. And it wasn't a long fall or float—whatever—it was, in fact, instantaneous and not at all unpleasant now that I knew what to expect. I simply stepped backwards and came to rest in the meadow.

There had been a curious sensation of heat, a kind of explosion of warmth inside me, as though I was being disassembled and put together again. A strange feeling, but definitely not unpleasant. Actually, I felt rather like one of those Fourth of July wands we used to whirl around and around, creating a dazzling shower of sparks.

I stood still and examined my inner self. My heart thumped, but with excitement, not fear or alarm. I was breathless again, but it was a sweet, natural reaction of childlike amazement and delight. This was all the

Christmases of my life rolled into one, a wild celebration of the rebirth of Roseanna Bently Tait.

I tasted it with my mind and body and soul, and I found it good. Good? It was fantastic!

Wanting to savor every second of this adventure, I turned in a slow circle. My breath caught at the beauty around me. When I touched a pink primrose and its pollen turned my fingertip yellow, I felt a touch of awe. Something as familiar as pollen had a reality all its own.

Although Carasel was struggling against my clasp, I did not free her. Now that the initial reaction of joyous wonder had passed, I realized I had problems. Nathaniel didn't know I was coming, and I didn't know where he lived. I also had no idea what day it was in his world. Dear Lord, I asked in awe, looking appropriately upwards, where is his world?

Wherever it was, it was very, very real. I couldn't think beyond this concrete fact, nor did I want to. If his world was real, then so was Nathaniel. That's all that mattered right now.

Carasel's squirming brought me back to the immediate problem of finding Nathaniel. After putting the dog on her leash, I took a few steps and stopped, undecided and a little anxious as I listened to the whispering beeches. To find him, I had to leave the safety of the boulder and venture out into this unknown land—but where? And for how long? My watch read four o'clock. Was it four o'clock here? There had been a time lapse, I remembered. When I'd returned to my closet that other time, I had been gone an hour and a half by the bedroom clock. But I'd spent several hours, perhaps four or five, with Nathaniel.

The eerie wind ruffled my hair. Or was it eerie? I laughed aloud. It was a very Earthlike wind. The question nagged at me again—was this Earth, then? My Earth? I knew nothing of time and space theories. Overlapping universes, parallel realms, time warps, and the like were all words from science fiction novels.

My head spun with confusion. Only for a moment, however. So I didn't understand all this, so what? Why demean miracles with questions or doubts, or tacky demands for explanations?

Carasel tugged at the leash, eager to get on with this. So was I. Soon I would see him, hold him, watch his smile and listen to his laugh. . . . Or would I? This was just his summer cottage, he'd said. By now he might have returned to wherever he called home.

Doubt flooded me. How on earth was I to find a man in a strange, unknown land? How was I to find him even if he was still at the cottage? Where the devil was that cottage? I looked around again. The meadow sloped downward and spread out on each side of me, rimmed with trees which effectively blocked my exploratory urge. What lay beyond those trees? People? Cities? Or emptiness?

No, not emptiness. There were those electric towers marching across the land like lacy steel giants. A warm symbol of familiarity, they carried electricity to homes, and homes had people. Somewhat reassured by this reasoning, I reconsidered the most immediate problem, locating the cottage.

Nathaniel had walked to the grove when he left me, so I headed in that direction. Judging from the angle of the sun—of which I am a poor judge—it was early afternoon here. I had to be back at the boulder before dark. And I must not get lost. Oh Lord, what if I got lost? I could wander around for days!

"Oh, shit," I muttered. Carasel promptly went into a frenzy of barking. I saw nothing to warrant her fury. Maybe she just hates that word.

Nearly dead center of the grove I came upon a little spring seeping water into a scooped-out pit rimmed with stones. Polluted? It didn't look to be. In fact, it was utterly charming with those lacy little ferns and yellow buttercups encircling it. Pale blue butterflies, exquisitely tiny and fragile, flitted around the flowers. Some very earthy-looking frogs scampered about in the grass as Carasel dashed to and fro.

Seeing her drink, I was suddenly ravished with thirst. I dipped a hand in the water and tasted. Delicious. I drank. If I died, I died, I thought airily.

Pulling Carasel along behind me like a toy animal on wheels, I left the pool and soon came upon another empty stretch of lea. Farther on, a small hillock obscured my vision. We headed full tilt toward that hill, Carasel and I, laughing, delighted fools racing through a froth of white daisies. "Just like that perfume commercial," I told my dog. Except that the perfume ad had a definite ending. I was supposed to be met by an equally delighted man.

I kept going, my spirits soaring as I became aware of the physical and mental change in myself. I was all lissome grace and radiantly lighthearted, both body and mind fueled by the exquisite energy of youth. It swept through blood, flesh, and bone in an exuberant flood of renewal.

The change I felt in myself was wonderfully visible in Carasel. I laughed aloud as this little arthritic canine matron transformed into an eager, curious, wildly rambunctious puppy. Six months old at the most, I thought, struggling to keep up with her mad dash. My hair came loose and streamed out behind me. I had changed into a pretty yellow sundress and white sandals, and it was this sight that greeted Nathaniel as he came over the crest of the hill.

He abruptly stopped, and stood watching us. Carasel broke into a furious greeting. I knelt and freed her from the leash. With heart-warming agility, she ran ahead, leaping up on Nathaniel in a delirium of affection.

I followed more slowly, a little shy, a little scared, my heart beating loud enough to hear. I stopped in front of him.

"Hello again," I said simply.

"Roseanna. So, you're back."

He was cool, even aloof; my punishment, I suppose, for not keeping our date. "Yes, I came back."

"Why?"

I blinked. "To see you, of course. Nathaniel, I'm sorry, I'm really, truly sorry—but God, I'm so glad to see you!"

Giving him no time to answer, I flung myself into the arms that instinctively came up to catch my flying person. Still laughing, I grabbed his face and spread kisses over it like butter on hot toast. Then I was scooped up and whirled around while we both went a little crazy and Carasel darted wildly between Nathaniel's feet.

"Roseanna," he whispered, and kissed me. It went on and on in a glad reunion of mouths. I burrowed into his chest and he held me tightly. I felt his lips moving on my hair. He smelled so good, so very good! I looked up at him, flaming with joy, drinking in his beautiful green eyes, his smile, him.

Realizing the depth of my affection for him made me uneasy. Nonsense! I chastized my overreactive self. Of course you adore him—you *created* him, for heaven's sake! Conjured him up from pure wishful thinking, I concluded, tasting the wedge of tanned skin exposed by his unbuttoned shirt. Dark, dusky, delicious male mystery. I buried my nose in it.

Ever so gently, his big hand cradled my cheek, lifting my face to his gaze. I put my hand over his and smiled at him.

"Oh, Roseanna." He shook his head, his struggle for control so plain I bit my bottom lip. "Where have you been?" he burst out. "I came back that night at seven and I waited. . . . Dammit, I searched all over for you, but no one had ever heard of you!"

"I'm sorry," I said lamely.

"Sorry doesn't cut it, Roseanna," he returned with some heat. "I'm not used to being stood up."

"I don't doubt that," I said wryly. His dark frown made me remember how much I hate feeling defensive. My chin snapped up of its own accord. "Look, I said I was sorry and I meant it. But if that's not enough, if you'd rather I leave—"

"No!" he blurted. He dragged a hand through his glossy chestnut hair. "Dammit, I don't want you to leave, I just want some answers! Why didn't you meet me?"

"Oh please, Nathaniel, no questions." I implored. "I don't have long, I . . . what time is it? My watch seems a bit slow."

"It's one-thirty." Taking a breath, he raked through

his hair again, a calming gesture, I was to learn. "I was mowing the yard when I heard Carasel. That's how I knew you'd come back."

"You heard Carasel? Where is your house?" I asked. "May I see it? You were mowing the grass? Ohmigod, I can't believe you were actually *mowing grass*!"

"What's so strange about mowing grass?" he growled.

I laughed and he threw up his hands, defeated by the excitement spilling out of every pore of my body.

"Oh, come on, it's just over this hill. You look thirsty and I've got some very good wine, all chilled . . . oh, Roseanna!" He hugged me fiercely and I could feel him hardening against my belly. He muttered something and kissed me again, in a different way this time. When he drew back, his eyes were intense.

"The wine?" I prompted. I was too shaken to think straight. He was going to ask me questions and I didn't have any answers.

Why hadn't I thought up a story? Because I didn't believe I'd ever see him again, not really.

"Yes, the wine. Roseanna, I'm so damned glad to see you!" he exulted. "And you, too, Carasel," he added, laughing as she put her front paws on his leg and barked. He looked so boyishly happy that I had to hug him again just to feel him, solid and warm in my arms.

"You're not mad?" I asked hopefully.

"Hell, yes, I'm mad. I must be, to be this glad to see you," he replied with a gruff, ironic laugh.

I squeezed his hand. Then, linking fingers, we walked down the other side of the hill and across a mowed strip of meadow grass. A rustic fence framed the equally rustic cottage sitting under its umbrella of tall, spreading trees. Flame-red geraniums rioted; wild roses clambered over fences and shrubs alike. It was charming, like a painting, or a scene from a book. A scene from *my* book, I realized. Except that my fictional Nathaniel had a sprawling ranch house standing under a lone cottonwood tree. . . .

A sleek, black pickup truck was parked beside the house. Behind it, the meandering dirt road became lost in the terrain.

The cottage was so isolated, we might have been alone on his Earth. And it was Earth, of that I was certain. The fat squirrel flicking its tail at Carasel before leaping nimbly for a limb, the tree itself, and the grass under my feet were the flora and fauna of my Earth. I wished I knew where we were, what state, I mean. But I didn't dare ask. Likely he'd find it odd that I didn't know what state I was in.

He opened the door and ushered us into a delightfully warm, inviting room. A gray stone fireplace took up one entire wall. Windows dominated another. The view was down the side of the hill, curling up and down and on and on across ranks of hills, until it merged into deep blue haze.

The fireplace stone was rough and uneven, but when I ran a hand over it, I marveled at its cool, satiny texture.

"This is beautiful, Nathaniel!"

"Thanks, I take full credit for it. In fact, I designed it. You thirsty, Carasel, hum?" He laughed, eyeing the little red tongue lolling piteously. Carasel whined, and he stepped into the kitchen to fetch her a bowl of water.

I stood looking around the room in something of a daze. It was simplicity itself, with rattan furniture upholstered in green and white ticking. There were splashes of blue here and there, some earthy heather and gold tones in vases and rugs, a tall white ceramic floor lamp with a wisteria-patterned shade.

The black pit of the fireplace was filled with an enormous basket of dried flowers: roses, hydrangeas, larkspur, Queen Anne's lace, all of which could have come from my own garden.

The windows boasted plantation shutters folded back to bring the stunning view indoors, and a white porcelain lion with an opalescent gleam guarded the rear door.

"That's Chatera," Nathaniel said as though introducing me to royalty. "He's very old and probably crochety, so leave him alone, Carasel. He belonged to my great-grandfather."

He had a great-grandfather! Why did I find that so

astonishing? "He's beautiful," I said, gliding a hand over the smooth head. "His eyes, what are they?"

"Opals."

"But they're precious stones!"

"Yes. And you're right, of course; they've been replaced twice already. The original eyes were emeralds."

"Like yours," I murmured.

I shivered as realization struck me anew. I was actually here, with Nathaniel, in his home. His home, not mine. Shivering again, I reminded myself that I had to be back at the boulder before dark.

"Sit down, honey," Nathaniel invited with a quick kiss. My skin thrilled. I knew I wouldn't be sitting for long. He was aroused and it showed quite clearly. Heat drizzled through my belly and lodged in the confluence of my thighs. Dismay mingled with anticipation. Getting back to the boulder before dark, without explaining to Nathaniel why I must, would be a devilish task.

"I'll get the wine," he said.

As he moved away, I watched him, delighting in his strong back and tapering waist. He wore a light green shirt, and his hair curled just at the collar. I kicked off my sandals and sat down on the couch. Then I leaped up again. Carasel was exploring the cottage, so I decided to join her.

The hallway had an arched ceiling with stained-glass insets. Lovely! The walls were plaster, roughed to the texture of suede. Gleaming tile floors led me past several closed doors, then into the master bedroom. The bed was huge, the walls white-paneled, the bathroom large and functional. A colorful quilt served as a bedspread, and thick, whipped-cream carpet cushioned my bare feet. The simple cotton drapes were the same shade.

No photographs in evidence, I noted with relief. I didn't want girlfriends infringing on my fantasy.

Books tumbled over the bedside table to pile upon the floor. One lay open, a mystery by an unfamiliar author, written in clipped, no-adjectives style. Rather dry reading, I thought, replacing it.

The headboard of the bed caught my attention. The

muted glow of old brass polished by time, and bas-relief figures sculpted in shadows, put this work of art in Chatera's class. Intuition told me it was another family treasure.

It was situated in front of a large window that offered a breathtaking view of the mountains. Leaning a hip against the bed, I stood enthralled.

"Sometimes I see deer from this window. Free, unafraid, browsing at the edge of the woods," Nathaniel said quietly from behind me.

I wondered how long he'd been standing there.

"Your wine, ma'am. It's very good. Local stuff. Here, sit down. We have no reason to leave this room for a very long time."

I quivered at the import of his words, but made no verbal response. Sitting on the bed, we sipped wine, enjoying its fruity taste, enjoying even more the sweet warmth that flowed between us.

There was none of the uncertainty that plagues new lovers. We were immediate friends, with a warm rapport already established. That sounded impossible, yet it was true. If I closed my mind to the eerie way I'd met this man, ours could be a normal relationship between any two people. Well, sort of.

I knew Nathaniel was churning with questions. I also knew he was eager to make love to me. And I knew one more exciting thing. Reflected in the dresser's mirror I saw a radiant, youthful woman; me, Roseanna. After wasting several seconds pondering this wonderful mystery, I gave myself a bit of sage advice. Don't question a miracle, Roseanna Noelle. Just say thank you and enjoy it.

"This is so nice," I murmured, sighing.

"Yes."

Looking up at him, I tipped the last of my wine into my mouth and licked my lips. He said my name, soft and low. Then, setting our glasses aside, he stood up and drew me to my feet.

I stood quietly while he undressed me. When my teddy fell to the floor, his swift, indrawn breath was audible, and intensely gratifying. Only one other man had

ever looked at me as he was doing and that was so long
ago I'd forgotten how it felt. I am small but lushly
curved, a ripe rounding of flesh that is not evident when
I'm clothed.

Still, I wondered why he was so mesmerized; he'd
seen me nude before. My eyes questioned.

"Roseanna, you are beautiful," he said very softly.
"Every time I recalled how you looked, I thought surely
I was letting my imagination run riot . . . but it's
more. . . ." His voice tailed off into a long exhalation
of sighing breath. He was looking at me not only with
desire but with a startled awareness I could not fathom.

Tenderly he traced the rounded contours of my
breasts. The caressing finger trailed up my throat and
around my cheekbones as if learning the symmetry of
my face. When I smiled, he leaned down and just as
tenderly kissed it.

He gathered a handful of my hair and let it run
through his fingers like molten gold. "I thought of you
so often. Even when I didn't want to think of you, there
you were, tormenting me. Such sweet torment. When I
could find no trace of you I thought perhaps I'd
dreamed you," he said in that soft, husky, faraway voice.
"Why did you come back, Roseanna?"

"Because I had to, because I couldn't stay away."

"You liked my loving?" he asked, but that didn't seem
to be all he was asking. However, it was all I was going
to answer.

"Yes, oh yes, I liked it!" I said. An erotic impatience
swept over me. "Your clothes, Nathaniel."

When he undressed, the lean, sinewy beauty of his
body was a hot slash of excitement flaming through me.
We stood close, kissing, touching lightly, satisfying this
hunger first. And then we fused together in a surge of
passion that tumbled us onto the bed.

It was a swift, hungry coupling. I was starved for this
and I responded with utter abandon to every deep
plunge, coming with him in an explosion of such ecstatic
pleasure, it wiped everything from mind except the body
grinding mine into the sheets.

My fingers were welded to his back. He was heavy on

me, but I relished the weight. Dreamily I wondered what he thought of me, what he felt for me, how he would accept my refusal to answer his questions.

He raised his head and kissed me, first with his eyes, then with his lips. I explored his mouth, tasting all around, licking his lips, tongue delving deep and delighting in the goodness of him. We were becoming aroused again by this erotic pleasure. His kisses roughened into that hungry taking again. I was honey-filled, and he was intent on draining every drop.

"Oh, baby, baby," he whispered.

David never called me "baby."

"My Roseanna, my little Roseanna, my sweet, sweet. . . ."

David never talked during intercourse. Shutting down my mind, I grabbed Nathaniel's taut cheeks and rode my wild, rapturous whirlwind.

Afterwards we lay quietly for a time. He had rolled off me and gathered me close. I didn't get up and go to the bathroom. *I always get up and go to the bathroom, then David does his cleansing. . . .*

I didn't want to be cleansed. And I damn sure didn't want to be thinking of David. But I couldn't help it. Having the privilege of comparing men was still a new and fascinating experience.

Nathaniel's hand moved up and down my back in mindless caress. "Pretty Roseanna. Who are you? And what have you done to me? Have you bewitched me? I feel . . . strange, as though this—you—are unreal, a mythical being. I find you in a meadow. You know my name. We make love. Beautiful love. You disappear for three weeks, then reappear in my meadow. I don't know who you are, where you're from, what you do, what you're like. I don't know you. And yet I know you."

His voice was quiet and bemused. I couldn't even find mine. His words had stunned me, and I was struggling to keep my balance. He'd said I had been gone for three weeks. On my Earth, it had been one. More confusion.

"That night you left, I watched you," he went on. "I went into the grove and then I stopped, because I meant to follow you back to the lake, make sure you got safely

home, you and your little dog. I waited for you to start
in that direction. But you never appeared. I came back
to the boulder and you were gone. Gone where? The
meadow was empty. Gone where, Roseanna?"

Oh, God. My throat tightened. *Gone where, Roseanna? Gone home, Nathaniel.* "I . . . the boulder must
have screened me," I floundered. "I walked that way,
not down through the meadow."

Watchful green eyes narrowed. "Why? The lake's
downhill."

"Well, sometimes I—I lose my sense of direction, you
see," I said lamely.

His voice roughened. "The hell you do. You don't live
at the lake, Roseanna. No one there knows anything
about you; I checked it out thoroughly. Why are you
lying to me? I mean, all I'm asking is where you live."

He tipped my face, and I promptly lowered my lashes.
My eyes are so darn truthful, they simply don't know
how to lie. David always catches me when I try it, just by
watching my face.

A poker player I am not. A quick thinker I am. When
you can't lie decently, you have to be fast on your feet.

"Nathaniel, why all these questions?" I asked irritably. "I mean, what does it matter where I live? Isn't this
enough? I'm giving you some damn good sex with no
strings attached; a pleasant interlude, a fun time—why
must you question it?"

"Because I don't want just some 'damn good sex'! I
can get all the sex I want," Nathaniel growled. "And you
know why I question. Good God, I'd have to be an idiot
not to question! Roseanna, I like you, I enjoy you, but
you're a mystery and one that's eating hell out of me.
You pop up today out of thin air—"

I put a chiding finger to his lips. "Oh, come on now,
I'm no mystery. You know there's a logical explanation
and that it will likely be a boring one."

"Why don't you let me be the judge of that? And I'd
like to, if you don't mind."

He was beginning to look quite grim.

"Oh, good grief, Nathaniel!" I snapped, feeling more
desperate with every word he spoke. "Look, bear with

me? Let me be a mystery lady—it's sort of fun!" I gave him a mischievous grin. "In due time, I'll explain it, but believe me, it's just an ordinary tale."

"I like ordinary tales," he said evenly.

"If you keep on with this, I'm leaving," I said, driven to panic. There was still a good chance that I might be crazy, and I didn't want him to know. Even if he was part of my madness . . . oh, Lordy. "Please?" I inserted into the throbbing silence.

"All right," he said reluctantly. "For now I'll drop it and let you be a mystery lady. I must admit you're a very sexy mystery lady." He grinned. Devastating. I kissed it. He kissed me harder. Relief rolled over me like breakers on a shore.

Freeing myself, I sat up and looked him over. A superb creation, Roseanna. Now you know how God felt when He looked upon Adam. "Nathaniel, may I kiss you? Anywhere I like?"

"Help yourself," he invited with a lazy, curling grin.

I helped myself. Over his chest and down his belly, and there. The moist, aromatic smells of sex and sweat and Nathaniel, with a little dash of me, were richly erotic. Such an *intimate* smell, I thought happily.

The penis I held was undergoing some interesting changes. Fascinated, I watched it. I had never seen an erection in the making. It began rising, very slowly, swelling, getting bigger and thicker. The tip was sort of splitting, the eye enlarging—my goodness!

I looked at Nathaniel, who was watching me with perplexed amusement. "I've never seen this happening in such detail before," I explained.

"You're doing it, baby," he said huskily. "Come here, Roseanna."

"I'm hungry," I said sometime later.

He had made this mating a long, deliciously drawn-out affair. I felt marvelously bruised all over from writhing like a maddened leaf upon that long, hard body. Even my mouth felt swollen.

"Are you! And here I thought I'd completely satisfied

your appetites! Damn, honey, I don't know if I can go another round or not, but if you insist—"

"Oh! You're outrageous, Nathaniel," I sniffed.

"Yes I am. And if you have any notions of leaving this house anytime soon, I suggest you discard them."

Startled at his flat tone, I drew back. "I really don't know you," I told him lightly. "You could be a terrible man, a ganster, a thief, a mad rapist—"

"Yes, I could," he pleasantly agreed.

I laughed. I knew he wasn't a criminal. I would never create a mean-spirited hero.

He cupped my face, his expression grim. "Roseanna, you're teasing, but, honey, it was a very real possibility. The woods are full of animals these days, and I don't mean four-legged ones. A woman was attacked just a few hundred feet from the lake colony last week. That's why I was so concerned when you just disappeared like that."

"I'm sorry you were worried, but I'm okay, really. Besides, I have Carasel to protect me."

"Yeah," he said dryly, glancing at the gray bundle of fur asleep beside the bed. We both laughed, but his laugh was strained.

"It's okay, Nathaniel. Believe me, I'll be careful." I gave him a quick kiss. "I'm still hungry. What time is it?"

Scooting off the bed, I headed for the bathroom.

"Three-thirty," he called after me.

Three-thirty, I repeated silently, which meant—what? When did I have to leave? I checked my watch. It had stopped precisely at eleven o'clock. My watch had never stopped before.

"Roseanna, the next time you come here. . . ."

I didn't hear the rest of it; I was dazed by his implication. The next time I came here? Would there be a next time? Heavens, I hadn't thought—but how long could this go on?

I'll think about it later, I decided swiftly. Evading Nathaniel's reaching hands, I escaped into the bathroom.

The medicine cabinet caught my eye. Intensely curious, I opened it. Deodorant, shaving cream, aspirin, mouthwash—the usual. Not a familiar brand name among the lot. I shut the door and peered into the mirror. My face was unlined, my skin firm and dewy with youth. How old was that face? Remembering that seven years ago, David had paid an outrageous sum of money to have a large crown put on my back tooth, I leaned closer and opened my mouth. The tooth in question was innocent of a crown.

Jolted, I expanded my investigation. I'd always had good teeth, but even so, I had a few cavities. Where were the fillings? My first had been done when I was . . . what, twenty-four? I had married David and was already pregnant . . . yes, definitely twenty-four. Before that age, I had no fillings, and I had none now.

"Lord!" I exclaimed softly. I washed myself, my mind going at a fast clip, examining, discarding, making no sense out of anything, but trying so hard.

Nathaniel tapped on the door. "Hey, honey, I'm next."

I opened the door and bowed him in, then left him alone.

When he emerged I was in the kitchen rummaging through his refrigerator. It was well stocked with not only the basics, but assorted cheeses and gourmet snacks as well. Lodestone beer. Timson's Dairy milk. Springtime margarine and Timson's butter. I grabbed the beer bottle again. These were packed somewhere and that somewhere would be listed on the container. Lodestone beer, Austin—

Barefoot and blue-jeaned, he took the beer from my hand and kissed my nose. He carried a robe over his arm. I realized I was naked only when he draped it around my shoulders.

"I thank you," I said, turning so he could help me into it. Laughing, he pinched my bottom before covering it with the soft red garment. The hem touched my ankles, and by the time he finished rolling the sleeves, I could barely lift my arms under the weight of those cuffs.

"Adorable," he decided. "Find anything to eat in there?"

"This ham looks good," I said brightly.

While I made sandwiches and light conversation, my mind ran along on two different tracks. Austin what? My Austin? In my Texas?

We sat down at the table and I reclaimed my icy beer. Wiping the bottle with a determinedly idle gesture, I peered at the raised figures at the bottom of the brown glass bottle.

Austin, Texas.

Giving up, I took a swig. It was delicious, and I was more confused than ever.

Chapter 5

We were having coffee when I spied the newspaper folded neatly beside an odd-looking instrument that appeared to be a telephone with a viewing screen. Casually I asked, "Are you through with that newspaper? If so, may I have it?"

"Sure."

As simple as that. I relaxed and crossed my legs with a languid air. "Nathaniel, tell me about you. Do you work? Or don't you have to?"

"In a manner of speaking, I guess I don't have to," he said.

Of course he didn't. I always made my heroes independently wealthy. Who wanted the grubby details of poverty interfering with their passion?

"You're rich?"

"Comfortable," he conceded. "But I do work. I'm an architect. I have my own firm, courtesy of my grandfather. I joined it right out of college. When he died, he left it to me outright. During the past six months or so, things have sort of piled up on me and I was beginning to feel strung out, soured. So I took a sabbatical and came up here. I fly into the office once or twice a week."

"You have a plane?"

"No, but there's a charter service nearby."

Bewildered, I stared at him. I was still clinging to the theory that I alone had created this man sitting across from me; that I had, from some deep, subconscious strata of my mind, formed this world as well as my entry into it. It was the only theory that made a lick of sense. And right now it didn't make sense at all. This Nathaniel was an architect instead of a rancher, and very much his own man with his own life.

What was reality and what was illusion? I touched his hand. It was warm and hard, and I could feel his pulse. That was life beating under my fingers, and life was reality.

"Oh, Nathaniel," I whispered, my eyes filling with tears. Suddenly I was so afraid of what I'd done. What *had* I done? God only knew, I didn't.

Nathaniel was concerned, but I brushed away the tears and his questions. "Tell me more," I urged.

I listened with rapt attention. I thought, It's funny how easily we can talk. How enjoyable it is to listen to him, watching him unwind and become freer with me, laughing often, stopping to ask if I'd had enough yet! "Go on," I commanded.

He likes skiing, fishing, tennis, and tobogganing. He enjoys traveling and has made several trips to other continents, combining a small dash of business with a large measure of fun. He loves apple pie and chocolate anything, icy beer and thick pretzels spread with mustard; all kinds of cheese, good wines, and beautiful women; Italian food, Mexican food, Greek and Chinese food, and my breasts, which are small but so piquantly perky.

They really are, I thought, tickled at this marvelous alteration of my form.

Sunsets and prismed dawns exalt him. Roses, walking in an autumn woods, the crisp, cold quiet of a December morning, the color of my eyes and the wild blue columbine they resemble, all pleasure him. He's hooked on reading, any subject and mysteries in particular, Danzig concerts and Loreli, the famed folk singer. And he was married when he was twenty-four.

I straightened up with a snap of protest. "Married!"

"Yes. Oh, I'm not now," he hastened to reassure me.

"Did you love her?" I asked bluntly.

He was silent for a moment. I watched his fingers turn the coffee cup round and round. "I don't know," he said finally. "I really don't know what it was. She was warm, witty, intelligent . . . career-oriented and fiercely independent, but still a tender, feminine woman. We enjoyed each other's company, sex was good, we—well, after six months we decided the next logical step was marriage. At least it seemed logical at the time."

I sensed he did not often talk this frankly, and of course I thrilled to it. Thick, dark lashes veiled his eyes, but he looked up at my gentle question.

"What happened?"

He shrugged. "I don't know that either. During those six months we had great times together, laughing, talking, sharing. But once we were married—hell, who knows what went wrong." He poured another cup of coffee and heated up mine. "She was executive assistant to J. H. Natterly."

He looked at me as if I would of course know who J. H. Natterly was. I nodded faintly.

"Naturally she had to go on trips with him, so I was left with an empty apartment and no dinner, no wife, no nothing, sometimes as long as a month at a time, and I resented that." He gave a quick laugh. "Hey, this is getting pretty heavy. What say we change the subject?"

"No, please go on. I really do want to hear it," I coaxed. I was dying to hear it. Never in my wildest dreams would I have made him a divorced man.

"We just didn't mesh," he replied shortly. "There was no—no cohesion between us."

"No cohesion?"

"Maybe that's not the right word. But there's something I've seen between people who have really good marriages, something that makes you feel good just being around them. But we had nothing of substance, just endless friction." He paused to sip coffee, the cup held in both big hands. Over its thick rim, he gazed into his past, one I did not help create.

"It was as if we were testing each other and we both failed," he reflected. "Karmic tests, perhaps."

"Karmic tests?" I repeated, startled. "You believe in karma and all that?"

"Oh, hell, I don't know. It does go a long way toward explaining the inequities that exist between people, the pain, the suffering, the screwups." He shrugged. "This whole area is into metaphysics—some kind of a power vortex, or so they claim." He set down the cup and took my hand. "What about you? Are you into reincarnational realities?"

"No, not really," I said wryly. David and I were Episcopalians, with no leeway for religious adventuring. "Did you have children?"

"No. Another bone of contention; she didn't want any and I did. But she didn't have time, she said. And besides, in her opinion it was just another selfish male trait. I only wanted a son to carry on my name so I would have the illusion of living forever." Nathaniel's laugh hurt me.

"It's not selfish," I said, low and fierce, remembering David's eyes when our son was born, remembering his eyes when our son died. My throat was hurting. "It's not selfish!" I repeated.

Nathaniel stared at me. "Well, I guess it's personal choice. Anyway, she left, filed for divorce. A year later she was killed in a stupid car accident. I went a little crazy after that, but. . . ." He shrugged. "Obviously, I survived." He dropped my hand. "Do you know, you're the first person I've ever talked to like this."

"I'm glad you did," I replied warmly. "Do you have someone now? Someone steady, I mean."

"No. There are a few ladies I see on an irregular basis, but no involvements."

"In other words, you call the shots."

He shrugged, watching me with a quizzical smile. "That bother you?"

I aped his shrug. "Not as long as you don't try it with me." I poured the last of the coffee and took the pot to the sink. "Do you think you'll ever marry again?"

"I'm a little gun-shy," he admitted. "Lisa and I both had good heads on our shoulders, and look how we screwed up a perfectly simple thing."

"I've never thought of marriage as a simple thing."

"I guess it isn't. At least ours sure got complicated in a hurry."

"Do you still want children?" Leaning against the

sink, I watched his face with curious intensity. My questions—and his answers—were disturbingly important to me.

"I did when I was married, and not just for immortality's sake. I have a good relationship with my father. I always assumed that someday I'd have a son to do with me all the things I did with him." He shrugged again, a quick, hard dismissal of innocence. "But I guess I won't. Time does have a way of passing. Profound, huh?"

His quick, shy grin stroked all the way to my toes. I could see he was a little embarrassed at having told me such intimate things. Perhaps all men are like that, I thought. Certainly David always shied away from vocal intimacy.

I walked back to the table. "How old are you, Nathaniel?" I loved saying his name. Nathaniel Knight. A beautiful name for a beautiful man. I was suddenly filled with nameless yearnings.

"Thirty-four, honey. How old are you?"

I squirmed. "You should never ask a woman her age! Don't you know that?"

"Umm, I've heard that. I'd say offhand that you're . . . Roseanna, are you sure you're past the age of consent?" he asked, cocking an eyebrow.

I burst out laughing. It was so absurd! How old was I? Who the heck knew? "Just barely past," I drawled.

"Where is your family? Are your parents still living?"

"Yes, they have a ranch in New Mexico. A working ranch." He touched my nose. "You know all about me. Couldn't you return the favor?"

Unsettled by his request, I felt a pang of heart as I gazed at him. My fingers wove through his tumbled hair, continued slowly down his face to trace the firm line of his jaw and that magnificent mouth. Our eyes met in a look that shook me.

Withdrawing, I took our cups to the sink. Long shadows were marching across the meadow. "What time does it get dark here?" I asked without thinking.

"About eight."

"What time is it now?"

"Five-thirty. Why?"

"Because I have to be back at the meadow before dark." I said it baldly, knowing a barrage of questions would follow.

"Why?"

Just the one question, so much worse than a barrage. Logically I answered, "Because I would get lost in the dark."

I heard his deep sigh. "Roseanna, are you deliberately trying to drive me crazy?"

I ran to him and knelt at his feet. "Nathaniel, you are very dear to me. I feel so close to you."

"Yes, I know what you mean, honey. I feel as though I've known you a lifetime. Another lifetime, perhaps, or in some other world, but I've known you." Sighing, he shook his head. A finger tipped up my chin. "Stay with me tonight, Roseanna? Sleep in my arms tonight."

"No, I can't tonight." I stood up and he took my hands. "But I will, darling. Someday I'll spend the night with you," I said recklessly. *The next time David goes out of town, in fact,* I thought. *When I can make . . . arrangements.* I shivered. That sounded so tacky. Cheating wives made arrangements. I pulled free of his grasp.

"I'd like to ask one question, and I'd like an answer," he said flatly.

I sensed what that question was, and I certainly didn't want to answer it. "No more questions," I returned lightly, but firmly. "I really should be going now."

I did want to go. I was afraid of this feeling burgeoning inside me. Already I was so involved with this man that I was planning the night I would spend in his arms.

"All right, no questions. Maybe I wouldn't like the answer anyway," he said coolly.

He pulled me into his arms and kissed me hard. I looped my arms around his neck. Our bodies came together.

"But you don't have to go this minute," he said.

"No, not this minute, nor the next," I whispered.

"So, when are you going to pop in on me again?" he queried as he pulled on jeans. His voice was light and his question casual. I didn't know whether I liked that or not.

"Soon. Very soon." I sat down on the bed and wrestled with a sandal. He took it from me.

"What small feet you have. What size shoe do you wear?"

"Right foot, size five; left, size five and a half," I said.

"Hmmm . . . and when is very soon, pretty thing?"

"I don't know. Ouch, Nathaniel, you've caught my toe in the straps!" I pulled his hair for this and, a second later, I was tumbled over backwards on the bed with him half smothering me, demanding an apology.

Grateful for any reprieve, I gave him a juicy, smacking kiss with my apology. I would have liked to make love again, but Nathaniel was all tuckered out. This is the one awesome inequality between man and woman. Women are always sitting on "go," but men must first pass "start" before they get to "go." I advanced this theory to Nathaniel and he disputed it hotly. When I trailed a finger around the evidence backing up my theory, he threw up his hands and proclaimed me absolutely correct, so I kissed him and nearly got him past "start" again.

Driven wild by all the glad noise coming from the bed, Carasel began leaping around it. One of her more exuberant leaps carried her up and over the side. She jumped atop us, wriggled down between us, and licked us half to death.

"Carasel!" Nathaniel groaned. Putting the dog off the bed, he sat on the side of it and rubbed her silky head. His eyes were very dark when he turned to me.

"It's been a lovely day, Roseanna," he said softly.

Something fluttered wildly in my chest. "Yes—oh yes, it has!" I gave him my hands and he drew me to my feet. We stood holding each other for a long, exquisite time unbroken by words or movement.

Finally I uttered the words we both hated hearing.

"I have to go, honey."

Releasing me, he went to his dresser and took something from a drawer. When he returned to me, he held my gold chain. I caught my breath. I'd forgotten about

that chain! And now, like a bad penny, here it had
turned up again, to taunt me.

"No, it's yours," I said when he would put it round my
neck.

"Pretty expensive little keepsake, Roseanna," he said,
watching me alertly. "Someone might wonder what happened to it."

"No. I bought it myself, so . . ." I put it over his
head and drew the shining links down his throat to his
bare chest. I grinned. "Looks prettier on you than it
ever did on me!" Easing from his embrace, I scooped up
Carasel. "I really do have to go. Alone, Nathaniel.
Please, allow me this freedom? If you like me as much
as I like you, be patient with me."

"Patience never was my strong suit, but since this is
just fun and games. . . ." An almost imperceptible
pause. "I'll curb my curiosity. For the time being," he
added, his voice flattening. "You really don't know when
you'll be back?"

"I really don't. Circumstances. . . ." I waved a hand
vaguely. Watching his mouth quirk awry, I felt another
flutter in my midsection.

Naturally he had to walk me to the meadow. Then,
reluctantly—a mild wording—he stopped in the grove
and let me go on alone. At best, I suppose he considered this insistence on solitude one of my little idiosyn-
crasies. As for me, I felt marvelously exhausted, a little
exhilarated, and so confused that my mind cried out for
help.

But since my mind had gotten me into this lovely
mess, it was up to me to get out of it. The problem was,
I didn't want to get out of it. I stopped in front of the
glistening gray boulder and drew a deep, shoulder-high
breath of sweet air. I had created a superb Dream King-
dom, equal to or even surpassing Kubin's mythical
realm. His, however, was located in the vast Heavenly
Mountain area somewhere between China and Kazakh-
stan. Mine was simply Somewhere.

Or maybe Nowhere. After another deep breath, I
stepped into the space between these two chimerical
places.

Emerging in my closet provoked an odd little ripple in reality. For a microsecond or so I was neither here nor there, and it took a few heartbeats to orient myself.

Nathaniel's newspaper was tucked under my arm. After letting Carasel out, I poured myself a small sherry and curled up on my chaise lounge. Then, feeling as though I was opening something as mysterious as an ancient tomb, I took up the small paper and looked at the front page.

The date first. His world was ten years ahead of mine! Ten years and one month, actually. It was April here, the end of May there. I mulled that over for a while, but as usual came up with no explanations.

Hiller, California. I had been in California, then! Surely this was a local paper? The headline featured the "smoke and mirrors" policies of the County Highway Department. It seems Farm Road 102 was paved to a point just past the Commissioner's daughter's house, and left graveled the rest of the way. Below this dark suspicion of skulduggery was a short, black-bordered box informing me that a wing of the International Peacekeeping Services had been sent to Monswarda, Africa, to put down a "brushfire uprising." There was no drama in the story; it was just something that needed doing and was being done.

Swiftly I turned pages, pausing here and there whenever something of interest arrested my attention. I might have been looking at our own evening newspaper, I thought. Deaths, robberies, airplane crashes, a fifteen-car pileup on the Venasee freeway. Puppies for sale, kittens for free, pizza to go.

A politician pleads nolo contendere, which is Latin for "I do not wish to contest it," a plea by the defendant in a criminal case declaring that he will not make a defense but does not admit guilt either. A phrase with which I am well acquainted since it comes in so handy whenever David makes a federal case out of some little nothing of a crime I've absentmindedly committed.

Housewife wins lottery. An eighty-year-old man selects for his eighth wife a seventeen-year-old female, "obviously retarded." My opinion, not the paper's. To-

day marks the anniversary of the Second World War.
My God, they had that insanity, too? The LBA has is-
sued a report confirming massive abuse of funds in la-
bor training programs. Obscenity charges against
Marshall Ping have been dropped. A tornado struck
Dickensville High School, no injuries reported.

Injunction sought against pornography ordinance; al-
leged coverup in State Attorney trial— Lord! just like
home.

Pope Louis visits Mexico. My heart jumped. God
lived on Nathaniel's world too! I was so glad.

Desperation Prayer for today: Quote. God, if You
are, help me, if You can. Unquote. Succinct and covers
everything.

Another item caught my eye. The nineteenth-century
symphonic drama, "Keileen's Sixth Symphony," will be
performed tonight by the San Lio Philharmonic Orches-
tra. Viveca would appreciate that, I reflected. She loves
classical music.

The Congress of World Churches will be held in Vi-
enna. Shampayne says Mexico will be a world power
within the next decade. In another news flash, Irit Ming
has taken a fifth husband and seized power at the same
time, proclaiming herself Imperial Empress of the Re-
public of Haiti. That Irit is quite a gal, I mused. She
looks like a Hawaiian woodrose. Six feet tall, multilin-
gual, she was educated in England where she married
Lord Holinshed who subsequently died and left her a
dilapidated castle, an impeccable title, and two grown
sons. Irit's response to bloodshed is terse and unmarred
by conscience. "You cannot bring in the new without
sweeping out the old."

Another fascinating woman confronts me on page
four: Elizabeth Howell, president of the United States
of America, will address the nation tonight. Subject:
Health Care.

"My God, a lady president!" I whispered gleefully.
"David would blow a gasket!"

A foldout section of sparse but lush advertisements
came next. Impossibly thin women wearing lingerie that
might have come from Macy's appear. Beer ads, whis-

key and wines in full color are enticingly suggestive of the good life.

"To a man, Siren's Song whispers sex. . . ." Gets right to the point, that Siren's Song. Costly, too—one-half ounce, five hundred dollars. Hemlines are all over the place; sleeves are long and flowing. The natural look is in this year. Dresses just skim the body and waistlines are definitely there. Frothy, romantic swirls of pleated chiffon and misty watercolors are touted for an evening of dining and dancing at Mirabella's. Oh, and these absolutely beautiful pumps! If I were there, I'd rush right down and buy three pairs—the marvelous rust, that pale, satiny dove gray, and those sexy red ones. A bargain at ninety dollars a pair.

Slaighter and Jonge declare sex to be a rejuvenating force, as vital to the human body as food and water. Slaighter and Jonge needn't have wasted three years researching this, they could have asked me.

There are car ads, of course—sleekly styled, dark-windowed, jewel-like colors; cowboy-Cadillac pickups for the pseudo Westerner; or sleek and plain, like Nathaniel's. An article debates the pros and cons of owning an electric automobile. Pros: Noiseless, non-polluting, inexpensive. Cons: Initial lack of power, speed, and recharge facilities. Still, thousands have been sold as commuter cars, it is reported.

There's a page of personals: the Carl Lamont family wishes to express their gratitude . . . Judy Jordan wants a 1960 Captura in mint condition . . . the twenty-fifth annual Ladies' Quilting Bee will be held in Fuller's Hall at eight o'clock, May thirtieth . . . a welcome-home party is planned for Kate Marga—Kate's been tooling around in space for the past year. . . .

The telephone rang. Startled, I stared at it for four rings. I had left Nathaniel's earth at six-thirty. It was after ten when I returned to my own. My watch began running the second I was home again. An Einsteinian mystery, not solvable by me.

On the sixth ring, I picked up the receiver.

"Where on earth have you been?" our daughter asked.

Good question, Lexi. And one everyone seems to be asking me lately. "I ate dinner out," I said. *Yeah, right out of this world,* my mind taunted. "Why? Did you call earlier?"

"Only a dozen times," she said. And my answering machine wasn't on, I remembered.

I confessed to forgetfulness, and asked what she wanted.

"To ask you and Daddy to have dinner with Clark and me Wednesday night. I know you dislike him, but it's my life and he's an important part of it, Mother," she said defiantly.

I sighed. "Yes, I know. I just wish . . . well, he's so dry and humorless, Lexi. And by far too ambitious."

"He's quiet and self-contained," she corrected. "And ambition is certainly not a fault. Daddy happens to think he's excellent husband material."

"I see. Okay, dinner Wednesday night. Tony's?"

Tony's it was. She'd make the reservations. After a few minutes of chitchat, she rang off.

I lingered beside the telephone, one finger poised to dial, as I weighed the urge to call Viveca. Beside me lay an alien newspaper, bearing a date years into the future. The sweet scent of Nathaniel still clung to my body, and my hair was rumpled by the same distant wind that had brushed my cheeks with color.

Naturally I was being eaten alive by the need to talk with someone about all this and get another opinion besides my dizzy own. I could just imagine what that opinion would be, but, still, I needed to share it. The urge to say it aloud and hear myself say it was an aggravating itch.

Maybe an itchy feeling is what drives a Catholic to confession, I thought moodily. God, I wish I was blessed, if only for an hour, with this marvelous way of spilling one's guts with immunity! Since I wasn't Catholic, and there was no one to share this tremendous adventure into the realm of shadowed unknowns, I decided to shower and wash away as much of the itch as I could.

When I returned to the bedroom attired in David's

robe and smelling of plain soap, the sight of that little newspaper was profoundly unsettling. It lay there so starkly black-and-white, so *real.* An urgency came over me—I had to get rid of it! What would happen if David saw it, I asked myself, grasping at even a hint of logic. How could I possibly explain *that*?

Without further ado, I took the paper to the closet and thrust it into the shadowy space that led to mysteries and wonders. It disappeared. I let out my breath. Doubtless sheets of paper were even now blowing across the meadow, wrapping around bushes, sailing aloft perhaps, borne on thermal winds to litter pristine desert sands.

With a sound quite like a whimper, I closed the closet door and climbed into my big, empty bed. I felt six years old again, and fighting off the unexplained noises that always came in the dark.

Chapter 6

*I*t was four long days later, a lovely Saturday morning at home and I was about to jump out of my skin. Not only was I up at seven o'clock but I was downstairs in the kitchen brooding into a cup of coffee. David hadn't left me any. I'd had to make my own and it was atrocious. Besides that I had PMS. I was two pounds heavier than I was yesterday, and horny to boot.

Mulling over my mistake of even getting out of bed today, I heard his escalating voice with an inward sigh. He had been a turkey since his return from Austin, finding fault and criticizing everything until I felt strung out over seven counties.

I rushed upstairs to confront the problem. David was out of dental floss. I resolved it by lending him mine and promising to buy more today.

"Thanks," he said, displaying that sudden rare grin that had hooked me in the first place.

Feeling a pang of guilt at being so wrapped up in my own secret life, I stretched up and shut his mouth with mine.

It was a dead-fire kiss. Stepping back, I could see his mind already racing at a precise fifty-eight miles an hour toward his Houston office. It didn't matter. I patted his cheek and flopped down on the bed to watch him dress.

He was a meticulous dresser. The simple blue-and-white–striped shirt and tailored navy slacks looked as though they had been made for him by nimble-fingered elves.

Smiling, distracted and in a hurry, he moved gracefully around the bedroom, gathering his change, folding
a handkerchief and slipping it into a pocket with the
same precision a surgeon uses putting on that final ban-
dage. I wondered what he would say if I told him another man shared his bed? Only in my thoughts and
dreams, but still. . . .

Sharply I shook my head. Dreams and fantasies were
not sinful. Although the preacher did say lusting in the
heart was as bad as the real thing . . . oh, damn. I carried too much emotional baggage around already. Why
was I adding more?

Mother's sweet voice suddenly rang through my mind.
Because those who dance must pay the fiddler, Roseanna.

With a wry smile, I thought about how much I've
missed her since she "passed on," to use her much more
agreeable little euphemism. We'd had no relationship to
speak of, but she was always there for me, ever ready to
tell me that I had no right to be depressed, that David
was a gift from God Himself, and to count my blessings
while I still had them to count.

In other words, Roseanna, God will get you for that.

Then, tucking away the threat of Divine Retribution
with all the other nebulous guilts which served to keep
me humble and uptight, I would apologize for thinking I
was depressed and promise to be more careful in the
future.

I remembered that as a child I never missed Sunday
School. At the end of every year I had fifty-two gold
stars for perfect attendance. It was Mother who gave
out the gold stars for my wedding anniversaries. Each
one we passed was a milestone for her as well as me.
She was so fearful that I would screw up and lose this
splendid fish I had somehow managed to hook. From
the first, David had taken care of Mother. He had been
her security, too.

I was born in Alabama and spent the first ten years of
my life there. Mother's family were born-again Baptists,
old South, illustrious ancestors, genteel poverty, goddamn Yankees background. I have aunts so gently born
that no one says condom in front of them. I have cous-

ins so delicate they faint at the slightest provocation—even when their plans include having sex that very night with the stableboy. I have uncles so southern that they exist on bourbon and branch water—polluted, of course; where can you find an unpolluted branch now? They're all as poor as church mice, but since no one admits it, no one is discommoded by it. Aunt Mercy, coming up eighty, has a charge account at the local market and hasn't paid a cent on it in twenty years. One would sooner think of dunning the statue of General Sherman than Aunt Mercy.

Daddy blew into this miasma of yesterday's lost glory like a breath of fresh air straight off the Texas Panhandle. When he asked for Mother's hand and she gave it, there were prostrate aunts lying about his feet like faded bits of confetti from the last great ball. Amid weeping, consternation and dire predictions concerning Mother's glorious mane of golden hair and its chances of making the trip intact—the ratio of rape being put at one per every twenty-five miles—Daddy took Mother back to Texas. There, according to Mother, they lived happily, without a single harsh word between them until his death eight years later. Then she came home again, carrying me in her womb.

I never knew my daddy. I wish to God I had.

Mother married someone named Uncle Fred. At least that's what I called him. When he died, leaving her a pile of debts, she took off for Texas again, dragging twelve-year-old me with her. She worked, paid a monthly sum on those infernal debts, raised me with a Bible in one hand and a switch in the other. . . .

Feeling half waif, half matron, I got up and bathed. I was literally aching to see Nathaniel, an ache disturbingly close to my heart. But I couldn't. Like the past four days, this was too entangled in the spiderweb of mother-wife-friend-neighbor and whatever else I was to allow time for personal desires. I could not just up and go to him whenever I wanted, and I resented that. With a ton of guilt, of course. Every one of those labels were important to me.

After dressing in my oldest jeans and shirt, I went

downstairs and fell upon the chores of housewifery. It
was truly a lovely day here. Was it lovely in the meadow,
too? I stood before the kitchen sink watching three tiny
yellow butterflies flitting about the great, orange-red
trumpets of my amaryllis. I envied those butterflies. So
what if they were likely to be eaten by birds at any minute; they were free, weren't they?

"Lord, Roseanna, you'd shrivel up and die without
David and Lexi and this house and all your labels," I
muttered. Which was solid truth; I would have no iden-
tity without them. Hadn't I held Viveca in my arms
while she cried, devastated by this discovery?

*"Roseanna, I don't know who I am anymore! I'm not
Viveca Valante, housewife. I'm not Viveca Blake, young
college woman! Who am I? What am I? I don't know
anymore, Roseanna!"*

I shivered, remembering the haunting fear in her
voice. Like her, I had cut my teeth on the absolute fact
that a woman was just a cipher without a man. Still,
there are times, I admitted, hating that freewheeling
butterfly, when I wonder about that. This morning, this
beautiful morning, I would so like to be free.

Viveca recrossed her long, slim legs and idly scratched
her arm. But the gray eyes traveling over me were far
from idle. We had just wasted two hours at the River
Oaks Country Club. Neither Viv nor I were active members, but we're on the Autumn Charity Ball committee
benefiting a local hospice, and where the committee
lunches, we lunch.

One of my New Year's resolutions was a solid vow to
eschew any sort of committee this year. But Viv got
caught, and naturally she reeled me in with her. We had
stopped off at her house for a drink and a quick autopsy
of the meeting before I dashed home to dress for dinner.

I stretched on the redwood lounger with voluptuous
languor. The afternoon sunshine imitated warm fingers
stroking through the thin fabric covering my thighs. Six
days had passed since I had seen Nathaniel, six days of
growing urgency massing in my heart and loins. Glanc-

ing up to catch Viveca's intense, faintly puzzled scrutiny, I flushed.

"Isn't this gorgeous weather we've been having!" I enthused. "I love it! It agrees with me."

"Something is certainly agreeing with you lately," Viveca said, dry as the wine we were drinking.

I decided to let that pass. Viveca was wearing pale green linen and her obsolete look again. Standing silhouetted against the sun, she was sleek, sophisticated, Woman On Her Own. On her own and still terrified. I wanted to wrap my arms around her and tell her everything was all right, and maybe weep a little.

"Anything wrong, Viv?" I asked softly.

She shrugged and laughed. "I was just thinking. Have you ever heard of a man dumping his wife for an intelligent older woman? Ah, well . . . Qué sera, sera."

"Some men are just natural-born idiots," I said fiercely, getting up and hugging her.

She walked me to my car and we kissed cheeks. She smelled like hyacinths, I thought. As I wended my way around the circular drive, I glanced back and waved. She was still standing there, looking infinitely small and vulnerable against the backdrop of her enormous white-pillared house with its empty master bedroom. I wished she would acquire a genuine patina of toughness, for my heart's sake if nothing else.

My own house felt warm, loving, and lived in. I stood for a moment, just letting its aura of security diffuse the inner chill that came with deeper thoughts of Viveca. Still preoccupied, I showered and dressed for dinner at our own posh country club. Viv has lost her anchor, I mused, straightening the jacket of my white knit suit. She is a very small boat set adrift on a very large sea. Like me, she had no experience steering her own course in these uncharted waters. How would I fare navigating this very same sea, alone and without an anchor to hold me in place? A scary thought. I shuddered.

Contrarily, when David came in and said that Jack Valante was joining us for dinner, I saw red. My dislike for Viveca's ex-husband had in no way slackened. "Why?" I asked bluntly.

"Because he's joining the club tonight."

"Old Tightwad's putting out the money to join a club? Will wonders never cease!"

David rocked back on his heels. "Now how do you know he's a tightwad?"

"Because Viveca said so, that's how. Tighter than a rubber on Bubba's—" I stopped. It seemed prudent; David's mouth had tightened. "I truly don't know why you associate with him," I defied him. "You're such a decent man and he's—well, not only is he a mean-spirited penny-pincher, he's a womanizer to boot."

"Mean-spirited, penny-pincher, womanizer." David picked up his briefcase. "Those are some pretty harsh judgments you're flinging around, Roseanna," he replied mildly enough to ruffle my neck hairs.

"Oh, come on, David. Just because you went to law school together doesn't blind you to his character faults. You know he's stingy. You also know he cheated on Viv."

David regarded me for a silent moment. "Maybe he had good cause."

"Good cause! What possible cause could he have had for hurting Viv like that?" I demanded, ignoring the sudden unease my question evoked.

"Maybe she didn't excite him anymore. Or just didn't fulfill his needs. Who knows?" Shrugging, he turned toward the door.

"And maybe he didn't fulfill hers, David! But *she* didn't start screwing around—not once in all those years of marriage!" I shot back. But the fire had gone out of me. Not that I compared my recent activities with Jack Valante's tomcatting habits, I quickly assured myself. But *something* disquieted me.

"What about us, David?" I blurted out, as something roiled the tiny pool of insecurity that lay deep inside me. "Do you still find me exciting? Are you satisfied with our relationship, does it fulfill your needs, or do you—"

"Oh, for God's sake, Rosie, let's not get into this relationship crap!" he cut in. "You're exciting, I'm satisfied, we're fine, all right? And I'm late."

"Relationship crap?" I carried on, but he was already

mounting the stairs. Deflated, I sank down on the couch. "Relationship crap." That smarted. Well, don't take it personally, I advised myself, it's just his way. An attorney deals in logic, not feelings, so it's perfectly natural that he shies away from emotional discussions. . . .

Suddenly fed up with rationalizing David's aversion to intimacy, I walked out onto the terrace, blinking back the threat of tears. I was exciting, he was satisfied, we were fine. What more could a woman ask for? Well, hell, obviously *something* more! I literally ached with unfulfilled needs.

I had wanted babies, lots of babies. After two miscarriages and one stillborn birth, little David Hadley Tait the Fifth had been a miracle: healthy, lusty, beautiful. David had been so proud I feared he'd burst with all the beautiful feelings going off like rockets inside him! And when that brief, lovely time ended in ravaging pain, doubt, and unbearable loss, I had watched a part of him die, too.

We had borne our grief in such different ways. Viveca had wrapped me in unjudging love and I managed to hold on to my sanity. But David had been unable to even stay in the same house with me. After the funeral he had lived in the corporate suite for over a month before returning, gaunt, flinty-eyed, and sucked dry of love and joy, to take up our life again.

If only I'd been able to give him another child, I thought, retracing an old and well-used track. It would have made all the difference—I know it would have! Another son, to at least partially fill that gaping hole in our lives.

But it hadn't happened. My fault of course, I thought with a sudden twist of pain. It hurts to know you have failed your husband in such an important way.

Shaking free of memories, I looked up and smiled as he walked in, all showered, sleek and classy in a silk sport coat and tailored slacks.

"David, I'm sorry, I shouldn't put down your choice of friends. Who you like or dislike is your business."

"Apology accepted," he said lightly. "Ready to go?"

I turned on my heel and led the way to the car.

Both absorbed in thought, we drove in silence. I wanted something. But feeling naggingly needful was nothing new. Every woman, I suppose, has to cope with that peculiar, resistive ache. One simply busied oneself until it either passed or was pushed down a little deeper.

This ache, however, was harder, sharper, impossible to shove aside as unimportant.

I opened the sun roof and gazed up at the clearing night sky. A few stars shone through. I wondered if Nathaniel was looking at them, too. Or were they even the same stars?

Wednesday morning I was back in Nathaniel's California again, beside the great, gray boulder that stood like a sentinel at the doorway to my own world. For all the magic it contained, the semicircular patch of grass looked no different from the rest of the weeds and clover that carpeted this summery meadow.

I still held my breath while I was en route, and let it out in an audible whoosh of air when I arrived. Then I had to stand stock-still for a few seconds while I imagined all my scattered atoms collecting themselves and reforming the very special and unique being that was me, Roseanna.

Roseanna the blessed, I thought, feeling giddy from my swirl of kaleidoscopic emotions. I was so happy, so filled with anticipation. And guilty of course, for I had arbitrarily and without explanation canceled my whole duty-laden day to spend this time with Nathaniel.

Putting Carasel on her leash, I looked around with my usual sense of wonder. It was after nine when I left home. Here, dawn was just breaking over the meadow, a beautiful dawn, pink and gold and lilac. Birdsong was beginning to pierce the hush and a soft little breeze blew my skirt about my knees.

Nathaniel would be in bed. I started across the meadow on that stimulating thought. Nathaniel in bed and, very soon, me in bed with him. Hot chills ran up and down my spine as Carasel and I raced over the hill and down into the yard.

The familiar black truck was parked beside the little

cottage now bathed in a mist of gold. I felt a rush of relief, for there was always the possibility that he might be gone on the day I chose to visit.

Carasel's bark reached the door before we did. Nathaniel opened it and stepped out just as I drew up to the rosebush aglow with white, satiny blossoms. His face lit up. He held out his arms to me. I dived into them and clung mightily. His hair was mussed, his cheeks shadowed with sprouting beard. He smelled wonderful!

"Oh, Nathaniel!" I exulted. Dropping Carasel's leash, I laughed up at him, a merry invitation to share the glory of our reunion.

"God, how can I not respond to this!" he burst out almost angrily before his mouth claimed mine. Carasel romped in through the open door, but I had forgotten Carasel.

"I'm so glad to see you," I whispered, kissing his prickly cheeks and ending up on his mouth again. He tasted incredibly good. Within moments we were in his bed making love; hot, sweet love, quick to crest, quick to come in explosive fulfillment.

My face burrowed into his damp shoulder as I calmed my breathing. We make such a marvelous perfume together, I thought, inhaling deeply.

His back was satin-smooth under my fingers. I caressed him, kissed him, whispered to him. All my past yearnings seemed to dissolve in these primal pleasures.

We made love again, slowly this time, teasing each other to the peak of excitement, then soaring wild and free.

We rolled apart.

Turning onto his side, Nathaniel began the questions I didn't know how to answer.

"Please, Nathaniel, don't start this again. Just take me as I am," I said with a flash of irritation. Why was he so hung up on knowing where I came from!

"You're going to drive me insane," he accused.

But for another day, he would take me as I was.

He made coffee while I lounged in bed and thought lovely thoughts. I had hours and hours to spend with him! There wouldn't be any complications, I assured myself when doubts promptly surfaced. This time belonged to Nathaniel and me.

We showered together, a magnificent new experience. He soaped me, laughing as he watched frothy bubbles breaking on my breasts. Leaning down to take a rosy nipple in his mouth, he tugged and suckled until I felt fire streaking from that central point downwards. He moved the pale green bar of soap down my belly and into the delta of my thighs, making a froth of lather in my dark gold nest of hair. His hands glided over my back, my hips, my bottom, and down my legs, with kisses along the way. And then it was my turn.

I soaped his back and buttocks. I scrubbed his chest, then squatted to lave his long, muscular legs. His big toe was crooked. "What happened to your toe?"

"Horse stepped on it when I was a barefoot lad of twelve—broke the damn thing. I was too embarrassed to tell Dad, so it healed that way. Does it detract from my appeal?"

"Terribly." I sighed, and stood up to kiss his enticing grin. Gently I lathered his cheeks and the strong column of his neck. My slick hands moved slowly down his belly and into the dark hair of his genitals. "How do you like this?" I murmured.

"Baby, it's a full-time job if you want it," he muttered.

Oh, God, those hot, glowing green eyes! I trembled. He reached for me and brought my slippery body to his. His breath warmed my skin as he kissed my eyelids, my nose, the pulse throbbing at the base of my throat. Water streamed over us, adding another pulse of stimulation. The avalanche of sensation took my breath away. We stood kissing under the rain of water until the excitement firing our bodies surged out of control.

"Now, baby, now," he said thickly. We moved out of the compact shower and dropped to the floor.

It was wild and spontaneous and ridiculous. We were all scrunched up in a tangle of limbs. But we didn't mind. In fact, we didn't even notice. The slap of flesh against wet flesh, faster and faster and faster, was a symphony without equal.

"Roseanna, Roseanna, Roseanna!" he chanted, low

and hoarse and on my mouth. We were flying so high we would surely break our necks when we fell to earth again. And then he plunged deep and our entire world was only this glorious sensation of being sweetly, hotly, deliciously torn apart.

Our senses returned one at a time. "Ouch," I said with a blissful sigh.

"What? Why ouch?"

"I think my back is breaking," I mused. "I think I have a bruised bottom, too. Now, Nathaniel," I warned as he laughed and kissed me. "I cannot go another round on this hard surface!"

"Yeah. I think I broke something, too. My little toe, on the doorframe." He raised up on his arms to glare at me. "Roseanna, you're a witch! I'm much too old to be screwing around on bathroom floors!" he accused. "Good screwing, though."

I giggled. He licked me. Both cheeks, then my chin. The bath mat was carving canals in my skin. I wriggled. He grinned and licked my lips.

"Stop that . . . get off, you big lug, and feed me," I ordered.

With much hilarity we showered again, then made a lavish breakfast: scrambled eggs, ham, fluffy biscuits, orange juice . . . ambrosia for the gods. I wore his midnight blue fleece robe, ankle-length on me. He told me I was beautiful and I believed him. When I am with Nathaniel, I do not permit my mind to shatter this lovely pleasure. Stark reality would break through soon enough.

"Pour me another cup of coffee, wench," he commanded, and I hastened to obey. He chuckled. "Now and then the clouds of confusion peel back and I see why I put up with this outrageous indignity you do me," he observed as I sat back down.

"Why do you?" I asked quietly. "I've really wondered."

"Me, too. Everytime I think about you dropping in and out of my life—on your terms, not mine, when *you* want to see me, not when *I* want to see you—I wonder. Why the hell am I waiting around in a meadow like some dumb teenager hoping his dream girl will appear. . . ." He drew a ragged breath. "To put it succinctly, it's an ego-blowing situation. But then I remember how happy . . . how just plain fuckin' happy I am with you, how good the sex is, how much fun you are," he ended in a rush. "None of which existed for me until you happened along. I've been an emotional zero since my grandfather's death, and Lisa's. Everything's been so flat; no ups, no downs, just flat. And now? Deep valleys and wild, soaring peaks. I feel alive again, Roseanna, and you did that for me. So, if you want to keep on playing this really *dumb* little game"—he cocked an inquiring eyebrow, then scowled at my vigorous nod—"I'll let you. For awhile."

"You'll *let* me, hmm," I murmured, mouth atwist. But I thanked him and went on to something else. We talked for hours just sitting at the table with the sunshine pouring in and Carasel at our feet.

Of course we talked about him, for I was anxious to know every detail of his life. But we discussed my life, too, little things, safe things: my childhood, my adolescent years, my environment. I revealed that I, too, had once lived in San Francisco and thought it the most enchanting city on earth.

He leaned toward me, his face suddenly intense. "When did you live there?"

"When I was nineteen. I took off during the summer and lived the wild life for three months—if you can call it that when your mother drops in unexpectedly about every two weeks." I made a face. "I had lived a pretty sheltered life—private schools, summers at my aunt's château in France, guarded like the virginal maiden I was."

"Virginal maiden, hmm?" He grinned. "Good thing I wasn't around then. That wouldn't have lasted long."

I slanted him a glance. "You think so?" I was flirting and apparently successfully, for he laughed as if he found my murmur a delicious challenge.

"Your family's wealthy?"

"Poor as church mice. But I did have one rich uncle."

"Where'd you go to college?" he asked, casual enough that I answered without thinking.

"Texas."

"What part of Texas?"

I hesitated, suddenly wary. "Sneaky, Nathaniel, sneaky," I said warningly, shaking a finger at him.

He shrugged. "Can't blame a guy for trying," he tossed off. "You earn a degree?"

"Fine Arts Major, a Minor in Horticulture," I said.

"Ah, brains as well as beauty. What do you do now?"

His question rang in my ears, inducing a sudden wild urge to blurt out, *I'm a housewife, Nathaniel. A mother, a writer, a committeewoman—all manner of things. Nearly twenty years older than you are, my darling Nathaniel. And not even sure if I'm asleep, awake, or even where I am at this exact moment.*

I shook off the dangerous urge. "I guess I'm a professional volunteer," I said thoughtfully. "I don't need a paying job, so I work at the hospital, at the church, things like that." I shrugged. "I keep busy."

I longed to share more intimate details with him, but of course I could not. Closing off part of myself to him was painful but necessary. "Enough talk!" I proclaimed. "Let's get dressed and go for a walk." I glanced at his clock. "Good grief, it's after noon!"

"So it is." He stretched. "Let's walk down by the lake. I want you to meet some of my friends."

His words startled me. Could I meet other people here? I hadn't even considered expanding the boundaries of my magic circle. "I don't know if I can do that, or even if I'm allowed to," I half sighed at this intrusion of reality.

"Why not? And why wouldn't you be allowed to?" His eyebrows drew together. "Who's to say no to whatever you want to do here?"

Who indeed? "Well, me, I guess." Drawing a deep breath, I blew it out and made a decision. "Okay, let's walk to the lake."

Chapter 7

*T*hough apprehensive about deeper involvement in Nathaniel's world, I felt the same eager curiosity Carasel displayed as we made our way down the narrow, winding road to the artist colony. The closer we came, the faster my heart beat. When I spied a young couple and two small boys picking berries along the road, my breathing apparatus went haywire. I didn't know what to expect. Not from them; they looked normal enough in their unisex jeans, T-shirts, and sneakers. But could I actually get mixed up in these people's lives?

Nathaniel greeted them cheerily, and introduced me as his friend. The children promptly took off after Carasel, who cast me a panicked look and threw herself headlong into the shrubbery. Parental rebukes stopped the rambunctious pursuit. I called my dog back and held her while we conversed. Bravely I sampled a few of their berries. Just plain ole blackberries, I marveled, tart-sweet and warm from the sun.

"Don't forget my show on Saturday," the woman reminded Nathaniel. She was playing Nancy in a local theater production of *Down Under* and was darned good, her husband stated.

I assured him I had no doubt of that.

"See you later," I said as we parted. Such a simple phrase, but it shook me. I held Nathaniel's hand the rest of the way.

The colony was a cluster of pastel-colored cottages, leased year round by people of artistic bent and those

who only thought they were, Nathaniel said. I found it
all very charming. The yards were mowed clover, but the
setting was picture-postcard perfect with those graceful
old trees and the wildflowers romping right up to front
porches. Roses were everywhere, competing vigorously
with the weeds. It smelled heavenly, this rural Xanadu.
A parklike expanse of wild grasses separated the colony
from the lake, and the backdrop of mountains topped it
off like icing on the cake.

I fell in love with the place, of course. I'd love to live
in one of those timeworn cottages, I thought wistfully.

We met many people in the next hour or so, among
them a doe-eyed poetess, a painter in psychedelic over-
alls who immediately asked me to pose nude, a psychic
who told me I had a lovely aura and posing nude would
do nothing to dim its radiance. This started a lively de-
bate about the wisdom of my decision to pass up a
surefire chance of immortality.

They were a mixed group and I liked them all. But I
felt as though Nathaniel gave me a gift of great value
when he introduced me to Liz Chance.

Besides being gloriously, magnificently pregnant, Liz
was delightfully pretty. Looking at her face made you
feel good all over. She had enormous blue eyes and
dimples so deep you could plant petunias in them.
When she smiled, she lit up the whole room and everyone in it.

Her hair was a perennially tousled cap of fluffy curls.
Such artful disarray bespoke a most competent hairdresser, as did the streaks of silvery beige set in among
dark gold locks. Her yellow linen maternity top and
slacks increased her radiance until she seemed to glow
with health and vitality.

She was open, merry, an instant friend. I guessed her
age as early twenties. Young enough to be my daughter
in my world, I thought, savoring the irony.

She was also unmarried and not the least bit concerned about it. I could tell Nathaniel liked her, although once, when I looked at her stomach and then at
him, he shook his head with the same bemused smile I
wore.

Liz didn't mind being pregnant. Liz didn't mind being husbandless. In fact, there didn't seem to be a thing in the world worthy of Liz's concern. Within fifteen minutes of listening to her froggy voice, I adored her. Blithe spirit, Liz Chance.

"Gosh, you're pretty, Roseanna!" she exclaimed, looking bewildered. "So what are you doing hanging around with Nate?"

Nathaniel glared. She laughed.

"He just got lucky, I guess," I said.

We had popcorn and lemonade under a tree beside the lake. Life, fascinatingly diverse, bustled all around us. Lots of children; evidently artists are fertile as well as talented. Old and young mingled in what was to me a rare and pleasing harmony.

There were some bad moments, like when Liz asked me where I was from, where I lived, how long I was staying, and was I Nathaniel's girl?

I responded evasively, but then I caught Nathaniel's expression. I turned and kissed him, which answered Liz's last question, anyway.

About then another guest joined us. "This is my honey," Liz said, patting his cheek.

Her honey was close to forty, a quiet little man with a cherubic face and a wee bald spot, who perched at Liz's elbow and guarded her against the world. His real name was Matt Riener, a late-blooming artist as yet undiscovered, but whose sandy beard was coming along nicely. In reality, he was a CPA escaped from modern civilization and basking in the sunshine of Liz's voluptuous smile.

His cocker-spaniel eyes were almost liquid when they rested on the enchanting woman-child. I gave Liz a questioning glance. She shrugged a tanned shoulder and Matt kissed it as if he was adoring an icon.

The burning question in my mind was his relationship to the child she carried. We were so at ease with each other that I indulged my curiosity as soon as she and I had a moment to ourselves.

"What's with you and that darling Matt person?"

"It's my belly; he's enchanted with it. He wanted to

see it so I let him, and now he wants to eat me," she explained with a cat-licking grin.

My heart swelled with affection. "I'm sorry, but I'm a hugger, and I have to hug you," I said.

"So am I, so hug away!" she said.

When I tried, I couldn't get my arms around her girth.

"Matt can't either," she confided. "But he has one hell of a time trying!"

"What's so funny?" Matt asked, walking up with a glass of iced tea for Liz. He handed it to her with nothing less than a worshipful air. Liz caught my look and we dissolved in laughter.

There was no malice in our mirth. Matt was too openly sweet to ever inspire malice. Kindness so wreathed his beautiful, homely face that I doubted Matt Riener could bring himself to swat a fly. At that moment I adored the astoundingly innocent man who was worriedly patting Liz's convulsing back.

"Oh, Matt, I like you!" I gurgled. He flushed beet red.

"Well, uh, I like you, too, Roseanna," he stammered.

"Uh, me, too," Nathaniel said, wrapping his arms around my midriff. Resting his chin on my shoulder, he grinned at Liz. "Unlike poor Matt, I can get my arms around my girl."

They began wrangling while Matt and I laughed, and the wind blew softly around us. Incredible, I thought with throat-tightening wonder; I now had friends in Nathaniel's world.

"Am I your girl?" I asked quietly when we again stood in the grove where we parted each time I returned to my own home. What I meant was, Am I your only girl? But I couldn't ask that, it wouldn't be fair to him.

"Yes, baby, you are. My mysterious, lovely girl," he said somewhat moodily. "I wish I knew where you go when you leave me," he added after a small, rather wistful silence.

"Nathaniel, you said—"

"I know what I said." He sighed, his green eyes darkening. "I meant it, too. The fact that I'm going nuts wondering doesn't matter—"

"The fact that you're going nuts matters very much," I cut in. "But it's your own fault, Nathaniel. You're making too much over this."

"Sure I am. So we end each date in the middle of a field. Doesn't everyone?" he asked, his smile sardonic.

"Well, you have to admit it's different!"

I wasn't feeling nearly as lighthearted as I sounded. Despite his claim of tolerance, Nathaniel wasn't going to put up with this much longer.

My house was as I had left it that morning, quiet and empty. Dusk was gathering in the corners. I snapped on a lamp. A glance at the clock gave me a jolt: It was after seven! Never had I stayed away this long. Fervently I thanked goodness that David was working late tonight. Wondering if he'd called, I checked the message machine. I'd forgotten to turn it on again.

Swearing at my absentmindedness, I snapped on a lamp to cut the gloom. The telephone rang. David, I thought. Instantly on the defensive, I chirped a bright greeting. Viveca's distraught voice ripped through my ear like a rasp.

"Roseanna, where on earth have you been? We've been trying to call you since ten o'clock this morning! Where were you?"

"I was . . . Viv, is something wrong?" I asked, knowing already that something was terribly wrong.

"Hell, yes, something's wrong!" she half shouted.

I sank down on the bed in icy fright. "What? Tell me."

"I'm sorry, I didn't mean to shout at you. I guess David's mood was contagious. It's Lexi, honey, she totaled her car this afternoon—"

"Was she hurt bad? Oh God, she's not dead!"

"No, no, honey, she's not dead. She'll be all right, Rosie, I promise. In fact, she's more than all right, I mean, it's amazing, just amazing that she got off so lightly! She had all kinds of tests and they're all negative! Bruises, a broken wrist, dislocated shoulder—all bad enough, but certainly minor considering that they had to cut her out of the car. It was awful, Rosie, just awful—a pile of scrunched-up metal!"

It was awful, all right. It was a mountain falling on me. "Oh, Viveca! God, I'm sorry, I never thought— you're sure she's all right?"

I was crying and my voice was a hoarse plea. Instantly Viveca calmed down and began soothing instead of chastising. The image tormenting my heart was not the competent lady lawyer Lexi had become, but the vulnerable little girl I had so fiercely loved and protected. She had needed me, and I wasn't there.

I blew my nose and asked, "Does her father know?" Of course her father knew! *He* was around when she so desperately needed parental support.

"I'll drive you to the hospital," Viveca said. "I'm home now, so I'll be there in just a few minutes."

"Thank you, Viv," was all I took time to say.

I jumped in and out of the shower in two minutes flat. Toweling, I raged—against Nathaniel, who was innocent; against me, who was not (this awful, irresponsible me); against the company that made the car; against Lexi, who was probably driving too fast as usual; against David, who would be asking questions; against me again.

Viveca must have driven at warp speed because she arrived before I'd finished dressing. She hugged me extra hard to make me feel better. God himself couldn't make me feel better.

"She's okay, Rosie," she said as though inscribing it on stone. "The last time I spoke with David, our Lexi was doing just fine."

The sweetness of that reassurance was tainted with apprehension. She had told David I was home and that we would be there soon. There being the hospital where he had spent a good part of the day. Apprehension gripped me with steel talons. Doubtless he'd have plenty to say about that.

Viveca waited until we fitted ourselves into her little Porsche before she asked what loomed in my mind as The Question.

"By the way, where were you, Rosie? I tried to call

you several times today myself. We were supposed to meet Barbara and Shelly at the club, remember?"

"Oh shit! Oh double shit! Damn it to hell, Viveca!" I wept.

"Okay, okay, honey, it's not important. You had a good reason, I'm sure."

Resentment joined my explosive mix of emotions. "Yes I had a good reason! I spent the day doing what *I* wanted for a change! What's so damned wrong with that?"

"Why, nothing, so far as I know," she replied, obviously confused by my vehemence.

So was I. Sighing, I leaned my head back against the seat and closed my eyes. "Sorry, Viv. As usual, I'm being emotional."

"So what the hell's wrong with being emotional?" she retorted. "Your child's been hurt—of course you're upset! Jesus, Rosie, you're not a robot. Goddamn men. Friggin' assholes, every one of them. Hang 'em all, I say."

I gasped. "Viveca, what on earth are *you* so pissed about?"

"You name it, I'm pissed about it." She patted my hand, then concentrated on driving.

David's anger was expressed in the tight, thin line of his mouth as I walked into Lexi's room. "Hi, David," I said, feeling breathless as I hurried past him to the bed where my stepdaughter lay limply against a starched white pillow. My heart shook—she was so pale! Flooded with guilt, I kissed her soft cheek. Her dark hair, usually sleek and shining, hung in dull hanks about her face. When she turned her face to me, I saw a purpling bruise running from her eye to her prominent cheekbone. "Hi, baby," I said, touching her cast.

"Mom? Oh, Mom!" Pain hazed the dark eyes opening to my soft voice. "You weren't there . . . weren't home. Daddy called . . . and Aunt Viv, but you weren't there, Mom!"

I never do anything halfway. My guilt was swampwater blackening my very soul.

"I'm sorry," I managed to say with quiet dignity. "I

would have been had I known, Lexi, you know that. But I'm here now, love." My voice broke as her eyes filled with tears that ran unimpeded down her ashen cheeks. To me, this soundless weeping was ten times worse than noisy cries.

"Can I get you anything, sweetie, do anything for you?"

She shook her head and held out her uninjured hand. I stopped asking questions and concentrated on soothing my child's distress. Taking care not to jar her poor little body, I sat on the bed and began an almost forgotten ritual. Softly, caressingly, I stroked through her hair, down her temple and around the stubborn chin so like her father's. With lulling rhythm my fingertips moved up the other side of her beloved face and back through her hair, to begin again. And all the while I whispered, "Shhh, baby, it's all right, Mama's here. Shhhh."

David got up and strode to the window. Otherwise, the room was silent except for my soft croon. I had done this so often during Lexi's childhood when she was ill, or had a nightmare, or was just plain scared. But she was an adult now, and seeing her respond to my maternal ministrations somehow worsened my own distress. When she murmured, "Don't leave me, Mom," I couldn't bear it. My Lexi was tough as nails, dammit!

"I'll stay as long as you need me. All night if you want."

A nurse came in just then and gave her a shot to help her sleep. Wincing, Lexi said, "I don't need anyone staying the night. I'll be fine, I'm sure."

"Of course you will," I gave quick agreement. "But maybe just until you fall asleep, hmm?"

A long sigh rippled through her body as she relaxed. "Yeah, I'd like that." Her eyes closed. "I'm glad you're here, Mom."

"Me, too, love." I tucked the blanket around her shoulders.

"Daddy had to handle everything by himself," she remembered.

"Yes, I know." I glanced at David's stiff back. "It looks like Daddy handled everything very well, though."

"Of course he did. But you should have been here, Mom."

Oh God! Dammit, are You listening?

"Dammit, Roseanna, are you listening to me?" David rasped.

We were in the car going home. He had begun the minute we drove out of the parking garage. Well, he had a right, didn't he? Roseanna! Guilty, Your Honor, guilty as sin.

"Yes, David."

"Well? Where were you, then?"

"I just went . . ." A tiny hesitation. I turned my face to the window. ". . . to the mall. With Grace. We shopped, had lunch—you know, the usual." Oh hell. Oh hell and damn. I pressed my knuckles to my mouth and bit down hard. Right then I hated David. He had forced me to tell a bald-faced lie.

He swerved to miss another car and swore at the errant driver before focusing on me again. "Lunching and shopping. Great, Roseanna, just great. While you were out doing the goddamn *usual* the rest of us were racing around trying to save Lexi's life!"

"David, that's not fair!"

"Isn't it? What the hell do you think *I* was doing when this emergency came up? Not out lunching, although I was supposed to be, and with a very important client. While you were wasting time on frivolous pursuits, I was being jerked out of a meeting, canceling appointments, spending time I could ill afford doing your job instead of mine. An entire day's work, lost. Half a million in billings riding on that meeting and I'm sitting in a hospital waiting room."

"Not to mention your concern for Lexi."

"That's a low blow, Roseanna," he replied evenly. "You know damn good and well how concerned I am about Lexi."

I mangled my bottom lip. "I'm sorry, I know you love Lexi. That just slipped out." Feeling lower than any snake's belly, I stared blindly out the window. Lexi could have died while I was gone. And I had blatantly lied to David. I burst into tears.

"Ah, Christ, Roseanna, don't start bawling! My day's been fucked up enough as it is," he said with a hard sigh.

I clenched my fists. I'd always had difficulty withstanding disapproval, and here it was coming at me from all sides. Even from above, I thought furiously. Well, go ahead, God, get it over with—strike me dead, dammit! I have frequent disagreements with God. He never does what He should do when He should do it.

Sighing at my noisy weeping, David gave me his handkerchief and suggested I blow my nose, which I did, loudly.

"Feel better?" he asked sourly.

I turned my face toward the window. "To be honest, David, I can't think of anything that would make me feel better."

Later that night, I lay stiffly on my side of the bed, glad that he had fallen asleep and left me to wallow in my tenacious, Protestant guilt. How shallow, how frivolous, how *evil* my tremblings and comings and spurious yearnings!

It had been such a beautiful day. Such a warm, delight-filled day, I thought with poignant longing. I had been young and free and pretty. I had been desired, loved, teased, kissed, and pampered with that most cherished of all feminine luxuries, the complete attention of a charming man. Such a wonderful day, to have ended like this. Tears locked my throat.

Well, I had learned my lesson, I assured God. I would not go through the looking glass again.

When I returned to the hospital the next day, Lexi was withdrawn and noncommunicative. But she's alive, I reminded myself fiercely. That's all that matters. I made myself comfortable and settled in for the day.

The following afternoon she was released. Against my will I took her to her apartment. Clark would be there if she needed anything, she said.

Wondering why I could never remember his last

name, I greeted him and offered to make coffee as an icebreaker. No one wanted coffee. Smoothing his ginger mustache, Clark suggested I go home and get some rest. I'd spent too many hours already tending to Lexi. Let him take over now.

I looked at Lexi, seeing David's dark eyes in her lovely face. With her cuts and bruises, she still looked so vulnerable my heart ached. My gaze veered to Clark.

"I do need rest," I agreed. "But first, I'd like a moment alone with my baby."

Lexi's mouth twisted. "Baby?" She and Clark shared a look of silent communication. When he stepped out the door she came directly to the point. "I know you dislike Clark. That's your right. But it is not your right to criticize him. He's a fine man, Mother. And he's good for me."

"I don't doubt he's a wonderful man. And I'm not criticizing him, darling, I. . . ." Suddenly at a loss for words, I stared at this lovely, vibrant young woman. Concealed within that cool exterior was a vivacious spark of life, with an enormous potential for love. A smoldering sexuality peeked from those dark-lashed eyes. I could not vocalize my feelings, but I wanted desperately for this child to have a real relationship, warm, close, and deeply satisfying. A relationship that was sweetly, joyously intimate. Everything I didn't have with David, I thought sadly.

"Lexi, listen to me. I'm not putting Clark down, believe me. I just don't want you to settle for second best. Oh, Lexi, don't ever be fooled by something that is just —just *good*! I want you to have it all, my darling. Only the finest, the best!"

"The finest what, Mother?" Lexi asked, her tone irritable, but indulgent, too.

"Love, baby," I said softly, sitting down beside her and taking her hand. "Real love, the kind that transcends just 'good' and becomes something indescribable. Breathtaking magic, Lexi, pure, intoxicating delight—an enchantment from which you cannot escape nor will you want to. Something so powerful that you comprehend God's meaning when He says the greatest gift of all is love. I want this for you. I want it because I love you. You have the potential for this kind of love, Lexi. Don't ever settle for merely 'good' when you can have the best!"

I could see she was taken aback by my passionate outburst, but I refused to tone it down or degrade it with an abashed smile. I stared intently into her eyes, letting my need vibrate between us until she drew back from it, and me.

"Oh, Mother, this is the real world, not a scene from one of your books," she gently chided. "Clark and I get along very well indeed. But I do appreciate your concern, darling." She tilted her head. "Any more advice, or are we through with this?"

Gazing at that vivid face, I slowly shook my head. At this moment, I felt younger than she by a good five years. How could I possibly advise her? "No, nothing more. Just—just be more careful. And enjoy it, baby, enjoy your life. Despite all the prophets of doom and gloom and glorified suffering, I have a sneaky suspicion that's exactly what we were put on earth to do, to enjoy!" I declared, laughing to ease the awkward moment.

I hugged her. She smelled like a warm, perfumed puppy. I smiled to myself; how she would hate knowing I thought that!

Looking as cool and collected as ever, she pulled free and picked up her mail. "I do enjoy my life. You don't need to hang around here, Mother. I know you're tired. You've been an angel these past few days and I couldn't have . . . well, it would have been a lot rougher if I'd been alone. So thank you. God, all this junk mail. What a waste!"

It was a nice dismissal, as dismissals go. Perhaps my face betrayed me, for as I went to the door to let Clark back in, I heard her soft, plaintive voice saying, "Wait a minute."

I stopped and turned to face her, waiting.

"Thank you for being there for me, Mom. Not just yesterday, but all the times I've needed you."

I cleared my throat. "No thanks necessary, sweetheart. I promised you a long time ago that I'd always be

here for you, Lexi. I meant it then, I mean it now."
Blinking back tears, I opened the door and called
Clark's name.

David was home when I came in. "Sorry I'm late. I
stayed with Lexi awhile," I said, like an offering, I
thought with a nip of anger.

Maybe it was that snippet of anger. Or maybe it was
just that, while no one on earth can lay guilt on me like I
can lay guilt on me, no one can lift it faster, either. At
any rate, as the following week passed without incident
and Lexi's recovery was assured, my heart began to
wriggle all around my vow about the looking glass.

After all, some good had come out of this. Lexi had
learned a valuable lesson at a relatively cheap price, and
David had been forced to walk in my shoes for a few
hours. That's always beneficial to a wife, I continued my
circular self-argument.

But it was this unceasing need for Nathaniel that
threatened to overwhelm my good intentions. *To see him
again, just one more time, just for a little while, an hour or
so. . . .*

God, it was a tempting thought!

Resolutely I wiped away both temptation and tears.
Besides, an hour wouldn't begin to be enough to satisfy
my hunger. I wanted bogs of time—days, weeks, months
of time with him!

"At least another day. I'd settle for that right now," I
muttered wretchedly.

But promises were taken seriously in my family, even
ones I made to myself. Well into the next week I vacil-
lated between duty and desire, seeking to appease both
my heart and conscience by throwing myself into various
time-consuming, mind-distracting activities: doing another stint with Legal Services; entertaining David's cli-
ents; being the perfect wife and mother. I was a
pot-bound houseplant blooming all over my little corner
of the world.

David was pleased. Hallelujah.

Viveca wasn't. "Rosie, why are you trying to commit
hara-kiri by good deeds and housewifery?" she asked

when I turned down a lunch date to do whatever it was I felt duty-bound to do.

I had to smile, for I loved her drawling, if tart, wit. "Ah Viv." I sighed. "You wouldn't believe it if I told you. I don't even believe it myself."

"Try me."

My fingers tightened around the telephone receiver as I battled a sudden keen urge to do just that. For something else was eating at me. Something far more serious than sexual urgency, I admitted, responding to the soft, waiting quality of her silence. Facing the prospect of never seeing Nathaniel again had forced me to confront my feelings for him.

I loved him.

Scary as it was, denial was impossible. I loved him! The worst kind of love, too, that wild, soaring excitement of first love, when your heart throbs insanely at just the thought of him, and you're a glutton for his laugh, his voice, his mouth, his body—him.

"Roseanna?" Viveca prompted.

I gripped the receiver. "Just hang on a minute, Viv, I'm trying to think this out!"

Taking her grunt as agreement, I stared blankly out the window. I didn't know what to do about loving Nathaniel. It seemed such an appallingly *hopeless* kind of love. I could never be with him on a permanent basis. I had twenty-five years invested in my marriage. Nearly half my life, I thought despairingly. If I give up on David, then all those years will have been wasted.

And I knew myself. I knew I was incapable of casting aside ethics and duty for my own selfish purposes.

Yet I could not stop seeing Nathaniel. A life without him was too gray and bleak to contemplate. And I needed him. His warm, openly affectionate presence had a healing effect on my wounds, whether they were the constant paper cuts David inflicted on my tender psyche, or the deep, raw places carved by the knives of loss, grief, and failure.

I loved Nathaniel. I could not voluntarily give him up. End of argument, I thought angrily.

But Lexi's ordeal had taught me a lesson, too. If I

returned to Nathaniel, I would have to have an accomplice, someone who would know where and how to reach me at all times.

Which meant two things, both good for a shudder. I had to tell someone about my secret life, and I had to take that someone through the looking glass with me.

The first was ticklish enough, but the second was mind-boggling. My breath went out in a long whoosh as I made my decision.

"Viv, you still there? Oh, good. So all right, friend. How soon can you get here?"

I had just enough time to shower, dress and make a fresh pot of coffee before she came dashing in the kitchen door. Once we were seated at the table with steaming cups in hand, I found I could not immediately come to the point.

"How's it going with you, love?" I stalled. Eyeing her, so slim and trim in a geranium silk blouse and white slacks, I felt a swell of affection. "Colin treatin' you right?"

"Colin's treating me just fine." Her sculptured nails played a riff across the tabletop. "Now what's this crisis of yours?"

"Oh, yes, the crisis." Her penetrating gaze pinned me like a butterfly to a board as I squirmed in my chair. "Viv, will you just be quiet, drink your coffee, and, for God's sake, do not interrupt me once I begin?" I requested with enough urgency to widen her eyes. "It'll be bad enough trying to explain this without you asking questions."

"I knew it!" she crowed. "Didn't I say all that activity was hiding something? I'm listening, Roseanna."

I sipped coffee while my brain sought words that might possibly make sense. "Okay, I'll—oh my goodness, I just thought of something! Is your heart strong? I mean, you can take a shock, can't you?" I asked anxiously. I didn't need Viveca keeling over on my kitchen floor right now.

"Oh for heaven's sake, Rosie, get on with it!"

I drew a deep, deep breath. "Okay, here goes. Viv,

you are my best friend. I can and do trust you implicitly.
I know that what I tell you today will stay right here
between us and never go out of this room—"

"My God, you've gone and done it!"

"Oh, shit, gone and done what?"

"Why, had an affair, of course! And you're right, it is
one hell of a shock, Roseanna," she said with an ap-
praising look—a quite insulting look, actually.

"Viv, if that's your idea of a shock, then Lord help
you!"

"You mean it's worse than that?" Her sherry-colored
eyes lit with amusement. "Rosie, my love, what have you
gone and done! Killed Mims? Robbed a bank? Ran naked through the Galleria? Cut of David's—"

"Viveca!"

"Oh, calm down, honey. Listen, whatever it is, we can
fix it. I'll stand by you." She wrinkled her nose. "Although I can't imagine you doing anything worse than
missing Sunday School and losing a gold star."

I wish I hadn't told her about my perfect attendance
record. "That's back when I was a child, Viv. Do you
want to hear this?"

"Of course I do."

She wasn't taking me seriously. Well, who could
blame her? Whenever I did confide my problems to her,
I made the tale so amusing we both wound up laughing.

"All right. This is serious, so please just listen. Don't
interrupt. No matter how wild the urge, do-not-inter-
rupt. Okay? Okay. You know what you said about me
looking so, uh—"

"Like a peach that's finally been plucked? And you
do, Rosie. I've known you too long to miss it, but I
couldn't believe you were getting a little on the side.
Are you?"

"Well, in a manner of speaking, yes."

"I'll be damned! When? Where? Who? Start from
the beginning," she urged with undisguised eagerness.

I took another deep, deep breath. "Well, one afternoon I stepped into my closet. . . ."

Chapter 8

There was total silence when I finished my narration. Viveca sat rigid in her chair, her lovely face a battleground of differing emotions, all fighting for precedence. Disbelief, of course. Astonishment, confusion, even fear churned in her eyes.

She gave a gritty laugh.

I didn't laugh with her.

"This is a story, right?" she said slowly. "A fictitious tale you've made up for—for what? A new book?"

I put my hand over hers. "No, Viv, it's not fictitious, it's true. All of it: the passage, the meadow, Nathaniel, all true," I said quietly, my expression sober enough to enforce my sincerity.

"Roseanna." She shook her glossy head again. "My God, you're. . . ."

"Unbalanced? I thought so, too. I thought so for an awfully long time. Sometimes I still do. But Nathaniel is too real, too wonderful . . . which brings me to the second half of your shock. I'm going to take you there. I have to, you see."

Quickly I explained my reasoning, reminding her of Lexi's accident and the distress my absence caused. "You do see my problem, don't you?" I asked, squeezing her hand.

"Oh, I see your problem, all right. Jeez, Roseanna, you know I can't believe this!"

"I know you can't," I replied softly. "It's been going on for weeks now, and I'm still incredulous. But you do trust me, don't you? Enough to just try it? Go with me, Viv. All right, humor me, if you'd rather think of it that way. Will you?"

"We've been friends for such a long time." Viveca sighed. "Okay, honey, I'll humor you."

You poor darling, her eyes said.

You poor dear, my eyes replied. And I meant it. Viveca still had one hell of a shock coming.

She stood up and smiled at me. "Okeydokey. Let's get this over with. But darlin', I must make one stipulation. I'll do this on condition that you make an appointment with Dr. Muehler as soon as possible. He's really been helpful to me."

"I know he has, but I very much doubt he can fix this," I said flippantly. She frowned. Quickly, I capitulated. "Agreed. If, after we're through and you still insist, I'll go see your marvelous Dr. Muehler."

She nodded, her expression sorrowful as she patted my hand. "I love you, Roseanna, you know that. And I am your friend, remember that."

"'Tis etched on my mind for all eternity," I said. She winced. "Oh Viv, I can't help my levity. This is going to be fun, honest it is! Upsetting, but fun, once you've adjusted."

Another shake of her auburn head answered me. With increasing excitement, I hurried her upstairs to my bedroom. Rather than dread, I felt vibrantly eager. Just wait until she meets Nathaniel, I thought with a gleeful little laugh.

My pulse was racing, and I felt breathless as we entered the closet. Carasel romped in with us and stood expectantly, her ears cocked, her gaze on the shadowed wall.

"Carasel loves to go," I explained to Viveca.

"Ah, God." She sighed.

"Well, this is it!" I said with an expansive gesture.

Tight-lipped, Viveca stepped up beside me and peered into the passage, which was to her simply a gap between a shelf and a wall. The look on her face was fast daunting my enthusiasm.

"I have to admit it doesn't look very impressive if one

doesn't know what lies beyond it," I plowed on. "Now just step back, honey. Oh, wait a minute, a word of caution. Viveca, look at me. Look into my eyes and see that I speak absolute truth, because I do, darling. What I've told you is so real that you're going to be terribly shocked if you don't at least let a little belief, just a *possibility* of belief into your mind. I mean it, Viv. I've never been more sincere in my life," I said emphatically.

"I know you're sincere. I don't doubt it for a minute. Dammit, that's what scares me, that sincerity." Biting her lip, she stared at me for a long moment. She was, at the very *least,* quite sure I'd flipped out. I knew this, just as I knew she was going to be utterly wiped out herself in just a few seconds.

"Now, Viv, don't look so grim," I chided. "Just step into the wall."

Slowly, her gaze fixed on mine, she turned sideways and began inching toward the dully gleaming plaster.

"Don't be afraid, it doesn't hurt," I said as though gentling a horse. "All you'll feel is a kind of crackling sensation and some bright prickles of light. Just step back into the wall."

"Oh, shit, Rosie!" she cried in an agony of concern. Concern about me, not the fact that she was shortly going into an alien world.

"Shh, it's all right. Carasel and I will be right behind you, I promise. Don't be scared, it's just a sort of floating. . . ." My patience snapped. "Step into the damn wall, Viv!"

She turned to look at the wall just then, and had she done as I said, she'd have broken her nose. That wall was as solid as—well, a wall. Cautiously she edged back until her shoulder touched it, then stood staring at me, those amber eyes filled with resignation.

Frantically I stared back at her. What was wrong?

"Come out again, Viv, let me see." When she obeyed, I stuck my fingers into the gap and reached for the wall. Which wasn't there, as I expected. Yet Viveca couldn't get through.

"I don't understand this," I muttered.

"Roseanna, please, let's go downstairs and we'll have a nice cup of tea," she pleaded.

"No, wait a minute, let me think. Oh, of course—color me brilliant!" I exulted. It was so logical. No one else could get through to Nathaniel's world, not without me. If the space had been open to just anyone or anything, then all sorts of objects from both worlds would be drifting back and forth. My irreverent sense of humor surfaced. Imagine stunned people suddenly finding themselves standing in a closet. And imagine David's reaction to my closet full of people! I began to laugh, which distressed Viveca even more.

"Okay, I see the problem. Don't worry, honey," I said so cheerfully she whimpered. "I don't think anyone can get through the passage unless I'm with them. Now you just step back as far as you can go."

Viveca's sigh was so put-upon that I gave her a little shove. "Will you just do as I say? Now step back . . . well, do it, Viv!" I hissed. I had Carasel in my arms and she was squirming like mad, those sharp little claws digging holes in my skin. Viveca hadn't moved an inch. "Viveca, indulge me? Please?"

With an air of hopelessness, she backed against the wall and I squeezed in beside her. An instant later we were standing in the meadow.

Joy drizzled through me like melting honey as I breathed in the fresh, fragrant air of my own personal Eden. Releasing Carasel, I turned to face my friend, who was not so enraptured.

"Ooooh!" Viveca whimpered. Her face was chalk-white, her eyes dazed as she turned her head in a slow arc. "Roseanna . . . *good God Almighty, Roseanna!*"

She swayed and I caught her shoulders.

"Viv, now Viv! I said it would be a shock. I warned you. Sweetie, are you all right?"

"Oh, my God!"

"Oh, dear. Maybe I should have brought along some brandy."

"Yes you fucking well should have! What have you done, Roseanna!" Viveca half screamed. She shut her eyes. Opened them again. Squinched them tight and slowly, cautiously, reopened them. "We're still here!" she moaned incredulously.

"Oh, now, Viv, it's all right. Here, sit down. Take two or three deep breaths," I urged, gently pushing her into the grass. Carasel was digging again. "You stop that, Carasel! You'll get yourself all dirty again. David was furious that last time, remember?"

"David was furious," Viveca repeated numbly.

"You'd better believe he was. Come here, Carasel. That's a good girl. We'll go see Nathaniel in a minute— yes, Nathaniel! You like that, huh!" I laughed as her tail wagged in riotous agreement. Catching the wriggly little dog in my arms, I squatted down beside Viveca.

"Nathaniel," she whispered as if this was the last straw. "There really is a Nathaniel then. There really is?"

"There is indeed!" I sang out.

"And everything you've told me is true? You've actually been . . . here . . . where on earth is *here*? Good grief, Roseanna!" Her voice cracked. It was all crashing down like a rockslide around her vulnerable shoulders.

I stroked her cheek. Her skin was soft, silky, free of the lines of bitterness that had marred her mouth just moments ago. Her youthful appearance would be another shock, but a pleasurable one this time. "Yes, it's all true, honey. As soon as you feel up to it, we'll walk to Nathaniel's house. Oh, I do hope he hasn't gone off somewhere," I fretted.

This was a very real worry, one that hadn't happened yet, but was bound to sooner or later. Nathaniel couldn't just sit around the house day after day waiting for me to pop in.

"He really looks like you said? Like the character in your book? But then he can't be real! This can't be real! Ah, Roseanna," Viveca groaned, covering her face with her hands. "Not only have you gone crazy, but you've dragged me along. And the dog—even a dog!" she ended two octaves higher than when she began.

"Viv, let me save you that trip. I've gone through all this already. Now, though, I'm simply enjoying what I've been given. I didn't ask for this, I didn't plan it. It just happened. Whether or not it's real, I don't know. Even now I don't know. But this I do know, it's real enough for me to take desperate measures to keep it."

I swept a hand around the meadow. "I haven't begun to tell you all of it! I've met people here—yes, other people, some very charming, very real people. I've eaten with them, laughed and talked with them. If this be madness, then I thank Heaven for giving it to me," I finished softly, reverently.

"But this is so . . . merciful heavens, it's so . . . surely it's abnormal. At least supernatural." She gave up. "Weren't you scared? I mean, to just—just fall into this without even as much warning as I had. Weren't you terrified?" she asked, incredulous again.

I released Carasel to dig her way to China, if she so desired. I felt too buoyant to fret about a little dirt.

"I was never scared," I said reflectively. "That first time, well, I was bewildered. Finding myself lying here naked in a meadow, when all I did was stoop down to look for a purse! Sure I was confused. But never afraid. I just felt happy. And peaceful, like I belonged here, like somehow it was meant to be. Ah, no, I've never been frightened here."

"Well, I'm frightened. I'm scared peeless is what I am! Lord, I'm shaking all over," Viveca whispered. She was huddled in the grass, hugging her knees and rocking a little, a gesture of stress I recalled from the days when she was all strung out over Jack's betrayal.

I put my arms around her. "Don't be frightened," I pleaded. "It's not abnormal or even supernatural. At least, *I* don't think it is. In fact, it seems very natural to me. Don't you feel it, Viv? Don't you feel the warmth, that sort of friendliness in the air? It's a lovely meadow, a lovely world, what I've seen of it, anyway."

I gazed around with possessive pleasure. The grass was knee-high now, and sprinkled with pretty red flowers I did not recognize. In Houston it was May, hot, humid and very close to June. Here, it was balmy, with a wonderful little breeze fanning my rosy cheeks. I knew they were rosy. I felt rosy all over.

"I'm so happy when I'm here, Viv, so free-spirited

that sometimes I think I could fly if I tried hard enough!
Just relax and let it enfold you, too."

"But how did we get here? I don't understand that
either!"

"Me, neither. Maybe our atoms are scattered for a
second or two, then regrouped in another dimension.
Sort of like Star Trek," I added mischievously. "You
know: 'Beam me up, Scotty.'"

Viveca's choked laugh was not reassuring.

"Viv, all I can tell you is that it works and that it's
safe. So just share this with me, enjoy it with me and feel
blessed, as I do, that you have the chance to experience
it," I coaxed.

She straightened, and I could see steel creeping back
into her spine. Like me, she's resilient. And like me, she
bounces back fast, a fact I was counting on.

"Yes," she said wonderingly. "Damn it all, yes! It's
fantastic—incredible—unbelievable—but yes!" Her
head lifted higher. "Very well, Rosie, take me to your
Nathaniel. I can't wait to meet him!"

Her eyes were shining, her cheeks flushed dusky-pink.
When I took her trembling hands to assist her to her
feet, I could see she was beginning to respond to my
infectious good feelings. For a moment longer I held the
reassuring clasp.

"Okay, Viv?" I asked softly.

"Lord, no, it's not okay! But it is some kind of wonderful." She laughed. "So lead on, babe, whither thou
goest, etc.!"

"Atta girl, Viv! We won't stay long; I've got that
darn charity affair tonight. Carasel? Find Nathaniel,
Carasel!"

As we set off in giddy pursuit of the jubilant little dog,
Viveca laughed again, a lovely sound on the crystal-clear
air. She was already beginning to adjust to the situation
in which she so inexplicably found herself. I felt jubilant.
The thought of showing her my Nathaniel was an electrical current galvanizing my legs until I was racing with
the wind.

I could always outrun her. Pausing at the top of the
rise, I waited until she caught up with me.

She stopped dead, her face paling again.

"Viv, what's wrong?"

"You, your face," she half whispered.

Oh damn! I'd forgotten to tell her of my fabulous de-aging when I stepped into this world. "Yes, Viv, it's true. What you see is how I am when I'm here. Besides everything else, I've recaptured my youth. Can you imagine what people would pay for this kind of gift?" I asked with a gleeful laugh.

"Oh, sweet Jesus." Viveca breathed in awe. "And me? Have I been included in this magical transformation?"

"Well, of course," I said with a crushing hug. "You look like you should be striding across a campus, arms full of books and flirting to beat the band! How do you feel?"

"I haven't the foggiest idea."

"Oh, nonsense, you feel wonderful and you know it."

Carasel barked her hurry-up call and I knew at once she'd spotted Nathaniel. "Come along, then, Nathaniel is coming to meet us," I said, a little less exuberant as doubt assailed me. I'd been gone for nearly two weeks now. Would he be glad to see me? Or hurt and angry at my over-long absence?

Nervously I smoothed my wind-tossed hair, tucked my sleeveless lavender blouse into the band of my soft, full, hydrangea-print skirt. My heart gave a frog-sized leap when he came into view.

I guess Viveca was a shock to him. He stopped when he saw her. Viveca not only stopped, she sucked in her breath with an audible gasp. But I had already forgotten Viveca. My feet were flying down the hill toward the tall, green-eyed man who waited with Carasel in his arms.

He wore white duck pants and a sleeveless blue shirt that left his sinewy arms exposed to my hungry gaze. Drawing nearer, I searched his face for a hint of emotion, but it was a mask. Still, the searing light that flared in the green eyes now raking me from head to toe was evidence of his pleasure. And of his anger.

I simply kept on running, straight into his arms. He

had no choice except to release Carasel and hold me instead. I looked up at him, my blood pounding as our bodies touched and I felt his catch fire. His mouth came down on mine and I tasted the tempest raging inside him.

Our kiss was rough and heated. I thought I'd die if he stopped. But one part of my still-functioning mind remembered Viveca, and reluctantly, I pulled away. Refusing to acknowledge his anger, I curved an arm around his waist and turned to watch her halting approach.

I had already warned her that she must not give my background away. It was risky, but she had a quick mind and could field questions. At least I fervently hoped so. One step at a time, I told her when she questioned my small deception.

She stopped a few feet away, her eyes wide with amazement. "Oh, my Lord, another Mel Gibson!" she blurted. "Roseanna, he looks just like him!"

"Oh, nonsense, Viv. Well, maybe a little bit," I conceded.

Nathaniel's eyebrows shot up. "Who's Mel Gibson?"

"Her gardener," I said, zinging her a look.

Quickly I introduced them. Viveca was immediately struck dumb. When Nathaniel put out his hand, she placed hers in it as if she were possibly shaking hands with a ghost. In fact, she stared incredulously at the big brown hand covering hers.

I nudged her with my elbow.

"Oh! Uh, hello, Nathaniel, I'm glad to meet you," she managed. She even gave him a smile, for which I gave her one.

"It's my pleasure, Viveca. Am I going to get any answers out of you?" he asked, flashing that devastating grin.

Viveca swallowed. "Oh, jeez! Uh, no, you're not."

"Just what I need, another mystery woman," he teased a trifle grimly. "But a lovely one. Well. Come back to the house and I'll fix you ladies a drink."

"Nathaniel, we can't stay for a drink," I began.

"Oh yes we can! I want that drink—in fact, I require that drink," Viveca said strongly.

"Okay, one drink. Then we have to go, Viv," came my pointed reminder.

Nathaniel's mouth snapped open, and then shut. He exhaled. "I've just made a pitcher of sangría. It's nice of you to drop in, Roseanna," he said, killingly polite.

Tears stung my eyes. His tight jaw was visible evidence of the guard he had flung up against me. I traced the firm line with my fingertips, saying softly, intimately, "Nathaniel, I'm sorry it's been so long. You know only something very, very important could have kept me away. Please don't be angry with me?" My wet gaze met his in a plea for understanding. "Please, darling?"

His mouth twisted into a wry smile as he glanced at Viveca. "I'm a sucker for tears, always have been. Besides, Carasel needs a drink too, don't you, girl!"

He patted her head and Carasel quivered in rapturous submission to his touch. Well, what female wouldn't? Feeling more aggressive, I took his hand as we started for the house. He glanced at me. Then his long fingers entwined mine in a tight, hard, possessive clasp that was far more warning than caress.

Viveca and I laughed and chattered continuously on our short walk to the cabin. He could no more resist her lovely lightheartedness than I. Eventually, caught between two irresistible forces, he succumbed, enough to relax, anyway.

The cabin lay drowsing in pools of dappled sunlight. The white rose blooming at the steps sent its fragrance to greet us. I walked up the three steps with a lovely sense of homecoming. I glanced at Viveca, wanting to share my joy. She rolled her eyes as Nathaniel opened the door, and courteously bowed us in.

I had gauged the time to be about five o'clock. Close, I thought, glancing at the mantel clock. It was noon when we'd left Earth. I would have to stick by my one-drink timetable.

Viveca was admiring the porcelain lion. Rather proudly I told her its name and history. She needed the bathroom, which necessitated a trip through Nathaniel's bedroom. Her expression was a gem as she tried not to look at the bed.

"Isn't the headboard lovely? It's another family heirloom," I said so knowingly that she bit her lip.

"This is beyond comprehension," she said with a slow shake of her head.

"My point exactly. So why try?"

"I meant you, Roseanna, and this," she gestured to the bed. "This is all part of your reality, isn't it!"

"Well, it's my present reality. When I get back home, I find myself involved in an entirely different reality. And this one's just as precious to me. I can't give it up. Why should I have to, anyway? Am I doing anything wrong? I mean, truly wrong?"

"Lord, don't ask me," Viveca said.

"Well, I am."

She studied me, then defiantly tipped up her chin. "Hell, no, you're not."

"Thank you," I said sincerely.

With a warm smile, she waved a hand in airy dismissal. When she turned toward the bathroom door again, she was caught and held prisoner by her mirrored image.

Delighted by the stunned pleasure settling over her pretty face, I leaned against the doorframe and watched her. She looked so lovely. Her eyelids were taut again, her mouth soft and unlined. Her skin had a dewy sheen no makeup could bestow.

Her voice quivered as she said, "Some face-lift, huh! But it doesn't last, does it?"

I made a wry face. "No, not in our old reality. Everything sinks back to normal, unfortunately. But it's fabulous fun while it does last."

"Yeah," she agreed wistfully. "I've missed you," she told her image with such solemnity that I got a lump in my throat. "How did I ever lose you?"

"You haven't, Viv. It's still you—still us. Every woman cherishes that young innocent who thought that if you waved to the world, the world would wave right back. The years may have distorted it, but it's still the image we hold onto despite what a mirror says."

"Not the innocence."

"Yes, damnit, the innocence! Why else do we try to hold onto the romance, the sheer beauty of love?" I countered fiercely. We were getting too emotional; our eyes were polished by tears. With effort, I laughed and blew her a kiss. "You look wonderful, my friend. So relax and enjoy it."

I swatted her tight little butt and hurried back to Nathaniel.

We stayed an hour with him, loathe to give up this delight, but knowing we must. I could see that Viveca was enchanted. No wonder, I thought, watching him with my own peculiar pleasure.

Finally, hating to, I said, "Nathaniel, we really must go."

He stood up and pulled me up with him. "All right, but first—can I see you a minute? Viveca, excuse us, please?"

Dreading it, dying for it, I went with him to his bedroom. Contemplating his questions made me queasy. He no sooner shut the door than I was in his arms, pulling his head to mine, mouth to mouth, belly to belly as he lifted me up and plastered me against him. His sizzling assault on my senses was an exhilarating challenge to my attempt at dominance.

I heard him say my name, his voice fierce and passionate, hoarse with furious need. Oh, the power of that mouth moving so hungrily on mine! His kiss was hot, liquid, demanding. His hands were under my skirt, roaming with abandon. I was trying my best to get inside his clothes with him.

Any thought of dominance fled my mind. "Nathaniel, oh Nathaniel—my darling," I said drunkenly.

"When, honey, when? When are you coming back?" Urgency bridled his voice to a hoarse rasp and I felt a fiery jolt of woman-power. Before I could respond, that hot, wet mouth took possession again. My tongue liquefied and dissolved under his.

"Roseanna, I want you," he whispered. An unnecessary utterance. "When am I going to have you?"

"Soon, very soon," I gasped. "Tomorrow, maybe.

Maybe another entire day with you. I'll try my best, I promise."

"Roseanna, what the hell! Why must you *try*! Goddamn it, why all this secrecy?" he roared in a half-strangled whisper.

"Nathaniel, please, oh please, not now." I begged shamelessly.

"Roseanna, are you married?"

The question ricocheted around the room and hit my ears like a clap of thunder.

"No, Nathaniel, not here, not in—no, I'm not married," I floundered. The truth, wasn't it? All right, how about half a truth, then? I was desperate enough to settle for one-quarter truth right now.

Stormy green eyes commanded and held my gaze. Then, slowly, he nodded. His grip loosened until I stood on the floor again.

"Please, honey, I do have to go now. But I'll be back soon. I will, I promise. Nathaniel, please don't come with us to the meadow?" I asked in big-blue-eyed appeal.

"All right. But we are going to talk, Roseanna. I've played your little game long enough. It's reached the point where I feel like a fool. As if you're using me like a—a goddamned stud!"

Startled and hurt, I stepped away from him. I guess my face spoke well enough. His hand went to my cheek.

"I'm sorry, I didn't mean that . . . oh hell, Roseanna," he said wretchedly, pulling me into his arms again.

"What about what you said the last time I was here, about tolerating my little games?" I asked with noticeable coolness. "You didn't mean that, either?"

"Yes, I meant it. I don't say things I don't mean!" he snapped. His voice lowered. "I spoke the truth, you *have* changed my life and given it meaning again. But there's a limit to my tolerance. And I've just about reached it, baby."

His eyes were so dark and I ached from that. At the same time I felt a fierce resentment at his questions. Why did he have to be so inquisitive? Why couldn't he just take and enjoy? Why couldn't I have created a scoundrel who just screwed 'em and forgot 'em! Why was I standing here even thinking this crap? He was a fine, decent man, that's why. And I was feeling guilty again.

"You make it sound like this has been going on for ages." I sighed. "When, actually, I can count on one hand the number of times we've been together."

"That's not *my* doing, Roseanna. If you recall, I've had very little say in how often we get together."

"Well, then I'll give you some say. When I can come back again, do you want me to?"

"Goddamn it, you know I do," he growled, fierce and furious.

I had been holding my breath. Releasing it, I grabbed his face and kissed him.

He hugged me, then dropped his arms. "Your friend is waiting. But just remember, so am I, Roseanna. For how long is anybody's guess."

There was flint in that. Nathaniel's pride was undergoing some wrenching adjustment. "I always remember that. How could I ever forget it?" I murmured in quick response.

"Easily, apparently."

I couldn't take any more of this. "No. You're wrong, Nathaniel. But I can't make it any plainer than that."

Turning, I opened the door and rejoined Viveca in the den.

He really did have beautiful manners, I thought, watching him bid her good-bye. She had told him only that we'd been friends for years. When he would delve deeper, she'd smiled and chided, "Now, Nathaniel, you know I can't answer that. Rosie has sworn me to secrecy."

An honest answer, and he accepted it as such.

"Come back again, Viveca," he invited. Sea-green eyes flickered to me. "You, too, Roseanna."

His ironic smile tugged at my heartstrings. "You can rely on that, Nathaniel," I said.

* * *

Viveca and I climbed the little hill in silence. As one, we turned at the crest and looked back at Nathaniel. He raised one arm in salute, and we waved back. "Oh, God," I whispered yearningly. I wanted desperately to return to his arms. But home was waiting. And that black-tie cocktail-hour dinner. I hated cocktail-hour affairs. All I really wanted was to sleep in Nathaniel's arms.

"Tell me something, Rosie," Viveca broke the silence. "You asked me to share this with you. Enjoy it, you said. Does that apply to Nathaniel, too?" she asked mischievously.

"Nathaniel I don't share," I replied so coolly she stopped to stare at me.

"Are you in love with this man from . . . from wherever the hell we are?" she finished with a helpless shrug.

"Yes, Viv, I am. Deeply, wildly, terrifyingly in love. Head over heels, to be truthful."

"Well, well. Aren't you just full of surprises! What are you going to *do?*" Her eyes were troubled. Evidently all the questions that plagued me were just now hitting her.

"Like Granddaddy always said, all you can do is to play the hand you're dealt," I replied, far more carelessly than I felt.

"I doubt very many people have played this particular hand," she said, sighing.

Subdued, we walked on, each lost in thought. Carasel ran ahead to the boulder and renewed her mark on its flank.

Viveca touched a finger to the blue columbine now gone to seed. "At least you have a landmark," she mused. "Can't get lost with this thing here. Roseanna, it occurs to me that we've overlooked one vital point in your plans; how do *I* come and go freely? I couldn't get through alone, remember?"

"I remember. But I think we can change that. Anyway, we're going to try." I stopped in the boulder's shadow and ceremoniously stated, "Viveca, I want you to have free access to this world. I give you permission to come and go at will." For ticking seconds I waited; for what, I didn't know. Finally I looked at her and shrugged. "Well, let's try it. Just step into that patch of grass right in front of you."

She rolled her eyes. "Not this again!"

"Come on, Viv, this is serious. Just do it, all right?"

"I'm not going through there alone!"

"Oh, all right, take Carasel with you, then."

"That's not much help, Roseanna. And what if our atoms get all mixed up?"

"They won't, trust me."

"Well, I've trusted you up to this point, I guess it's too late to stop now. But I think I'll let you keep Carasel. So, beam me up, Captain," she said with a shaky laugh.

She took a step while I waited with bated breath. Another step—and she disappeared so fast my heart jolted into a new rhythm. Wasting no time, I grabbed up Carasel and pulled the same disappearing act.

Viveca was standing in the closet, pale and shaken, one hand clutching her chest. She gave a small yelp as Carasel leaped from my arms like an apparition from the beyond. Surging out of the passage, I grabbed my rattled friend in a fierce hug.

"We did it, Viv! You came through on your own!"

"Yes, I did, didn't I? I really did," she said wonderingly.

"And now you're going back on your own."

"Oh now, wait just a minute!"

"We have to *know*, Viveca. This is the only way to see if it's one hundred percent effective. I'll be right behind you," I promised with a tickling sense of déjà vu.

She nodded and blew out her breath. I could actually see her get a grip on herself. She stepped into the gap, and was gone.

I waited, not without my own anxiety. Seconds crept by. Then she was standing in front of me, laughing.

"Oh, Viv!" I said, choked up with relief. "You okay, honey?"

"Why, I'm just fine, Roseanna," she said, and disappeared again.

Feeling a bit sad that something so exclusively mine was now mutual knowledge, I followed her. "You're becoming a regular space jet-setter," I teased.

"Aren't I, though!" She tarried a moment longer, looking around the meadow in a long, still slightly incredulous sweep before her gaze met mine.

"Fan-tastic," she said.

"Fantastic," I agreed. "Time to go back, love."

"Back to reality."

"Another reality."

Pensively she looked around again. "Unbelievable. And yet, here it is. Here it *is*! That absolutely blows my mind." Her wandering gaze lit on me with a sudden spark of amusement. "My gardener, Rosie?" she drawled.

"Oh! Well, that's all I could think of, Viv. You blurt out that silly thing about him resembling Mel Gibson—what the devil was I supposed to do?"

"It wasn't silly," she said, haughty as hell. "He does resemble Mel. If you squint."

"If you squint," I conceded. "Come along, Viveca Lee, I'm taking you home before you get into any more mischief!"

I caught her hand, and a heartbeat later we were crammed into the space beside my closet shelf.

She stepped out first and leaned against the wall.

"Viv, you okay?" I asked, disturbed by her wistful expression.

"I'm okay, Rosie. Just a little overwhelmed, that's all." She stared at that shadowed, mystical space with a slow, bemused smile. "I haven't the foggiest idea how it works, but it's a lovely way to get around," she said softly.

Chapter 9

$\mathcal{T}$he lovely pleasure of that afternoon was not long lasting. I did not go to Nathaniel the next day or the next. Things came up, as things have a habit of doing, to prevent it. But Viveca and I had worked out a virtually foolproof plan.

"Now if only I just get the chance to use it," I muttered, wishing I could stop thinking and just go to sleep. Convinced that I was doomed to itchy wakefulness, I curled up in my favorite position and promptly felt my brain begin to fog.

The next thing I knew someone was nuzzling me out of my precious slumber. When I mumbled a protest, that someone laughed and for a startled instant I didn't know whose laugh it was.

"You awake?" David asked.

I mumbled something which fortunately he did not hear. He pressed against my back. Dandy. David had awakened with an erection.

I have never cared for early-morning sex. With my mind still asleep and my body undecided, by the time I get it together he is winding down. Whether for that reason, or some other, I did not want sex.

"Go pee," I suggested, flopping onto my stomach.

He swatted my bottom and went to the bathroom.

Then he turned on the light and looked at me lying there all sleep-wrinkled and blinking.

"Happy birthday," he said, pulling on the green silk robe that made him look like one of those classic ads for twenty-year-old Scotch. "You know, you don't look half bad for an old girl of forty-eight," he said judiciously.

"Idiot," I muttered, burying my head in a pillow.

After he had left me in peace, I poked a finger through a slat of my blind to check out the newborn day and found it utterly hopeless. Grayness. Garbage cans sitting curbside; sodden newspapers strewn on driveways. A drenched robin huddled on the lawn, waiting for a cat to come along and end its misery.

I dropped the blind and wrapped the tiny, vulnerable spirit of Roseanna in my arms for the cuddling she needed. Then, singing at the top of my lungs, I showered and toweled off so roughly it felt good.

My attempts at cheering me up fell flat. So I laid my naked self back down on the bed. I felt raw with longing, but I could not escape my cage today, even for a few hours, without hurting, disappointing, or disillusioning someone. And I'm too soft-hearted for that. Yesterday David had asked me what I wanted for my birthday and for a god-awful moment, I nearly told him.

A little while later Lexi called, then Viveca, with festive birthday wishes. Lexi would present me with a gift at our celebratory family dinner on Sunday.

"What did you get me?" I asked Lexi.

"Just what you want," she assured me.

I doubt that, I thought as we rang off. What I want isn't a material thing, or even the uplifting, sanctifying pleasures of the spirit. What I want are the lusty, wicked, voluptuously low-down pleasures of the flesh.

Confused by my perpetual inner conflict and in need of ballast, I reached under my night table for the photograph album I keep there for no specific reason. It's my personal album, given to me by my mother. The edges of the first pictures are curled with age, yet still clear and distinct.

Infant Roseanna, sleeping, crying, smiling, naked on a blanket, brand-new and beginning.

Roseanna at five, long sausage curls and mouth pursed in pure goodness. A Bible in one hand and a prissy white purse in the other. A white ruffled pinafore over a red velvet dress. So precious she sets my teeth on edge.

Roseanna at eight, pigtails, shorts, and T-shirt. Scabbed knees and a gamine grin with one tooth missing.

Roseanna at Sweet Sixteen party, hair atop head, eyes shining with anticipation. Roseanna at eighteen, boarding the train for college. A cool, poised, woman of the world with a half inch of slip showing below the pleated wool skirt.

A newlywed all in white. Blue eyes shining with wonder, she holds a bridal bouquet and the arm of a tall, black-haired man. David and Roseanna, brand-new and beginning.

My fingers flipped pages faster, skipping through years in the space of a heartbeat. Roseanna, eyes still filled with wonder, cradling a baby; Roseanna, standing with husband and little girl, all somber-faced. Picture of a tiny white casket, closed, a spray of tiny sweetheart roses on the lid, tall white candles burning in the background. Disembodied hand clutching the edge of casket.

Roseanna, hugging proud college-grad Alexis; say-cheese smile, puzzled eyes looking beyond David, looking beyond world, looking beyond—where? What was I looking for then? And what am I looking for now?

Gently I closed the album and put aside this pictorial record of Roseanna Noelle Bently Tait's life. I felt torn asunder by bittersweet sorrow, or maybe just self-pity.

I am forty-eight years old today. God, you know that's impossible. What happened to all my yesterdays? What happened to all the things I was absolutely going to do before I settled down to a matronly lifestyle? I never got to sleep my way through Europe. I never even got to Europe. I never swam naked in the Caribbean Sea or made love with a starving artist just because, or rode a horny dragon, or sucked a blood-red orange. I never rode in a baby-blue convertible with my hair blowing gloriously in the wind. And I meant to—I meant to do all that and much more.

But it's too late now.

Even more depressed, I sat in a huddle of limbs and

pondered the years that had slipped like sand through my fingers. It was still raining, that dreary, crying-type rain, a steady, drizzling bitch of a rain. Not the sort of day you'd choose to have a birthday, I concluded. But I didn't choose to have a birthday. I just got shafted with it.

"You're getting into the absurd, Roseanna," I warned. What was wrong with being over forty, anyhow? Why was half the world terrified at even the sound of it, despite all those enlightening articles titled, "I climbed the Alps at forty-five," or, "My unforgettable fiftieth birthday—I took up skydiving and *loved* it!"

Because forty is sitting square on top of fifty, that's why, I answered myself. And when you're six, you see your grandmother who is fifty and thus ancient; but that's all right, she's your grandmother and you love her exactly the way she is. When you're twelve, your grandmother is still fifty, still ancient and a goddess in your world, and it's *okay*. But when you're sixteen, your grandmother is gray parchment skin and your own eyes peering out of that skeletal face. Then it hits you. My God, someday I will be like that, which is fifty, which is ancient, which is a skull so thinly covered with flesh that you can trace the bony outlines with a mental fingertip. And it's *your* future face. And you *love* her. And she's *dying*. And she's *fifty*.

As always, memories of my beloved grandmother stuffed my nose with tears. Resolutely I reclosed that painful door.

Downstairs, Mims-the-maid was running the vacuum. I knew when I came down, she would smirk and say, "Well, how old are you now? Doesn't matter, you're only as old as you feel! Happy birthday!"

If she said that to me today, as she had for the past five years, I would fire her, by damn.

I considered getting up, but I couldn't think of any place to go. I didn't want to go downstairs and fire Mims. I'd love some coffee, but not at that price. She would probably refuse to be fired, anyway. Or maybe not, and then I'd have to do that damned vacuuming.

Still in a masochistic mode, I picked up David's list of

Things to Do Today, concluding with "check the Mercedes' right rear tire—it looks low."

Then there was my own list, concluding with "see GYN for Pap smear." Shit. Happy birthday to me. I loathe going to a GYN. That undignified position claws holes in a woman's ego. But it's necessary. So get your ass up, Roseanna and put some clothes on it, I advised myself. The world awaits.

The thought does not cheer me. The world waits, all right, but it is not the world I want to see. I want to see Nathaniel. I want to fly to a meadow where the sun is shining and a warm wind ruffles my hair. I long desperately to smile into emerald eyes and hear that deep, husky voice telling me I'm lovely and exciting, and know that in his world it's solid truth!

The child in me yearns for the magic of it all. The woman yearns for the man who is that intoxicating magic personified.

But sometimes magic has a dangerous side.

I let that thought slide by. In fact, I gave it a push. I had never felt threatened with Nathaniel.

I did, however, wonder keenly if he would want to see me. Nathaniel must be furious by now. Who knew how many days had passed in his world? If only I could synchronize his time and mine. But I can't. There is simply no continuity there. None that I can see, at any rate. It's like trying to establish logic by illogical means. David says I do that quite often, but still, even I can't make sense of Nathaniel's time.

Feeling both resigned and rebellious, I put on an artist's full white cotton shirt and a blue denim skirt without a stitch of underwear. If I got hit by a car and had to go to the hospital, Mother would just have to bear the shame of it, which she would surely feel even in Heaven. My temples were throbbing. After popping two aspirin with a mouthful of spit, I went downstairs.

Mims, engaged in dusting the mantle, turned to me and said, "Well, how old are you now? Doesn't matter, you're only as old as you feel. And I must say, you're obviously feeling very well lately. Happy birthday!"

"Thank you, Mims," I said with a winsome smile,

then stormed out of the house into one of Houston's miserable-weather days.

Just one more day until David takes himself off and leaves me to my own devices, I reminded myself.

Just one more day, Roseanna, I soothed when the right-rear tire on the Mercedes went flat in the parking lot.

After the man with the star had repaired it, I stopped by Viveca's and canceled my other appointments. The rain had settled down to a light drizzle that made for perilous driving. Viveca, being wise and likewise attuned to the astounding number of fender-benders now taking place on our freeways, had barricaded herself in her den with a good book, soft music, and comforting Bloody Marys.

"Happy birthday, darlin'. Join me?" she invited.

"Lord, yes!" I replied, collapsing into a chair. "What have you been up to lately? Besides having the good sense to hole up here and get soused?"

"Reflecting."

"Reflecting?" I stretched my legs, and on second thought, opened them a little. There was just no end to my defiance today. "Reflecting on what?"

"Life. Mine, mostly. Don't bother asking; I've not yet reached any mordant conclusions," she said dismissively.

While she filled another glass with icy red liquid, she gave me the once-over. "I must say you're looking good, Roseanna. A little nervy, but good."

I drank half my spicy tomato juice in one life-giving gulp. "I feel quite healthy, thank you."

Her throaty laugh rang out. "Honey, it has nothing to do with the state of your health. Only one thing on God's green earth can give a woman that particular look and that's being loved and being loved well. Cheers."

"Cheers. It's been awhile, though." I sighed.

"To risk repeating myself, I think you're crazy to be sitting here in my den when you could be in Paradise. If I had that option I'd be out of here in two seconds flat."

I tasted the sourness of frustration. "Viv, I told you, I can't just up and go anytime I please. I've got duties here, responsibilities—I'm a responsible person, dammit!" I half shouted.

"I know, honey. It's a shame the Peace Corps never got ahold of you. You'd probably have world hunger whipped by now."

"Very likely," I admitted, matching her droll tone. Forcing myself to relax, I sat back and let my gaze trail over the coral silk lounging pajamas she wore so well. "You look very good, too. So Colin must be attending you well."

She stiffened. "Rosie, don't go downgrading what you have by comparing it with what I have. Colin is a total zero when compared with Nathaniel and you know it. I do not care to be patronized nor insulted by oblique references to my lack of intelligence."

"Hey, Viv! I wasn't being catty or anything," I said in honest surprise. "But if you thought so, I apologize."

"Apologize to Nathaniel, not me. I know what I am and I neither ask for nor make apologies," she replied tightly.

"And what is that?"

"An aging, lonely woman, holding onto a witless young man with both hands because she's too gutless to stand alone just yet. And one who, if she didn't have her good friend Roseanna to lean on, couldn't have regained even this upright position." She glanced at me with a rueful smile. "Sorry, friend. It's the rain . . . or maybe the drinks. Anyway, enough soul searching. Drink up!"

"Viv, there is nothing wrong with your affair with Colin, not one bitching thing," I said furiously.

"There probably isn't, Rosie. And yet, me doth think you protest too much," she replied with a lilt of face-saving humor.

"Horsefeathers!" I said succinctly.

Shrugging, she let the subject drop in favor of my birthday and her gift to me, a scandalous red satin and lace teddy.

"Wear it in good health," she said, poker-faced.

On the drive back home I replayed the conversation and became stuck on one particularly disturbing point.

Several people had commented on how well I looked
lately. Even Mims had departed from her familiar
script. Yet the one most intimately close to me did not
see the difference. David viewed me as an extension of
himself, not subject to change; ergo, he saw no change.
If he had noticed my overflowing happiness at all, no
doubt he attributed it to himself.

I was being critical, even damning, and it bothered
me.

Nevertheless, I watched him closely that evening. Although he was home on time for a change, he still appeared tired and testy. I thought showing him the
royalty check that had arrived in today's mail might coax
a smile from him.

It did, a smile that practically reached down and patted my rump. "My little breadwinner," he said.

Shit. I poked a finger into the dimple that dots his
chin. "David, do you love me?"

"Of course."

"But do you *treasure* me?"

He looked pained. "Roseanna, we're not characters
in a romance novel. Now where's the evening paper?"

"It's on the arm of your chair where I have put it for
the last two decades."

"No need to get snippy, I haven't forgotten," he re-
proved.

"Forgotten what?"

"Your birthday present. Here, happy birthday." He
handed me a check. "I didn't know what to get you so I
thought I'd just let you decide."

I held my royalty check in one hand and his in the
other. "Whoopee," I said under my breath. One night
when we were first married, he had come home with a
pot of pink hyacinths still bearing the price tag, one
dollar twenty-nine cents, and I was stoned out of my
mind with happiness. I would gladly give both my checks
for one spontaneous pot of hyacinths.

"Thank you, David. I'm sure I can find something I'll
like. Maybe I'll spend it on hyacinths. Imagine, a whole
room full of hyacinths. They'll stink us out of the
house."

His heavy black brows tangled in a frown. "I asked you what you wanted and you said nothing. What the hell am I supposed to do, go out and buy you a nothing?"

He had a point. "No, I guess not. It's a very nice check," I said gamely.

"Yes it is." He picked up the paper and started toward his study, where he would sit down in his ox-blood leather chair with his unlit pipe jutting from the corner of his mouth and look lordly, a man in firm control of his world.

"Wait a minute, I'm not finished," I said, interrupting his progress. When he turned to face me I stared at him as if I had him under a spotlight. He wore even the most casual clothes with elegance. The open-collared shirt, tweed sweater vest, and pleated gabardine trousers were perfect for his businessman-relaxing-at-home image.

Slowly I raised my gaze to his immaculately barbered face. Impatience stained his deep brown eyes. Eyes that knew everything, I thought irritably. Nothing bothered David, while I was constantly aflutter with one demanding emotion or another. Did he never know the cold-molasses sense of incompetence that so often afflicted me?

"Roseanna?" he prompted.

He was looking full at me, but he wasn't seeing *me,* any more than he was taking note of our kitchen appliances. When did he stop? Was there a precise moment his image of Roseanna became the lump of butter on his toast? Who really looks at a lump of butter lying exactly where it should, doing exactly what it should, and takes note of it?

"David, do you ever look at me?" I asked intensely.

He sighed. "Since that sounds too obvious, obviously I don't understand the question."

"All right, I'll rephrase it. When you look at me what do you see?"

"I see my wife. Should I see something else?"

"No, I guess not." Tears stung my eyes. "I just wanted you to look at me and see *me,* not a goddamned lump of butter!"

"You are upset about the check, aren't you? Look, tear up the damned thing. I'll buy you something tomorrow."

"It's not the check, it's me, David. It's *us*!"

"There is nothing wrong with us," he said flatly.

"I think. . . . Oh, forget it," I said, backing away from the terrifying abyss opening in front of me. "I'm just in an odd-mood, that's all."

"Yes, you are that," he agreed, frowning. "I don't know what's gotten into you lately. You've become irresponsible—"

"Irresponsible! How on earth can you say that?"

"What would you call it then? We're a team, you and I, and a damned good one, too. Usually. But lately you've been dragging your feet on everything I ask of you. You've practically abandoned the Ladies Club. You refused to hostess that Japanese tea and sushi party for the firm. You've showed up late for two important dinners—"

"Political dinners—"

"Important, nonetheless. To top off all that you've displayed patent disrespect for me."

"When did I do that?"

"Yesterday, when you rebuked me in front of our daughter. At that charity benefit last week, when Lynn pinned on my nametag and you suggested she be careful lest she puncture me and let all the air out."

"David, for Pete's sake, that was a joke!" I protested.

"At my expense."

"Maybe you need a few jokes at your expense!"

"Now what's that supposed to mean?"

"That you need to loosen up?" I suggested. "Maybe even laugh at yourself once in a while?"

"I laughed, if you'll recall. And this diversionary tactic isn't working, Roseanna. Pointing up my flaws in no way mitigates your failures."

"Failures? I've been a good wife to you and you know it!"

"I didn't say you weren't a good wife. I'm simply stating a fact as I see it."

"Then you don't see too well," I said evenly.

"I think my vision is clear enough. Of course I could be wrong."

"Yes, you damn well could!" I flared. "I'm tired of this, tired of waiting around hoping for a bit of tenderness and caring, a little sensitivity on your part. And I'm damned tired of being alone and lonely."

"Roseanna, you know my work is demanding, and that it requires travel, which means leaving you alone from time to time. I'm sorry you get lonely, but I—"

"Oh, not that kind of lonely! I'm talking about the kind of loneliness that comes from lack of affection. Like right now, David. You're here, right here with me, and I'm so lonely I could cry."

"You're getting maudlin."

"You mean emotional, and heaven forbid we get *emotional*! I think you're afraid of feelings, David, I think you buried that part of you—"

"That's enough, Roseanna!" Shifting, he looked at the newspaper he held. Awkwardly. And awkwardness was alien to David.

I was caught in the same unease. Somewhere, some way, there was a small but deadly serious tear in the fabric of our marriage. How had that happened? Surely not from my puny charges. Alarmed, I stared at him. He averted his gaze and my anxiety increased. David was never defensive.

"David, let's talk? We never talk about things. Even after the baby died, we just . . . went on in our own separate misery."

"There are some things I don't care to talk about." He cleared his throat. "Anyway, I learned long ago that trying to communicate with you is utterly futile. You're a species unto yourself, Roseanna Noelle," he said with a dry laugh. "Let's have a drink, shall we? Gin and tonic suit you?"

"Fine." I went into the den and sat down on the couch. I knew from past experience that we were through talking. What had we resolved? Nothing, as usual.

We sipped our drinks in clotted silence, while he read the paper, front to back, thoroughly. I fixed myself another gin and tonic. Champagne would have been nice. After all, it was my birthday. But champagne gives David a headache.

Time dribbled on, splashing like wasted water on a desert floor. I had three drinks in quick succession. So I couldn't drink worth a damn, so what! Feeling furious, violent and dangerously sexy, I gulped down the last drink and threw the glass at the fireplace like I'd seen them do in one of those wild Russian movies. Then I glared at David in virulent challenge.

When, eyebrows atilt, he merely glanced at the shattered glass, my wrath increased tenfold. Why couldn't he at least care enough to *fight* with me? Rapidly reaching my boiling point, I stood up and stomped over to his chair.

"It's okay if you don't treasure me, 'cause I don't treasure you, either, not anymore," I announced, peering at him bulldog-style. "I've tried. God knows I've tried!" I swayed, and he shot to his feet. "But you just stay calm and cold and distant while I keep right on trying! You don't love me, don't need me, don't desire me anymore. Yet we're still married, still together. Now that's weird, David, that is downright—oops!"

Looking amused at my inebriated charges, he caught my arms to steady me. "You're being silly," he chided. "Our marriage is very important to me and so are you."

"Sure I am."

The bitterness I felt must have been noticeable, for his voice sharpened. "You are, Roseanna. And I do love and need you. Maybe not the way I used to, but our needs are different now. Because *we're* different; older, more stable. . . ." His mouth quirked. "At least one of us is."

I didn't smile. "I'm different, more stable. Stable enough to wonder why we're still married, anyway."

He looked surprised. "Hey, Roseanna, come on now. You know you matter to me, you know how much I value our marriage. We've been together for over two decades. We've shared so much, accomplished so much. We'd be fools to throw away all those years just because. . . ." He tried another smile. "Just because I neglected to buy you hyacinths for your birthday."

"Calm, cool, logical, that's my David," I said, pushing away from him. "About as much feeling as a turnip, but—"

"Dammit, that's not true. Sure I'm logical! And yes, I'm practical, *and* calm, *and* cool-headed. But that doesn't mean I'm a stolid lump, devoid of feelings."

"We haven't made love in months."

"I know that, I—" He dragged a hand across his face. "Roseanna, the partners are in the middle of some very complicated business negotiations right now. You know how hard I've worked lately, how busy I've been."

"Day *and* night?" I blurted, startling myself as well as him.

He sat back down. "Some nights, yes, I concede that."

I waited.

"Roseanna, I'm a logical man, I can't help that. Yes, I'm ambitious. I have goals I intend to reach or die trying. What's so wrong about that? I've always taken care of my family. Neither you nor Lexi have ever suffered from my drive to succeed."

"We haven't made love in months."

"Roseanna, for God's sake, I only have so much energy," he protested. Rising, he caught my shoulders and squeezed. "Look, give me some time, hmm? Let me get on top of things at the office, then we'll see what happens." His hands slid down my arms in that slow, sensual caress I remembered so well. "Maybe we'll take that trip you wanted. This fall, perhaps. We'll work it out." He tipped up my chin. "Won't we?"

"I—I guess so."

He brushed kisses across my mouth. "I know so. You're my wife and I love you. Now, why don't you go on to bed." He chuckled. "While you can still walk!"

Confused and lightheaded, I decided to take his advice.

Despite the alcohol I'd consumed, sleep eluded me. My mind kept replaying our scene, analyzing, searching for something solid to hang my hopes on. Once I would have accepted his words with joyous relief and even anticipation. But I'd lost too many of my lovely illusions. I was torn between wanting to believe, and wary of belief.

Someone was shaking me. Blearily I peered at the insensitive clod who should know I would awaken with a headache. "Roseanna? You awake?" David repeated.

I mumbled that I was, and what time was it?

"Eight. My flight's at nine, so I'm leaving now. For San Antonio," he reminded my blank look. "I'll call you tonight."

Firewater shot through my veins and brought me upright. "No, don't call. I won't be here." I looked at him through slitted eyes. "I have a date tonight."

"Humph. Very funny. But you and Viveca have fun. I'll be back late tomorrow. After midnight, I imagine."

Remembering our mini-brawl last night, I scanned his face. Opaque dark eyes and aquiline features revealed nothing but impatience to be on the road.

Coward! I denounced my relief. "What's going to keep you out until midnight?"

"Work," he replied shortly.

"Oh, David, you work too hard," I said with soft sincerity.

Instead of an immediate response, he fiddled with the clasp of his briefcase. Then, abruptly, "I love my work. Well, I'd better be going. 'Bye, Roseanna, take care."

"'Bye, David. You, too." Lying back against the pillow, I watched him leave the bedroom. Something, I sensed, was still out of kilter in his world. Whatever it was challenged him. Work problems, most likely. Which meant I wasn't going to hear about it.

Shifting my focus, I listened to his footsteps in the hallway and followed his progress down the stairs to the marble-tiled entry. I heard the door shut . . . the garage door open . . . the car start up. Only when the sound of his motor faded away did I relax into the crisp linen sheets that we fancied.

David was going to be gone overnight. And so was I!

I could not begin to describe the way I felt at that moment. I only knew I was lighter than air, a radiant lightness centered in my heart. Anticipation poured more of that firewater into my veins. Jumping out of bed, I rushed to the kitchen for a cup of coffee. On second thought, I grabbed the pot and took it back upstairs.

Then I called Viveca. Her line was busy. I refused to be daunted by this snag in my plans. It was a lovely day. The rain had stopped sometime during the night and the sky was pure, newly washed blue. White clouds drifted around that azure vault like clean laundry hung out to dry.

Carasel put her front feet on the bed with a pleading whine. She is such a tiny bit of a dog, and a beautiful one with her platinum fur and fluffy beige feet. Heart softening to Jell-O, I lifted her up beside me. "We're going to see Nathaniel, Carasel! Yes, we'll spend the entire day and night with him!" I said with lilting joy.

Another call to Viveca went unanswered except by her message machine. After I left my urgent message, I took a bath in scented water. Five minutes of inactivity was all I could stand. Filled with an irrepressible sense of eagerness, I decided to let my skin dry naturally while I packed an overnight bag.

What should I take? The basics, of course: toiletries, a complete change of clothes. My birthday gift from me, a filmy gown and peignoir. Perfume—Joy, I decided. I bought the extravagant little bottle of scent for myself.

While I packed, bubbling laughs escaped me much as if I had gas. But a sudden dark shadow of fear intruded upon my gaiety. Reality. I had tried to push aside any qualms about what I was doing and was largely successful. But the sheer magnitude of what I planned suddenly hit me like a hard thump in the gut. I was actually going to leave my world, my real life, my family, to spend an entire day and night with a fantasy man in an alien realm.

What if I should become trapped there?

In a mild sweat I examined that possibility and eventually discarded it as incompatible to the situation.

What if David somehow found out what I've been doing?

Another dismissible concern, I decided. How on earth

could he possibly find out? And even if by some remote
chance he did, would he believe it? Of course not.
Something like this was simply not in David's belief system.

To my intense pleasure I was able to shake off my
darkening cloud. Part of that ability came from the fact
that I simply could not resist the irresistibly sweet temptation to visit my other world. Because I'm in love, I
thought dreamily. And being in love is a song in your
heart, wings on your feet, dancing under exploding stars
and fly me to the moon.

It is not stable, nor does it come with a guarantee.
Even so, there is nothing on earth to equal being *in love*,
and I am falling-down drunk with it. My stomach is
churning, my legs are shaky, and I can't breathe right.
This also describes me when I have the flu. But the flu
doesn't grip me with a fevered urge to go out and hug
the whole damn world and give away all my clothes to
poor people. I do not break out in little snatches of song
as I skip nimbly from bathroom to bedroom to closet.

I do not, when I step on Carasel's little foot, get down
on my knees and implore her forgiveness and kiss her
ten times. Usually I say, "Well, damn, Carasel, stay away
from my feet, will you?"

My stomach really was churning. "But I'm not sick,
I'm just in love!" I sang in what David calls my god-
awful Texas twang.

After dressing in a feminine red sundress with only a
clever arrangement of straps across the back, I added
gold hoop earrings and pirouetted in front of the mirror. Perfect.

"Viv, come on!" I groaned, antsy with impatience.

Immediately the telephone rang.

"Are you going?" Viveca asked.

"Yes, in just a minute."

"For the night?"

"For the night. Oh, Viv, I'm scared," I confessed.

"No need to fear, Viveca's here," she intoned. Then
she added softly, "Vaya con Dios, Rosie."

My heart winced at the wistfulness in her tone. "You,

too," I said with a liquid gush of love. "God, you cry at the drop of a hat, Roseanna," I scolded, wiping my eyes.

Tucking Carasel under one arm, I picked up my overnight bag, and headed for my closet.

Although it was nine o'clock when I left Earth, the meadow was rosy with the first glow of dawn. Carasel took off the instant I released her, and I was right behind her. We raced headlong past the spring and on through the whispery grove. The combination of joy and anticipation gave me such a heady rush that my feet barely skimmed the dew-damp grass.

Carasel's bark shattered the hush as we crested the hill. She rushed ahead, but I stopped so abruptly that I stumbled.

Nathaniel wasn't in bed. Nathaniel wasn't even there. His black truck was gone.

Chapter 10

$\mathcal{M}$y excitement dissipated on the instant. For a few minutes longer I watched Carasel yapping at the door. Then I called her back and we returned to my closet.

I was nearly crying with disappointment. I was also going crazy with wondering. Where was he? And at dawn? I paced the room and wrung my hands. By ten I was in such a state that I returned to the meadow again.

Bright sunshine rayed across the land, but storm clouds were gathering. A long roll of thunder quivered the air as we reached the hilltop.

The truck was still gone. I knocked on Nathaniel's door without any hope of an answer.

For awhile I simply sat on the front steps lost in my misery. Another peal of thunder finally jerked me to awareness. Only minutes away, a gray curtain of rain was sweeping down from the mountains. I had to seek shelter. But I couldn't bear to go back home. Surely Nathaniel had a door key hidden somewhere.

After searching the front steps, I walked around to the back porch. Beside the door was an old-fashioned galvanized milk can holding a wilted plant. The can was heavy, but I managed to tip it over. Bingo, a key! Not very original, Nathaniel, I thought fondly.

It was hot inside, and the air had that faint, musty smell that permeates a closed house. How long had he been gone? I rushed to the bedroom and slid open the door to his closet. His clothes were still there. A quick search of the bathroom revealed that his shaving gear was missing. "Well, at least he hasn't left for good," I told Carasel.

So relieved I felt sick, I opened the windows to let in some of that marvelous stormy air. Then I approached the air-conditioner thermostat and checked it out. Although unfamiliar, it had a knob that said OFF and one that said ON, which seemed simple enough. I turned it ON and the unit purred.

A moment later the rain began and I had to close the windows. It was a gentle rain. My night had been restless; I was coping with sonic emotional letdown, and there was Nathaniel's bed. Another irresistible combination, I confessed.

Not even attempting to resist, I stripped down to my carefully chosen black silk underwear and slipped beneath the sheet. The lulling patter of rain and the good smell of Nathaniel soon put me to sleep.

When Carasel's sharp bark awoke me, I was confused as to place and time. But not for long. The sound of an engine cutting off brought me from the bed in a single bound. Through the window I could see Nathaniel getting out of his truck. My heartbeat stumbled into a new rhythm. Shushing Carasel, I ran to the front door and flung it open just as he climbed the steps.

His foot froze in midair, then slowly came down on the porch. Carasel raced through my legs and hurled herself upon him much as I longed to do. But I wasn't that sure of my welcome. Nathaniel's face did not light up. In fact, he looked at me with a calculating coolness that shivered my spine.

"Roseanna. This is a surprise. I didn't expect such a reception committee. Hello there, Carasel. How you doing, girl?"

He stopped to pat the prancing little dog before coming in.

I closed the door behind him and snatched a calming breath. "Hello, Nathaniel." Suddenly shy, I offered a tremulous smile. "I hope it's all right for me to—well, it started raining, you see, so I found the key and let myself in. I hope you don't mind." I was babbling and I knew it. But his face was so expressionless!

"Of course I don't mind. Can't have you getting wet, can we!" His gaze flickered over me. "That's some costume. You usually answer the door dressed like that?"

"You know I don't!"

"How would I know that?" He slung the briefcase on the couch. "When did you get here?"

"At dawn, I came at dawn. And then I went back home and I came back about ten, I guess." In my nervousness I ran the words together on one breath and had to gulp another lungful of air. "Then I laid down and fell asleep. In your bed."

"I see. Where have you been, Roseanna?" He removed his tie and tossed it atop the briefcase. "I waited a week, figuring that 'tomorrow' of yours must surely fall into a specified length of time."

"Nathaniel, please, I'm sorry. I couldn't come, darling. Honestly, I couldn't! But you know I wanted to!"

"Sure I do. Any coffee?" He walked to the kitchen and checked the pot.

Rattled, I shook my head. I hadn't made coffee—why the hell would I make coffee? He hadn't been here to drink it.

"Where were you?" I asked.

"Where were you?" he countered. We stared at each other. I wrapped my arms around myself, feeling chilled by that cold green gaze.

"I couldn't come, Nathaniel. That's the truth. I'm sorry you were upset."

"Upset?" He laughed. "Such an innocuous little word." He slammed down the coffeepot with such force, I jumped. "I waited for you, goddamn it! I sat here waiting day after day, feeling more and more like a double-damned fool, waiting! In fact, baby, I got to feeling such a fool that I said to hell with you and I packed up and went home. Then I went on the worst binge I've ever lived through. I even tried to pick up a woman! But I was too drunk to even pull that off. I spent all day yesterday trying to stand on my feet and glue my skull back together again. Yes, in retrospect, I'd say I was a mite *upset*!"

I ducked my head to hide the tears filling my eyes despite my furious blinking. His scathing tone did not hide the fact that he had been deeply hurt. And I had done it. Turning quickly, I walked to the sink for a glass of water. The small act gave me time to gain some control. Swiping at my wet cheeks, I sipped water and stared out the window. There was a magnificent rainbow arching over the hills nearby and far away.

"There's a rainbow," I said. He didn't answer. I returned to him and stood with trembling hands clasped behind my back. "Nathaniel, if you don't want me—"

"Oh, cut the humble act, Roseanna. You know damned good and well that right this minute I want you more than I've ever wanted any woman," he said, disgusted with his weakness. "So? Why did you come back this time? Need a little more stud service?"

His voice was clipped and flat, with none of that melodic resonance I so loved. "I'm sorry, Nathaniel, I—I'd better go."

"Oh now, don't let's be hasty, honey. We might as well do what you came here for." With a harsh laugh, he began unbuttoning his shirt. Hard emerald eyes raked me up and down. "No use wasting such a sexy getup!"

Tearing off his shirt, he balled it up and threw it on the floor. I flinched, frozen to my spot by his anger. He stepped close and cupped my breasts. Those mocking eyes cut deep, but I held his gaze unswervingly. When he ran his hands over my body, I knew it was meant to be insulting. Yet, when his fingers slid down inside my panties and molded my buttocks, I swayed toward him. The heat in him fanned my own smoldering fires.

I had to feel him, taste him! His naked chest was manna to my hungry mouth. My fingers were lost in the satin of his back and I was acutely aware of his arousal. Blindly I turned my face up to his.

Instead of a kiss, his sardonic chuckle warmed my lips. "Um, hot already, aren't you! Just like you were in the meadow that day, lying there waiting for a man. Any man, not just me. Open invitation, huh, baby? Come and get it, whoever the hell you are!"

My eyes flew open at this. His smile was a tortured twist of lips. "That's not true!" I cried. "Just any man wouldn't have—I'd have fought tooth and nail if it had been anyone but you!"

"Would you?" His teeth flashed. "Somehow I doubt that."

I gazed at him, wide-eyed and stricken by his words. And suddenly, ragingly angry. "Well, you can go to hell, Nathaniel," I said with a lilt of that fury.

He swore, spitting out the oath as if it were a mouthful of bitter aloes. Before I could react, he clenched his hands in my hair and kissed me, hard and bruisingly rough. The big hands left my hair to slide around my back and crush me into his body. For an instant I was overwhelmed by my own hot-blooded response. But his savage kiss was hurting me. When I cried out, he drew back immediately.

"Don't kiss me like that, Nathaniel! You hurt me!"

He winced, then dropped his arms. "And what about me? It's all right for you to hurt me?" he grated. Suddenly he looked so young and vulnerable, my heart twisted. "Oh, hell," he ended tiredly. "I'm sorry I hurt you."

I felt pretty damn young and vulnerable myself at that moment. "I didn't know you had such a temper. Well, live and learn. Maybe I really had better go," I said, sighing.

"Yeah, maybe you'd better," came his level response. "And don't bother coming back, Roseanna. We'll just end up hurting each other again."

He might as well have slapped me. I stepped back and tried desperately to react in a sensible way. He was right. Of course he was right! This had gone far beyond lighthearted frolic. He had been hurt, and any deeper involvement would only add to that hurt.

Even as I acknowledged this, my heart was engaged in frantic denial. The pain of giving him up was astoundingly acute. I wanted to run to him, fling myself at his feet and plead with him. Pride didn't matter. It wasn't pride that kept me silent.

Carasel chose this taut moment to come romping back into the room dragging one of Nathaniel's shoes with her. She flopped down and attacked it with ferocious growls.

Quickly I knelt to rescue the shoe. When I glanced up again, Nathaniel's face was inscrutable as he watched me and my little dog. I was hotly aware of the ridiculous picture I must present, clad in these scanty black undergarments, tangled hair obscuring half my face. Trying to ignore my discomfort, I stood up and put the shoe on a table.

"Nathaniel, I'm sorry, truly I am. I didn't mean to hurt you, I just—I. . . ." I drew a breath and burst out, "I'm not that cheap person you tried to make me out to be! I've only known two men in my life and you're the second. If it hadn't been you—Nathaniel, I gave to you freely, like a wanton, I know, but it was only because it was *you*!"

His expression shifted. I was crying, even though I didn't want to be crying. "I'll go now. I'm sorry, so very sorry."

"Oh, Roseanna. Oh hell, come here," Nathaniel said. He held out his arms and I flew into them without a second's pause for thought. He clasped me tightly, with our cheeks pressed together and my tears wetting his face.

"Roseanna," he repeated, sighing. "Please stop crying? I'm sorry I was cruel. You know I didn't mean to be."

"Oh, I know, I know! And you weren't, not very much." Standing on tiptoe, I groped for his face, his mouth. Finding it, I kissed him in a wild fever of relief. I was berserk with happiness, aglow and soaring on his forgiveness.

"God, I missed you," he muttered. Scooping me up in his arms, he carried me to the bedroom with his mouth locked to mine. My body slid sensuously down his until we were both standing. When his hands moved to my breasts in greedy caress, cupping them to point the tight nipples to his mouth, I felt consumed with hunger for his touch. Part of my mind was still aware that, except for this obvious need flaring between us, I didn't know where I stood with him. But for now, this was enough.

Sensations, both given and taken, flowed over and through me in intoxicating waves. His smooth chest was dewy with a film of sweat, his hair a feast of crisp, entangling softness. His tongue probed my mouth as if seeking to discover my innermost being, and mine returned the quest.

"I love this outfit you're wearing," he murmured.

"It's for you. I've never worn it before," I replied breathlessly. He was already taking it off me. And then his hands were all over, moving, caressing, kneading, curving around my hips to press me into his erection.

I pulled at his belt, trying to open the buckle, eager to get him undressed so I could fill my aching hands with him.

"Clothes," I moaned at some point in time.

With a low, rich laugh, he took off the belt and trousers that were aggravating me so. I grasped his shorts, sliding them down his long legs, sensually slow, pausing to kiss here and there. His knees were erogenous zones, imagine! I was driving him crazy and exulting in it.

Then he was nude except for his socks. I wasn't inclined to worry about socks. Sliding my hands down his flat stomach, I filled my tingling palms with the marvelous heft of him.

He sucked in his breath. I felt him tremble, a powerful stimulant to my femininity. My own breath stilled as he began to kiss me, a line of torrid kisses that began at my chin and meandered down to my thighs.

"Oh, love, love," he said thickly. "The feel of you, the smell of you, sweet perfume and ready woman . . . like an aphrodisiac, your skin, your hair . . . mine, goddamn it, all mine!"

His rough, possessive words struck me like drops of molten gold. A quiver of confusion arrowed down my spine. Then there was only his face, taut with passion, hovering over mine again. Hooded green eyes watched as I responded to his urgency. I was aflame from head to toe. My shameless wanting poured into the hot, wet, open-mouthed way I kissed him. His hands moved down the curve of my buttocks and edged under the soft mounds, lifting me up until he was snug in the damp triangle of my thighs.

His eyes glazed, smoky with excitement. His breath came in soft, heated gusts. Suddenly he pushed into me, holding my body fused to his as he drove sweet and true, deep into the core of my most intimate femininity.

No one had ever touched this secret place, I thought with a swirling sense of bewilderment. My entire being was focused on the excitement radiating outwards until I felt etched in fire. What was he doing to me? Whatever he wanted. Engulfed in this most incredible pleasure, I curved my legs around his hips and opened my body completely, taking him in, pulling him deeper and deeper, moving my hips in a provocative swivel as I rode him in delicious abandon.

It was swift and torturously sweet, building in seconds to unparalleled heights, then flinging us over the edge to share an earthshaking climax.

Under its onslaught, he staggered backwards and we fell onto the bed still locked together. A tremor shook him from head to toes as he held me against him.

"God! I've never, *ever* . . . experienced anything like that."

"Me, either," I said with the same trace of awe.

"My little darlin'," he whispered. "Roseanna, I'm sorry, I didn't mean to take you like that."

"Hah! Macho male," I muttered darkly.

"Ah, God," he half laughed, half groaned.

I raised my head to huff, "You deny it?"

"Hell, no! The more the better, I say." When I huffed again, he buried his face in my hair, kissing through it until he reached the super-sensitive flesh behind my ear. I squirmed. He sighed and licked it. "You squirm so nicely," he explained.

He turned us on our sides. "I don't understand what you do to me or how easily you can do it," he murmured wryly. "I was ready to strangle you—hell, strangle you several times over for what you'd put me through. Instead I find myself making love to you. Imagine! Kissing instead of strangling. Amazing!"

"Well, you're an amazing man, Nathaniel." Eager to delay any serious discussion, I touched my nose to his. "I can spend the night with you . . . if you want?"

He smiled. I went weak with the pleasure that smile gave me.

"You know I want." His voice deepened. "Oh, babe, you know I want."

For some crazy reason I remembered I had a daughter who thought babe was a four-letter word. Personally, I loved it. All of it. The joy of being in his arms, being in his bed—just being! This was *right*. To be together was perfectly *natural*.

With a luminous sigh I melted into him for a leisurely session of tender, romantic lovemaking. Later we fell asleep under the magic of soft rain and sweet exhaustion.

When my eyes opened again, Nathaniel was lying beside me staring at the ceiling. Noting his set face, I felt a minute drop to solid land. "Hi, honey," I whispered. His arm was under my shoulders and I cuddled closer. The bed smelled rampantly delicious. I sniffed like an ecstatic puppy, and tried to wriggle under his skin.

Nathaniel did not respond beyond a glance my way. "You said you weren't married. So why does your overnight bag bear the initials R.T.? Is your name a lie, too?"

My heart sank. "I've never lied to you, ever!"

"No, you just don't tell the truth," he agreed flatly. "Roseanna, let's be honest with each other? Say exactly what we feel and think, and have felt and thought from the beginning?"

I lay back and flung an arm across my brow. "Okay, let's. You first."

"I figured you'd say that," he said, beautifully wry. "But okay, here goes. This situation has become flat-out intolerable to me. When I first found you in the meadow —hell, it was a romp, babe. There you were all naked in the grass, looking like something from a man's horniest dream. You wanted loving and I was ready. What the devil did I care who you were or where you came from? Oh, sure, I was curious, but that didn't mean I cared.

"When you didn't show up that next night, I damn near tore the lake colony apart looking for you, but I put it down to being hot and bothered about being stood up. It is not a familiar experience," he said with just enough arrogance to tickle my affectionate funnybone.

"Then you came back and it was fun and excitement again. I said to myself, what the hell, she's good sex, so leave it alone. I even began to enjoy your little mystery act. Why not? Made it even more exciting. After all, we were just balling each other, so what did it matter what you were up to? I'd screwed a lot of women without giving a damn who they really were. . . ."

Then, mockingly, "Yep, that's what all I told myself."

I kept very still, lying beside him as though I were merely an interested listener, while eddies of icy dread filtered through my bones. When I shivered, Nathaniel reached for the sheet and drew it to my breasts. I rolled up against him and kissed his shoulder in sudden wild desperation.

"You sure do make it hard for a man," he said, whooshing out a sigh.

"I try, Nathaniel." I listened to his groaning laugh with rabid pleasure. Then I nipped his shoulder.

"Oh, sweetheart," he said huskily. Turning onto his side, he drew me close again. "I've already told you the real reason why I tolerated the situation. Just realizing how much I loved life since you came along, how vibrant and even happy I felt—at times, anyway—was reason enough. But it has to change, Roseanna, you know that. It has to change because we have changed. It's no longer fun and games; it's not a game anymore, period. Not to me, at any rate. I don't want to play anymore."

"What *do* you want?" I asked warily.

"I want a normal relationship. I want to do things with you. I want to go dancing, to the movies, cook dinner with you, shop with you, just the normal things a man and woman do together."

"Cook with me?" I repeated the one thing that snagged my attention. I had never cooked with a man or even shopped with one. Enchanted, I asked, "You can cook? I mean, really cook?" I checked. After all, the only thing he ever fed me was sandwiches and lemonade. And tart lemonade at that.

"Yes, I can really cook."

"And you like to?" I couldn't imagine David cooking.

"Yes, I like to. Why so incredulous?"

I just shook my head.

He spewed out another hard sigh. "I guess the bottom line is that I want a relationship that has a lot more meaning than a romp in the hay."

I needed help and quick as a flash, my irrepressible sense of humor kicked in. "We've never romped in the hay. At least, I haven't. Have you?" I asked, wide-eyed.

That odd half-and-half sound broke through his lips again. "No, I haven't romped in the hay! Dammit, get serious!"

Getting serious was the last thing I wanted. When I did not respond, he tipped my chin up. "Look at me, Roseanna. I'm a man, not an adolescent who can forever enjoy a mystery lady. I'm finished with it. I cannot and will not endure another week like this one. It's time to start behaving like adults."

"You have no idea what you're asking, no idea!" I said hopelessly. "Do you know how long it took me to just convince myself that this was real, that you were real? I mean that literally, Nathaniel. I had to convince myself that you were actually *real.* Oh, what can I tell you?" I ended, defeated before I began.

"Why not try the truth? After all, how hard can it be?"

How hard could it be? I closed my eyes. When I re-opened them, he was waiting. I could sense the avalanche of questions forming, lining up, eager for their turn. And all I had to succor me was an enormous dread of the truth. Good lord, I couldn't tell him the truth! Telling Viveca, whom I've known half my life, was hard enough. Telling Nathaniel was impossible.

"Because the truth is too—too . . . I *can't!*" My

voice picked up a stammering urgency at his impatient movement. "Nathaniel, please listen, please just listen? You put your finger on the truth that first day in the meadow, but you didn't know it. I did drop from the sky, in a manner of speaking."

His mouth tightened. Sitting up, I hugged my knees. "I wasn't quite truthful when I said it would be dull or even logical. It isn't. In fact, it's so incredible, you couldn't possibly believe it if I did tell you. I have two worlds, Nathaniel. In yours, I am as you know me. In mine, I'm someone else altogether, and that Roseanna has . . . obligations which keep her from moving freely about."

Oh, Lord, I was skirting all around the truth without accomplishing anything other than adding to his frustration. "I can't just up and come to you when I want to. You wouldn't believe how complicated these visits have become."

"I probably wouldn't," he agreed, achingly wry.

"Oh, Nathaniel, please! Darling, I feel deeply about you."

"I don't think you give an emotional damn about me."

"You're wrong, so wrong. My feelings about you are strong enough that I-I want your respect, Nathaniel. I value your good opinion of me. I love the way you look at me and I want to keep that look in your eyes. I do want it so badly! But there are things in my past, things over which I have no control, things I c-can't—" I started crying.

"Ah, Christ. Please don't do that," he requested quietly.

"Well, I can't help it! I can't stand to hurt you. I can't stand seeing you frustrated and angry, and you have a perfect right to be f-frustrated and angry! And this isn't just sex to me! You aren't a *stud*, goddamn it!" I wailed, pounding his shoulder with an impotent fist. "What we have together I value beyond price!"

"Do you?"

"Yes! Yes I do! If I didn't, I wouldn't be trying so hard to explain to you something I simply cannot explain! I would say to hell with it, to hell with you and to hell with this screwed-up world of yours! Oh damn you, damn you! Why couldn't you just let it alone, let it b-be! Just let it be like it was!"

I spread my hands over my face, crying hard, hurting with a fiery desolation. Why did he have to ruin it!

"Roseanna, I simply can't cope with your crying. Please don't do this to me."

When this only increased my distress, he gathered me to him with a resigned sigh and let me weep all over his chest.

"I'm sorry, I'm not doing this on purpose, I just c-can't stop!" I sobbed.

"Yes you can. Hush now, darlin', shh . . ." He kept making those soothing little noises until my weeping ebbed to hiccups. I was all stopped up and probably looked a mess. Crying is not something I do prettily, or even gracefully. When he stuck a handkerchief in the vicinity of my nose, I blew so lustily that he laughed and squeezed me.

"Whatever is in your past, I can't believe it could be so bad I can't forgive you. Why can't you trust me enough to level with me? I'm not such an ogre, am I?"

"Because . . . because. . . ."

"Well, that's a start. Because?" he prompted.

Nathaniel's voice, thin with impatience, suddenly blended into David's. *Yes, Roseanna? Because? I'm waiting, Roseanna.* . . . My jaw set as old wounds flared to life.

"Because I can't," I said stubbornly. "Why can't this be enough? It's so wonderful, why can't we just go on like this?"

"Because I want more."

"I can't give you any more!"

"Because you don't have it to give." His level voice masked the hurt in his eyes.

"I have it, believe it, I have it. But. . . ." I gave a helpless shrug.

He lay back and folded his arms under his head. "Sometimes it occurs to me wonder: Am I really tolerant, patient, understanding, all that gentlemanly stuff

I'm trying the fuck-all to be? Or am I just plain stupid? Maybe you're getting your kicks by playing me for a fool and I'm too dumb or too enamored or what-the-hell-ever to know it!"

Fighting his fire with fluid softness, I asked, "Is that what you really think, that I'm playing you for a fool?"

He closed his eyes and sighed. "Only in my ego-tantrums. Christ, Roseanna, how could I stand believing something like that?" His eyes opened, and looked straight at me. "If I did believe it, I'd walk, baby."

Such fine arrogance in that! I lowered my head. "I don't doubt that. Oh, Nathaniel, I *do* care for you." Fizzing with frustration, I leaned over and kissed him hard on the mouth. "And what I can give you is so enjoyable, so much fun. Can't that suffice?"

He swore. "Not by a long shot! Didn't you listen to a thing I said? What I'm asking is so common, so *ordinary*! I want us to be open with each other. I want stability, dammit! Is that too much to ask?"

"No," I admitted.

"Then why can't I have it?"

"Because you can't. And you never will," I said with saddened finality. Freeing myself, I got off the bed. At that moment, I literally ached to give him anything he would ask of me. But my family's needs took precedence over his. And over mine.

Turning, I looked at him. I hated seeing his eyes so dark and flat. But there was no such privilege as "ordinary" for us. Gathering up my underwear, I walked to the bathroom, acutely aware of my swaying hips and the hair tumbling around my naked back.

When I emerged again, he was still on the bed. I reached for my dress without speaking.

"Where are you going?" he asked, quiet now.

"Home. And I'm not coming back. This is too unfair to you to continue it." *I can't believe I'm being so noble, so stupidly noble!* "It was, as the song goes, great fun, but just one of those things," I continued in the same asinine vein. Well, hell, I didn't know how one ended an affair. I'd never had one to end before.

"I don't know that song, but it does not apply to us," he growled.

I stilled. How funny. That song had been around for years and he didn't know it. I raised the dress over my head, feeling terribly honorable and hurting all over.

"It does not apply because I love you," he said very, very softly.

Chapter 11

The dress just hung there like a shroud around my face as I tried to cope with his statement. I never dreamed that he might actually come to *love* me. Seconds passed one by silvered one. I was being punctured with arrows of incandescent joy, and I didn't know how to cope with that, either.

I dropped the dress in a cherry-red pool around my feet.

"Now why did you have to say that?" I cried wildly.

"I love you," he repeated.

"Well, I love you!" I accused.

We had stunned ourselves. I just stood there staring at Nathaniel, who just stared back.

"Come here, darlin'," he said with throat-hurting huskiness.

I stumbled over the entangling dress and I ran pell-mell into his outstretched arms.

"Roseanna, trust me," he whispered into my hair.

Oh dammit! I was plummeting again, and getting dizzy with all this up and down motion. "I do trust you. But you wanted honesty, didn't you?" I caught his face in my hands. "Nathaniel, listen to me? Hear what I'm saying? To change this situation I would have to do unspeakable harm to other people, people who have given me their trust, their love. I am incapable of betraying them, even for you, whom I love so very, very much. Please accept that fact."

"Baby, we can work it out," he said soothingly.

I didn't want to be soothed.

"Oh, shit, Nathaniel! Aren't you listening? It's not workable, not changeable. This is it, all of it, right here, right now." Releasing his face, I clasped my hands together, pleadingly. "But this is such a lot, such a very lot. Darling, why can't we just enjoy what we've been given? And we have been given it. For reasons I can't begin to understand, we've been *given* this beautiful experience," I said with all the urgency I felt.

After a short silence, he flopped onto his back. "You baffle me," he said musingly. "This relationship baffles me. In fact, I'm a goddamn baffled man. Confused as hell, too."

He stared at the ceiling some more. I was thinking furiously, my mind sorting through and discarding the flotsam of pure desperation, until finally a lucid thought emerged.

"You're confused because you've stumbled into something that has no rational explanation. But you're not alone, I stumbled into it, too. Fell into it is a better word. Nathaniel, I just realized I've told you far more than I ever dreamed I would, went farther than I ever intended. So maybe it is possible that in time. . . . But it has to be at my own speed. It is simply too tremendous a thing for me to be rushed."

I kissed him softly. "Please give me time? You asked me to trust you, so why can't you give the same privilege to me?"

"Do I have a choice?" he retorted.

Stung, I flung myself off the bed. "You have choices. So make one, Nathaniel. I've said all I have to say."

I stalked out of the room.

He didn't come after me. My dog did. I picked her up and buried my face in her fur as the weight of all my years of experience bore down on me like a runaway freight train. "This is ridiculous, *ridiculous*!" I choked. I felt ancient; I felt terrifying young and vulnerable; I didn't know anything about love; I'd written the goddamn definitive book on love! Muttering every oath I knew and a few I invented, I walked outside and let Carasel run a minute.

That I was naked didn't matter. Nathaniel's doing, I thought with an unruly little smile. He had no hangups about nudity; to him the human body was beautiful clothed or unclothed.

I picked one of the huge, lacy white roses from the bush entwining the porch railing and inhaled its evocative fragrance. My temper cooled as I remembered how eager I had been to see Nathaniel again, how much I had needed the warmth of his arms.

"So why the devil are we wasting our precious time together quarreling?" I whispered into my rose.

I peered inside the open door. Naturally, being the quintessential female, I wanted him to come after me. But he didn't. Well, this wasn't a power play. When Carasel finished her business, I stashed her in the kitchen and returned to the bedroom.

Nathaniel still lay on the bed.

"Hi," I said.

He gave me a one-sided smile. "Hi, yourself."

I walked closer. "Are you still mad?"

He was silent for a moment, thinking. "Are you involved with another man?"

Startled, I shook my head. "Absolutely not. There's not another man in this entire world who can claim this kind of involvement with me. Or any other kind for that matter. So shut up and stop ruining our day. Here, I brought you a rose."

I could see him relaxing. Although his eyes still resembled unpolished jade, that familiar, tender smile began curving his mouth. His eyes crinkled at the corners and I longed to kiss him right there. But I was held suspended. Would he give in to my pleas this time?

He took the rose, sniffed it, shredded it, strewed its petals over my pillow. "You're a stubborn-assed woman."

"Yeah. Mule-headed, Mother used to say."

He laughed. "Come here, stubborn woman!" Pulling me down beside him, he caught fistfuls of my hair. "God, I love you. It stunned me, you know. I kept examining it, this feeling, kept thinking I couldn't love you in so short a time. But I think I began loving you that second time you came racing across the meadow into my arms, your hair flying around your shoulders, your pixie face glowing. I felt like I was choking on something as I watched you running to me. Do you love me? Tell me again," he commanded fiercely.

So I told him, each word a shock to my simplistic self. How could I be vowing my love for another man? Doggedly I blotted out the how of it and just savored the fact of it.

"Nathaniel, please, I don't want to fight with you. I want to spend our time together enjoying each other, not bickering and saying hurtful things." I gazed deeply into his eyes. "No one else can make me this happy, no one can fulfill me like you do. Just being with you is such bliss! Please let's don't spoil it, okay?"

"You're as elusive as quicksilver." His smile was tender, wistful, a little bewildered. "I can't resist you, isn't that something? I'm a proud, strong, reasonably intelligent and reasonably sane adult male and I cannot find the will to throw you out of my bed, much less my life."

"Oh, good!" I said, and he laughed. I pulled his hair. "No more discussions, right? We just enjoy. Deal?"

"I guess we could deal . . . if I knew for sure it was going to be enjoyable. Ouch! Damn, Roseanna! I'll be bald as well as baffled if this keeps up."

"I'll love you bald." Reacting to the sweet wash of relief, I let go of his hair and kissed him all over his face. I buried my nose in his chest and inhaled his good smell; I ruffled his hair and smoothed it again. I licked and kissed and nibbled in a ferocious abandon of self-indulgence.

His richly pleased laughter filled our sun-misted room. One big hand eased up the nook of my thighs and parted the cleft within the tawny nest of curls. How lovely, I thought in one of my whimsical asides; I was still blond down there, too.

A long finger delved deeper, making me shiver. And how lovely, I thought, to be able to explore the astounding depths of my sexuality without fear of embarrassment. I started to kiss him. He shook his head.

"Uh, uh. This time I shall do the loving, pretty lady. This time you just lie there and enjoy it."

Which is just what I did.

"It's frightening, to feel this deeply," Nathaniel's reflective voice slid into our euphoric hush.

Freed now of mind-hazing passion, I drew back from his words with a shrinking of flesh and spirit. The love I felt when I gazed into those soft green eyes was too big and bulky to handle. I had to reshape it and make it more tractable. Rising to my knees, I trickled my fingers through his chest hair and down his belly while I spoke in lilting cadence with my fingertip steps.

"To look directly at the sun is foolishness, for its glory is blinding. Therefore it is wise to be satisfied with its gift of shining warmth and not seek to probe its fires. For lo, men of science have stripped the moon of its gossamer clouds and pronounced this shining luminescence nothing but a bleak, barren rock dependend upon the sun for even a speck of light. Has this greatly benefited mankind?"

Nathaniel's arms tightened as I paused to see how he was taking this. I flashed him a quick, saucy grin.

He goosed me. "Tell me, little oracle, do you have a point to make, or are you just rambling?"

"I happen to have a point, Nathaniel. I'm surprised you haven't caught it already. Really!" I fumed.

"I beg pardon, madam. This poor, unlettered savage walks roughshod through the tall grass of subtlety," he proclaimed with deepest sorrow.

My mouth twitched, but I firmly disciplined it. "I quite agree with that. However, I will try," I said, sighing. "Even the most fervent and dedicated lotus seeker prays he shall ne'er find that which draws him onwards, for the fun, oh wild stallion of mine . . ." Lowering my lips to his ear, I whispered lustily, "The fun is in the seeking, the chase, the wild thrill of searching through endless honeycombs for that pure essence of honey, a honey made from the sweetest of nectars, the pure, innocent lust of an undefiled flower whose pollen sacks drip strawberry ice cream, which brings us back to the lotus again—"

Nathaniel's roar of laughter cut off my liturgical chant. "Oh *Lord,* I love you!" he groaned.

I propped up a knee and lay a hand prissily upon it as I gazed at him from an imperious distance. He lay on his back, arrogantly nude, splendidly at ease. His manhood slept upon its furry cushion, so sweetly harmless that only a natural-born lotus seeker like myself could imagine the dastardly deeds this soft length of pink flesh had done. When his hand snaked up my leg, I slapped at it.

"Humph! Really, Nathaniel, I had hoped to capture for myself a gallant knight who rides a white charger. Instead, I have a horny charger who rides me," I muttered.

How I loved his laughter! Nathaniel is capable of mischief. David is not. Were I to spout such nonsense to him, he would look askance and charge me with nipping at the cooking sherry again. Poor David, I thought sadly. Maintaining his dignity had cost him an awful lot. And he didn't even know it.

"I love you when you're playful like this," I said fiercely. "I love to hear you laugh and act a fool without fear or embarrassment. And the best thing about it is, you give me the same privilege, the same freedom. That's some kind of wonderful, Nathaniel Knight."

He looked at me, a half smile tilting his mouth. "I get the point, Roseanna."

"Huh. It's about time. God, I'm hungry," I accused in a lightning swift change of mood.

"So am I. Are you a good cook?"

"Yes I am."

He whistled. "All this and she can cook, too. Why are you just lying here? You know where the kitchen is. Oh hell, I forgot! My groceries are still in the truck. Go get them, will you? I don't think I have the energy to carry an egg."

Rolling off the bed, I threw his pants at him and suggested he put them on. After I'd dressed in brief yellow shorts and a tank top, he brushed out my hair, an act as intimate as a hand between my legs.

While he fetched the groceries from the truck, I went out to his garden and picked several ripe tomatoes. Then we fired up the lovely antique stove and scrambled eggs, fried potatoes, sautéed some spicy little sausages. We baked biscuits, sliced some tomatoes, and opened three different kinds of homemade jams. The thick slice of honey-cured ham sizzling in a skillet tortured us unmercifully. We set the table with white napery and flowered china, and kissed all the way through it.

And we laughed. God, how we laughed! At anything, at everything, at each other, knowing the richness of an enjoyment that absolutely must be expressed, either in mirth or the most self-abashing display of emotion.

We chose laughter and the hills rang with it as we strolled hand in hand through sunny meadows and shadowed glens in late afternoon. The verdant land was cleansed by the rain that had started my day. I was as far removed from the weeping Roseanna in my bedroom as the first stars piercing the still blue sky.

As the long twilight settled around us like a soft blanket, our mood settled with it. Rather than waste time on a trip to town for dinner supplies, we raided the refrigerator and prepared a tray of assorted cheeses and leftover ham; several varieties of pickles, my especial delight, and flaming hot peppers, Nathaniel's especial torment. Crisp, buttery crackers, chunks of toasted French bread, and tart green apples made up the rest of our ambrosial feast.

He opened an earthy red wine that did not whisper but sang out strongly of sun-ripened fruit and dark, musky caverns. I adored its smokey taste and savored Nathaniel's spicy kisses. Sitting on the deck watching the sun go down made it all the more memorable.

During a wildly rambling conversation, we discovered we were both foodies. So we talked of epicurean delights, both plain and fancy, and I loved it.

David never talked food with me. The alluring perfume of a perfectly ripe melon meant nothing to him.

"What's your favorite comfort food?" I asked eagerly.

"Macaroni and cheese. The real thing, of course, made with elbow macaroni and thick slabs of cheese baked until brown and crusty on the bottom."

"Oh, yes," I said, practically salivating. "Can we have some for lunch tomorrow? Do we have the necessary supplies?"

"Elbow macaroni and a wedge of sharp Cheddar."

"Oh, God, a purist yet! You know what I've always dreamed of? Sitting at a table somewhere with a huge platter of Florida stone crab claws and pots of horseradish and red sauce. And as soon as I finish the last one—no, just as I'm *finishing* the last one—in comes someone with another platter. And so on until I'm absolutely stoned on stone crab claws," I said with an orgasmic sigh.

"An easy enough dream to fulfill, I'd say."

"Ho! Have you priced stone crab legs lately?"

"Don't worry, I can afford it," he said grandly.

I stared at him. David could afford it, too, but that didn't mean it was ever going to happen.

"Can and will are two different things," I pointed out rather wistfully.

"Not in my case."

I just laughed and tickled him. Faith in a man's intentions was not one of my strong points lately. It was sweet enough that he took my fancies seriously.

We refilled our glasses and let the deep purple dusk enwrap us in its soft silence. We held hands. I looked up at stars sparkling in the midnight blue sky and thought of another sky in another world. I thought of David and Lexi and Viveca, of the Roseanna they knew and the Roseanna sitting here beside Nathaniel. They could not possibly be one and the same. And yet, a connective force, like a very thin umbilical cord, bound the two and stretched from that world to this one.

What if that cord should break?

A deep shiver raked me as my mind latched on to this possibility. What if I should become stranded on this world! I loved Nathaniel, true enough. But I also loved my family. And my house, my neighbors and friends. They made up my very *life*.

Nathaniel squeezed my hand and brought me back to him. Gripped with apprehension, I had been holding my breath, and now the air flowed painfully into my lungs. *Exhale, inhale, relax.* I ached from the tension I had just created.

"Are you cold?" Nathaniel asked. He slid an arm around my shoulders and pulled me into his side.

"Umm, not now," I murmured.

Letting his warmth fill the icy little hollows carved out by my "what if's," I shoved aside my fears and relaxed into his embrace. The same force that brought me here would no doubt see me home, I told myself firmly. Distrust was not only corrosive but insulting.

Sweetly cocooned, we began talking about the constellations. I was relieved to know that he too recognized the Big Dipper and knew that the Milky Way wasn't just a candy bar. The conversation grew ever deeper; of God and man, of the stupidities, the abominations, the dreadful, laughable, puffed-up caricatures of men who would be rulers at any cost; and the helpless pawns whose lives hung on the contingency of whether or not the emperor–king–czar–despot–dictator–benevolent tyrant had enjoyed breakfast, sex, or a good bowel movement that morning.

He thought we were discussing the same California, the same America, the same Middle East, indeed, the very same world. In truth we might have been. It was eerie how evil maintained its parallel paths.

Carasel was asleep at our feet, and I could not contain a yawn. Chuckling, Nathaniel put us to bed, her on a rug in the guest bathroom with the door closed, and me in the heavenly comfort of his big bed. As the rising moon spilled its light across our windows, its splendor bound us with silvered ribbons. We lay close and shared the singing silence, and I kissed, slowly and lovingly, each long, slender finger of his hands.

Midnight. I couldn't sleep. My nerves were exquisitely fine-tuned, sensitive to every night sound both inside and outside the bedroom. Nathaniel was restless too, and decided a moonlight swim would be fun. Lying

bonelessly in bed, it sounded like fun to me, too. There
was an urgency in us, a driving need to try everything, to
miss nothing that might prove pleasurable.

Very soon I found myself standing buck naked on a
small sandspit that extended out into the lake, preparing
to step into its dark depths. Was this me? I wondered.
Ordinarily I would never stick so much as a toenail into
that witchy black water.

Nathaniel went first. I stalled, still none too sure I
desired to join him. Who knew what lurked down below
that inky surface? Well, Nathaniel lurked there. Responding to his jeer, I gritted my teeth and waded out to
my knees. Before I could scream, he caught me, lifted
me high in the air and plunged us both down, down
. . . and then, thank God, bore us upwards again.

I clung to his shoulders and hissed ferocious threats.
Like giddy children, we romped.

But when he pulled me against him and sought my
lips, we were no longer children at play. There was
nothing between our bodies but the silken kiss of water.

"Let's make love," he said on my mouth.

"You mean here? In the water?" I asked on his.

"Yes, here. We're alone. Don't you want to?"

"Well of course I want to."

It was an out-of-time experience. The cool water
made little splashes around our movements. Night birds
called softly. A full moon shed its radiance upon our
Eden and glossed his hair with silver. His face was in
shadow, but his eyes gleamed like a cat's.

Moonlight. Madness. Love. The trinity of pure delight. We were drunk with its intoxicating magic.

The the wind came up and raised goosebumps on wet
skin. We hastened back to the haven of our cottage.

The shower we shared was sublime rewarmth.

Utterly exhausted, we fell asleep in a sweet confusion
of limbs, the deepest, most relaxed slumber I have ever
known.

I awoke first and instantly knew where I was and with
whom. For a lovely while I dwelled upon his features,
liking the rough cut of them. I loved the way his hair

grew in a whorl that fell over one side of his brow. His firm mouth was molded by sleep to a vulnerable softness that pinched my heart.

I retreated from this soft pain and turned my face to the window. The alien landscape touched me with an icy sense of awe. The sheer audacity of my actions was a nerve-tingling stimulant. I was here, actually *here*! In another part of space, in another time, in another realm. I'd actually *slept* here. For some reason that seemed the most incredible thing to do. I felt the chill of fear cool my skin as I lay awake and supranaturally alert, in a strange land in a stranger's bed.

"Hi, Blue Eyes." Nathaniel's husky voice broke through my unease like sunshine through shadow. He gave me a piercingly sweet smile.

"Hi, yourself." As I kissed him my apprehension faded into the rightness of being exactly where I was. Live for the moment, I advised myself. Snuggling my head on his shoulder, we savored the sweetness of this waking.

Carasel's demanding bark finally stirred us to action. When Nathaniel let her outside I stepped out too and drew a deep breath of country air. My first morning in a new world! A lovely world, I thought joyously. Flowers bloomed in great pink and yellow drifts across the meadow. Every grass blade had its very own diamond. Nathaniel, splendidly naked and as magnificent as any other element of nature, stood beside me on the porch.

Driven into raptures by the intoxicating scents in the yard, Carasel raced madly about. Laughing, Nathaniel watched her. "Wouldn't it be something if she took off and I had to go chase her?" he half shouted.

I threw back my head and laughed out some of my uncontainable happiness. Sunlight and soft blue skies, butterflies hovering over the fragrant white roses; birds singing hallelujahs and the wind blowing, and my love beside me all golden in the sunlight. God, I was lifted to astounding heights. Fear promptly etched my exhilaration, for too much happiness was surely dangerous. Mother said so. Why make the gods jealous, Roseanna?

Because I couldn't help it, that was why. When I flung

my arms around his neck, he picked up both me and
Carasel and carried us back inside. The dog romped
over to the porcelain lion and lay down in cozy friendship. I patted Chatera's gleaming head, then Nathaniel's
rumpled one.

"Let's go back to bed," he proposed with vast enthusiasm.

"Nathaniel, we're both going to be sagging wrecks if
this keeps up," I warned.

"True. Let's make breakfast first then," he suggested
with a devilish grin. I longed to kiss his feet but he was
standing on them.

We cooked another gargantuan breakfast. After dis-
posing of every crumb, we cleaned the kitchen and
made the bed. He shared each task with me. David had
never shared a household task . . . I suddenly realized
this was the first time all morning I'd thought of David.

I made up for my neglect while I bathed. My mind
traveled all the way back to our first halcyon days of
marriage when it had been so good between us. David
had listened to what I had to say as if each word was a
pearl of great wisdom.

No, I corrected myself, he had never done that. It was
just the newness of me he listened to, for I actually said
very little. David was so overwhelming when newly met
that I couldn't think of much of anything that might
interest a man like him. What was I but a vapid virgin all
wrapped up in the heat of my loins?

Well, what was I now? Certainly I was still wrapped
up in that same heat. But Nathaniel had listened to me
last night. He made me feel my opinions were valuable. . . .

I began to laugh. I had twenty some years of living to
add substance to that starry-eyed virgin. If I hadn't
grown a little in all that time, I chided myself, then I was
hopeless.

Nathaniel came in and perched on the edge of the
tub. "Lady, do you intend to hibernate in here? If so,
move over and let me join you. If not, get that gorgeous
bottom out of there so I can shower!"

I got out. He wrapped me in a towel that covered me from head to toe.

In the bedroom, I took out the change of clothes I had brought, a halter-style blouse and a full skirt of darker coral. Did women wear bras here? My breasts were so high and perky, I tossed my bra back into the suitcase.

Nathaniel came strolling in. He stood easy in his nudity, a towel slung over one shoulder, hair still damp. "You look like a peach," he said.

I felt like a peach, sun-ripened and juicy. I gave him a flirtatious glance that came so naturally I was inordinately pleased. Maybe flirting is like riding a bicycle— you may get a little rusty, but you never forget how.

My nipples were saucy little peaks against the sunset-colored fabric. Astounding, I thought, how they fall in limp defeat each time I return to my own world. Instant transition from up to down.

Nathaniel's fingers were caught. This passionate friction was always between us. As he untied my straps, I curled my arms around his neck. Then, perversely, I pulled away with a nose-wrinkling laugh.

"Really, Nathaniel, I've just bathed and dressed," I chided, retying my straps. "And you promised to take me to see Liz," I reminded as I glided from the room. An instant later I was lifted off my feet and flung over a caveman's shoulder.

When we finally arrived at the lake, our new friends were lunching outdoors under a huge eucalyptus tree. To my vast pleasure, Liz was glad to see me while I was tickled to see her. She was enormous! That belly was a monumental glory, the eighth wonder of the world. Her eyes were still that soft, credulous blue. Her dimples still flashed like neon lights and her dark gold curls were still a masterpiece of disarray. A bewitching woman-child.

After a lunch of sandwiches and iced tea, we took in an art exhibit by the resident artist who had wanted to paint me nude. After perusing his work, Liz decided I had been unwise to refuse his kind offer. Being depicted with three melon-sized breasts and an arm growing out of her navel would delight any woman.

Nathaniel gave her a pained look. "This exhibit is pure crap. What say we all take a walk along the lake, get away from this crowd? Can you still navigate the path, Liz?" he asked, casting a dubious look at her belly.

"Certainly I can. And if I can't, Matt will carry me."

Matt muttered a despairing word.

"Never fear, Matt, between the two of us we can drag her back home," Nathaniel gravely assured.

Liz's smile was nothing less than angelic. "Well, screw you, Nathaniel," she invited.

He considered it. "Best not. Roseanna is hellishly jealous . . . like a little wildcat when she gets riled. I have scratches all over my back."

Innocence shone in those dancing green eyes. I was forced to fling my arms around him and kiss him right there in front of the whole damn world.

With the help of both men, Liz lumbered to her feet and we started off. Nathaniel and I held hands. "I love you," I was compelled to say.

"I love you, I love you," he went me one better.

"You're both crazy," Liz stated. "Damm it, will you stop for a minute? I've got a rock in my shoe and I need a rest. I *am* pregnant, or haven't you noticed?" she inquired testily of Nathaniel.

"You're pregnant? Good grief, I thought that was your natural shape!"

Warm, laughing, teasing fun. The newborn intimacy between four fairly new acquaintances was ripening into firm friendship. Beautiful. And it was all as fragile as a soap bubble.

The day was ending, and Nathaniel's attempts to prolong it were so transparent that I had to hide a smile.

"I can't believe we're continuing this charade of walking you to the meadow and then off you go," he grumbled. "There's no reason you can't just drive up to the cabin now, is there?"

"There is. Drop it, Nathaniel," I warned crisply. I didn't intend wrangling over this subject, too.

I must have sounded like I felt, for he dropped it with only a few under-the-breath mumbles. When I gave him a look, he flung out his hands. "What? Can't I even mumble now?"

"I guess," I relented, laughing. "But try to keep it short."

After picking up my suitcase we took a roundabout way to the grove. Carasel ran ahead and stopped to drink of its sweet spring waters. We drank, too. Kneeling in this hushed place, I felt uplifted beyond a human level of joy. It is so pretty in the grove. Ferns and violets carpet the moist, alluvial soil. It must be the perfect environment for violets, for they grow with luxurious abandon, offering glossy, heart-shaped leaves of deepest green and enormous velvety blossoms which retain that dew-wet look even during the hot part of the day.

Nathaniel gathered a handful for me. Then he picked some more and began placing them in my hair, around my bare shoulders, between my breasts. He caught my chin and kissed me while he played with the flowers. I could see his face tightening with that look of intense sexual arousal.

Green eyes were so very green, with golden flames leaping in their depths. His mouth took mine, roughening, parting my lips until I gave him what he wanted in our kisses.

"Roseanna?"

"Yes, love." What other reply could I possibly give?

He took off my clothes, then laid me down on the soft cushion of flowers and grass. I closed my eyes as I felt the small, cool splash of violets being strewn all over my body. When his lean nakedness moved atop mine, the crushed blossoms released a cloud of perfume.

There were no words to describe it. Yet I knew I would never forget how I felt right then.

I held him to me while we regained our senses. Looking up through the canopy of leaves which formed our roof, I could see it was getting late.

Reluctantly I brought this to his attention.

Reluctantly he brushed away the wilted flowers and we redressed in silence.

"Ouch," I muttered, scratching at the tiny welt on my backside. "Even Paradise has insects!"

"Sorry," he said with a brief smile.

I touched his quiet face. "Nathaniel, it was lovely, so lovely I can't find words. Thank you."

That eyebrow slanted at an absurd angle. "I really do think I found it quite as lovely as you did, therefore I see no need for thanks," he returned dryly.

He walked me to the edge of the meadow. "Good-bye for now, darling," I said, beginning to feel anxious again. His eyes were darkening. Such a telltale sign of distress, I thought. I would always know when he was unhappy.

Always? In this situation "always" is a frightening word.

"I'll see you as soon as I possibly can. Nathaniel, remember all the things I said? Just let it work in your mind and maybe. . . . Well, come on, Carasel." I gazed at the dog sitting cozily by his feet. "She doesn't want to leave you any more than I do."

"Then don't leave." He cocked his head. "What have you got at home that's better than me?"

"I don't think there *is* anything better than you," I said with a very wry smile.

Chapter 12

*M*y bedroom was pitch-dark. I hadn't expected this and when I eased open the closet door, my catch of breath was loud enough to be heard if anyone was within hearing distance. Questions pounced on me with cat-claw urgency. What time was it? Was David home? And if he was, what on earth was I going to *say*?

Flattening myself against the wall, I listened so hard it hurt. *Was* anyone else in the room? Was David even now preparing to rear up out of a sound sleep to demand an explanation as to my whereabouts these past hours? Hours? Maybe *days,* I thought, appalled as I realized I had forgotten all about the time differences between Nathaniel's world and mine. God, how long had I been gone?

My pounding heartbeat and quick, shallow breaths were the only sounds to be heard. Frozen to the spot, I peered into the concealing darkness. Gradually, with agonizing slowness, my eyes adjusted to the lack of light until I could make out the shape of furniture. My bed was flat and smooth and empty, just the way I left it.

I leaned against the wall and gulped air into my starved lungs. "Really, Roseanna, calm yourself!" I chided with a credible laugh. "Viv would have come after you had something gone awry."

Drawing another ragged breath, I ran to my bedside table, snapping on lights as I went. The electric clock was blinking; apparently there had been a power outage while I was gone. David was due in from his business trip around eleven Tuesday night. For all I knew he had already returned. To an empty house. And called Viv, who was lying comatose in some hospital because of her reckless driving. . . .

Having worked myself into a state of incipient panic, I was all thumbs as I snatched up the telephone and pushed the quick-call button that connected to Viv's number. Four rings later I let out a pent-up breath as she mumbled hello.

"Oh Viv, oh thank God!" I cried hoarsely.

"What?" she muttered. "Who—Roseanna, is this you? What the devil! Do you know what time it is?"

Aggravated by her indignant query, I said furiously, "No, Viv, what the fuck time is it?"

"It's almost four. Three forty-six, to be exact. Are you home? Why are you home?"

"Shouldn't I be home?" I asked, feeling more and more confused as weariness fogged my wits.

"No, that is, not unless. . . ." She paused, and I could just see her sitting up and pushing at her hair. "Is something wrong, Rosie?"

"God, I don't know," I moaned. "You tell me."

"Not as far as I know. But you're home a day early, honey, and at four in the morning, too. What's up?"

"Early?" My voice rose. "You mean David hasn't been home yet? And no one's out searching for me?"

"Well, no, not as far as I know."

"Oh, Viv!" I sank down on the bed as another gale of relief sucked the strength from my legs. "God, you don't know how worried I've been!" My mind shifted gears with blink-of-an-eye swiftness. "Wait a minute! You mean this is still Monday? I just left here this morning?"

"Well, technically speaking, it is after midnight and therefore Tuesday morning, but yes, in a sense you just left."

"You mean I could have spent another whole day with Nathaniel? Well, damn, Viv!" I exploded, outraged at having been cheated like this.

"Well, don't blame me, Rosie, I didn't tell you to come back so soon. Why did you? What happened?"

"I forgot about the time differences," I said and

sighed. "It was later afternoon of the next day when I left there."

"Oh, honey, I'm sorry. You could go back."

With a leap of excitement I considered her suggestion.

"No. We already said our farewells and stuff. Besides, he's getting antsy about my background and if I popped back in again so soon, no telling what would happen. Anyway, I don't know if I could climb back on this particular roller coaster without a breather," I ended wryly. "I assume everything's okay on this side of the universe?"

"Everything's fine. So, Roseanna, how was it?" she asked, low and intimate.

"Paradise," I said simply.

"No snakes?"

"No. A few rough moments, but no real snakes. I'll tell you all about it tomorrow, Viv. Right now I need to unkink. My nerves have split ends despite all that bliss," I confessed.

We agreed on a meeting time, and rang off.

I was too keyed up to go to bed. So I worked awhile in my office outlining a new book. Nathaniel's book, I conceded, was as good as dead. My mind simply froze whenever I tried to animate its characters.

I didn't have much luck with the new one. At the moment I was more interested in living life than writing about it. I turned off the computer and returned to the bedroom.

Too tense to sleep, I undressed and slipped into the delicious warmth of the hot tub that sat just off our bathroom. When we built the private, second-story deck to accommodate this addition to home, I had visions of David and I being stimulated by the tub's erotic, liquid heat to the point of sexual gymnastics on its slick bottom.

Poor David. His libido was so impacted by that stone-hewn environment he'd been reared in that he was actually embarrassed by my attempts to introduce us both to the delights of hot-tub sex. Such red-faced chagrin, I mused, feeling a little puff of tenderness as I recalled his strained laugh when I teased his balls with my toes and even went underwater to see what was up. Noting his arousal, I had simply flopped on top of him with a sultry, sensuous smile and wonderful expectations. But his discomfort was too intense and it ended in deflated annoyance on his part, and abashed disappointment on mine.

"Well, live and learn," I murmured, yawning. At least I derived enjoyment from this lovely extravagance.

I wasn't scheduled to work at the hospital tomorrow. Maybe I would anyway. As my own somewhat stony background was fond of reminding me, service to others was mandatory if one was Heaven-bound.

I knew Viveca would be wild to hear all about my grand adventure. So as soon as I finished my shift the following day I headed for her house. We settled down beside the pool with a pitcher of sangrías. As I suspected, she was avid for details, living vicariously each pleasurable moment I shared with her.

"He says he loves me, Viv," I ended on a desolate-delighted note, an impossible combination.

Viveca sat back and stared at me from under the wide brim of her woven-straw hat. "Whew! I have to hand it to you, Rosie. When you decide to have an affair, by damn you *have* an affair! Makes the rest of us look like kids fingering each other," she drawled.

"I'm glad this amuses you so, Viveca," I stated.

"Oh, all right. I'm sorry, honey. I'm not really amused, except that . . . well, hell, Rosie, it is funny. In a way it is. It's just like you to be so different! You go to another world to find a man to romp with. And then you make that poor soul fall in love with you!"

"It's not a laughing matter, dammit. He wants a relationship, a normal relationship. He's hurt, angry, baffled, frustrated; you name it, he's feeling it. I'm going to have to tell him, and when I do, how much less is he going to be frustrated and so on? And hurt, of course. Especially when I tell him I'm a married woman."

"There is absolutely no need to tell him you're a married woman," Viveca said so firmly that I slid it to the back of my mind for later consideration. "But I do see your point. I liked Nathaniel. Even though I've only met him that one time, I do like him. He seems a decent guy, too much so to play games with. And this is a game to you, isn't it?"

"No!" I bit my lip. "Well, at first it was. It's all so damned incredible, what else could it be? But it's getting beyond game stage now, Viv. It's getting out of my control and I don't know what to do."

"I guess you don't, honey," Viveca said softly. "But I have one very important question, which I'm sure has occurred to you by now. How does it end, Roseanna? How does this fantasy of yours end?"

Viveca's question gnawed at me with tiny rat teeth. I had given no thought to an actual ending. I couldn't even fantasize an ending. It hurt too much.

Like Scarlett, I decided to think about it tomorrow. Right now I was too busy anticipating my next visit with Nathaniel.

Thursday morning I put in an early call to alert Viveca to my absence for the day.

"You're going to see Nathaniel again so soon?" she asked.

"Something wrong with that?" I asked, instantly combative.

"Hold your fire, Rosie. I was just surprised because you got into such a dither when you came home from your last visit."

"I know, but I'm prepared now, Viv. Since there's not much I can do about our time differences, I will just have to trust that you'll take care of me. So I'll be going now."

Silence.

"Wouldn't you go if you were me?"

"Rub it in, why don't you?" She sighed. "But yes I would. In fact I'd have probably gone yesterday."

"I couldn't. Mims was here yesterday, remember? Can't very well let the maid watch me step through a closet wall," I said shortly. "I didn't mean to rub it in, Viv, I just . . . well, it just feels good knowing someone else would do the very same thing. I intend to come home around three, but give me until five, okay? And Viv, drive carefully, huh?"

Enjoying her throaty laugh, I hung up and put Carasel out on the sunporch. She was staying home this time.

She gave me a reproachful look, well aware that she was being left out of the fun. I gave her a "good girl" pat, then hurried upstairs to dress.

I chose new bikini briefs and a scrap-of-lace bra; shorts, sweater, and sneakers, all in the same pale shade of blue. I worked my hair into one braid that hung like a beribboned pendulum between my shoulder blades. After a quick spritz of perfume in the area of my thighs, I headed for my closet.

Ten minutes later everything but the perfume lay scattered over Nathaniel's bedroom floor and my hair was streaming around his taut face.

I had knocked on his door, he yelled come in, and from there things just went beautifully to hell.

"Come lay on me," he was urging. "I love the feel of your skin on mine."

Instant obedience. My flesh spread out over his like melted butter, warm, receptive, oozing around every hard, exciting plane and jut of his body.

His hands moved down my back and I quivered all over. "You have such a delectable little ass," he murmured, his hands molding and kneading.

"I'm so glad you think so." I grabbed his hair and kissed him without mercy.

"I'm going to love you my way," he said when I let him speak.

I raised my head. "Your way? You haven't been loving me your way?"

"Yes, but now . . . in a different way, baby."

That thick, husky voice acted like a probing finger between my legs. He rolled over, and I lay beneath. I was eager, but a little wary of this "different way." I sensed what he meant to do and although I could write a swinging love scene when necessary, my actual sexual experience was really quite limited. Deviate a few degrees from the norm and I was painfully ignorant. Cunnilingus and fellatio were only words in a book to me. To be honest, I wasn't all that sure they were pleasing words.

"All right, Nathaniel," I said trustingly.

He smiled that get-right-into-your-panties smile. I sighed; I am besotted, utterly helpless before that smile. Green-gold eyes caressed me so hotly, I was running over with cream.

"Ah, sweetheart," he whispered through soft, brushing kisses. I wondered if he knew how much I loved being called sweetheart. I even thought about telling him. But about then my brain shut down and I became pure, exquisite sensation.

When I lay limp and drained, Nathaniel moved up on me and began kissing my breasts.

"Oh, darling, that was lovely, so lovely." I sighed.

"Was, baby? It's not over yet," he said with another soft, sensuous laugh.

"Oh, but I can't! Nathaniel, surely. . . ."

"Can't you, darling?" he murmured, sucking a nipple until it practically stood up and saluted.

I did feel a tiny touch of that divine fire. But my mind was working again and little knots of distress were demanding attention. Had Nathaniel done what he did to me because he liked to or because he wanted to please me? And either way, was he expecting me to reciprocate? I definitely had mixed feelings about that. But if he wanted me to, then I had to, didn't I?

I was trying to think through all the tumult going on in my body. It wasn't easy. Then Nathaniel kissed me deeply and I tasted myself, which meant I had to analyze that quiff of Roseanna on his mouth. He was hard and hot against my sex. His intense excitement was stirringly visible in his smoldering gaze.

"You are going to come with me," he said in a rough, thick whisper.

Ah, jeez. I'm so completely satiated I'll have to resort to pretense, I thought just before he thrust into me with a marvelous male power that filled me to the point of a husky little cry. His smile was beautifully triumphant. Wordless, I turned my head from side to side. I couldn't be feeling this heavy, swelling, seeking heat already tightening around his penis until he had to fight his way out of me and back in again. This was straining reality and flowing over into the pages of *Hot Purple Passion* by Noelle Bently. But I was soaring up to meet his plunges, clawing his back, devouring his mouth and exulting in his response. Reality and fantasy merged into a flood of stunning pleasure. With shameless abandon I urged him on, kissing him with hot, open-mouthed, stabbing-tongue ferocity, and flying, oh flying! We were borne up and up on the crest of this mountainous wave that might very well destroy me when it splintered.

It was the most astounding orgasm of my life and in some way, a frightening one. This went far beyond or-gasmic sex. Such intensity, such involvement of mind and body, such penetration of soul, was a power un-leashed from the very spark of creation.

"Le petite morte," Nathaniel said raggedly.

I couldn't make out the words. His breath came in short, hot blasts and his voice was muffled by my hair. "What, darling?"

"Le petite morte . . . the little death!" he gasped.

"God, yes," I whispered, awed at such a magnificently fitting description. Naturally my mind chose that mo-ment to scamper off on its own tangent and my thoughts went from the sublime to the absurd.

I didn't want to go down on Nathaniel. Would he take that as personal rejection? But it isn't, I thought defen-sively, not really. It's just that I've always been very par-ticular about what slides down my throat into my stomach. There was a very good chance that I might throw up all over Nathaniel's penis if it started sending slimy stuff down my throat.

Oh, hell. I chewed my lip and fretted over my lack of sophistication. At age twenty-two it wasn't that bad. But at forty-eight? Laughable. Damn you, David! You were my teacher! Why didn't you *teach*?

"What's the matter?" Nathaniel asked. He had wedged between my thighs and lay with his eyes level with mine.

"Nathaniel, I tasted me on your mouth and—well, it's

sort of odd. You didn't mind that?" I asked, merely curious, of course.

"Ah no, honey, I love the taste of you. Why do you ask?"

"Oh, no reason. I was just thinking . . . do you like to . . . that is, is it the same—" He quit smiling as I stammered on. "Do you like to make love that way, have it done to you, I mean?"

"Yes I do, honey. Providing of course, that the lady feels the same way."

His eyes were asking questions his mouth kindly did not. I felt the blush working its way up from my belly to my cheeks in a fiery wash of color. My gaze dropped before that inquiring green look. He wouldn't believe how dumb I am, I thought with another vivid flush. Dammit, I wish I'd never started this!

"Oh, darlin'," Nathaniel whispered in tender comprehension. "Roseanna, listen to me. I don't want you to do anything that you honestly don't want to do. If anything displeases you or makes you uncomfortable, then say so. Surely you know I wouldn't ask anything of you that you didn't want to give."

"Oh. Well, it's nothing personal, Nathaniel," I said most earnestly. "It's just that I—well, I can't even eat boiled okra because it's too slimy, you see. I start gagging—"

Nathaniel's outburst stilled my voice. Burying his face in my breasts, he roared with laughter, his shoulders shaking so violently I became alarmed.

"Nathaniel? What's the matter with you?"

"Oh God! Roseanna . . . okra is t-too slimy? You start gagging? Oh, Jesus help me," he burbled.

Still wary, I forced his head up so I could see his face. Sparkling, somewhat wet green eyes relieved my worry. "Well, it's the truth," I said indignantly.

"Oh, God!" Nathaniel groaned.

I held my tongue. Eventually he rolled to the side of the bed and pulled me up with him.

On guard against his ornery grin, I asked, "Now what?"

"Now we shower. Then, my delicate little flower, we

are going to find out all about your likes and dislikes."
His grin widened. "And mine too, while we're at it."

The kitchen clock read quarter till five when I next
glanced at it. It had read one when I arrived, although it
was eight when I left my closet this morning. So now it
was five o'clock, which meant four hours had passed
. . . Nathaniel's time, that is. . . .

"Oh, foot!" I muttered. My stomach growled. My
breakfast coffee was long gone, and I'd had nothing else
today. Not even semen.

"Hurry up!" I commanded Nathaniel as he walked
surefootedly across the grass to his tomato plants. Naked, of course; the man had no modesty, thank goodness. I stood in the doorway wrapped in the top sheet
that formed a fetching sarong covering everthing but
one slim shoulder.

After we dressed, me in my shorts and sweater and
Nathaniel in the oldest, softest, sexiest pair of jeans ever
painted onto a human body, we paired the tomatoes
with pasta and a Velveeta-like cheese. Although it was
marvelously satisfying, I still let Nathaniel apologize for
his wretched lack of foodstuffs. But I stopped eating
when he told me why he had run so low. He was getting
ready to return to the city when I came "busting in" on
him.

"A little problem," he acknowledged, seeing my dismay. "For some reason I didn't expect you today," he
added ironically. "But the real problem is this: I've been
working as a trouble-shoot consultant on a friend's job
and I intend to keep on doing so since it does give me
something to think about besides you. If I knew this love
affair was going to last. . . ." He glanced at me, waited,
then went on dryly, "at least for a few more months, I
could set up a communications center in the spare bedroom."

"You could work with that?" I asked.

"Most of the time. Certainly it would cut down on my
trips to the city. So, Roseanna, how long is this relationship going to last?"

Sea-green eyes, watchful and intent, bored into my face. I had to look away.

"Well, certainly for a few months longer," I said, forcing a laugh. Getting up, I rumpled his hair. "Look, love, you do what you think best and we'll work around that, okay? I told you when I arrived that nothing has changed." I glanced at the kitchen clock again. "Well, I must go. Sorry it's such a short visit, but. . . ." I lifted a shoulder apologetically. "Want me to help clear up?"

"I'll do it later. Roseanna—"

"You promised," I reminded, forestalling further questions.

"So I did." His eyes glinted. "But the next time you come, you can at least park your Skyecraft in front of the house. That secret's out, anyway!"

I fiddled with my sheet. What on earth was he talking about? "Skyecraft?"

"Yeah. I saw one fly over just a few minutes before you walked in the door. I have to admit I'm surprised, though. Those little jobs are expensive. Are you rich, babe?" he asked, cocking his head.

"Not hardly," I grunted, carrying my plate to the sink. "I don't have a Skyecraft, Nathaniel. A car, maybe, but. . . ." Shrugging, I headed for the bedroom to rebraid my hair.

He followed me in and sat on the bed, watching. Flustered by his steady regard, I chattered. "Are you still going to the city today?"

He was.

"Well, then, you don't need to walk me to the meadow. I know you're anxious to get started. How long did you say you'd be gone?"

"I didn't say. But probably until early next week if I decide to buy that communications system."

"Nathaniel, don't be upset with me, please?" I implored softly. "I'm always so utterly delighted to see you, to be with you again. Please don't let's part in anger."

He stood up and took me in his arms. His cheek rested against mine and I could feel him sigh before he replied. "No, I'm not angry with you. And you know how glad I am to see you. So. I'll see you next week?"

"Next week for sure," I said, and kissed him with all the tenderness my heart held for this tall, green-eyed man.

When I was once again standing in my own bedroom, I recalled his question with a sense of melancholy. *How long is this going to last, Roseanna?*

How on earth was I supposed to know that?

Frustrated by yet another unanswered question clogging up my airways, I stumped downstairs and took Carasel for a long walk.

David and I turned in early that night, but I was too keyed up to sleep. So I turned on my light and tried to read. My attention kept shifting to the man lying beside me. I could tell by his breathing that he, too, was awake. When he reached for me I was so startled I dropped my book.

"David, wait, I want . . ." What did I want?

Not to make love with anyone but Nathaniel.

Made breathless by this shocking aversion to conjugal relations, I flattened my hands against David's shoulders. "I want to talk a minute," I ad-libbed desperately. "When you make love to me, are you making love to a woman or to your wife?"

He grimaced. "Oh, hell, Roseanna, you're not going to start some foolishness, are you?"

"No, I'm not going to start some foolishness. Answer my question, please."

"Since you are both woman and wife the question answers itself."

"The question does not answer itself!" I pulled up the blanket, feeling a sudden desperation I didn't understand. There was a sense of now or never in it that stung my eyes. "I don't want to forget it, it's too important to forget." I bit my lip and tried again. "Let's make love then, but this time we'll do it my way. First we go shower—together, David. Then we'll come back to bed and we'll . . . I want you to kiss me all over and then I'll do the same to you. And I don't mean stopping at

bellies, I mean all *over*," I said defiantly. "I want you to
kiss me here and I want to come from just your kisses.
And then I'll make you come, maybe in my mouth, I
don't know. I'm not too sure how I'd react to that, but
for you—for *us*, I'm willing to try it and see."

"Roseanna, that's quite enough!" David said sharply.

I stared at him. "Are you embarrassed?"

"Of course not. I just find this conversation distasteful, that's all."

"But—but why?"

"Dammit, quit looking at me like that."

"Well, I can't help it! I think it's odd that you find it
distasteful to talk to me about sex. We've been married
forever, why can't we say these things to each other
without getting embarrassed?"

"I am not embarrassed," he snapped. "Goddam it,
you're my wife, not some whore! What the hell's so odd
about me finding it distasteful when you begin talking
like one!"

I stared at him in open dismay. I knew he was sexually
repressed; I had sensed his antipathy toward anything
except the most conventional sexual practices. But I had
no idea it ran *this* deep! I studied his face, plainly seeing
his discomfort. Suddenly I felt such pity for him, it
rocked me like a strong wind. To feel pity for David was
somewhat akin to pitying God. It was the height of arrogance.

Confused, I touched his shoulder. "I'm sorry."

"Yeah, so am I. Roseanna, I'm neither ignorant nor a
prude, but you're my wife and I do have strongly set
opinions about that. I know you're a woman, but first
and foremost you're my *wife*. Do you understand?"

I understood far better than he would ever know. The
things he could enjoy doing with a *woman*, he could not
enjoy with a *wife*. How very sad, I thought, remembering
Nathaniel's lusty enjoyment of everything we had done
this afternoon.

Filled with a curiously maternal compassion, I looked
at David's quiet face. I felt like crying for him, for the
lovely things he missed by closing so many doors in
himself.

"Yes, I understand," I said with a sad sense of finality. "I just thought that maybe, well, that maybe if we tried something new. At least kept an open mind." I glanced down his body. "I'm sorry, are you deflated?"

"Like a flat tire, thanks to you." Rolling onto his back, he yawned and ruffled my hair. "Good night, Roseanna."

"Good night." I turned onto my side.

David was soon snoring softly. But I had a lot of thinking to do, some of it painfully tender. I had always considered myself by far the weaker vessel in this marriage. Wouldn't it be strange if that turned out to be untrue.

Chapter 13

The sense of finality I had felt with David plagued me, filling my mind with questions. What of loyalty? Responsibility? Commitment? They were words I honored, words I loved. And yet, and yet. . . .

As I dressed the next morning I repeated those words and wondered why they weighed so heavily upon me. They were part of my security. David and marriage and family were all my security, I reminded myself angrily. *So why do you feel so insecure, Roseanna?*

Startled by my little voice's pointed question, I automatically began preparing an argument, which was drowned out by insightful truths. All my life I had tried harder, worked harder to please, bent over backwards to avoid confrontation. I had sought to Do Right in whoever's eyes were turned judgingly upon me: Mother's, my stepfather's, David's, Lexi's. Only Viveca knew the real Roseanna.

Big deal, I summed up. What had I gained by this spurt of self-analysis?

Perhaps nothing. Yet ten minutes after David left for the office next morning, I was in the meadow. The elating recklessness that had borne me here swiftly faded; the boulder was only a huge shadow blending into even blacker shadows. I had arrived long before dawn.

All that darkness made my skin prickle. Suddenly breathless, I leaned into the safety of cold, hard stone while I revved up my courage. Having left Carasel at home, I was alone and acutely aware of it.

"Oh, Roseanna, really! Since when have you been afraid of the dark?" I chided my apprehensive self. I was perfectly safe on Nathaniel's world. With a breath for courage, I stepped out of the magic circle and started across the meadow.

The glow of a quarter moon was far too dim to illumine the way. My feet seemed to take perverse pleasure in encountering every obstacle within a ten-inch radius of my step. After three stubbed toes, I was cursing my idiocy in wearing sandals.

When I reached the grove, I stopped to look into the dark mass of trees. I was not known for my valor, but Nathaniel lay on the other side. I was so eager to see him that I plunged into the grove without further hesitation.

The well-worn path led me to the spring. I stopped to remove a stick that had lodged between my bare toes.

As I straightened, a twig snapped sharply off to one side. I froze. My gaze darted from shadowed mass to shadowed mass seeking to find the source of that breath-stealing noise. It was hard to hear over the accelerated beat of my heart. But I heard it again, softer now, as though the maker of that sound was using stealth!

A bush rustled. Then silence fell like a smothering shroud.

The total lack of sound was even worse. Everything was that hazy shade of gray on gray that gave me the sensation of being blind as well as deaf. Nathaniel's tale of an attacker at large shrilled through my mind and I was fast becoming terrified. Was there a darker shadow among the fringing leaves?

I could be imagining this. God knows I have an overactive imagination. Bolstered by this admission, I began breathing again. It was really quite unlikely that anyone would be hiding in the grove at this time of night.

Something moved in the darkness. My breath caught —it was moving toward *me*.

My feet refused to run despite my mind's frantic urging. I was caught in the gluey grip of indecision. I could flee back to the boulder or I could run ahead to Nathaniel. The distance was about the same. It—whatever *it* was—was on the other side of the spring, so I could go either way.

My eyes burned and stung from staring into the dark, trying to distinguish between tree trunk and specter. It could be just an animal. . . . Terror welled up when the brush rustled again, closer now. I screamed at the top of my lungs.

And then I was flying to Nathaniel, stumbling, running, screaming his name, without ever making a conscious decision to turn back or go on. I was just *going*.

Something crashed heavily through the brush as I burst out of the grove. I raced full speed up the rise. I was still screaming Nathaniel's name, but I heard clearly the thud of feet behind me. Once I stumbled over a tree root and fell to my knees. I don't recall getting up again, but I did, and, totally panicked now, I flew downhill to the darkened house just barely visible in the first feeble glow of dawn.

When I saw the light come on, it gave impetus to my feet and renewed my lung power tenfold.

The door opened and I cried his name. Then I fell down and the world went black.

When I opened my eyes again, I was in Nathaniel's bed. The face looming over me was blurred at first. Then it cleared and I lunged into his arms.

"It's all right, honey, it's all right, you're here with me. Roseanna, it's okay," he said, shaking me.

With a muffled cry, I burrowed into his bare chest and let the warm, sleepy male smell of him cleanse my fear-fogged senses.

"Oh, God, I was so scared, Nathaniel! It was after me! It was hiding in the grove and I heard it moving toward me!" I gulped air. "And I started running and t-then it started running, chasing me—oh, Nathaniel!" Shuddering, I locked my arms around his neck in a stranglehold.

He tensed. "It? What do you mean, it?"

"I don't know!" I wailed. "I never saw it, just a shadow in the trees! But it was big, too big for—" I stopped.

"Too big for an animal? Ah my God, Roseanna!" Nathaniel crushed me against him. "What the bitching *hell* were you doing running around alone at night!"

"I miscalculated the time—I thought it would be daylight in your world! Your time is so confusing, Nathaniel! It was past seven in my world, so I thought it would be noon or so here. That's why I never know when I'm going to be here—even your days are different! I keep getting so confused!" I cried in unthinking hysteria.

"What in God's name are you talking about! My world? Your world? Different times! Roseanna . . . good Lord," he said in a stunned whisper.

I was still shaking. His arms tightened until I felt smothered, but I wanted it. "Did you hear me screaming?"

"Yes, I heard you," he said heavily. "It woke me."

"Did you see anything?" I maneuvered myself until I could see his face. His hair stood on end at the back of his head and his jaws were stubbled with the beginnings of a beard. Love assailed me and I kissed his chest. "Anything at all?"

"No, you were just lying there. I saw nothing or no one. Are you okay? Were you hurt, honey?"

"I don't know. I guess not." I laughed shakily. "Maybe we better check me out."

"Yes, I guess we'd better. Here, stand up, love. Legs all right? Arms, hands, shoulders? His hands were moving over me as he spoke. "Do you hurt anywhere?"

"It hurts all over," I said quite truthfully.

"Here, let's get these slacks off and check you out. Roseanna, I feel like—like spanking you!" he burst out.

Startled, I mouthed a silent, "Oh!"

He kissed it, hard and fast. "I also feel like loving you and God knows what else I feel." Kneeling to pull off my shoes and slacks, he glanced at me, his face grim. I could read his thoughts very well. I shuddered.

He kissed my scratched knee, then buried his face between my trembling legs. "If anything had happened to you—"

"But nothing did. I'm fine. Might have a bruise or two, but I bruise easily and that won't be unusual, so no

one will notice," I said more to myself than to him.
When he raised his head I gave him a bright smile. Bits
and pieces of what I had said to him were popping up
and demanding attention.

But I couldn't handle that right now. Tears ran down
my cheeks as I implored, "Please, just let this go for
now? I'm too shook up to even talk about it." I touched
his hard jaw. "Okay, love?"

His face tightened to a mask of lines and angles as he
struggled with his need to know versus my obvious need
for comforting. He dropped his hands and stood up.
When my pleading gaze entangled his, a half-smile softened his mouth.

"Okay, babe. As usual, you win," he said so wryly, I
hugged him.

Carefully he removed my shirt and underwear. He
wiped my bruised, dirty feet with a wet cloth and dried
them with warming tenderness. I held on to his shoulders. My legs were not yet steady. It was still dark outside and I shivered again as I looked into that
concealing opacity. Only the bottom part of the bedroom windows were curtained. The tall, higher portion
was left open since no one could see in. At least I hoped
no one could. Another shiver clawed my shoulders.

"Come on, honey, get into bed and let me warm you,"
Nathaniel ordered.

Gladly obedient, I lay back down. He peeled off his
jeans and got in beside me. It felt so good to have his
strong arms around me, drawing me close to his warm,
naked body. He just held me until I stopped trembling.
Then he made love to me, slowly, tenderly, his hands so
gentle on my body. I loved him beyond expression. Everything hazed, blurred, and faded softly from mind. My
other world, my family, even my attacker ceased to exist
for me. Nathaniel was my sole reality.

Afterwards he held me until I fell asleep.

Bright sunshine washed the bedroom when I awoke.
Nathaniel sat in a chair beside the bed, drinking coffee
and watching me. Through my lashes I gazed at him,
liking immensely what I saw, a rumpled, virile man clad

in cutoff jeans and red felt house slippers. Bare, tanned legs sprinkled with brown hairs, sinewy arms bronzed by a hot summer sun. Sexy with a capital S, I thought drowsily.

A tray on the bedside table snagged my attention. It held a pewter coffeepot, cream and sugar, and another cup. The fragrance teased my nostrils unmercifully. I perched up on an elbow.

"Hi," I said, yawning.

"Hi, yourself. Coffee?"

"Um, yes, thank you." Much too aware of his strained smile, I sat up and smoothed my tangled hair. "Didn't you sleep?"

"No, honey, I have too much on my mind to sleep."

I remained silent and watched him pour coffee. His hands were steady and sure as the stream of aromatic brown liquid precisely filled my cup. He added a spoonful of sugar and a dollop of cream, gave it a quick stir. Eagerly I accepted the perfectly brewed results of his labors.

An incautious sip promptly burned my tongue. "Delicious! You make marvelous coffee." He smiled. With care, I edged back against the headboard. "I guess you want to talk."

"You guessed right," he returned dryly. "Roseanna, I have to know what the hell it's all about, what *you're* all about. Last night was just too much, you being in danger, risking your life to come to me. Just too *much*, goddamn it! I can't allow that, don't you see? I can't let you take chances like that!"

The emotions raging in his voice—anger, frustration, fear—prompted my instinctive denial. "Nathaniel, you're getting a little dramatic, don't you think? Look at me, love. I'm okay, truly I am." I managed a convincing chuckle. "Granted I was scared. Petrified to be honest. But I'm not a brave person and it was spooky out there in the dark. So when something made some noise I freaked out. Besides, we don't really know that that something was dangerous."

"Yes, we do," he cut in grimly. "You know as well as I

do that you could have been hurt! Hurt badly, or even. . . ."

He didn't finish it and I could not. I was caught in a storm of jolting wonder. Could I actually die in Nathaniel's world? God, what if I did! The implications of this thought were absolutely staggering.

Nathaniel's rough voice finally penetrated. "Roseanna, I mean it. This has gone beyond foolishness. I have to know. Beginning with what you were doing out there in that spooky dark in the first place."

I sighed, a long whoosh of air between pursed lips. He was right. He had to know. Some of it, anyway.

"All right, darling. Come lay down beside me? It's easier talking when we're in bed."

Taking our cups, he set them aside, then slid into bed and drew me close. My mind spun a web of beginnings, yet I had no idea how to begin.

"Roseanna?" he prodded.

"Okay, I'll tell you. But you're going to be stunned, maybe even think I'm unbalanced. No maybe about it, you *will* think I'm unbalanced," I said with bleak certainty.

I turned until we lay belly to belly in a closeness that sizzled with tension. His warm breath played over my face as he placed tiny, encouraging kisses here and there.

"I doubt I'll think you're unbalanced," he teased.

"And I doubt that you won't. But remember I can prove everything I say. Keep telling yourself that because I really can prove it."

I paused while my mind sorted through details suitable for telling and those that were not. I could not bear to tell him that I was almost fifty, a wife, a mother. I could not destroy his illusions to that extent! But slowly, softly, I related the rest of my story, along with a graphic description of that first wild trip through space, and the stunning wonder of meeting—and then loving—him.

It was his turn to release a long, noisy sigh. I had felt his body growing rigid during my narration. Every muscle was hard and tense with his struggle to make sense of what he had heard.

"Nathaniel?" I queried softly.

"I don't know what to say, Roseanna. You said once before that you'd dropped from the sky. I studied on that for hours, but I couldn't take it literally. I kept skirting all around it. And now?" His grunt of a laugh came mostly through his nose. "Jesus Christ—and I do not say that irreverently! Roseanna, I can't accept this. I just can *not.*"

"But you have to. Because it's true." We rolled apart, and lay on our backs, the inch of space between us suddenly a chasm. "Don't you believe me?"

"I believe that *you* believe it."

"Remember, I said I could prove it," I reminded him, not at all gentle. "Did you notice how shaken my friend Viveca was that day? Well, you don't know her, so probably you didn't notice, but her nervousness, her anxiety is not Viv's true nature. But that day, she'd just been told what you've just been told. And then of course, I had to prove it. So I did. That was her proving visit. That's why she said 'Oh, Jesus!' when she touched your hand. She was still shocked and stunned and trying to force her mind to believe."

I twisted around until I could see his face. His eyes were closed, his mouth a thin line. Doggedly I pushed on.

"We're just ordinary people like you, just ordinary people going about our daily routine. And then *this* happens. The first time I met you I thought I was caught in a dream. That's why I accepted it so calmly when I fell over backwards in my closet and landed in your meadow. In your arms, eventually. I said either I'm dreaming or I've gone crazy. Dreaming seemed better than crazy, so. . . ." I shrugged. "For the longest time I simply thought you didn't exist, that you were a delusion, a fantasy, a creation of my mind. I'm still beset with the question. *Are* you real? Is this world real? Or am I still yet dreaming?" I asked with quiet intensity.

"One thing I can tell you for certain, you are not dreaming," he said, exceedingly wry. "And I am very much real. Real enough to be in love with you, at any rate."

"That's the worst part of it. If only we could have kept this just a romp, a lark, just great fun."

"Why? Mind you, I'm not saying I accept your story. I can't accept it, to be frank. It's simply too bizarre to accept. Although I admit I'm not as shocked as you thought I'd be," he said, surprising us both. "I guess, subconsciously, my mind has been arriving at some conclusions of its own. But still, going on the premise that it is true, why is our being in love such a terrible thing? Couldn't you change worlds? For me?"

I felt off-balance, as if walking on ice. How could we be lying here discussing this so calmly? And what on earth was I going to say next? When I realized what it was, I hated it. But I said it.

"No, Nathaniel. I have . . . obligations in my other world."

I sighed as the promise I had made to Lexi threw its shadow across my mind. *I'll always be here for you, darling. Always.*

"I can't just walk away from them."

"Ah yes, I remember: 'Other people you can't hurt or betray,' he quoted with steely softness. "A man, Roseanna?"

The sting of his question coincided with the hurt of my own. Did he think my "other world" existed only in my imagination, that it was just another city somewhere down the road from here? Was that the reason for our calm discussion?

My slight movement put more distance between us. "My other-world life is private." My tone softened as I caught his pained grimace. "Remember, please remember, I did not want this. I never asked for this! It just happened to me; I had no say-so or control in the matter. Well, I guess I did have some control. I didn't have to return after that first time." I pushed at my hair. "But, my love, I tell you truthfully, no power on earth short of death could have kept me from returning to you."

He was silent far too long. Covertly I watched his face. It revealed nothing. At last I burst out, "Well, do you believe me or not?"

"Roseanna, I love you," he said helplessly.

"But do you believe me?"

"Sweetheart, don't put me on the spot like this. I believe that you're sincere, that you believe every word you've said. Now I do, Roseanna. But I . . . God!" He exhaled the exclamation. "Look, just talk to me, huh? Tell me more about how you felt. And, remember, even you didn't believe it at first."

"That's true. It took a while to face up to the oddities of even a dream," I confessed.

He asked questions. I answered as best I could. I told him of my panicked reaction, of my attempts to deny the awesome space in my closet, my fears and doubts. Then we fell silent.

I got up to go to the bathroom. As I walked across the cool, tiled floor I felt an odd sensation of being disembodied, a sense of unrealness so profound that I turned to look at Nathaniel just to check his existence. He was staring at the ceiling.

We did not discuss the matter further. While I dressed, he put his jeans back on and went to the kitchen to make breakfast. Just toast and orange marmalade, but even that was too much. Mostly we drank coffee. I would look up and find his eyes on me. He would look up and catch me watching him. Warily, wonderingly. For the first time in our acquaintance we had nothing to say to each other. Nothing safe, anyway.

Nathaniel set down his cup and abruptly stood up. "All right, prove it to me."

His eyes were flat and dark. I hated that look.

"Please, oh please, don't look at me like that!" I cried, throwing myself into his arms.

"Oh, sweetheart, I'm not looking at you like anything in particular. I'm just . . . who the hell knows what I'm just," he sighed. "Come on, let's get it over with." He tipped my chin and kissed me before escorting me out the door.

The air was hot and utterly still, reinforcing the warning from storm clouds massing over the valley. Perspiration beaded my brow as I tried to keep up with Nathaniel's long strides. When we reached the grove he stopped and asked me where I was standing when I first heard noise, and from which direction it came. We searched, but found nothing more than an empty cigarette package. The grove wasn't all that private; anyone could have dropped it. We saw matted-down grass, but deer were plentiful here. Taking his hand, I led him from that pretty place and across the meadow to the boulder.

Again we stopped and he looked around, at the ancient gray stone, at the spot just in front of it where he had found me lying in the grass that first beautiful spring evening.

"This is it?" he asked softly, huskily. "It's *here*?"

"Yes, love. This is it."

He sighed, and I heard all the things that sigh said. *All the times I watched you leave. . . .*

Another long sigh conceded a little more merit to my claim even before he said it. "I have to admit this makes it seem much more possible." His mouth twisted with courageous humor. "So what happens now? A fiery chariot?"

"Nothing so dramatic. Just this." Stepping away from him, I reached the magic circle and simply disappeared from sight.

A moment or so later I stood before him again. His face was ashen beneath his tan. He couldn't speak. Taking his hand I drew him to me. Then I took him on a trip he would never forget.

My shadowy closet drew a strangled but reverent oath from him. I flicked the light switch without effect; evidently the power was off. I opened the door to let in a little light and immediately closed it. For in that brief instant I saw his face, the face of a man twice his age.

I gave him no time to question. Stepping in beside him, I took us back to his world, a trip that deepened his pallor, if possible. He had not moved so much as a muscle during our departure and return.

"Nathaniel?" I probed gently. "Are you convinced?"

He drew a shuddery breath. "God, I don't know what I am! Stunned, I guess."

I could see him trying to take it in. Like trying to

ingest a bitter foreign substance into your body, I thought, watching his face. I could see the exact moment when he fully comprehended the distance that separated us, an unimaginable distance, a dreadful, appalling distance. He saw the temporal nature of our love. In the same instant I saw the annihilation of his hope for a future together. He groaned, anguished with realizations. I wanted to go to him, but I reined in my instinctive urge to soothe. He had to be totally convinced, beyond-a-shadow-of-doubt convinced.

I returned to my closet again. When I reappeared in the meadow, Carasel was with me. She dived from my arms to his like a delighted child.

He buried his face in her fur. "Dear, God," he whispered.

"Oh my love, my love," I murmured, putting my arms around them both. We stood there in the sunlight, silent, afraid, lost in a situation that surely had no parallel on any earth.

"That place was your closet? And that's all there is to getting here, just that . . . fizzy feeling?"

"That's all. Sheer simplicity, which makes it all the more incredible." Mentally I checked my watch. "Nathaniel, maybe I'd better go on home now. You need to be alone, I think."

He shuddered. "Maybe that would be best. I've got to assimilate this, I . . . yes, I do need to be alone. But you'll be back soon? I need you, Roseanna. God, how I need you!" He grabbed me, crushing Carasel between us. She yelped. "Sorry, Carasel," he said with a weak chuckle.

The first hard drops of rain spattered our shoulders like a handful of pebbles. I don't think he even noticed.

"I'll return as soon as possible, you know that." I took my little dog and raised my face for his kiss. It was too forceful and his grip too tight, but I didn't complain. His hands fell away from my shoulders.

"Good-bye, Roseanna. I love you. Don't forget that, please? Not in your world or in mine. Just don't forget I love you, goddamn it!" he said roughly.

"Oh, darling, how on earth—any earth—could I forget that? Soon, love," I promised, and left him standing there in the rain.

For once, Viveca listened to me without interruption, eyes big and lips softly parted as I spun my dramatic tale. We were in her kitchen with tall glasses of iced tea and the rest of her spice cake.

Late afternoon sunlight created lacy patterns on the tablecloth. Idly I traced a leafy outline while Viveca offered up her opinion. Knowing me so well, she dismissed my wild night flight as the product of an overactive imagination and my pursuer as an animal. A large dog, perhaps. But her eyes were somber as they rested overlong on my face.

"Roseanna, this frightens me."

"What frightens you?"

"This. All of this. At first I thought it was a fantastic romp, a fine tonic for you in fact. But now. . . ."

"But now?" I jerked erect. "What about now?"

"Now it's beginning to really disturb me. Your life is here, not in that fairy tale you fell into. It is here, isn't it? I mean, you're not thinking of going there to live or anything like that, are you?" she asked tersely.

"I think about it sometimes. It is a very lovely fairy tale, you know," I replied with a smile so wry it hurt.

"But it is still a fairy tale, not real life. Isn't it?" she persisted, watching me alertly.

"Viv, I don't know how to answer that. All the sleepless nights I've spent pondering it and I'm still not one hundred percent sure, not about anything. Not even about Nathaniel. He might not even *want* me to come live with him."

"But if he did? Let's assume he does, and I'll play devil's advocate for you. I mean, this is important, Rosie, this is radical-lifestyle change we're talking here. So what's stopping you from joining Nathaniel if he wants you?"

"Lexi and you, for starters. My home, which I love. How could I just walk away from it all? Abandon my Lexi? Break the promises I've made, the vows I made before both God *and* Mother?" I added with a stab of humor.

"Vows and promises are broken all the time," Viveca reminded me. "But okay, let's change perspectives. What if you did go to live with Nathaniel and it all went sour between you? Maybe you couldn't return. You don't know how long that passage is going to remain open. You could be stranded in a strange world, no family, no identity, really. Do you love him enough to risk that?"

"Oh, jeez, Viv." A shiver raked my shoulders as I considered the picture she so vividly painted. "It isn't a question of loving him that much, it's *trusting* him that much. Do you realize what an enormous amount of trust that would require? Even if I could find an honorable way to leave my life here and go with him, would I have the courage to give so terribly much of myself into someone else's safekeeping? Could you do that? Leave everything—even your own world—for a man you've known such a short time?"

"I doubt it. I'm not all that brave, either. But, Rosie, you're taking a pretty big risk with David, then. The man has his faults and plenty of them. And since I've practically lived in your pocket these umpteen years, I know them nearly as well as you do. He's a pompous ass most of the time, a domineering chauvinist the rest of the time. Well, you know my opinions about David. I've voiced them often enough," she conceded, flashing me a look. "But, honey, flawed as he is, David Tait is one hell of a catch. There are half a million women in Houston alone who'd give their right tit to have him. Throw him up for grabs and they'd trample you getting at him."

Her voice thinned. "Take it from the voice of raw experience, Rosie, it is bloody hell to lose a husband."

Her vehemence was as startling as her words. Hot coffee sloshed all over my fingers. "Oh, shit-fire!" I swore. Shaking them, I turned my ire on her. "Viv, I have no intentions of throwing David up for grabs. Nor of losing him either."

"Maybe not intentionally, but David must have noticed something by now. He's not *that* dense."

"No, he's not that dense. But he is that complacent. Or at least he was. I think I shook him up the other night, at least enough to swear to me that it was going to get better. Even enough to promise me that romantic vacation I've been wanting."

"Well, I guess that's something to hang on to," Viveca allowed.

Chapter 14

*A*fter Viveca left I felt edgy and distracted. There were errands to do, phone calls to make. Instead I went to my office, sat down at the typewriter and wrote so fast and furiously that I lost track of time. The first chapter of my new book was finished by the time David came in, late as usual.

He looked tired and cross. I told him he worked too hard, a charge he answered with a one-sided smile. Following him into the bedroom, I lounged on the bed and watched him undress. When he paused before the mirror to comb his hair, I came up behind him and put my arms around his middle, almost experimentally.

"Did you have a good day?" I asked, kissing his back.

"Fair." He put down the comb and reached for the blue silk pajamas I had placed on his dressing table. "What did you do today?"

Social chatter to cover the shift of body that removed him from my embrace, I acknowledged. But he couldn't very well put on his pajamas with me glued to his back, could he? I tilted my head and met his gaze in the mirror.

"What would you say if I told you I'd spent the day with another man on another planet, and I meant it?"

He grunted. "I'd say that what I've been predicting has finally come true—you've become certifiable. What are you doing, starting another book?" He laughed and gave my braid a tug. "Just reading that kind of stuff is enough to turn your brain to oatmeal, much less writing it."

I started to let it pass. After all, I was used to it. But the same imp that had taken control of my tongue before spoke in an even, almost musing voice. "David, do you really think I'm too dumb to know what you're doing?"

Puzzled, he asked, "I don't know. What am I doing?"

"Veiling insult with humor."

"I do nothing of the sort."

"Oh? What do you call it then?"

"Roseanna, I was merely tweaking *your* sense of humor. Although I will point out that I've made no secret of my preferences in reading material."

"Certainly not cheap paperbacks with lurid covers featuring half-naked women and bare-chested Neanderthals," I intoned.

He laughed and swatted my rump. "Exactly." He yawned. "Are you going to work some more tonight?"

"Well, at least you know it is work," I said, and swatted *his* rump, quite forcefully too, seeing as how there was only thin silk between it and the palm of my hand.

He didn't seem to enjoy it. I did. In fact, I was astonished at how good it felt.

In between these little marital moments, I was being eaten alive with anxiety. I kept wondering, without hope of an immediate answer, how Nathaniel was dealing with my revelation. A logic-resistant quill of fear had lodged itself in my heart. What if he *couldn't* deal with it? What if he decided to quit this relationship, decided that it was simply too bizarre?

That was the word he had used—bizarre. . . .

Despite my inner agitation, two full days passed before I could escape the entangling mesh of my life and head for the meadow again. Before leaving I took down my hair and dressed in red shorts and a sleeveless T-shirt. The saucy outfit didn't invite close inspection in my bedroom mirror. But in Nathaniel's world my smooth, firm thighs and slim arms would please me as well as the man I traveled such a monumental distance to see.

I was surprised and very pleased to see the large brass bell that hung in the shadow of the boulder. I knew instantly that Nathaniel had put it up for my use should I ever again return at night.

Recalling the fright of my last visit, I was cautious about approaching the grove. But it was a meadowlark kind of day and nothing but a rabbit lurked in its whispery shadows. Carasel chased it with a great deal of verve and no success.

Laughing, running after her, I gave in to the intoxication of an expected lover's tryst. Nathaniel and I would have so much to talk about, I thought excitedly. But when I crested the hill and spied the cottage, my throat tightened with disappointment. His truck was gone.

Carasel ran to the front door with blithe disregard to the meaning of the missing truck. I followed her on leaden feet.

No one answered the door. I hesitated, hating the thought of going home. I decided to go see Liz.

The sky had become overcast and the day mercifully cooler. I found Liz working in her roses, her tawny hair perfectly tousled and her eyes red and watery.

"Allergies," she explained.

She waddled to the gate to meet me, a wayward angel decked out in blue cotton shorts and a huge white smock. Matt Riener followed behind her like a faithful collie. We hugged, kissed cheeks, exclaimed over how long it had been and how wonderful everyone looked.

"I'm glad Nate's taken off," she declared. "Now I get you all to myself. It's so good to see you, Roseanna!"

Arm in arm, we walked up the path to her minuscule front porch. This was the first time I had been to her little house, and I was surprised to discover that what resembled worn, even raddled wood steps was actually a clever disguise.

"Prefab, of course," she said when I commented. "With the price of wood? You'd better believe it!"

"The price of wood?" I asked before I thought. "I mean, why is it so darned expensive, anyway?"

One eyebrow rose ever so slightly. "Because the bastards have cut so much of it down, that's why. And then the last redwoods! Can you imagine that kind of greed?"

"Oh, no! The redwoods are gone?" I half cried. Then I remembered this wasn't my world and they weren't my redwoods. But still. "I hate that, really hate it," I said fiercely. "Your child has the right to see a redwood, dammit."

She shot me an oblique look. "Well, at least there are people who cared enough to raise seedlings. So maybe my children's grandchildren will get to enjoy them. And it will be worth your life to cut down one of *those* trees. So maybe we did learn something. Come on in, honey. Matt, skedaddle, huh? Roseanna and I have lots to talk about. Woman-talk, so you beat it," she admonished the chubby little man.

Marvelously obedient to her slightest wish, Matt brought us iced tea, kissed her, smiled at me, and beat it.

I looked around the living room with open curiosity. It was shabby but clean and so homey I felt the tension oozing out of me. A plump couch and two chairs; tile flooring washed and buffed to a honeyed gleam. Above the fireplace hung a lovely painting of water lilies, bewitchingly close to the Monet reproduction in Lexi's old room. With the soft yellow couch cover and the coral, beige, and pale green color scheme, the room was as voluptuously warm as the inside of a full-blown rose.

"I like your house, Liz. It's exactly like you!"

Baby blue eyes twinkled at me. "Well, thank you. I think. It isn't much, God knows, but it's cheap, which is of paramount importance. I get a small stipend from Daddy each month I stay away from home. It doesn't buy penthouses, but it's enough to live on." She laughed, jauntily dismissing something that sounded unpleasant to me.

The dining room was a nook behind the couch. We carried our drinks to the glass-topped table.

Curious, I asked, "Where are your parents, Liz? And

why do they pay you to stay away? This tea is delicious by the way."

"It is good, isn't it! Matt makes it. I can't make tea worth a damn. Tastes like weak pee for some reason." She took a long drink. "My parents live outside the city, on a big ranchero there. Big wheels, Roseanna. And they pay me to stay away because one, I won't conform to their standards; and two, I insist upon bringing little bastards into the world when I have alternatives. Well, fuck 'em," she said with a charming smile.

"Your parents are wealthy?"

"Filthy with money, burdened down with it. Daddy even craps pure gold," she quipped, laughing.

"Jesus! You're amazing, Liz!"

Her mouth quirked. "Yeah, ain't I though? Roseanna, everyone in this colony is to some extent a nonconformist like me. A dropout, if you will."

"What are you dropping out *of,* Liz?"

"All of it. A success-driven, high-tech society. Power trips and no-fault irresponsibility. The system itself. I think half the population is out of it by now. But the other half still hangs in there, grabbing with both fundamentalistic hands." She leaned back in her chair and eyed me. "Don't you agree?"

"Oh, yes, indeed. But if you're out of it, then what are you in to?"

"Simplicity. Freedom. Love. Karma. Forgiveness. The divine right to happiness."

"Those are beautiful guidelines to live by."

"Hey, it works for me." She eyed me over the rim of her glass. "So, what's with you and that sweet Nathaniel? He must not have known you were coming, or he'd never have left. Would he?"

"Of course he wouldn't. How long has he been gone?"

"Almost a week, now."

"Well, he should be back in a day or so," I said with assumed confidence. "But when he does return, will you do me a favor? We had a little spat last time I was here so, well, just tell him that if he wants to see me again to leave a note by the bell."

"A note by the bell?" she repeated, eyebrows arching.

I lifted my hands, palms out. "He'll know."

"Okay, I'll tell him, but. . . ."

"Thanks, I'd appreciate it. So what's with you and that sweet Matt?" I rushed on. "Any more tea? I'm parched with thirst."

"In the fridge. Bring the pitcher with you. I'd play hostess, but getting up is a pain in the rectum these days."

The two-door refrigerator was ancient, the stove positively baleful. The Formica countertops had seen better days. Better years, in fact. But pretty yellow china filled the open shelves and sparkling, brass-bottomed pots hung on hooks beneath. Plants on the windowsill happily shared space with ripening peaches.

Windows were opened to the breeze, for she had no air conditioning. Overhead, though, a huge white-bladed fan turned with willowy grace.

I refilled our glasses and returned to the table. The day had become even grayer, but as I sat down, her smile was sunshine to bask in.

"Matt," I reminded.

"Ah yes, Matt." She grinned. "He came on the scene about three months ago. Poor baby didn't have anywhere to go. The cottages were all taken. He had been staying with Nella and Jerry, but their tiger fights were getting on his nerves. He spent most of his time sitting outside to avoid being hit by flying objects. So I took him in."

"Without even knowing him?" I asked (squeaked).

"Oh, sugar, look at Matt. Could something that innocent be a madman in disguise? He's so gentle I wouldn't be a bit surprised to see birds nesting in his hair."

We shared an indulgent laugh. "But I sense more than a platonic friendship, don't I?"

She dimpled. "Yeah. One night I let him rub my back, which aches like hell all the time lately. Then I let him rub my belly just because it feels so good. And then, well, he was absolutely fascinated by my belly. It turned him on something fierce! So then I let him fool around a little and now he's fallen insanely in love with me. Or my belly, whichever. But he's so sweet that I don't mind. Besides, it's fabulous luxury having him around to clean house and cook and rub my back. He's pretty good at fooling around, too, so tender and patient."

She sugared her tea and absently stirred it. "He's a little lost soul, you know, tired of running on his treadmill but not knowing exactly what he's looking for. That witchy wife of his—"

"My God, a wife?"

"Ex-wife. Screwed him good when she divorced him. I never could understand a bitchy woman," Liz mused. The delft blue eyes fixed on me again. "Now, what's between you and that gorgeous hunk, Nate? You don't know how hard I tried to get him into my bed! But he isn't turned on by big bellies, damn it all. Brooke got him first."

"Brooke?" I cut in, deeply interested. "He was messing around with someone here?"

"Well, sure, honey. He'd been here awhile before you came along. Had to mess around with something. Better Brooke than a chipmunk!"

"Huh. What did she look like?" I naturally had to ask.

"Gorgeous. Long legs, yards of black hair, swivel hips, and flag-saluting tits. She's gone now. When you appeared on the scene they had a quarrel. At least Brooke had a quarrel. Nate just walked off. He does that, you know. When it gets to be too much of a hassle, I mean. I think he had a witch-wife, too."

Liz abruptly changed subjects. "Roseanna, what is it with you? I mean this act of yours, just popping up out of nowhere and then you're gone, then here you are again. Nate searched the entire colony for you that first time you disappeared. Despite the fact that he wouldn't sleep with me—or maybe because of it—we've become pretty good friends. Sometimes he comes up here just to sit and talk. About you quite often . . . how you wouldn't tell him where you came from or anything. It amused him at first, but I don't think it amuses him anymore. In fact, last time I saw him he seemed exceedingly uptight."

I set down my glass, hard. "When was that?"

"Oh, a few days ago, Tuesday, I think." Her gaze leveled on mine. "So what's it all about, Roseanna? What are you up to?"

I leaned back in my chair to regard this pretty woman I knew only slightly and yet, inexplicably, so well. Apparently Nathaniel hadn't shared his new knowledge about me. Looking into those velvety eyes, I felt an intense urge to confide in Liz Chance.

"What do *you* think I'm up to?" I asked lightly.

"More than Nate thinks," she said with a cryptic smile. "And more than meets the eye, that's for sure. I sense something. You're much deeper than you appear. Maybe just a very old soul, maybe just someone I met once upon a long time ago, eons ago. Certainly a person I like and want to know more about."

My attention had snagged on something. "Eons ago?"

Her lashes dropped. A faint, secret smile curved her lips. "Just a phrase."

"No it's not. You meant that." I watched her alertly.

"Okay, personal philosophy, then," she conceded. "I believe we've all lived many lifetimes, Roseanna." She shrugged. "As I said, personal stuff. So what are you doing here in this quiet backwater?"

"Oh, Liz." I sighed. "I like you too, very much. And because I do, I . . . I want to tell you a story. A fictitious one, of course. I'm a writer, by the way. Stories are my natural milieu. This one is about a woman who walks into her closet and—and stumbles over backwards and lands up against her closet wall. Only there is no wall. She keeps falling, falling . . . and lands in a meadow. Since her little dog was scampering around her feet the dog too lands in the meadow, on another world, under another sun."

My throat was dry. I drank some tea before continuing.

"Well, she lies there awhile wondering if she's gone crazy, wondering if she's caught in the middle of a dream, wondering all sorts of things—like why grass is tickling her bare ass, why her little dog is digging like mad at the base of a huge gray boulder. Normal things one might wonder about if one merely walked into a closet to find a purse and landed in a meadow."

Liz made a curious sound in her throat. I glanced at her and took another quick swallow of sweet, icy tea.

"She was curiously unafraid," I went on, still simply telling a story. "In fact she felt wonderful. So she just laid there and closed her eyes, musing, wondering. Along comes a tall, dark stranger who discovers her lying naked in his meadow. Naturally he is quite bemused at this, but also quite willing to . . . well, they spend several hours together in the warmest, most delightful interlude. Then she begins to panic because the dream is getting out of hand. She sends him on his way with a wild promise to meet the next night. Then she stands up, steps back toward the boulder with her little dog in her arms, scared now, wondering what the hell—and suddenly she's back in her closet again."

I shot another glance at Liz. Her glass was suspended in midair. Jolted into awareness by the splash of cold liquid, she quickly set it down and wiped her hands with a napkin, finger by long, slender finger.

"Well don't stop now, Roseanna!"

"To shorten my tale, after a week the woman gets up enough nerve to investigate the small space in her closet, which is a nook between a tall shelf and the closet wall. Knowing it's only a figment of her possibly deranged mind, she gathers up her little dog and steps into the space. An instant later she's in the meadow again. She locates the tall, dark stranger and they . . . well, so forth and so on. The door between the worlds is real. She can come and go as she pleases from her world to his. End of story. What did you think of it?" I asked brightly.

"I think you have one hell of an imagination." Liz had worked the napkin into a shredded ball. Grimacing, she tossed it on the table and lit a cigarette. "Sun Lights" was the name on the package.

"May I?" I asked. Although I seldom smoked, I was dying to try these.

She nodded. I lit up and inhaled. Very mild, slightly

sweet and pleasant. "These aren't marijuana, are they?"
I asked suspiciously.

She laughed. "Nope, I don't go that route. Bad for
Baby. These probably aren't that great, but I've already
given up tobacco and alcohol. What more does the little
darlin' want?"

The cigarettes had a minty flavor and I wondered
what they contained. Certainly not the harshness of tobacco. We smoked in silence. Liz looked at me, at
Carasel asleep at my feet, back at me again.

"That sure was some story," she said musingly. "Be
something if it was true, wouldn't it!"

I smiled. "Wouldn't it, though!"

We finished our cigarettes. "When is your baby due?"

"Another month or so. I haven't seen a doctor yet so
I'm going on my own reckoning."

"My God, Liz, you haven't seen a doctor?"

"Oh honey, what can they do that I can't? I take good
care of me. Matt certainly does, anyway. I'll get around
to it, don't worry. Maybe next week," she said languidly.

I was stunned, of course.

She laughed and placed a finger over my gaping
mouth. "Catch you a fly if you keep that up. Roseanna, I
think I'm your friend, at least I feel like one. I'm not a
gossip; I detest dispensing nasty little tidbits to people
about people. I only told you about Brooke because I
honestly thought you should know. Besides, if I didn't
tell you someone else would. I don't repeat stories, no
matter how fictitious they are. You're a writer, you said.
You're going to use that plot in a book, I hope. Jesus, I
do hope."

I shrugged. "Who would believe such a farfetched
tale?"

"Yeah, who would believe it?" she agreed. Blue eyes
inched over me. "Can you stay for lunch?"

"I'd love to. Liz, tell me something. You and Matt,
are you. . . ." Unbidden, my gaze landed on that enormous belly.

She shrugged. "No marriage if that's what you're asking."

"And the baby's father?"

"A jerk. Fantastic body, gorgeous face. I thought there was a man hidden in all that splendor," she said, not so lightly. "When I told him I was pregnant he came apart."

"So what did you do?"

"Went back and told him I wasn't. After a dramatic scene with Mother and Father I waddled on down here, and here I am."

"But this is such a—I mean, you must have had the best of everything!"

"Oh, yes. A proper nanny—British, stiff upper lip and all that rot. Private schools in New Hampshire, Switzerland, England. The latter dismissed me summa cum disgrace on account of my bad character. I coasted along, finished college, went to wicked L.A., and came home four months later tanned and pregnant. End of story. Now why don't you call my honey? I'm famished, and he makes marvelous kreplach."

"He's Jewish?"

"The best," she said simply.

I laughed and hugged her. "Well, of course he is," I said.

Chapter 15

Two days passed without a message from Nathaniel. Each time I dashed to the meadow and back, Liz's words would echo through my mind in chilling reminder. *Nathaniel just walks away if it becomes too much of a hassle. . . .*

Miserably I wondered if he considered our relationship too much of a hassle. Could he just walk away, go on with his life as if I had never been? Why not? I was never all that important to anyone else, I raged in midnight despair. Why should this be any different?

With the return of morning sunlight, despair faded and hope took its place. Saturday morning, lying alone in my big bed, I listened for sounds of David's presence. He was working at home, which meant I was tethered to home and hearth today.

At noon I prepared his lunch and took it to his office. I hung around long enough to remove his tray and carry it to the kitchen. I even washed his utensils. That was the limit of my patience. Throwing caution to the winds I ran upstairs to my closet. A moment later I was standing by the boulder, searching vainly for a message.

It was dusk here, making my search all the more difficult. I had about given up and was very close to tears when I heard him call my name. Gasping, I whirled around. The instant I saw him my heartbeat escalated, becoming wild and violent as I watched him approach. I was hopeful; I was fearful and apprehensive. I wanted to fling myself into those golden arms and kiss his firm, unsmiling mouth. Instead I spoke with a cool dignity that cost more than he would ever know.

"Hello, Nathaniel. It's good to see you again." Was my heart going to flail its way right through my chest? "I wasn't sure that I would. See you again, I mean."

"Neither was I," he said quietly. Very carefully he lifted the curl clinging to my cheek and placed it behind my ear. His eyes flickered over my mouth. "I wasn't sure of anything for awhile there."

My throat was too full to attempt conversation. In the soft light his bronzed skin seemed to glow against the pale yellow fabric of his shirt. Sheathed in lean, black slacks, his legs went on forever.

Desire, honeyed, hot and insistent, burned at the base of my belly. My breath shuddered out as he leaned against the boulder and thrust his hands in his pockets.

"Liz said you and she had a nice visit," he remarked.

"Yes." I coughed. "I came to see you but you were gone. Why, Nathaniel? Why did you go away for so long? Business? Or something else?"

"Some business. And some something else." His somber green gaze moved over me in oblique appraisal.

"You haven't even kissed me yet," I said so low that I didn't know if he'd heard it or not.

He did not speak for a very long moment. When he did, his voice was achingly gentle. "If I kissed you, baby, I wouldn't stop with kissing. And before you ask again, I'll tell you. I went away because I had to. I had to see what I felt about this, about you. It seemed such a screwed-up mess, such a god-awful, incredible mess I'd gotten tangled up in. I told you I've avoided involvements since Lisa's death. And here I'm not only deeply involved. . . ." He gave a short laugh. "But what an involvement! I needed to think it out."

"With someone else?" I asked, an involuntary, impertinent, but absolutely irresistible question.

"I haven't been with another woman since our first meeting," he replied with leveling gaze.

Tension seeped out of me like globules of sweat. "I'm sorry, that wasn't any of my business. I didn't mean to ask it, honest I didn't. It just slipped out before I could stop it. I apologize, Nathaniel. Do you—that is, what did you decide?" My nails were cutting into my palms. I uncurled my fingers. "About us, I mean."

Nathaniel sighed. "I didn't make any decisions. Nothing concrete, anyway. I just walked around missing you like I'd miss the sun should someone take it from me."

His flexible mouth quirked in self-mockery, but there was hunger in those smoldering green eyes. With sure instinct I put my hands on his arms.

He stiffened. Then, as though a wall had been breached, he reached for me. At last I was in his arms, being held tightly, kissed with passionate wanting, drowning in the glory of his need for me.

Instant combustion. Flame and wildfire, searing my skin, enveloping my body, blazing in the wet delta of my thighs. My fingers curved deep into his hair. His mouth tasted so good, so good. Hard, heated flesh pushed into mine, straining through the fabric between us.

"Roseanna, I love you," he muttered. "God, I do love you!"

I had heard all I needed to hear. The wild, singing joy in my heart was such intoxicating relief that I laughed, raw, husky and blazingly sexy. "I love you, Nathaniel Knight! Oh, damn, damn, *damn*, how I love you!"

His mouth curved into that heart-shaking smile. "Come home with me?" he asked, and I was plunged into the icewater of reality.

"Darling, I can't, not tonight. But soon, very soon, I promise. That is, if you still want me around?"

"Oh, hell, Roseanna, you know I want you around." His arms loosened; he cradled my face. "Once you asked me if I loved my wife. I said I didn't know. Well now I do know. I've found out that you can't walk away from love and I could have walked away from Lisa at any time without excessive pain."

His hands cradled my face. "But with you—it would tear my heart out to lose you! I couldn't give you up even if I wanted to. And I did want to, Roseanna. So damn much hassle." He leaned his brow to mine. "I don't know why we met. Hell, I don't understand any of this. But I do know one thing for certain. I love you.

And it's the deepest, most profound, most frightening thing I've ever felt. I can't see our future; it's shadowed and impossible to see what's ahead for us. But whatever it is I want it. And I mean to have it whatever the cost."

He dropped his hands to my shoulders. "I sense that you had a full life before I ever came into it. I really don't want to know about your other life," he added quickly. "But I do want to know; what if it comes down to making a choice?"

I felt the blood rush from my face. "A choice?"

"A choice between me and whatever holds you to your world. Me and our love, or. . . ."

I sucked in a breath. "All right, Nathaniel, you've made your point. With an icepick, I might add."

"That bad, hmm?" His eyes veiled. "Which brings me to another icepick question, inverted this time. Do you have children?"

"I—well, Lexi, she's . . . yes, a daughter," I ended in a firming voice. "Whom I love very much."

"I see. Well, that pretty much nullifies my first question, doesn't it! Only a beast would ask a woman to make that kind of choice." His voice and smile were sardonic, almost bitter.

My heart hurt as I remembered my promise to Lexi. *I'll always be here for you, darling.* I did so love my girl, but that promise's bindings were cutting into my very flesh.

"I can't give you that." I swallowed; the hurt had reached my throat. "I can give you an honorable out if you want it. If you think that best for you, then we'll end it right here."

He shook his head. "No, we won't end it. Like I said, whatever the cost, Roseanna."

My knees were trembled. I exhaled and swiftly drew in a breath. "Nathaniel, listen to me. I have never loved another man as I love you. I do have a full life, but it's—oh darling, it's as if there was an empty place inside me that had never been filled, that lay fallow and waiting. For you, Nathaniel. It's a private place that can't be touched by anyone else ever. It's yours for all time, love. No matter if you want it or not, no matter how long we're together, it belongs to you and you only. I swear by all I hold sacred, that part of me belongs exclusively to Nathaniel Knight forevermore. Amen."

I made these solemn, quite frightening vows with a sincerity as disturbing as the situation. Neither of us knew quite what to say next. It was too intense. Beyond more rather extraneous declarations of love, words were impotent right now. By habit I glanced at my (stopped) watch.

"I've got to go. Oh, thank you for the bell, Nathaniel," I said warmly. "It's a lovely gesture of concern. I assume it was you who put it up?"

"Yeah, it was me. Now you use it, you hear? Anytime you're scared or even just uneasy about walking alone, you ring that bell," he ordered gruffly. "Three rings, a ten-second pause, and three more rings. I'll hear it."

"But so will others," I pointed out. "Or they'll see it."

"No problem, not around here. They'll just think it's a private shrine. You promise to use it to summon me? No more wandering about in the dark, Roseanna."

"I promise. Well, I really must go. But I'll be back very soon. Oh, my love, I've missed you so much!"

"Have you?" he demanded.

"Oh, yes, yes!" I whispered, kissing him wildly. Then I leaned into his cuddling embrace and savored every lovely sensation. I hated to end this. But I had been here far too long already.

"Nathaniel? What's a Skyecraft?" I asked the thought that popped so incongruously to mind.

"A personal helicopter, a little vehicle you can put down anywhere you have a few feet of bare space. Dandy little things. Maybe I'll buy you one."

I shuddered. "No, thanks. If at all possible I keep my feet planted solidly on the ground."

"So do I, but lately it's been a mite more difficult," he drawled, a crooked smile forming.

The next morning I canceled my appointments with a ruthlessness that would have amazed me earlier. After a quick call to Viveca I left for my own private version of Eden.

To my delight, Nathaniel was as passionately eager for
love as I; to my chagrin, after lovemaking he was just as
eager to delve into the mystery of our separate worlds.
For the moment our situation took a backseat to his
avid curiosity.

That night, lying sleepless in my own bed in my own
world, I tossed and turned in a welter of confusion. Nathaniel's curiosity was a powerful force, infusing my own
up-until-now blind acceptance with disturbing questions. The most obvious one was why. Why had I been
chosen for this out-of-world experience? Wouldn't it
have made more sense to choose someone with the in-
tellect to grasp the overall concept, or at least ask intelligent questions? Why me? Was there a reason? Was I
supposed to be doing something other than having a
marvelous time? Or was it merely chance, a simple case
of being in the right place at the right time?

From what Nathaniel and I had been able to con-
clude, we inhabited similar Earths, differing only in minor ways that seemingly made no impact on the future.
It was as if his Earth zigged where mine zagged and
fitted sweetly together again.

The maps of our worlds dovetailed with only occa-
sional changes in names. The great land masses, the
oceans, the polar caps, the tropics and deserts and jun-
gles; the holy places, the bloodied lands, the volcanic
islands strung like jewels in an azure sea were all exactly
where they should be.

His was without a shred of doubt the planet Earth
with its corresponding theory of evolution, and sometimes dismal, sometimes glorious past. The recorded
centuries matched with some insignificant changes as to
exact dates. The industrial revolution paralleled ours
right up to the present rate of advancement, including
the fuel shortages and escalating buildup of nuclear
arms.

Then something went awry and our paths parted. On
his Earth new fuels were developed; gas and oil were no
longer dire necessities. Even more astounding, the nuclear threat under which I spent my entire life had simply evaporated into thin air. Russia fell apart; Europe

smoldered, fought, separated, coalesced into new nations; China clung stubbornly to its ideology until that too was vanquished under the new and revitalizing winds of freedom that swept over his world.

Religions were beleaguered by new insights into old truths. Belief in unconditional love was overcoming belief in hellfire and damnation, and God was definitely not dead.

I wondered what my Earth's future held. The same? Or would we yet blow ourselves to smithereens in a nuclear holocaust? How far did this similarity extend?

We had discussed another intriguing possibility. If our worlds were identical, there should be another Roseanna on his earth and a Nathaniel on mine. Could I meet myself in his world? There was a name for that. Doppelgänger. An ugly name. And a deflating possibility. But we were going to check it out. Through Viveca I intended hiring a private agency to seek out the existence of the Knight family in New Mexico. Nathaniel was going to check Alabama and Houston for his world's Roseanna Bently. What would he do if he actually found her?

Instinctively I felt this would come to naught even though I had no tangible reason for this feeling. Maybe it was vanity, but I was quite sure God had made only one Roseanna Bently.

"Oh, dammit, Carasel!" I muttered as I tripped over the little dog for the third time. It is odd how she senses my imminent departure for the meadow. She stays underfoot the entire time just in case I have intentions of sneaking off without her again. I patted her head as I put another book into the box. We were in David's study, which also doubles as our library, selecting reading material for Nathaniel.

Since any work of fiction, no matter how farfetched or trivial, does reflect upon some area of our society, I took selections ranging from Welles to Sinclair to Bombeck.

As soon as we arrived in the meadow I sent Carasel on ahead to fetch Nathaniel. My laughter was indescribably sweet as I watched her run like a gamboling puppy, head up, ears flying, tail in continuous, riotous motion. I felt a bit riotous myself. When we came to this mysterious place we shed more than years. Cares and worries dissipated like fog in bright morning sunlight.

Well, not all of them, I conceded, noting the puff of gray clouds that besmirched the horizon. A particularly apt metaphor, I thought. "So what the fuck am I supposed to do about it!" I asked Carasel so ragingly that she whined. Composing myself, which mostly consists of shoving it to the back of my mind to fester in private, I strode onward.

The box was heavy and I had barely made it to the grove when Nathaniel appeared to relieve me of my burden. After half a dozen kisses with scorched edges, he strode across the meadow so exuberantly that I took two steps for his one.

In his living room he began unpacking as eagerly as a child opening a Christmas gift.

"Well, don't start reading now, Nathaniel!" I scolded, taking a book from his hands with a petulant pout. Suddenly serious, I caught his face and asked softly, "Are you okay, love?"

"I choose to be okay, therefore I am okay. Words of wisdom from Liz."

"From Liz? I don't understand."

"They had me to dinner the other night and seeing I was a tad low, Liz said, 'Nathaniel, you can be down or you can be up. The choice is really up to you.' She said something about while you can't *control* outside circumstances, you can choose how you *react* to those circumstances." He shrugged. "I decided what the hell, why not try it? It couldn't hurt and might even help. Especially in this case. And to be brutally honest, right now I'll grab any potential lifeline that comes my way."

"And thank you for that load of guilt," I said, swatting his shoulder. "God knows I'm only knee-deep in the stuff on any given day."

"That wasn't my intent, Roseanna."

"Oh, don't feel bad, I'm used to it. I think our Liz is one smart cookie," I mused. "The lady is deeper than she looks. Well! Enough sobriety. Let's do something fun."

He relaxed, smiling. "Well, we could make love. That's always fun."

It was. Glorious fun, this celestial dance, as Nathaniel termed it. Then he looked abashed and I chastised him for being embarrassed by such beautiful sentiment. I told him I loved my own sexuality, even though I had to admit that at times I'd been abashed myself at being deemed oversexed, or, in kinder words, a "peculiarly horny wench."

"Who said a thing like that?" Nathaniel growled.

"Someone who obviously didn't appreciate my lusty nature," I said with an echo of sadness in my careless laugh.

Like one who has lost control I was back in Nathaniel's cabin the very next day. I was pleasantly surprised to realize that he was taking our situation in stride, as much as possible, anyway. Such equanimity on his part attested to a far greater depth of maturity than I had suspected. We were together and we made the most of it. We swam in the lake and played in the water until we were exhausted, until to lie down on the quilt and stretch like supple cats was voluptuous pleasure. We made a soft, drowsy, sun-warmed kind of love. Afterwards we plunged back into the pleasantly cool water.

Such simple pleasures, I marveled. "Skinny-dipping at our age," I scolded as we splashed our way to the opposite bank.

I put on his shirt while he spread the quilt under the lacy fronds of overhanging willow branches. We laid down again. I stretched my arms, my legs, relishing the sleekness of lithe young muscles, remembering, as I flexed each knee, the small *pop*! of bones when I did this in my world.

"God, I feel good!" I exulted.

"Umm, me too." Nathaniel sighed. Folding his arms as a cushion for his head, he closed his eyes. "I've been doing some thinking. Do you want to hear my thoughts?"

"Do I have a choice?"

"Don't get cute," he admonished. "It's your fault I've been doing so much thinking. Sitting around waiting for a certain young lady to drop in on me now and then gives me a lot of time for thought."

"Huh." I rolled onto my belly to watch his face. "Well, I've been doing some thinking too and my opinion is that you're doing too much thinking."

His scowled. "Roseanna, I'd have to be a moron not to think about all this. My God, it's fascinating!"

Because I was feeling so blissful and because his eyes were the same color as the grass blade he chewed on, I went along with him. "So tell me a thought, my brilliant Thinker."

He cut me a look. "Last night I was sitting on the terrace having a drink and feeling kind of low. Or maybe just contemplative. Anyway, it was a beautiful night, clear, starry, mysterious, a 'thinking beyond' night, you know? And I began thinking of history as a tapestry, unfolding inch by inch, each inch a hundred years of recorded history. Then I began questioning the identity of the weaver and the ultimate pattern on the tapestry. The weaver," he repeated thoughtfully. "Who or what is the weaver? Some say it's God and some say mindless chance. Some say we ourselves are the weavers."

"What do you say?" I asked with genuine interest.

"I can't say, not for certain. But I sure don't go for that mindless-chance crap. The tapestry stretches all the way back to the creation of the world itself and I tell you, honey, that night sitting there looking at a million trillion stars, chance was a joke, and a retarded one at that. This earth, those stars, the order of it—the beautiful, awesome *order* of it could not be chance. Perhaps my opinion is a little biased—an architect knows full well the intricate planning that goes into creating even a small office building. Just try slapping up an eighty-story skyscraper using mindless chance!" He looked at me and laughed. "Have a helluva lot of hard stuff falling down around your head!"

I moved closer and laid my cheek on his bare chest. "So what conclusions did you reach?"

"Nothing definite other than that falling building. And the need for a mastermind to make it all work. And that the weaver, whoever and whatever it is, is a creator if we include this planet as part of the tapestry. History is simply the lives of people and what they do with those lives. Each life intertwines to make up the threads the weaver uses to create his designs. As for names, in most cases I don't think names are all that important. It is Man who colors history, so what does it matter if a mother named her son Bill or Dick or Plato? It's that particular man at that particular point in time, the one needed to provide a vital change of design in the tapestry. . . . Gets a little convoluted, doesn't it!"

"My head is spinning," I agreed. "Could be the wine, but it is definitely spinning."

"Well so did mine, honey. Because if we acknowledge a Master Weaver—a Creator—then we have a Creator who creates two identical worlds, two identical tapestries. Why? What's the purpose?"

"Beats me. Do you believe in predestination?"

"No, not really. Because it shortchanges a man, gives him no reason to struggle. But whatever theory we accept, there's still one solid fact behind this: there has to be a guiding hand behind the sum total of that tapestry to prevent chaos. But identical tapestries? Or nearly so, because I've just discovered a bigger difference. We had no Vietnam War."

"You didn't! How did you escape that?"

He shrugged. "We considered it an internal Vietnamese affair. Anyway, I decided to visit Liz and Matt and rifle their library—a rather astounding collection of reading material, by the way. Books on religion—all religions—and past lives, future lives, spirits, reincarnation, myths, theologies, aliens! I knew she and Matt had farflung interests, but this! They let me browse and I found this book on parallel worlds. A fascinating concept," he mused. "Outlandish, I guess, but . . . you want to hear it?"

"I love fascinating concepts, outlandish or not," I assured him. His eagerness gave my voice a lilt.

"Well, according to the author there are many Earths, all created by points of crisis. If we go along with that, then your world and mine took separate paths because of Vietnam. Your government became involved; mine decided against involvement—that's one theory. Then there's simple personal choice; maybe on your world I made a dumb decision and died. And maybe on another world I'm married with six kids. Hell, anything's possible! If we go along with this concept, that is."

I gave him a quizzical look. "Do we?"

"I don't know. Do we?"

"As good a reason as any, I guess. I like your idea of a tapestry, though. There is a Master Weaver, but maybe all It does is supply the cloth for the tapestry. It's up to humanity to supply the design."

"Hmm, good theory. But what about the identical designs?"

I snuggled closer until I was half-sprawled on him, making myself more comfortable, if not him.

"Suppose there isn't any master design. Let's say that people are the threads and they do the weaving. So suppose the Creator decides to experiment and supplies two identical cloths, which are our Earths, and a handful of threads, which are people. Now, always remembering that He also gives free will to the weavers. . . ."

I had gotten lost. Flushing, I glanced at Nathaniel. He displayed no amusement, just quiet, attentive interest.

"Well, let's make it more simple, since I am basically a simple person," I went on. "We have two Earths, each containing a group of similar people. From this point, the tapestry—history—begins. Now out of two given groups of people, no matter how dissimilar in looks or background or even nationalities, the same dominant traits would surface, wouldn't they? On your Earth or mine, the group would reshuffle until the dominant people, both good and evil, would rise to the top. Regardless of names, they would be alike in their ruling drive to dominate, to take command, to *do* rather than to *be*. Does that make sense?"

"Yeah, it does. Some. And over thousands and thousands of years, the dominant genes would pass from generation to generation, keeping pace more or less with the other Earth."

"But still, would each group do exactly the same things, weave the same pattern of history? That's carrying it a little far, don't you think?" I argued with myself.

"The genetic makeup would be altered immensely as time passes, but the basic genes would never be totally erased. Have you discovered yet that the original genetic blueprint is coded in every human cell? And every other living thing, for that matter. I find that astounding fact a direct finger pointing to an original Creator."

"God," I said firmly.

His smile was gentle. "All right, God. But the point is . . . damn, I wish I knew more about genetics!"

"I don't because then I'd have to listen to a discourse on that, no doubt."

Nathaniel began laughing and pulled me down on his chest.

I nuzzled his throat and said thoughtfully, "But I think you're wrong about names being unimportant. Would Confucius have been Confucius if he'd been named Joe?"

"Would an apple still be an apple if we'd named it a pear?"

"Huh. If a man named Amerigo Vespucci hadn't roamed around our Earths, would we be living in America?"

"Good point. You got an answer?"

I scowled. "No, I don't. All I have is the good point."

"You certainly do have good points," he murmured. "Any wine left?"

"It's all gone. Which is just as well, love. It's time for me to fly away home," I said lightly.

He laid his cheek on my breast. "I wish you wouldn't. I have this fear—"

"No fears, Nathaniel." Gentling my voice, I bit his chin and murmured, "Remember, there is nothing to fear but fear itself."

Nathaniel smiled and nipped my nose. "Bullshit. When we were kids, my brother and I used to—"

"Whoa!" I exclaimed, rearing up. "You didn't tell me you had a brother!"

"Well, Michael is sort of the family black sheep," he said in that offhanded way that masks something important. "A defrocked priest, much to Mother's everlasting shame."

I blinked. "Good heavens! What happened?"

"Oh, it's a long story." He shifted, and gave me a lopsided grin. "Well, actually it's not. His opinions were deemed a little too unorthodox even for our liberal times."

"My goodness! What were those opinions?"

His grin grew more crooked. "Just about the opposite of everything that's been preached since the beginning of recorded history."

My interest fired by my own sly wonderings, I asked, "You mean he doesn't agree with traditional teachings? Why not? Is he just not religious? Or has he developed a totally new philosophy?"

"He's still very religious. A fool for God, you could say. No new philosophy, just new insights. Man evolves and so does religion." Nathaniel shrugged. "Or so he believes."

"And you? What do you believe?" I asked intensely.

"I believe. . . ." He laughed and nipped my chin. "That I'm a fool, too, baby. A fool for love," he said, not quite teasing.

Chapter 16

*T*here were times when I was as big a fool for love as Nathaniel claimed to be. For Lexi's birthday the following week, I proposed a party, a hearth and home, good friends and parlor games affair that I thought might bring us closer.

"Oh, Mother, really!" she exclaimed. "Parlor games?"

"I'm glad I'm still capable of amusing you, Lexi," I returned crisply. "Your father thought it a fine idea, but if you disagree. . . ." *Unfair, Roseanna.* "What's your idea of a celebration, honey?"

"More on the order of dinner and champagne at Maxim's. Did Daddy really like the idea of a party?" she asked skeptically.

"Who knows? Handling family fetes is *my* job, not his. He's annoyed that you and I don't get together very often. Maternal neglect and all that. He just harrumphed when I tried to explain that you don't have time for me," I said, chuckling to show I too could be amused.

"We're both very busy people, Mother. But thanks for thinking of me. Although it really isn't necessary: Daddy's taking me to lunch, and Clark is doing the champagne dinner."

"So you don't really need me at all," I said, listening to her answer with something deeper than mere ears.

"I guess not. But let's do lunch next week, Tony's perhaps. We both enjoy that. Then we could stop in Nei-

man's for a spot of shopping and you can buy me
something outrageously expensive," she suggested
cheerfully.

In my mind's eye I could see her—shiny black hair,
long, sleek legs and slender feet in expensive pumps; a
designer suit with an important gold pin on the lapel;
small, round, horn-rimmed glasses perched prettily on
her straight little nose. All grown up and still a precious
part of my life.

"My chic, brilliant, superbly altogether Lexi, willing to
take time from her hectic schedule and 'do lunch' with
her old mother. Be still, my heart." I laughed, still
amused. "Tell you what, I'll pass on lunch. But I will buy
you a nice present."

"Oh, shit, Mother, I didn't mean . . . hurting your
feelings was not my intent. Why are you so idiotically
tender-hearted, anyway?" she teased. "Look, I meant to
announce this later when we were all together, but . . .
Mom, Clark and I have set the date for our wedding!"

My idiotically tender heart caught at the "Mom" and
sank at the news. "You're really going to marry him?
Does your father know?"

"Of course he knows. And approves, I might add. Oh!
But only that we're getting married. You're the first to
know we've set the date," she added, her voice suddenly
small and chagrined.

"Oh, goody!" I said lightly. "So when is the date,
love?"

It was June of next year. I wondered, suddenly and
painfully, where I would be in June of next year.

"So that gives you plenty of time to cope, Mother.
Not that it's going to be a huge blowout! Think small,
quiet, elegant. Orchids and champagne, that sort of
thing. Well, must run, so terribly busy you know," she
said drolly. "We'll talk later."

"Later," I agreed. "'Bye, sweetheart."

I hung up and dashed at tears. Why was I so blasted
weepy lately? If my strong-willed Lexi wanted to marry
that cinnamon stick of a man, then she'd do it. *No big
deal, Mother.*

I went to the bathroom, blew my nose, flipped on the

shower. When I opened the cabinet for a new bar of soap, a box of tampons fell out. I stopped dead, my mind suddenly buzzing as I replaced the box. It was August sixth and I had not yet begun my menstrual cycle.

Anxiety created odd little hollows in my stomach as I backed out of the bathroom. Lots of women could shrug off eight days. But you could set your calendar by the rhythm of my cycle. Menopause was still just a word to me.

"But not an impossible word," someone said—me, I realized. Discovering that I was now sitting on the edge of my bed, I took a breath and blew it out.

Menopause. "What else could it be, Roseanna?" I chided with strengthening humor. As much as I had wanted and prayed to give David another baby, it never happened. My last pregnancy had been very difficult and delivery even more so, leaving me incapable of bearing any more children.

I was only twenty-six then, and it was unlikely I would ever conceive again. I was now forty-eight and practically celibate in my marriage, which brought the chance of conceiving again down to zero. So.

Well, no wonder I'm so weepy, I thought, gratified at this firm thread of logic. Entering The Change, as Mother had termed it, was bound to upset hormonal balances and cycles and such. Likely David was right when he accused me of being neurotic!

I stood up, discovered my legs weren't boneless after all, and walked back to the bathroom. Maybe I ought to call my doctor, see if I should be taking hormones or something. . . .

I no more thought it than I forgot it. For that very evening David told me he was going to New York for a week. He would leave Sunday morning and return the following Sunday. He was explaining the strictly business aspects of his trip when I stopped listening.

In fact, I almost stopped breathing. The idea had come like a shot of pure adrenaline and my heart was pounding so hard that I was sure he could hear it. One week! An entire week of my own, minus a day for caution. Six nights, six days—oh God! I clenched my fists and fought to calm myself.

"No problem," I assured him. "I have no desire to go to New York." Finding myself draped over the arm of a chair, I stood up. "Do you know what I *would* like to do, more than anything else in the world?"

Visibly startled by my intensity, he asked, "No, what?"

"I would like a week to myself. One week, David, one week that belongs to me. No one to interrupt, no one to steal little drops of time from it; one week entirely my own. Just Roseanna's. Not Roseanna the wife or mother or friend, just Roseanna. A week entirely alone."

He shrugged. "So? While I'm gone you'll have the house entirely to yourself."

"The house, maybe, but not me. Lexi will call, Viveca will call, you will call. You see?"

He frowned. "Maybe you do need to get away at that. Lately you've become downright unstable at times," he added with a pointed look. "All right, you may have this week."

The words "pompous asshole" flashed across my mind, but I managed to contain them even if it was akin to swallowing a mouthful of sharp little stones.

"Thanks, David, you're a prince," I said dryly. I jammed my hands into my pockets. "You're sure it's okay?"

"I'm sure. But I do have to know where you are, in case of an emergency if nothing else. Surely you can see that."

"Yes, I agree. Viveca! I'll tell her and she'll act as my go-between," I settled it with an airy wave.

My heart was going crazy. A week with Nathaniel! I hugged David in fierce appreciation, aware of incongruities but too happy to confront them.

"I don't believe it!" Viveca said when I told her that David had promised me an undisturbed week to myself. She could not resist the delicious irony of it and several minutes were wasted stating the obvious.

When she sobered we made plans. We put in as many escape hatches as we could think of, the main one being a secret place for emergency messages.

"That large hole at the base of the boulder." I suggested.

We worked out any remaining bugs in our plan with half a dozen more calls that day. Eventually we had it as foolproof as possible.

"Viv, you don't know how much I appreciate this," I told her.

"No sweat, honey. I'm getting something from this too, you know. Vicariously, I'm going to enjoy every minute of that week with you! Have you told Nathaniel yet?"

"No, not yet. There hasn't been time. Honest to God, Viv, you wouldn't believe what a trial this has been, arranging for one measly little week to myself. David just packs a bag and goes. Me . . . a thousand details," I said, sighing.

"Don't I know it! Roseanna, what would you have done had David denied your request?"

I thought about it, then made a decision that rocked us both. "I'd have gone anyway, Viv."

"Well, well, aren't we getting spunky, though! While I naturally applaud that. . . . Just take care, hmm? Just take care that your life doesn't wind up a mess. A real mess, honey. After all, you're juggling some pretty heavy tumblers. Fragile ones, too."

I just laughed and hugged her. Nothing was going to spoil this precious gift of time. Nothing.

Sunday morning David left on the ten o'clock flight to New York. I waved him off and rushed back upstairs to the bedroom. Forgotten were confusions, frustrations, minor hurts. Feverishly packing, I refused to allow even a sliver of doubt to invade my slightly delirious mood. Nothing would go wrong. Viveca was guarding the homefront. Nathaniel would be there when I arrived and very glad to see me. Amen.

I dressed in white shorts with sexy little cuffs, and a knit halter top. Both were a bit too tight, but they'd fit just fine in Nathaniel's world. The shopping spree I managed to work into my busy schedule had included a new camera, a sleek, costly little thing that was totally automatic save for installing and removing the film. I put the camera and six rolls of film in my cosmetic bag. I had no idea whether or not one could photograph a fantasy, but I was going to try.

After I finished packing I dashed off a note to Nathaniel. Next I took Carasel to the meadow and held onto the excited little dog long enough to secure the note to her collar.

"Go find Nathaniel," I instructed.

Catching my excitement, she took off, legs flying like pistons, yapping all the way. For good measure I rang the bell three times as instructed.

"He'll be there," I told myself fiercely. "He *will*."

After sending my bags "down" by simply dropping them, one by one into the opening, I made a quick, wifely check of the house.

When I reached the meadow I found my luggage gathered up and placed in the truck that stood off to one side of the boulder. Nathaniel lay on his back in the grass, eyes shut, a blade of grass in his mouth. He pretended sleep. Carasel romped up and began licking his unprotected face.

"Oh good grief, Carasel!" he groaned.

Laughing, I walked over and placed a sandaled foot on his chest. "Have you been here long?"

"Forever. But it's worth it." Deep green eyes met mine with an impact that struck both of us an emotional blow. "You're really spending the week with me?" he asked softly.

"I really am," I replied on a strained breath.

The moment was too intense. Just when I thought I couldn't bear it any longer, he grinned and ran a hand up my bare leg to the hem of my shorts. "Hey, lady, those are some shorts!" he said with an edible leer.

Tension shattered. Laughter engulfed us. Dropping to my knees, I removed the grass blade from his mouth and tickled his nose with it. I felt so powerful, so giddy, so unafraid. So many good things, I thought, flinging up my arms.

"Hi, terrific-looking man!" I crooned.

"Hi, terrific-looking lady!" he half shouted. He pulled me down atop him and we went rolling over and over like maniacs in our delicious excitement. I wound up on top.

"Really *nice* shorts," he marveled, hands moving.

We wrestled some more and it was pure fun, a mischievous, high-spirited, sensual fun that was fully as intoxicating as any nectar the gods might whip up.

When we finally reached the cabin, he bounced out, raced to my side, and plucked me from the seat with an ardor that left me breathless. We didn't get the luggage into the house but we did manage to reach the bedroom before I was gloriously assaulted.

"God, I did miss you," he said, sighing, eons later.

"What did you miss?" I asked saucily.

"You. This lovely face, this wild hair, these wicked blue eyes, that absurd, definitive giggle."

My nose wrinkled. "Definitive giggle?"

"Oh, most definitely definitive. It is the last word on giggles, the defining sound of what a giggle should *be*! If I heard that giggle in a bar on Jupiter, I'd say, "That's my Roseanna!" He sobered. "I missed this closeness, too. And sex, of course. But mostly I missed you, all that you are to me."

I blinked, wanting to hear more and afraid to hear any more. I still had this almost superstitious fear of acknowledging how much we needed each other. To expose the full depth and breadth of our love would be tempting the gods.

Not to mention the burden it puts on me, I thought with an odd tinge of bleakness. How could I bear it if this lovely, magical interlude brought him pain and regret?

A mental shake of head rejected even the possibility. "I missed you too, way too much." I sighed. "Darling, what do you expect from this week together?"

"Passion and pleasure, of course," he replied readily.

"But also to become better acquainted, to get to know each well enough to be able to make some intelligent decisions. Fair enough?"

"Fair enough." I knew he was asking more of this week—and of me—than his mild response implied. But for some as yet unexamined reason I didn't feel panic or even anxiety. Somewhere deep inside, a change was taking place in me. I didn't question. Soon enough I would know, I suspected. "We didn't unload the truck," I reminded him.

Lithe as a cat, he stretched. "We'll do it right now. I want the pleasure of putting your shoes beside my shoes and your little silk panties beside my little cotton shorts," he exulted, patting my bottom. His hand lingered. "On second thought we have all week to unload that truck."

A wicked grin curved his mouth and his eyes danced, agleam with mischief.

"You truly are wonderful," I said with all my heart. Then I bit his chin. We laughed, kissed, and teased our way into lovemaking again.

Time passed without notice, golden minutes dropping into a bucket that would never be filled, not for us, I thought languidly.

Stretching, I asked, "My love, shouldn't we get up?"

"Why do we have to get up?" he asked lazily.

"Because . . ." I stopped in surprise. "We don't have to, do we! Nathaniel, we can do anything we want!"

His laugh was inexpressibly tender. "Anything we want."

We lay silent, a little awed at our great good fortune. When he spoke again, his voice was quiet and sober.

"Roseanna, something's been gnawing at me. That first evening in the meadow when I came upon you lying in the grass, according to what you've told me, that was the first time you'd come here and, thus, the first time you saw me. Yet you knew my name and accepted, even invited, my loving. At the time I thought you'd just seen me around town and that's why I was familiar to you. But now I wonder: How did you know me even before we'd met?"

"Why can't you ask me something easy for a change?" I muttered, sighing as I grappled with the always perplexing question of how much to tell Nathaniel about my life. "Like everything else I've told you, this is going to sound crazy. But here goes. You remember I told you that I'm a writer? I write . . . well, what we call women's fiction. Historical romances, to be precise. I've published fourteen so far—"

"Fourteen novels? That's fantastic! Why haven't you told me about this? It's an honor to know you, Miss Bently!"

I stiffened. "Don't patronize me, Nathaniel. They will never be classics, but I enjoy writing those books tremendously."

"I wasn't patronizing you. I'm truly impressed," he said quietly. "But what does your writing have to do with knowing who I was?"

"You have to understand how I go about plotting a book. Sometimes it's the plot that first begins to take shape and sometimes a specific event, an anecdote, a newspaper item; just some little something that acts as a catalyst. But this time it wasn't plot or incident or any of the usual. This time it was a character, Nathaniel. A man who began forming in my mind, who began to grow, to assume personality, habits, and character traits, all the things that make a person real."

Nathaniel had become very still as I spoke. After a quick glance, I went on. "This character began to assume such substance in my mind that I swam in the beauty of his eyes. I knew intimately the shape of his head; I had mentally kissed the curves of his mouth. My fingers knew the feel of his skin, his hair, the smoothness of his back and shoulders," I half whispered. "My body began to hunger for the touch of his hands, I . . . *knew* him, you see. I wanted his lovemaking. I craved him, even. There was no story, no plot, no romantic adventure, just this man, this vividly known man."

I took a deep breath. "Then a name came to mind and I knew immediately that it was his name."

I smiled and nodded to the question in his green, green eyes. "I tried to write about this man, to make him come alive in a story. But he wouldn't. Only in my mind was he alive. I wrote several chapters, trying to fit him into a certain place, a time, a lifestyle, but he simply would not fit. I was damned aggravated, believe me, so much so that I decided to scrap that stalled manuscript and start another. But before I could act on this thought, I fell through a nonexistent hole in my closet and landed in a meadow . . . and met Nathaniel Knight, a man I knew well over a month before that actual moment of meeting."

He gave a slow, awed shake of head.

"My God! It's only at times like this that I'm aware of what a terrific shock this was to you. Just look at my reaction that one brief time I experienced it. It was a helluva shock, traveling to your world and returning to mine, all in a heartbeat of time! No wonder you had to work at convincing yourself I was real! How on earth did you manage to take it so calmly?"

"I alternated between thinking I was crazy, or dreaming," I returned dryly. "Staying with either of these options helped me keep my cool."

"I guess so!" He whistled. "Awesome! Just plain awesome! You actually knew me before we met; I wasn't a stranger at all! But how? How did the awareness of my existence seep into your mind even before our worlds touched?"

He reared up with his intriguing thought. "Or did it? That first time, baby, it was the first time you had *used* the passage, but that doesn't necessarily mean . . ." He paused. "Is it possible the passage could have been open a month or so before you discovered it?"

Was it possible? I remembered the sound I'd heard upon waking each morning, weeks before I fell into that narrow little gap between wall and shelf. A soft, silky whisper of sound, like a gentle wind rippling through tall grass. A mystifying sound that had no definable source, I reminded myself.

"It's possible, I guess. The way that space is constructed, I have to have a specific reason for getting into it. Remember how it's tucked into the corner?"

"I don't remember much of anything about that

space. It's a blur, really. Here, draw it for me," he said, bounding from the bed to fetch pen and paper.

I shook my head. "I can't draw worth a damn."

He sat down on the edge of the bed. "Happens to be my specialty, ma'am! Just give me some measurements."

As I talked, he drew, and soon my tall shelf and narrow gap were neatly defined. "Fantastic!" he declared. "So it's possible that during that month I began assuming shape and substance in your mind, the passage was open. And somehow, though God knows I can't begin to explain that *how*—"

"But somehow the essence of Nathaniel Knight began to seep into my mind," I finished for him. "And thus when I finally did meet you, I knew immediately who you were. Oh, God, darling, I have goosebumps all over," I whispered.

He gave a great shout of laughter and threw down the paper. "So!" he exulted, rolling over and squashing me against his chest. "You were indeed lying there just waiting for me!"

"You had doubts, then?" I asked rather coolly.

"It was a situation made for doubts, Roseanna. I think I did pretty damn good keeping mine to an escaping few," he replied with an irony that made me flush.

Chapter 17

We did not leave the house that day, nor the following day. We were too blissed out to do anything other than lie in a hammock and snooze and talk, and anticipate the evening's entertainment, which was dinner with Liz and Matt at Savoyn's, a local club of some repute.

Around six, revived by a long shower, we dressed and headed for the lake colony. Nathaniel had bought a new car during my absence, a sporty blue convertible. I was enchanted! The wind blew gloriously through my hair in solid fulfillment of a long-held fantasy. I closed my eyes and let the layers of Roseanna peel away until only the girl I once was sat beside him.

Liz's little house had the patina of pewter in the evening sunlight. Liz herself was even more enormous, a magnificent blimp walking around on two slender legs. Matt escorted her with the same awe and respect due such a luscious, geranium-pink wonder. She was now, by her own reckoning, either due at any second or two weeks' overdue. Which added an extra fillip to our evening. Giving birth on Savoyn's dance floor would be a spectacular windup to Lakeview's celebratory fete.

Savoyn's was as far removed from elegance as one could get and still be civilized. It was mismatched chairs, scarred Formica-topped tables, ersatz pine floor, and a band composed of escapees from a mental asylum. The clientele would have been at home in any Texas dancehall.

The hours spun by on ribbons of laughter. Nathaniel,

by now happily intoxicated, needed desperately to dedi-
cate a love song to me despite my expressed reluctance
to be the center of attention. Shushing my protests with
loving forebearance, he drew me to the edge of the
bandstand.

"Play 'My Heart Belongs to Roseanna,' " he instructed the uncouth, possibly syphilitic leader of the
band.

"I don't know 'My Heart Belongs to Roseanna,' " he
protested.

"That's all right, just fake it," Nathaniel said grandly.

The uncouth one faked it. Nathaniel and I danced to
an exceedingly simple air sung by a blond, lanky person
—male, I think—a song which began:

> My heart belongs to Roseanna,
> my lungs belong to Roseanna,
> my liver belongs to Roseanna,
> my kidneys belong to Roseanna,
> my navel belongs to Roseanna,
> my balls belong to Roseanna,
> my—

"That's enough!" I shouted.

"Let him go on, honey," Nathaniel said, "he's just
coming to the good part!"

I felt the sudden sting of tears even as I laughed, for I
could well imagine David's reaction to something like
this. Not once in all these years had we ever shared this
particular kind of laughter, so deliciously naughty in its
promise of things to come. He could not unbend to this
extent. How sad.

The compassion that stung my eyes reached my heart
and held for an instant. Nathaniel's husky inquiry broke
the spell and returned me to my present reality. I slid
my arms around him in a needful hug.

By the time we left, both Matt and Nathaniel were
levitating. Since Liz could not get behind the steering
wheel, it was left up to me to drive.

I peered at the dashboard with all its little buttons.
There was no gearshift, just more buttons located in the

console between our leather bucket seats. Baffled, I slapped at Nathaniel's hands and asked, "How does this car work, Liz?"

"Jesus, Roseanna, you do know how to drive, don't you?"

"Of course she does," Nathaniel said with blind loyalty.

"Of course I do," I said. "But this is Nathaniel's car, you know. It's entirely different from the cars I drive."

"What do you mean, different? Different how?" Liz asked.

"Oh, Liz, use your head, huh? I already told you that story," I said impatiently. "Now how do you drive this thing? Where's the key? And the keyhole, for that matter?"

"*Can* you drive this thing, darlin'?" Nathaniel murmured.

I smiled with love spilling all over my indulgent lover. "Ah, sweetheart, yes I can drive this thing, never you fear! I shall drive like the goddess Diana, winging her chariot among the stars and around the Milky Way and down through—"

"Roseanna, for God's sake, can you drive us home or not!" Liz shouted. "I have to go to the bathroom!"

"Well! Just hold your horses, Liz. I said I would drive us home and I will."

"Well then, *do* it!" she moaned. "PC, Nate?" she prodded when he lazily stretched.

"PC?" I questioned, wishing I'd paid more attention to how he drove this ultramodern vehicle.

"Program combination." Grinning, Nathaniel leaned over and punched some numbers aligned in a square on the dash. The car started. "Wow!" I said, impressed. "What if you forget the combination?"

"You don't forget," he said.

I let that obvious assumption pass. After I distinguished the headlights from the windshield wipers, the windshield washer, the overhead lights, the rear defrosters and the sunshields, Nathaniel made a bemused suggestion. With an exasperated, "Huh!" I pushed the D button on the console. The car made a smooth-as-silk change of gears and we set out for the lake.

Although Nathaniel pestered me all the way, I managed to get us to Liz's, where she and I propped up Matt and dragged him indoors.

Then I maneuvered Nathaniel and myself home, after which he took over and got us to bed posthaste.

Alcohol played its usual sneaky trick of inflating the libido and deflating the equipment. "Just hold me," I said. So he held me. Eventually his breathing calmed. He's asleep, I thought. I needed the bathroom. When I moved, his arms tightened.

"No, don't leave me, Roseanna. Don't ever leave me again," he muttered thickly. "Don't go back there. Stay with me, be my wife . . . live with me, love me. Together all the time, Roseanna, no more loneliness, no more hurting. . . ." his voice mumbled off into wordless whispers.

I lay rigid in his embrace. This was the innermost Nathaniel speaking, the secret heart's desire, firmly denied, but now released by alcohol and tormenting to my ears.

"You won't leave me?" he asked quite clearly.

"Shh, hush, Nathaniel, I'm right here," I whispered. "Sleep now, beloved."

I too eventually slept, but it was haunted slumber.

The sun was high when I awoke. Easing from beneath the arm flung over my hips, I made the much needed trip to the bathroom. A swirl of nausea made me clutch at the sink. Straightening, I inhaled shakily as it passed. Something I'd eaten—or perhaps just imbibed—last night, I reflected.

A shower would feel wonderful but the sound of running water might disturb his rest. I sponged off until I felt refreshed enough to put on some clothes and make a pot of coffee.

Still he slept. He smells like a brewery, I thought wryly. Leaning down, I kissed his prickly cheek, and softly, his mouth. How beautiful he was! Sunlight struck auburn flints in his tousled hair. His lashes lay like dark fans across his cheeks, his fine mouth relaxed into a half smile. I fancied that I could glimpse the little boy who lived within this long, powerful body.

"Oh, beloved," I whispered hurtingly. After another soft kiss I went to the kitchen for a cup of coffee.

The golden day outside the window beckoned like a magnet to my capricious mood. Gulping down my coffee, I grabbed an apple from the basket and took Carasel out to the small rear deck.

The day really was golden. A wash of sunlight burned off the violet mists fringing the foothills. Dew sparkled like diamonds on long meadow grasses, and everywhere birds sang in joyous accompaniment to this fresh, clean wind cooling my flushed face. I sat lost in nature's soul-music, unwilling to face just yet the worrisome knots I still had to untie.

"Good morning." Nathaniel stood beside me, clad in his red robe, a coffee mug in one hand and the pot in the other.

"Good morning, love. How do you feel?" I touched his cheek. He had showered and shaved, and he smelled wonderful.

"Um, I'm not sure yet. Not even sure I want to investigate." He grimaced. "I have an unnerving suspicion that I made a jackass of myself last night. More coffee?"

I held out my cup. I wore a filmy white peignoir with voluminous sleeves and lavish froths of lace at my wrists and throat, an outrageously expensive bit of feminine fluff but worth every penny, the look in his eyes assured me.

"You weren't alone. I think we were all a little crazy last night. But it was wonderful fun." I blinked, my eyes suddenly wet as I wondered if I would ever feel like that again. "The most fun I've ever had, in fact. Thank you, darling, for giving it to me."

"You're welcome, but I think it was mutual giving. Hey, Carasel, you having a good time, hmm?" he asked as she came racing up the steps. Tail wagging her entire body, my little dog greeted him, then lay down beside me. Smiling, Nathaniel took the other chair. "You look so pretty, Roseanna. I often have my morning coffee out here, and to wake up and find you sitting here waiting for me is like one of my midnight dreams come true."

Heedless of the tears spilling down my cheeks, I stared at him. Long, tanned fingers touched my face. "Why the tears, sweetheart?" he gently inquired.

"Last night you said things, Nathaniel. You were nearly asleep, and drunk, I know, but you said things that hurt. Beautiful things, love, but they hurt. You asked me not to leave you, to stay here and be your wife. Never to leave you, because you were so lonely. . . ." I turned from him to gaze out over the tear-blurred meadow.

"I'm sorry," he said quietly. "But you must know how much I want that. I never said it because I knew it would hurt, but I'd give anything to have you as my wife. That's God's honest truth, how can I deny it? If I just had something solid to hold onto—please don't cry, Rose-anna."

"How can I not cry! I know you're manipulating me and I hate being manipulated, and here I can't even work up a decent batch of resentment. Don't you think I want to be with you, too? I do, Nathaniel. But I can't, I . . . Oh dammit!" I muttered, swiping at tears. Managing a smile, I looked up at him. "This is a fine way to start the day, isn't it?"

"I know a better way."

His gallant, teasing response only deepened my pain. But if he could ignore it, so could I. "Yes, come to think of it, Mr. Knight, we do have some unfinished business from last night," I said with what I hoped was an impudent smile, wobbly though it undoubtedly was.

"I flubbed up, huh?"

His abashed grin had to be kissed. "You flubbed up good," I said crisply. "However, I never hold grudges and I'm always willing to give lavish second chances."

"A saintly woman. One thing, though, do you think I'd survive it?"

"I think if we conduct ourselves in a dignified manner we might just pull it off. Tell you what, you just lie there and I'll do the rest. You won't have to move a muscle.

Well, one muscle, but that's all. What say you, Sir Knight? I'll be gentle, I promise!"

"I'll try anything once," Nathaniel decided.

How could we be carrying on this frivolous conversation when our hearts were hurting so? "We merit medals for valor," I murmured on the way to the bedroom.

Later, I was loathe to continue our painful discussion simply because I didn't know what to *do* about it. Or even what to say, I admitted, resenting the never-ending sting of guilt.

Nathaniel, apparently sensitive to my feelings, did not bring it up even though, being a fair woman, I afforded him several opportunities. Like me, he gave himself wholeheartedly to the magnificent, unhurried pleasure of just being together.

Sometime during that day he walked with me to the boulder to check for messages. There were none. Lighthearted from a lessening of anxiety I had not been aware of feeling, I suggested we clean up his garden. For some reason I needed the connectedness of working with nature.

That evening we prepared a light dinner: roasted vegetables aromatic with olive oil and crushed herbs; chopped avocado and tomatoes nestled in beds of tiny, tender lettuces, and a crusty loaf from the colony baker. Afterwards we sat on the deck watching the sun go down in a splash of scarlet glory. Our wine was as extravagant as the evening, golden pink with a delicate, wild-berry flavor, like summer on the palate. Linking fingers, we sat richly content in the gathering dusk.

Or so I thought.

When Nathaniel broke the silence, his quiet voice held a hint of urgency. "Roseanna, I need to talk about us, about our future." His grip tightened. "As my friends can tell you, I'm a long way from being perfect, but I think I'm a fairly decent man," he said with endearing awkwardness. "I take full responsibility for my actions, I believe in justice—which doesn't mean I'm weak, only that I'm fair—and I'm capable of commitment. I also think I'd be good with kids."

"I'm not sure I'm following you," I said with a nervous laugh.

Rising, he walked to the railing and leaned against it, his taut form betraying the frustration evident in his gaze. "I think I'd be good with your daughter, too. I'd sure try, anyway. So." The hand he ran through his hair came to rest on the back of his neck. "Your choice would be a lot less drastic, should you have to make one, I mean."

"Oh, Nathaniel. Oh, God." I sighed, rubbing my brow as I thought of my twenty-nine-year-old daughter. I knew I ought to explain Lexi to him, but that would just open another can of worms, and I was getting awful damn tired of explanations. Eyes narrowing, I peered at him. "You said should I *have* to make a choice?"

His voice smoothed into that subtle, velvet-wrapped-blade so useful in handling a balky female. "Roseanna, I think we both know we're reaching a crossroad, one that's going to call for some of those 'intelligent decisions' I spoke of earlier. I'm not pressuring you—"

"That's good, because the only pressure I'm responding to is what I apply to myself," I replied with scatter-shot fury. "I've fuckin' well had enough of people telling me what to do. This is *my* life, goddamn it!"

His eyebrows shot up, as did his palms, in comic fear. "Whoa! Who's been telling you how to live your life?"

"Who hasn't? Up until the day Mother died she was giving me instructions. My daughter has reversed our roles and my . . . well, suffice it to say I'm considered an airhead most of the time. I'm not aggressive enough, not pushy enough, not bitchy enough. I don't know how to be shrewd and calculating. I'm too trusting, which translates to dumb, and I flunked cynicism in college. It's a dog-eat-dog, devour-before-you-get-devoured world, according to my advisers. . . ."

"Do you believe that?" he cut in softly.

"No, but then, I'm an airhead." I laughed, my anger subsiding. "I'm not, but because I'm small and easygoing, my opinion is usually ignored. Or at best, listened to and politely discarded. So I get a trifle irritated when told I *have* to make choices. Let's use this week like you said, to make some intelligent decisions. But no forced choices. No power plays, Nathaniel. Because I tell you right now, I won't stand for it."

"I don't force people to do anything," he said rather stiffly. "And I'm not into power plays."

I didn't reply. My assertive stand had surprised me. Even more surprising was realizing how much stronger I was here than at home. But no one had pounded me down with condescending love here. My spirit was still untrammeled and I felt spunkier, more powerful, taller, even.

Looking into green eyes that could turn me to vanilla pudding, I laughed softly. "Of course you're not. Can you help it if you don't know your own power?"

"Can you help it if you appear soft and fragile and desperately in need of guidance and protection?" he countered, cocking an eyebrow.

A torrent of anger and frustration swirled upward, volcano style, and erupted in heated words. "Well, appearances can be deceiving! I'm not soft and fragile, I'm *resilient.* A willow, not an oak, able to bend with the wind. And there have been some rough winds, Nathaniel. I buried three babies; one miscarriage, one stillborn, and one just four months old. I never knew my father; he died before I was born. My stepfather was strict, never pleased, harsh and critical of childish endeavor. He also had a temper. Both Mother and I were scared to death of him. When he died she took over his role. Out of fear, I've decided with the help of hindsight. She was so vulnerable and needed so much from me. I tried, I really did, but we just couldn't communicate. She died last year and I. . . ." I blinked at tears. "I miss her, even so."

Nathaniel's face wore a look of soft astonishment. "I never suspected! Such trauma, Roseanna! And to one so young, too."

"On my world, I'm older," I said shortly.

He thought about that. "And a gentleman never asks a lady's age, of course."

"No, he does not."

He raked at his hair again. "I guess I really *don't* know you all that well yet."

"You don't know me at all." I stood up and curved my hands around his neck. "But then neither do I. Maybe this week we'll both get to know me better. Meanwhile let's table this and get to bed. Last night was a helluva night, Nathaniel," I accused.

He grinned a sheepish grin and my heart eased. It would be all right, I soothed myself without examining what that "it" was.

Despite my weariness, I was too keyed up to sleep. My every nerve was alive and vibrating to the presence of the man beside me. Even the ticking of the clock was loud in my hypersensitive state. Each quiet ticktock echoed the refrain my heart pulsed with every beat; time was running out. The last of this week would mark either the end or the beginning. And I was a mass of confused and contradictory desires.

Thoughts leaped across my mind like cumulus clouds, piling up, collapsing, building again. Thoughts of the past, the present, the shadowed future. And suddenly, disconcertingly, thoughts of David. He did not belong in this bed with Nathaniel and me. But he was vividly there. Too much so. I eased from the bed and found my slippers.

Moonlight illumined the den. Shushing Carasel, who slept beside the fireplace, I took her out on the terrace with me.

My mind was still on David. Once he had loved me. I in turn had loved him so very much. And now?

I couldn't answer for him, but I could for me.

Wrapped in my own arms for both warmth and courage, I acknowledged the truth I had struggled so long and hard to deny.

The man I had loved and married no longer existed. That warm, affectionate, giving part of David had died and been entombed in the nursery he had locked with such bitter ferocity.

The deep void left in my heart and soul had been filled by Nathaniel, of that I had no doubt.

But what did I still owe David?

And what did I owe myself?

Chapter 18

The next morning Nathaniel informed me we were going shopping for clothes. For me.

"Oh, that's really not necessary—I have plenty of clothes," I protested.

"You have no clothes, because from now on, what you wear here will be clothes that have been bought and paid for, by me."

With quick comprehension, and rather liking the touch of arrogance in that, I said, "Manipulation again! But what the heck. After all, if there's one thing a woman loves to do, it's shop," I informed him with such glee he winced. Sobering, I reminded, "Nathaniel, I haven't made you any promises."

"So? What I said still stands, my clothes or nothing. So we go shopping . . . or were you planning to walk around in your birthday suit the rest of the week?"

I laughed and tickled him. The dark clouds of last night had faded in the sunlight of his good spirits and I welcomed this respite.

When we began preparing breakfast, I felt a little queasy at first. Then abruptly, nausea sickened me to the smells emanating from the lovely omelets he'd whipped up from yolkless eggs.

"I must have eaten something at Savoyn's that didn't agree with me—I felt a little queasy yesterday, too. Just let me . . ." Jumping up, I rushed to the bathroom, but nothing came up. I was grateful, for Nathaniel was right behind me, concerned, speaking of doctors and clinics and even the emergency room.

Wiping my face with a cold cloth, I shushed him. "Oh, for goodness sake, it's just a tummy upset. I'll be fine in a minute. Just get me a cola. And maybe some dry toast."

The cola and bread acted as an absorbent; my tummy settled down; I felt okay. "Certainly capable of shopping," I told him.

At last convinced, he agreed to the trip.

The town of Serena was larger than Lakeview. It seemed a prosperous place, with shops ranging from Nessby's, a large department store similar to Sears, to Madelaine's, a chic, first-story establishment whose preciously old-fashioned decor set my teeth on edge. But there was nothing antiquated about the merchandise, nor the prices.

As we swept into the shop, Nathaniel gave a curt nod to the approaching saleswoman's, "May I help you?"

"Yes, you may," he conceded. "This lady will require your undivided attention as she needs to be outfitted from the skin out. You may bring me a chair and place it here by this mirror, and a cup of coffee to ease my pain," he said imperiously.

I hid my grin as the snippy young woman melted into servility. Madelaine, sharp of eye and round of figure, sized up me, then Nathaniel, and promptly took over this special (obviously a prince and therefore meriting her valuable attention) customer. My grin got loose. Waving a careless hand, he commanded me to get on with it, he didn't have all day.

We spent two hours and fourteen thousand dollars in Madelaine's shop. David would have gone berserk by now, I thought, but Nathaniel enjoyed it immensely. With a lazy grin and flick of fingers, my prince selected or discarded frocks, skirts, sweaters, negligees, and underwear. He grew more lordly with each bite of the cheesecake that had appeared on his coffee tray.

Consqueen jeans, eighty bucks a pair and fitting like a second skin, five pair with different pocket designs; a certain sweater he liked, in six different colors, whether or not I concurred.

At his urging, I changed from my earthly dress to a peachy vanilla sweater and a chocolate brown skirt. The soft fabric cupped my plump little apple breasts and the slim skirt sheathed my hips and buttocks in a way I hadn't allowed in two decades. Sleek brown pumps, a paisley print silk scarf in bronzy autumn tones, and big gold earrings. "Jeez," I said, quite struck with my appearance. At *that* age twenty-four, I had looked a little raw and unformed; at *this* age twenty-four, with all my earthly years tucked neatly beneath supple skin, I looked ripe enough to pluck.

When I presented myself for his inspection, I said, suddenly shy, "Well?"

He stood up and surveyed me with a curious expression flitting across his face before he smiled. "Well," he agreed.

Leaving Madelaine a much happier woman, he steered me down the street to a jeweler, where, to my consternation, he selected a diamond solitaire mounted high on a wide gold band. When I urgently protested this lavish expenditure, his eyes met mine with an intensity that stilled my voice.

"I know, no promises. Just wear it, wherever you are." He laughed, breaking the tension. "It'll keep me on your mind."

"You're always on my mind, even without this. But thank you," I said, turning my hand this way and that. "It's quite the most beautiful ring I've ever seen."

But he wasn't through yet. Seating me in a chair, he selected a delicate rose-gold chain entwined through two tiny hearts, and fastened it around my ankle. I had not worn an ankle bracelet since I was sixteen, when they were all the rage.

Smiling up at me, he clasped my ankle with both hands and asked, "Do you like it?"

"Oh, yes, I like it. Thank you, darling," I said softly.

"You're welcome," he growled, signing a ticket. "Now that you've bankrupted me, how about some lunch?"

Hungry, I quickly agreed. He chose the Lighthouse

Café, a small place all bright yellow and orange, slick plastic and shining tile. It was all very modern and impersonal, except for the black, potbellied stove sitting in the center of the room. From its open lid sprung an enormous begonia that dripped white flowers from every arching stem. It was such a magnificent incongruity in this enameled ambience that I was entranced.

He was well known here. The waitress, a lissome redhead, greeted him warmly, while a plump woman with a frizzy halo of carrot-colored hair gave a welcoming cry similar to a frog's mating call, and enveloped him in her fat, golden arms. His long arm barely encircled her waist as he introduced us.

"Millie, my love, meet Roseanna, my love." His grin grew wider. "Brace yourself, Millie, the wench has trapped me. No longer can I run wild and free in the moonlight!"

Millie's shriek turned every head in the café. "I'll be gawdamned! You done got caught, didja? Summabitch! Hi, honey, I'm pleased t' meetcha. Pretty little thing, ain't she!"

The next instant I was squashed flat against the most magnificent bosom in California.

Breathless, I sank into the chair Nathaniel pulled out, and turned my attention to the well-endowed waitress now laying the table. She gave me an oblique glance, and I knew that he had sampled the delights she had to give a man. But that was before I came along, I reminded myself. This was all before I came along—a natural part of his everyday life, these people, this place, this town. It all served as a painful reminder of how little I knew of Nathaniel Knight.

But I was learning to know him. The kiss of autumn made the day an intoxicating pleasure, and we were both a little drunk with it. In late afternoon we wandered hand in hand through the woods, romped in tawny grasses, drank from the crystal spring hidden deep in the grove. Wonderfully tired, we came home to a supper of cold chicken and wine, followed by delicious little pears from Liz's tree.

The night was crisp and cool and arrestingly lovely.

We sat out on the deck for awhile. Gazing at the star-spangled sky, I wondered where in that black velvet vault lay my Earth. Or was it even among those glittering bits of light? The mysteries of time and space and universes beyond imagination were profoundly close at such moments. I was always chilled by the vast unknown I held in my two small hands.

At midnight we went to the Night-Owl movie and had hot buttered popcorn and colas that were potent shots of caffeine. The film was a comedy, slapstick absurdity and great fun. We came home and made love and then cuddled up, spoon-style, to talk until dawn.

It was as close to Paradise as I'd ever come.

We were up at seven, and by eight had decided to spend the night in San Franscisco.

My little inner voice expressed alarm, but my sense of recklessness had increased until it was a wildness inside me. I felt rebellious and restless, almost feverish in my determination to block out thoughts of the future and enjoy this priceless *now*.

We had a chartered plane and pilot at our disposal, a luxury I decided I could do without in favor of much bigger planes.

Miraculously, San Franscisco looked the same, improbable, enchanting, and childishly fascinating to me. But I was nothing less than thrilled when Nathaniel directed the cab to a sleek, modern edifice that soared forty stories high. Standing out in stark relief against the gold glass façade, tall black letters spelled out simply "KNIGHT."

Like a rubbernecking tourist, I stared up at the glowing tower and those impressive letters until he laughed at me. But there was pride in his laughter.

"Oh, Nathaniel," I said just short of an undignified squeal, "I had no idea, no idea at all! Is this really yours?"

"Um, not entirely, baby. I have a few partners. But we designed it, my grandfather and I. In fact, this was his last triumph. He died just two days before we were to take possession," he said with deceptive matter-of-factness.

We walked through a functional but elegant lobby and took the elevator to the top floor. Nathaniel's office colors were an electric blue and soft dove gray, a combination that at once stimulated and soothed. As I wandered around reading the documents on his wall, both Nathaniel's and his grandfather's, I was suddenly touched with a peculiar chill. For a startling instant, the man who sat down behind that enormous desk and began going through his mail was a stranger to me.

Perhaps my stare was noticeable, for he looked up questioningly. Feeling absurdly awkward, I smiled at him.

"You like my office?" he asked with flattering eagerness.

"I love it. Did you choose the colors?"

"Yep!" Rising, he took my arm and escorted me through the door. "Gray is one of my favorite colors, the right shade that is, not that industrial gloom spread on defenseless walls."

Pausing at the desk of his very pretty receptionist, he plucked a rose from the arrangement of pink-on-pink lilies and roses, and presented it to me with a bow. "A rose, for a rose."

As we left the premises, I caught the looks from his female office staff, and wondered how he'd remained unsnared all these years.

After a fabulous lunch of lobster and a dry, sparkling Valley wine, we went to his apartment. I was eager to explore it, but immediately we were inside, he swept me up and carried me to the bedroom. I caught a glimpse of a magnificent four-poster bed before being laid upon its silken linens.

"I've dreamed of making love to you in this bed," he whispered as we nestled into position.

Feeling strange, almost uneasy, I forced myself to concentrate only on this sweet, sweet moment.

Later, wrapped in one of his robes, a deep-napped velour the color of a winter sky, I roamed the spacious living area with a renewed sense of being outside time and reality. This was another side of Nathaniel, this sensual indulgence of sparkling glass and gleaming silver, tawny velvets and buttery soft leathers, and meticulously chosen artwork.

The leather-bound books in floor-to-ceiling bookshelves, the complex stereo system, the circular bar with its fine crystal and exotic liqueurs, the bronze winged Pegasus, the exquisite alabaster sculpture of a man and woman embracing, this luxurious apartment lost in the clouds now veiling the windows—my Nathaniel? I had not suspected this love of sybaritic splendor. It seemed set apart from the man I'd met in a meadow, and the simple cottage we shared. I supposed I had considered it a reflection of his character, for this complex, multifaceted Nathaniel was a surprise to me.

A lovely surprise, but dismaying, too. Like any normal woman, I wanted total possession of the man I loved. How could I possibly feel I possessed this man, or even knew him, for that matter? I grabbed his face and kissed him so fiercely my lips stung. And when he whispered my name, I knew we'd known each other forever.

That night we dined high atop one of the city's tall buildings. Nathaniel in a dinner jacket had the potent effect of straight tequila on my womanly senses. We sipped champagne, we kissed, we danced for hours. Eyes followed us, envious eyes, yearning eyes. For our love was visible, implicit in every look, every touch, in our faces as he held me in close embrace and we moved languidly to the strains of some soft, unknown melody.

It was an enchanted evening, worth any price. But none was exacted. It was given to us like a magnificent Christmas gift.

My sense of time passing had never been so acute. It made me sad, wistful, ragingly eager to taste and savor every moment of being with Nathaniel. When we arrived back at the cottage the following afternoon, he called Liz and Matt and invited them to dinner.

Of course we had to go to the market for supplies. By the time we finished, I had decided he was the most passionate man I'd ever known. Not just sexually: what-

ever his pleasure, he lustily enjoyed it. Every time I
mentioned something I liked, it went into the basket
along with his pet likes. Soon we had a selection of
cheeses and wines that would do justice to a gourmet's
kitchen. From there we drove to a fruit and vegetable
stand and bought some beautiful melons. Valley-grown
lettuces, yellow and orange tomatoes, and pearly green
onions finished our marketing. Feeling fabulously rich,
we hurried home to begin preparing our feast.

We both cooked, cleaned up, set the table with the
new placemats and napkins I'd bought him at the market (with his money, but my intent was good). I snapped
pictures with abandon, using an entire roll of film just
on the preparation of, and the subsequent demolishing
of, our stupendously successful dinner.

Afterwards, we ordered up a splendid sunset and took
our guests to the deck for raspberry liqueurs. Liz was a
vision in flowing chiffon the color of the sparkling cider
she sipped. She sat beside Matt and I cuddled into a
lounger with Nathaniel for some small talk, peace and
quiet.

But not for long. Liz suddenly bolted up from her
chair with a surprised look and a startled gasp. The gasp
escalated into outraged words. "Sonofagun! I've wet all
over my dress! And your chair—ah, jeez, I'm sorry, Nathaniel—oh hell!" she wailed as the river continued
flowing down the chair and onto the floor.

"Omigod!" My screech joined hers just a second later
as I, too, bolted from my chair. "Liz, you're not—Nathaniel, that's amniotic fluid, her water's broken! Liz,
are you having pains?"

"No . . . well, sort of an ache, all through dinner, in
fact. Real low, about here." She spread a pretty hand
across her lower abdomen and stared confusedly, then
fearfully, then delightedly, at me. "Amniotic fluid?
Roseanna, I'm having a baby!"

Everyone else panicked, including me. After a wild
ten-mile ride down a curvy, narrow road, we reached
the hospital still four in number, thank God.

Liz refused to allow Matt in the delivery room, seeing

her all yucky and sweaty. After all, it wasn't as if they were married.

Minutes crawled into hours, which crept into years. Matt paced through another layer of linoleum. I took Nathaniel's hand and held it, smiling at him, delighted to be sharing this splendid thing with my love. What if I hadn't returned when I did? I'd have missed this grand and often hilarious night.

At twelve-forty, a doctor-looking person appeared in the doorway wearing greens and a stupefied look. "Mr. Chance?" she wearily inquired.

"Ah, no, that is, I'm, uh . . ." Matt replied.

"Oh, hell!" Nathaniel snorted. "Yes, we're all Chances! What? What is it?"

The woman shook her head. Matt instantly went insane. "Oh God, she's dead, Liz is dead, she didn't make it—why did you let her die? Why didn't you do something, why didn't you—"

"Mr. Chance," the woman said, removing his hands from her green coat. "Mrs. Chance is fine. You have a daughter—"

"Oh, thank God!" Matt cried.

"You also have a son—"

"Lord!" Nathaniel whispered.

"And another daughter."

Silence reigned supreme. The woman nodded kindly. "Triplets," she said.

Matt made an odd little sound and sank gracefully to the floor.

It was two A.M. when Nathaniel and I finally got to bed.

It was a little after seven when Matt called to rehash the prior night, mourn Liz's lost belly, and tell us he was going home and get some sleep.

We, on the other hand, were now wide awake. So we decided to have breakfast and go visit Liz.

Nathaniel heated some sweet rolls with a honey-and-cream sauce, which smelled and tasted heavenly combined with aromatic Maui coffee. For a bite or two, a sip or two. Then my stomach rebelled. Rushing to the bathroom, I made it just in time to retch and heave dramatically.

Nathaniel insisted I see a doctor.

"I don't need a doctor, I've always had a bit of a stomach problem." Which is true; that's where my body stores the residue of negative emotions. "Just stress," I dismissed it.

He disagreed, but I obviously felt so much better after my cola-and-toast routine that he grudgingly let the matter drop. While I showered he cleaned the kitchen instead of the other way around, and we left for the hospital.

Liz was sitting up in bed, looking like a madonna in her white gown and that beautiful, satisfied, obscenely smug smile. Her gaze caught mine in feminine communion.

"Triplets, Roseanna!" she chortled. "Hello, Nate!"

"Hello, lady of the year. Heck, lady of the *century*!" He leaned down and kissed her apple cheeks. "You look gorgeous. We may have to bury Matt," he informed her. We laughed together as he related Matt's dejection concerning the demise of her magnificent belly.

"Roseanna suggested he might make you another one," he said.

"Darn, Roseanna, you got it in for me or something?" she groaned.

The drab little room was mellow with love and laughter. A huge vase of yellow roses sat beside her bed. In unconscious esteem, Nathaniel took one from the arrangement and handed it to Liz. "To you, little mama," he said.

She blushed prettily. As we talked she held the long-stemmed rose to her lips and I couldn't decide which was lovelier, Liz or the flower.

Nathaniel left to get some coffee. I settled into a chair beside her bed and we replayed the hilarious drive to the hospital. Apparently she was feeling wonderful. Giving birth to three babies was a snap of fingers for Liz.

What she was going to *do* with three babies was given the same light concern. "I'll just love 'em. Besides, there's Matt."

"Is there Matt? They're not his babies," I gently reminded.

"No, they're not, but I'm his Liz and the babies come with the territory. Anyway, I could get along all right if he decides otherwise. Matt sent Daddy a telegram this morning, so all hell should be breaking loose on the homefront right about now," she said with an impish grin. Imagining that stiff parental shock, I joined her in a rich round of laughter.

The babies' names were Matthew, Lacey, and Elizabeth Roseann, to be called Rose. "Lacey is my grandmother's name, I've always adored it and her, too. And Elizabeth Roseann is the best—hopefully—of you and me. Well?"

I brushed at my eyes. "Lovely names. Which is which? The girls, I mean?"

"I reversed it. Lacy is the blond and Rose is the dark-haired one. Roseanna, I'm famous! Had reporters from all the local papers trying to get in this morning—everyone's agog! God, I can't wait to get them home."

"Oh, Liz! Goodness gracious, have you any idea of what awaits you? I remember when I came home with—" I stopped.

"Oh, I'll have help, of course," Liz said smoothly. "Daddy can just fork over some more money. After all, they're his only grandchildren." She dropped her gaze. "Roseanna, I'm not a nosy person. At least, I don't think so. But I am open-minded, and maybe even a bit credulous. Daddy was fond of saying that if someone walked up to me and told me they knew how to fly by just flapping their arms, I'd stare in wide-eyed wonder and beg them to teach me. Maybe he's right, because I. . . ."

She gave me a tiny smile. "I believe your story, Roseanna. That is, I believe it could happen . . . maybe even that it did happen. Matt does, too. Believes that it's possible, I mean. So I—I just wanted you to know that Matt and I, well, we're your friends. And always will be, no matter what. I love you, Roseanna, and I love Nate, too. It's that simple." Her dimples flashed neon bright. "Like me, huh."

Measuringly, I studied her. Then I relaxed. "Yes, it's that simple, Liz. And it is a true story. You remember that I told you I didn't know the why or how of it?" I spread my hands in a helpless gesture. "It just simply happened."

"Are you going to stay here with him?" she asked softly.

"God, I don't know, I—oh, Liz, I love him so much, so very much! But to desert my own world . . . it would be treachery of the worst sort, a betrayal that I just don't think I'm capable of. Yet, to give up Nathaniel would be death itself." I shook my head. "As you might have guessed, I exist in utter confusion." I twisted the ring I still wore. "Look, honey, I'd really prefer you not speak of this. I'd hate for it to leak out," I said nervously.

"Well of course it won't leak out. You know Matt and I wouldn't blab your secret. It does baffle me, though, how Nate can stand knowing you're just a—a visitor here and how transient your love is. He's such a proud man, not one to take what scraps you give him. I'm not being cruel, honey, I'm just trying to understand, that's all."

"If you do understand it, any of it, would you tell Nathaniel and me? We certainly haven't had much luck sorting it out."

I sat up and assumed a brisk air to vanquish the threat of tears. "Enough about me. Let's talk about those fabulous babies of yours. Really, Liz, three at once? Wasn't that a trifle ostentatious?"

When Nathaniel rejoined us, he took me, not to the car but to a clinic that abutted the hospital. Because of her fondness for Nathaniel, the pleasant-faced senior citizen who ran the place had graciously agreed to slip me into the doctor's busy schedule.

I was annoyed, but since we were here, being ushered into an examining room without delay, I went along with it. It would be entertaining, I thought, to see Nathaniel fill out the information sheet she brought along.

He answered her questions with an aplomb that tickled me, never actually lying, but skirting devilishly far from the truth.

Then they left, and the doctor, gnomish, bald, and sharp-eyed, came in with a younger nurse. We discussed my very minor symptoms. I peed in a teeny little cup for him and another nurse bore it off like an offering to the gods.

As instructed, I hoisted myself on the paper-wreathed table and endured some poking in my midsection. I lay perfectly still while an unfamiliar instrument was passed over my belly and held there while pictures were generated on a screen off to my right. I couldn't actually see the pictures but from his comments I assumed that was what transpired during those few moments.

Empty-handed, the nurse returned, and conferred privately with the doctor. I put on my clothes and followed her to his office.

We both sat down. He read his chart, grunted a couple of times.

Then he told me I was pregnant.

Chapter · 19

I knew that my high, startled laugh was an inappropriate response, and the doctor's expression confirmed it.

"I beg your pardon. What did you say?" I asked.

"I said you're pregnant. Eight weeks, in fact."

He looked quite stern and spoke with authority. But I simply did not believe him. "I'm sorry, Doctor, but that's impossible," I said easily. "I'm too . . . that is, uh, well, actually, I can't have children, you see."

"Whether it's good news or bad news, I don't know, but you *can* have children, Miss Bently. And you are pregnant. Do you want to know what it is?"

"Human, I hope," I said, absurdly light and gay. Actually I was numb. He frowned, and I decided to humor him. "Okay, what is it?"

"A girl. Perfectly normal and healthy, too. I foresee no problems."

Another laugh gnawed at my throat. I cleared it. "You can tell all that from that short examination?"

Of course he could. The clinic's technology was very up-to-date. "Well." Avoiding his quizzical gaze, I stood up and extended my hand. "Thank you, Doctor. Oh, you are not to tell anyone else about this, of course."

"If you're thinking of aborting, we have facilities for counseling, as well as an adoption agency right here on the premises."

"My goodness, no! I'm just going to. . . ." I drew a deep, deep breath. "Nathaniel isn't to know because he's not involved in this. It's really none of his business," I asserted.

Accepting this—since he was given no other options —the doctor segued into prenatal care and I shook my head, my voice rising. "You're not going to be my doctor, so don't worry about it. Not that you're not a perfectly nice doctor, but I'm not from here, you see, I'm from . . . quite some distance away."

With the aid of another deep breath, my voice strengthened to empower my command. "I'll tell Nathaniel I've got a touch of summer flu or something like that. Naturally I expect you to respect my wishes in this matter."

"Naturally." He wrote out a prescription. "These capsules will quiet your nausea. Take two immediately upon rising until this passes." He stood up and took my hand. "I wish you luck, Miss Bently."

I thanked him and hurried back to Nathaniel. "See, I told you it was just a tummy upset," I chided. "Let's get this prescription filled, then go have lunch. I'm starving!"

It wasn't until that night, when we were lying in bed in concealing darkness that I let my thoughts loose to fly about the room like confused bats. Using willpower as a net, I gathered them in and calmed them down, sifting through the turmoil until I could make sense of my feelings.

I still couldn't believe I was pregnant. I was menopausal and that in itself protected me. Granted, I wasn't very well informed on the subject. Still, I felt fairly confident of my conclusion.

And even if by some crazy chance I really *was* pregnant, it was only as long as I was here with Nathaniel. All sorts of strange things happened in this world. My Earth, however, was sane and logical.

A little girl, he'd said. I immediately thought of Lexi and the wedding I was presumably planning right this minute. From there my mind wandered through the past, all the way back to her first day of kindergarten. She had clung to me so fearfully and I'd wanted to kill that unsympathetic teacher who'd pried her tiny arms from my neck.

Swallowing over the lump in my throat, I reminded myself that she didn't need me to defend her, not anymore. But who would plan her wedding, help choose her dress, find the perfect shoes, select the flowers, if not me? Who would weep all those maternal tears? Tears I felt clogging my nose, even now, for who would rock her babies, if not me?

But what about *my* little girl? If she did exist, if I really was carrying Nathaniel's child. . . .

I backed away from the thought. It was just too far-fetched. Surely there was still a middle-aged body hidden in this smooth, supple skin? Didn't it simply mask all those years?

But still, a little girl. Imagine. . . .

I suppose I did sleep. Yet I saw the pink of dawn glaze the windows and gradually become soft white light. Turning onto my side, I watched my love's face with the kind of pleasure that aches something deep inside.

Had we, during this lovely week, laid the foundation of a lasting relationship?

Or had we just been two lovers playing house?

Eventually he stirred, stretched and yawned himself toward wakefulness. Although I was troubled, I could not deny the simple joy of snuggling closer to him, feeling his instant response, which was to turn, and, with sweet naturalness, gather me into his arms.

"Good morning, Nathaniel," I murmured, allowing the timbre of my voice to expose the delight I took in his presence.

"Ummm, good morning, pretty thing." He yawned mightily. "Been awake long?"

"For awhile. I've been watching you sleep. Do you mind? It's a terrible invasion of privacy to watch someone sleep," I admitted.

"No, I don't mind. I do it quite often, you know."

"You watch me sleep?"

"Yes, love. I call it making memories, though, not invasion."

We lay close, talking in low voices befitting this soft

intimacy. Our bodies began to rouse as we touched. He buried his face in my hair and held me as if savoring the sensation.

"I could stay like this forever, just holding you, so warm and sweet in my arms . . . drowning in the smell of you, the feel of you against me. Sometimes in the night I wake up and touch you just to make sure you're there. And sometimes I want so much to wake you and love you, but you sleep too sweetly." His mouth touched my neck and left a mark before moving up to my ear. "Do you want to make love?"

His skin was so hot and smooth, I tried to get inside it with him. "I love your breasts," he said from the depths of them.

"I'm glad you don't call them tits. Or even worse, titties."

His laughing face raised to mine. "Umm, sometimes I do, but these are too lovely to describe that way. I love your belly, too . . . also your navel," he said, tasting it.

"Have you found anything you don't love?"

My impish query was rewarded with another husky laugh. "No, but I'll keep looking. Bound to be a flaw somewhere!"

"Huh. It's my turn now. Turn over, I want to kiss your back." Laughingly he obeyed, and I memorized, by taste and touch, every square inch of his body before my inquisitive need was satisfied.

Feeling swollen with woman-power, then and only then would I surrender to the fiery sweetness of mating.

The telephone jerked us from our soft drowse. Nathaniel answered, his grin widening as Liz's voice shrilled through the wire. She was home? I couldn't believe it! It had only been three days.

"That's not all you won't believe!" Nathaniel exulted, but more than that he would not say. After quick showers, we dressed, ate a hasty breakfast of bagels and coffee, and piled my suitcases in the truck.

Since I had so many new clothes, I didn't need the ones I'd brought with me. So I sent them "up" to my closet, made a quick check of my house and the date—right on target—and rejoined Nathaniel. Too late I remembered my camera was in the luggage. Not inclined to return for it, I decided I'd taken enough pictures for now.

The babies were still in the hospital, which was a good thing, because her little house was a wreck. Boxes sat everywhere, some sealed, some half empty. Matt fetched coffee and rolls. A jubilant Liz, looking luscious in yellow velour, bade us sit down and she'd tell us all about it.

First of all, yes, she was moving. Seems Daddy and Mummy Chance had flown into Serena to see for themselves the ghastly fact of not one, but three illegitimate grandchildren. They were appalled at practically everything: Lakeview, the three babies, the unrepentant Liz and glowering Matt, and especially the squalor in which their only daughter dwelled.

Daddy swung into action. Knowing Liz would not budge from the lake colony, he stalked through the small cluster of homes, and selected the one most appropriate for his errant offspring and his three (she'd had a *litter*, for God's sake) grandchildren.

That the house happened to be occupied was immaterial; it was a large two-story residence with four bedrooms, three baths, a screened veranda and a fenceable backyard. Ceiling fans cooled its airy rooms, and a monstrous attic fan sent a roaring current of air whipping through the upper hallway. Peeling paint, slumbering dogs and questionable stains on questionable carpets notwithstanding, the house had definite potential. Daddy said he'd take it.

The owner of the house was understandably reluctant to evict the present tenants on such short notice (Daddy wanted them out by tonight), but his protests just died away when offered a three-year lease at double the rent. The stunned tenants in turn swallowed their protests when Daddy dropped a stack of hundred-dollar bills on the three-legs-and-a-stick table, and suggested they start packing; the painters would arrive in the morning.

The power of money is astounding. Like faith, but a whole lot quicker, it can move mountains. And men. Within forty-eight hours the tenants were gone and a gaggle of plumbers, electricians, carpenters, and painters battled for territorial rights in the old house. When they withdrew, carpet-layers and furniture men moved into the void. Triplicates of everything known to be necessary to a baby's survival filled the large sunny nursery (formerly the master bedroom). The storage room held nothing but disposable diapers. The nurse recommended by Liz's doctor passed muster, along with a girl to fetch and carry, both to be semipermanent fixtures in the new house.

Serena and Lakeview were agog; Liz reeled, but not in surprise. She knew her Daddy.

Daddy and Mummy, satisfied that they had done their duty, fled Serena for their Palm Springs retreat to recuperate for a year or two.

While Liz related the magnificent feat Daddy had accomplished in less time than it took God to create land, I looked around this shabby little living room with a wistful pang. The new ecru, mauve, and seafoam green decor she'd described, while likely a feast of understated but powerfully good taste, just didn't sound like my Liz.

"Oh, don't worry," she said. "There's nothing like three kids to give a house that lived-in look. Doubtless little Matt will burp all over the new couch first thing," she said complacently.

How dear she was! I adored her, and Matt, too. What a superb mismatch, I thought, regarding the pair. She the gorgeous goldfinch and he the brown wren, quiet, self-effacing, not a shred of handsomeness or sex appeal, yet she loved him.

More importantly, they both loved Nathaniel.

"They're your friends, Nathaniel," I said softly, earnestly, when we had returned to the cottage. "They'll always be there for you, in case you need them. They know about me, you know."

"Yes, Matt and I talked about it. I answered his questions as best I could. Does that bother you, that they know?"

I'd been caressing his arm and my fingers stilled as I pondered his question. "Well, not bothered. Uneasy, maybe. That's two more people who know about me now."

"Three. I told Michael."

"You told your brother about me?"

"Yeah, during that week I spent in the City. He was passing through and we got together and, well, I was pretty damn low, Roseanna. All bollixed up but good. I needed to talk and he's a great listener."

Wide-eyed, I asked, "And he believed you?"

"Mike has placed no limits on his mind, so he's capable of belief," he said simply. "He was intrigued, to say the least. In fact, he'll be coming to visit us any day now." He grinned. "I can't imagine why he's so hot to meet you, but he is!"

"Well, I—I'll be glad to meet him, too, but now it's three people. I really think that's enough, don't you? I mean, I'd hate to be a freak show!" I laughed, but I was serious. The thought of what the press would do with me if they ever caught on to my eerie existence in Nathaniel's world was unnerving.

"I agree. But Mike's okay, and I'll speak to Matt tomorrow, make sure he realizes the danger . . . you smell so fuckin' good!" he said, voice thickening.

My body stirred, but my mind had its own agenda.

"What *would* they do if they found me out, Nathaniel? You have immigration laws, don't you? Would they deport me?"

He raised up on his arms. "Well, yeah, we have laws, but . . . deport you back to where?" he asked, beginning to laugh. "Be the first time in history a person ever got kicked off an entire world!"

Our laughter grew uproarous as we envisioned armed guards escorting me back to my boulder, and bidding me depart and never return. Would they station a guard at the boulder to enforce their order? I wondered aloud.

But the more I thought about what we'd said, the more serious it became. "Nathaniel, if I did stay with you," I said slowly, "wouldn't we really have those problems?"

"We'd find a way to resolve them." His voice was flat, and I realized I'd hurt him with my tenuous question.

I pulled his head to my breast and closed my eyes while my mind raced along at lightning speed sorting through pros and cons. I did love my Earthly home, the life I'd built for myself. But I could overcome that. David, too, was relatively unimportant. It was the other choice I had to make that ached my heart. I had to choose between my two daughters.

I saw it with such cruel clarity. With or without me, Lexi's life would still go on, but if I was pregnant (and why should that good doctor lie?) I'd have to stay here with Nathaniel to give *this* daughter life.

My decision made, I vented the hurt in a long, long sigh.

"Well, you'd better get busy finding a resolution, then," I told him. "Because I rather like your Earth and plan on living here on a permanent basis before too long."

He tensed, muscles knotting under my hands. When he spoke, his voice was unbearably gruff. "I'll take care of it, don't worry. Roseanna, you mean it?"

"Yes, I mean it. I can't say just when because I—I have matters to take care of at home before I become your wife," I said, inwardly shuddering as I acknowledged just what those *matters* were. I pushed at his shoulders until his head came up. "You were planning to marry me, weren't you?" I demanded suspiciously enough to ease his taut features.

"Yeah, I guess so. Liz would likely get out her shotgun if I didn't make an honest woman out of you— ouch, Roseanna, that's tender stuff there, you know!" he yelped, and we got into one of our wrestling matches, a shield to hide behind until we had mastered our quite devastating emotions.

He took my ring off, and solemnly swore to love, honor, and cherish me for all time to come, before slipping it back on my third finger, left hand. "You are now my wife.

"Well, not quite, Nathaniel. I don't see a preacher."

"Nevertheless, we're husband and wife . . . as soon as you promise to love, honor, and obey, of course."

"You really need this?" I asked very softly.

"I need it, babe, I really do. It'll do for now."

So, deeply affected by the vulnerability he made no effort to hide, I promised to love, honor and cherish him.

"You are my wife, as long as I shall live," he said.

"As long as I shall live," I repeated over the lump in my throat.

Then we consummated the union.

Was it different?

"Oh, yes," I whispered. "Wonderfully different."

I had kept mum about the baby. Even though I had to fight a fierce urge to tell him, I didn't. My decision to make his Earth my home was quite enough to cope with right now. The many complexities of it all kept assailing me even while we talked of where we'd live, here, or San Franscisco; and what kind of wedding we'd have; a small one, with his brother Michael officiating, and Liz, Matt, and Viveca as witnesses. . . .

"Omigod, Viveca!" I jumped up off the couch and strode to the window, staring blindly through the rain-streaked glass as I considered my beloved friend's opinion on what I planned to do.

"How can I possibly get along without my Viv? We're practically sisters!" Turning my head, I gazed at him through a blur of tears. "Sometimes the only reason each of us kept our sanity was because of the other! I wonder if she'd come with me? If I could persuade her to live here, would she be welcome?"

"Of course she would. Who knows, she might even take a fancy to Michael. Like me, he's quite a lady-killer," he warned, coming up behind me. His hands slid around my midriff, pulling me back against him. "Rose-anna, I know this is going to be difficult for you-"

"Yes, it is," I cut in sharply. "Do you have any idea, any idea at all, what I'm giving up to be with you?"

"Everything. Everything except the man you love."

"Yes."

My stark response evoked a sigh from him. "Regrets, already?"

"No, no regrets, but I get pissed off when you seem to take this lightly, Nathaniel."

"I don't take it lightly, I just can't stay down there in that slough of emotion for very long. It's too intense—it hurts, dammit!" His arms tightened. "I've assumed that you're divorced, but maybe not. Maybe there's someone else who loves you, someone who's going to lose something he'll have a helluva time living without," he said roughly.

Turning to face him, I replied with an inner sigh, "No, darling, no one who can't get along without me."

"I'm glad to hear that. I'd hate to think I'd messed up some poor bastard's life. But your daughter, tell me about her, so I'll know what to expect. Will she resent leaving all her friends?"

I groaned. Why must everything be so complicated!

"Nathaniel, I've allowed you to assume certain things that are incorrect, about my daughter, I mean," I said a little stiffly. "She's not a child, she's an adult. A brilliant attorney, in fact, engaged to another brilliant attorney."

His eyebrows shot up. "She's an adult? An *attorney*?"

I flushed. "Yes, well, she's my stepdaughter, you see."

"I see," he said, none too convincingly. "But you love her."

"Yes. She means a lot to me." Resolute, I met his watchful gaze. "But our child means more."

The silence hummed, taut with questions that were answered by the expressions on our faces. His registered disbelief, wary of believing, the possibility of belief, and then, a great, joyous gulp of belief that encompassed his entire face.

"Our child?" He drew a shuddery breath. "Oh, God!" He exhaled it and caught me in his arms. "Roseanna, you're—"

"Pregnant. I don't have a touch of summer flu, I have morning sickness," I said thinly. My heart was beating fast and light, and I simply could not draw enough air. I had made no conscious decision to tell him; the time just seemed right. "I didn't tell you because I . . . well, it's just such a tremendous thing that I had to absorb it first. Are you pleased, my love?"

"My God, am I pleased, she asks?" With a sound somewhere between a laugh and a groan, he caught me close and lifted me off the floor. "Yes, I'm pleased, oh yes, I'm wonderfully pleased, Roseanna. *My* Roseanna," he finished in a rasp of triumph.

"Because it ties me down, clips my wings so to speak?" I asked, forcibly light.

"Yes, that, too. I crave security as much as the next man. But to know I'm going to be a father—I'll be a great one, you know, just an absolutely incredible father! We'll go fishing, boating—I'll teach him to ski, of course—"

"Her."

"Her? It's a girl? I'll have a daughter? Now that's scary, that's really scary. What about boys? And dating? No makeup until she's sixteen, Roseanna, I'm firm about that. But we'll still go fishing, boating. I'll have to get a bigger boat! What'll we name her? When will she be here? We'll have to buy a house; that apartment won't do. And this place is too small . . . unless we remodel it. . . . I'm babbling, aren't I?"

He was. But he was also riding an incomparable high and I wasn't about to diminish his pleasure.

My own shivery excitement was tinged with fear at the very magnitude of my life change.

Relationships do sour, Rosie.

I know, I answered Viveca's remembered warning. *But if you love, you must trust. And I do love.*

The die was cast, I told myself. I was totally committed to this earth, this time, this man and our baby.

I was in no hurry to return Sunday. In fact, I didn't even fret about the time difference. It had come down to only a matter of hours now, anyway. If I was a little late, no one would care. It was Matt's birthday and we were having a fabulous cookout this evening, with the whole colony invited.

I'd leave after that, I told Nathaniel. Just thinking about confronting my family chilled my soul. Reminding myself to focus solely on the present—to live in the now —as Liz said, kept my laughter light and ready.

We helped cook and set up tables. Then we returned to the cottage to dress in our finery, a pretty frock for me, a voluminous white poet's shirt and black cords for him.

Neither of us had wanted to spend precious time going into town for a gift, yet I wanted very much to give Matt something. I had become exceedingly fond of the quiet little man.

Suddenly I remembered the rod and reel I'd bought for the gardener's birthday. This gift would require only a quick trip through light-years of space, rather than the five-mile trip to Lakeview. When I told Nathaniel, he indulgently agreed to escort me to the boulder and wait while I fetched it.

We walked across the meadow hand in hand, with Carasel racing hither and yon in frantic enjoyment of whatever it is dogs enjoy. She forged ahead of us through knee-high grasses like a ship through a foaming sea.

Nathaniel was rather feverish himself, ill-put to contain his personal joy and satisfaction. We stopped to kiss, to hug, to laugh. His shirt had three buttons unfastened at the throat and I tugged at the dark curls wisping through the gap. Placing sweet, moist kisses right there was a singing pleasure.

As for me, I was acutely aware of everything around me, my senses fine-tuned to my environment as well as to the man. Near the boulder there was a lark singing in piercingly sweet voice, and I looked around until I located it on the slender limb of a sapling just beyond the gray stone. Its joy seemed to match the explosive happiness racing through our veins like some fine old wine, heady, delicious, utterly impossible to contain, or express. Lingering apprehensions drained away, leaving my heart light and sure. In time I'd learn to love this world. In time, I told myself fiercely, it would assume all the beautiful connotations of the word "home."

We kissed again, taking our time to enjoy it. Kissing Nathaniel was not something to rush through.

"Back in two minutes," I said.

He patted my bottom, then squeezed it for good measure. "Two minutes, darlin'."

When I stepped into the passage, Carasel romped in

with me, and we arrived together in my closet. Skirting my luggage, I hastened downstairs to the coat closet where I'd stashed the rod and reel. Matt liked fishing and he'd enjoy this, I thought.

The rod was tall, and kept hitting against the bannister as I rushed back upstairs. I had insisted the salesman assemble it for me; I detest getting things in bits and pieces. Half impaled on the handle of the blasted thing, I scrambled into the closet, knocking against the door frame, the shelf and the wall with the tip of the rod.

One of the walls I knocked against was the wall beside my shelf.

Uncomprehending, I struck it with the metal tip, listening to the tap-tap-tap, not yet believing . . . refusing to believe.

The tip slid slowly down the wall . . . down . . . still hitting solid plaster, while I watched, frozen in the grip of something indescribable. And then it went through the pale glimmer of wall, but at this point, the rod was level with my knees.

Still confused, I released it, letting my gift fall into the space, and disappear. In fearfully slow motion, I stretched out a trembling hand and felt for the passage.

"No!" My deep, atavistic cry denied even as my mind did. No, this was not happening, could not be happening, the wall was not, *could not* be there!

But it was. There was less than two feet of empty space from the floor to where solid wall began.

The door was closing between our worlds.

Chapter 20

$\mathcal{M}$y agonized scream ricocheted around the small room. Carasel put her front feet on my leg and whined her distress, but I could not respond. I was engaged in a desperate struggle with an irresistible force.

Flattening both hands against the wall, I shoved upward with all my might. Even as my fingers hooked around the plaster's edge, I felt a gentle but inexorable pressure, as another inch of space closed between my love and me.

"No! No, oh no, God no, please don't, please don't, please!" I was screaming, frenziedly hammering on the wall, crying aloud to whatever controlled this abominable force barring me from Nathaniel. The pain of it! The hot, slashing, furious pain of trying to stop something that mocked my raging efforts by gently, gently, descending! I went a little mad then, alternately cursing and praying; pleading and crying and down-on-my-knees begging.

And all the while, the closure continued.

Up until this point, I have always thought the most difficult experience I have survived was the morning Dr. Wagner stood before me in the blue and white nursery saying, "Roseanna, give him to me now. The baby is dead, you must let him go now," and I backed against the wall holding my baby with fiercely denying arms. He was swaddled in a soft blue blanket, I remember, and even through that blanket I could feel the total absence of warmth. And then David was there, holding out his arms and saying in an utterly indescribable voice, "Give him to me, Roseanna, give my son to me," and I released the tiny body of our son into his hands.

It had been at that precise moment that my baby had really died, and I had instantly accepted it. There was no way not to, not with David standing there staring at me with those eyes from hell.

And now, as my fingers touched the gritty edge of the wall and measured the small space that was all that remained of the passage to Nathaniel's world, I accepted it on the instant and began functioning again.

Nathaniel was so vulnerable, he needed to know—he *must* know that this was not my doing. There must not be a shred of doubt left to torment him. No sooner had the thought flashed across my mind than I scrambled to my feet and ran to my desk for paper and pen. Knowing I was in a race with time, I wrote without regard to coherence or punctuation. The entire letter was an agonized cry from my heart.

"My beloved, the passage is closing between us. I must hurry—I must not give into—oh, Nathaniel I love you I love you I love you! Darling, darling, I'm so sorry, so sorry, our baby—how can I bear this double grief! There are so many things I want to say, but I don't have time. But then I don't have to say them, you know them, don't you, my only love? Because we are one forever—*forever*, Nathaniel—oh God, I love you! The passage is so small now. Darling, you know I am weeping, you know I am dying inside, you know I love you with an agony too terrible to bear! Why we met, I don't know—if we'll meet again, I don't know—but I do know this. I thank God with every breath that we did meet and love and between us created that beautiful symbol of our love, your daughter. Oh God, why couldn't you have known your child!"

Wiping tears with my shoulder, I checked the passage again. About eight inches . . . quickly I finished the letter.

"Beloved, I am sending down pen and paper for your reply. We have time for this last communication. *God has to give us this!* Please, my love, oh please don't regret a single minute of our time together. I know you will be in agony and, Oh God, that hurts, that hurts. I feel your pain as my own. Don't worry about me, Viveca will take care of me. I won't say good-bye, I'll just say until we meet again. I love you, Nathaniel Knight, and I will wear your ring for the rest of my life. Your wife in spirit, Roseanna Bently Knight."

It was an awful letter, maudlin, hysterical, blotched with tears, the paper torn by my frantic haste. I dropped it, along with pen and paper, into the passage.

Then I waited. Holding myself in tight restraint, I waited.

Imagining his anguish, imagining his face as he read it, feeling his pain with my own heart, I waited.

I was being torn apart from the inside out.

Carasel licked at my tears and that rough little tongue provoked a long, keening cry from me. I imagined I heard a corresponding cry crossing space and arrowing into my innermost self. Was it only imagination? No, I decided. I heard that cry with other than the normal sense of hearing. I had *felt* that cry!

Minutes stretched into eternities, exquisitely long and painful, filling my heart with aching suspense. I was on my knees, keeping a hand in the passage to prevent its closing before I received his reply. I would lose that hand before I permitted it to close, I vowed through clenched teeth. That door *would not close* before Nathaniel answered me!

Eons passed in slow, languid motion. I was suspended in limbo.

The letter was suddenly just there, floating gently into my hand.

"My beloved Roseanna—oh my darling, thank you! Thank you for managing to say good-bye, thank you for loving me, for giving me the sweet pleasure of knowing our love created a child! You can't imagine how I feel about that—oh yes, you know, don't you, my own! So many things to say! But no time, and you know them already. Only one of importance, I will love you always, Roseanna, as I have since the day I found you in my meadow. And no, sweetheart, I regret nothing—noth-

ing! I'm almighty glad we met and loved. I will miss you
with an intolerable ache, I will die a little each time I
remember, yet I will live because I remember. We will
meet again, never doubt it. I don't know whether it will
be here in the meadow or in some other world, but *we
will meet again,* now goddamn it, we *will*! Until then, I
love you. And our baby. And Carasel. I must send this,
God, I don't want to send this, you will be gone—Roseanna, I love you! Nathaniel."

I folded the paper and slid it into a shoe. My tears
were wetting the paper and it was too precious to permit
even one word to be erased. Carasel whined harder as
she sensed my deep anguish of soul. Still on my knees, I
caught her face and looked into her age-clouded eyes,
remembering what he'd written. *I love you. And Carasel.*

"Oh, Carasel, I love you, but he does, too," I whispered. "And you love him. You love Nathaniel, don't
you?" The tiny stub of tail wagged in riotous agreement
at his name.

I felt the passage again. It was barely wide enough,
but she would fit. But how could I bear to lose her too! I
stood up and grabbed my velvet cape. It smelled faintly
of my perfume. Rubbing the soft fabric against my
cheek, I wet it with my tears, then slipped it into the
opening. A silly gesture, perhaps, but he would know its
meaning.

I held Carasel to my chest and kissed her, accepted
the little red tongue's moist kisses in return. " 'Bye,
Carasel, love him for me, take care of him for me."
Gently, I slipped her through the narrow space. She
yelped once, and then I was alone in my closet.

I imagined it. I saw him walk across the meadow,
holding my ridiculous cape, his shoulders hunched under the burden of pain.

I imagined it; Carasel, finding herself at the boulder,
began barking, and I saw him turn, seeing her, knowing
instantly what a sacrifice I'd made. Solaced by it, running to meet her—my Nathaniel, my Carasel, together,
a symbol of—what? I could go no further in my im-
agery, and it ended with Carasel wrapped in his strong
arms, his tears mingling with mine in her silky fur.

For a fleeting time I was sustained by that beautiful inner vision. Then the hell of anguish broke loose in killing force.

They were gone! My Nathaniel, my love; Carasel, my constant companion, gone from me—oh, Jesus, it hurt! I was weeping wildly, my keening cries the sounds of an animal in ghastly pain. Nathaniel and Carasel; my heart torn from me and carried across a meadow under an alien sun, a meadow from which I had been barred.

My fingers were still in the passage, still fiercely resisting its progress. But they were being slowly forced down, down . . . and then, there was only solid wall.

The passage was closed.

Green-gold eyes, the color of spring leaves in sunlight. A smile curving his beautiful mouth, dark hair springing over his brow. "Roseanna," he whispers, his voice deepening in that special way. . . .

But I could not hear that whisper now. My closet wall was only a white plaster wall.

The cry that tore from my throat was wild and primitive. Memories flowed through my mind in endless succession and I was caught in the throes of a grief too awesome to be borne.

Mindlessly, half-mad, wrapping my arms around my knees, I rocked and cried in loud, wailing lament, letting the anguish pour from my heart in jagged clots of pain.

At last I could cry aloud no more. So I simply held myself, rocking with soft, whimpering moans as madness and images blurred into a single, tuneless dirge.

It was the pain of death, come again. A tiny, blackhaired son with eyes the color of brown velvet, lying motionless in his crib . . . unresponsive to my glad greeting . . . cold to the touch. I remembered it, relived it all, the fear, the rising anxiety, the keening cry shredding a summer morning.

The horror of that long-ago day blended with this one: death come again.

Nathaniel, oh my Nathaniel, my love, my heart. Gone. Gone *where*? I had a stone on my baby's grave, something I could touch, something that said, "Here lies an

enormous piece of my heart." But for Nathaniel I had
only memories. . . .

When David came home, he found me sitting in my
closet wrapped in my arms, rocking gently back and
forth, mourning in soft whimpers. His voice buzzed
around my ears, but did not penetrate a mind that was
not in his world, but that roamed far beyond the sun.

He carried me to bed and I knew I was in my bed, but
I was *not*. When he tried to tear my arms from around
me, I resisted mightily. I needed those arms around me!
Without them I would shatter into pieces and I fought
the hands which would tear them away and leave me
vulnerable to unspeakable desolation.

He said my name over and over, his voice growing
sharper and sharper. Gradually it penetrated, and I
looked up into anxious brown eyes. "Roseanna, what is
it? What's wrong? Roseanna! Tell me," he kept saying,
shaking me when I hit out at him.

"Carasel . . . Carasel!" I whispered hoarsely. That
was the only answer I could give him.

"Ah, God. I'm sorry, Roseanna. How did it happen?"

I blinked at his question. What on earth was he talking about? Oh, of course, I thought wearily, he assumed
Carasel was dead. I shut my eyes and curled up in a fetal
knot. Let him assume, then. It didn't matter.

That shattering weeping began again. It tore at me; I
felt the rending and fully expected to bleed from the
knives carving up my soft inner self. David was forcing
brandy down my throat, setting it on fire, and I struck
out in wild rage.

"Leave me alone! Go away and leave me alone!" I
screamed. God, I hated him! Of course I didn't, but I
had to focus this explosive rage on something, and since
God was beyond my reach, David was that something.

He left the bedroom. I curled up in my knot of isola-
tion, withdrawing into a black circle no one could enter.

"Roseanna, you've got to stop this. All right, you're
grieving, but you're going to make yourself ill." He was
back, trying to lift me up, to hold me, all the time saying
I had to get ahold of myself, I was making myself sick.

I didn't want his comfort—I loathed his sensible logic! But he was stronger and I was forced into his arms, held against his chest. At once I quit fighting and went limp, so ravaged with grief I couldn't think straight. When he released me, I turned away and sought my defensive curl again.

Then Viveca was there, sitting on the side of the bed, her hand gentle in my hair. "Roseanna, what's wrong, darling?"

When I heard that dear, familiar voice, the voice of one who would understand, I grabbed her like a person going down for the third time. David was standing behind her, so I could not tell her outright.

But I looked into her eyes and said, "She's gone, Viv, Carasel's gone. It's over. I can't get through anymore!"

Comprehension filled her eyes. "Oh, love, I'm so sorry. It's all right, I'm here now. I'll take care of you," she whispered.

I heard her talking to David about taking me home with her for the night, explaining this excess of grief as best she could, reassuring him, caressing my hair as she spoke.

David's baffled eyes rested on my face for a moment, then he sighed and nodded. All this grief for a dog, those eyes said.

But he was gentle with me, helping me downstairs, into Viveca's car. "Poor David, to have missed so much and not even know it," I said sadly, and started crying again.

Viveca maintained her silence on the drive. I simply huddled against the seat and cried. I don't remember getting to her house. We were just suddenly in her bedroom, and she was undressing me and putting a gown on my unresisting body. I watched her from a great, glassy distance.

"All right, darling, tell me," she said softly, and I came apart in my friend's arms.

A long time later I managed to smile for Viveca even though I felt raw and sore inside and out. She did look relieved. But sadly, I wasn't finished yet.

"I haven't told you the worst part yet, or maybe the

best part, I don't know. Oh, Viv, I was pregnant—I was
going to have Nathaniel's baby! On his world I was
young, you know, fully capable of bearing children. The
doctor said so!"

I didn't hear her reply for my tears welled up again
from an apparently inexhaustable source. They grew
into racking sobs that shook me like savage hands as I
told her about my lost little girl. Both of us took it for
granted that she existed only on his world.

Viveca held me until at last I was totally drained and
exhausted. "Sleep now, darling, I'm here, right here," I
heard her murmur from a far distance. A black velvet
cloud was pressing down on me, a smothery sensation,
but I welcomed it.

Viveca understood, I thought, dimly comforted. She
knew I was grieving for more than a beloved little dog.
In all the world, only Viveca knew I was in deep mourning.

"Viv, I love you," I said, or perhaps only thought it.
The cloud descended and I wove myself into its dark
folds . . .

*The darkness vanished, to be replaced with soft, golden
light, and I was drifting through it, splashing through its
radiance, insubstantial as thistledown. I looked back from
a great distance and saw Viveca holding the tightly curled
body of Roseanna like an infant in her arms. Both were
infants, I thought tenderly, for I was filled with an ancient
wisdom which has no name, which just Is.*

*Then they were left behind as I soared upwards, into a
familiar realm, a familiar place. Liz and Matt's little cottage, I thought, filled with joy to be here again.*

*Liz and Matt were in the kitchen when Nathaniel burst
into the house. The gay smile of greeting was wiped from
her face by the expression on his. He was burdened with
Carasel, a fishing rod, a velvet cape, and a sheet of paper.
Bewildered, she stared at this odd assemblage. Matt shot to
his feet as she questioned, "Nathaniel?"*

*"Here, this is for you, from Roseanna, a birthday gift.
She had to get you a birthday gift," Nathaniel said, thrust-
ing the rod at Matt. When Carasel gave a complaining*

yelp, he clutched her tighter to his chest, and held out my letter.

Liz took it. Her low moan mingled with Matt's groan as they read it together.

"Oh, Nate, oh, God, I'm sorry, so sorry," Liz said. She turned into Matt's arms and wept. Nathaniel stepped up to the two in an agony of need, and their arms reached out to gather him in. After a moment, she sat him down on the couch and nestled beside him, holding him as he wept.

"She's gone, Liz, she's gone!" he cried.

"I know, I know, darling," Liz crooned.

It went on and on, his raw, ragged voice, and her soft, sweet, soothing croon. Matt sat in his own anguish, as did I, wanting to help, incapable of helping. He didn't know what to do. Neither did I, for they could neither see nor hear me, nor did my touch make any impression. I could only watch.

Suddenly the door burst open and a tall man much like Nathaniel in appearance hurried into the room. His rugged face was carved with far more lines of experience, and I knew immediately this was his brother Michael.

Nathaniel turned in surprise. "Michael! How come you to be here, now, at this moment?"

"I just felt an urge to come, Nate. What's happened?"

Michael's attractive face was bleakly impassive as he took the outthrust letter and read it. Only the tightly clenched jaw gave evidence of his pain. When a harsh, choked sound came from Nathaniel's lowered head, Michael gathered his brother in his arms. "Let it out, Nate," he said gently, and held him as Nathaniel cried the deep, wrenching sobs of a man in great pain.

Placing a hand on his shaking shoulder, Liz stared helplessly into Matt's wet eyes.

"She's gone, Michael and I need her. I need her, goddamn it!" Nathaniel raged. "And I'll never see her again, never hold her again—why? Goddamn it, I want to know why!"

"Nathaniel, why do you say that? What makes you think you won't see her again?" Michael asked gently.

"Because I won't! Don't give me a bunch of crap, Michael!" Nathaniel bitterly rebuked.

He leaped to his feet and strode to the window. Liz glanced from his rigid back to Michael's hurting face with a little whimper of despair.

"Nate, listen to me," Michael began urgently.

"Don't you preach at me, damn you! You and your God —He took her from me, He—oh, God damn Him, God damn Him!" Nathaniel ranted, the ludicrous image of God damning God lost in his chaotic fury.

"But He gave her to you in the first place, didn't He?" Michael countered.

"Damn you, Michael!" Nathaniel exploded in impotent fury.

I could read his thoughts, feel his feelings. The muscles of his neck stood out like thick cords as he clenched his fists with his ravening need to hit something or someone.

"Don't you see, you blind fool?" he shouted. "She wasn't just a woman, she was my wife, my beloved wife! Even though we didn't get around to making it legal, she was mine. She wore my ring, dammit! And He had no right, no right! to take away my wife, my child—oh, Christ, I'd like to—keep your hands off me, Michael," he warned as his brother stretched out a hand in appeal. The hand dropped before those blazing green eyes.

"Nate, don't, please, don't," Liz said softly.

"Liz, just—just stay out of this? Just leave me alone," Nathaniel grated. He wheeled to the window again.

He's like a wounded animal that will bite the hand that dare gives aid, Michael thought. He was neither insulted nor outraged at the words hurled at him by his brother; they were only howls of grief and loss.

"Liz, do you have some wine?" Michael abruptly asked. At her nod, he smiled. "All right then, would you get it, honey? And bring four of those paper cups, please? We're going to celebrate."

Nathaniel swung around in disbelief. "Celebrate! What in God's name are we celebrating?"

"Many things, Nate. The first being the sustaining power of hope. Did you ever stop to think what hell a man's life would be if he was denied the existence of hope?" Michael smiled at Liz as she opened the wine and poured four glasses. "Next, we're celebrating the marvelous fact that we

were all given the pleasure of knowing and loving Roseanna. Mine was vicarious, shared with me by my brother,
but it certainly brought joy into my life. Even with the pain
we feel right now, does anyone regret meeting our pretty
little Roseanna?"

Nathaniel lowered his head as he remembered my plea.
"Don't forget, please don't ever regret, a single moment
we've spent together. . . ." But he could not yet give up
his sustaining rage.

"Personally, I wouldn't have missed it for the world!"
Liz said. Smiling through tears, she handed round the
wine.

When they all held glasses, Michael lifted his and
sipped. "Very good, Liz," he approved. Glancing at Nathaniel's stony countenance, he chided, "Nathaniel, this is
a joyous occasion."

"Joyous!" Nathaniel shook his head in weary amazement.

"Yes, dammit, joyous! Read that letter again. My God,
she's carrying your child. Have you forgotten?"

"I'm not likely to forget that," Nathaniel said with a
bleak smile.

"You are so blessed, my brother. You know the joy, the
delight, the sweetness, of a great and passionate love,
something few of us have ever or will ever, experience. Just
one night of such love must be priceless. I've never known
it, and I wish to God I had. I envied you, Nathaniel, I
envied you every time I watched you say her name. To feel
so deeply! To share such a profound experience, such joy,
such happiness! Men would sell their souls to have what
you do."

"What I did," Nathaniel corrected in grim reminder.

"What you do. Does love die the instant a loved one
vanishes from sight?" Michael retorted. "Now lift your
glass and drink to that love, Nathaniel, or you're the big-
gest fool in the world, this one, or Roseanna's."

"To Roseanna and Nate," Liz ventured. A real smile
was her reward as Nathaniel met her eyes with a softening
of his countenance.

"And to the conception of Nate's child," Michael said
softly. He raised his glass in a salute that was just a touch

defiant. "Let's drink to the daughter of my brother, Nate, and to his wife-in-heart, Roseanna," he continued. "Let us drink to the product of their love, and perhaps, the reason for it."

It was morning, a confusion of sunlight and shadows and haunting-echoes morning. I sat up in bed with the cry of a bewildered child.

Viveca moved swiftly across the room, a breakfast tray in her hands. "Good morning, honey. Here, some juice and coffee, and some of those kolaches you love so."

"My ring, where's my ring?" I cried, suddenly frantic at its possible loss.

"I put it up for you, last night, when you fell asleep."

"Oh, thank you, I was afraid . . . oh God, Viv, last night I went back and I—Viv, he was so hurt, so hurt! Nathaniel was crying, can you imagine David crying?" I asked incredulously, proudly. "But Nathaniel was. Oh, and Michael was there! Yes, I met Nathaniel's brother! Well, I didn't exactly meet him, but I saw him, and, Viv, he's beautiful, like Nathaniel, only older! And he said. . . ."

What had Michael said? It was fading, fading. . . . I stared at Viveca's pale face. "They were all sad, but Michael said it was a joyous occasion and they were to be happy. Because of the baby, you see, they were drinking wine and toasting Nathaniel and me." What else had he said? "I can't remember anymore," I ended in tearful desolation.

"It's all right, love. Here, drink your juice, you'll feel better soon," Viveca replied soothingly.

Hurt and angered by her refusal to say what I needed so desperately to hear, I caught her hand. The splash of cold liquid made no impression on my embattled senses. "Don't talk to me like that! I tell you, I saw him—I was *there*! It was real, truly it was. But I can't remember . . . oh, Viv, it's fading and I can't remember!" I wailed.

Methodically she began blotting up the juice I'd

spilled on her expensive coverlet. "Roseanna, it was a dream, and dreams do fade upon awakening."

"It wasn't a dream, I was there, I tell you! I was there. . . ." Massaging my aching temples, I lowered my head against her sweet, tolerant smile. Sunlight hurt my eyes and confusion swirled in dizzying eddies in and around my mind. What was real and what was illusion?

"Drink your coffee, honey," she said.

"It wasn't a dream," I stubbornly repeated.

But then again, maybe it was.

It was August, or maybe September. Days were simply to get through, nights just long, aching hours in which to remember and stifle my sobs lest David hear.

He slept down the hall most of the time. I didn't care. I had withdrawn from him, although to be truthful, he didn't seem to notice. I didn't care. In fact, I didn't care about much of anything. Except the closed-up space between my wall and shelf, of course. That I cared about, that I checked every morning upon awakening and every night before sleeping. The only thing it got me was another deluge of hot, choking tears.

My other abiding interest was the pictures I had taken on Nathaniel's world. Viveca had the film developed, reporting that the developer was mystified by the peculiar blurring effect on each and every picture, as if the objects I'd photographed had, background and all, been moving, and moving in sync.

"I didn't tell him where they were taken," she had said with deliciously dry humor.

Even though blurred, these pictures were an enormous help to me, both as balm to my wounds, and insurance for my sanity. I wasn't crazy, it *did* happen; I had pictures to prove it.

Turning onto my side, I read the luminous face of my alarm clock; four-fourteen, still dark outside, and raining. I heard a car drive by, and the *whack!* of the newspaper hitting the driveway. I might as well get up and work some more, I thought tiredly. It had been Viveca who started me writing again, by saying simply, "Write your story, Roseanna. Give it a happy ending, for both of us," she'd added with a wry, gentle smile.

So I did, plunging into the task with fierce gratitude for its thought-blocking escape from reality. Driving me was the fear that I would forget, and I couldn't bear to lose even the smallest memory of Nathaniel's world.

Yawning, I stretched, feeling tired and apathetic.

A strangled breath later I was sitting up in bed, my heart hammering so violently it jarred my chest! Something had moved deep inside me, a curious, fluttering something, something alien.

I blew out a breath in quick, fiery annoyance. "Just a gas bubble, you idiot," I muttered in harsh rebuke. I'd had lasagna for dinner last night and it always disagreed with me.

The movement came again, light as the touch of a butterfly wing, something tickling my belly from the inside.

Idiocy or not, the effect that soft movement had on me was startling enough to bring me out of bed. I knew it was nothing; my menstrual cycle was still all screwed up and I'd lost weight instead of gaining. In fact, I was rather gaunt at the moment, just two huge blue eyes in a small, pale face. For I had felt the loss of this child just as much as I had the others. It might have occurred under different circumstances, but the bottom line was, I'd still lost a baby. Both my appetite and my will to live had been severely damaged by this new trauma.

Swinging my legs to the floor, I shuffled my feet into house slippers and walked to the bathroom. Its bright light and mirrored walls made me wince as I pulled off my gown. Standing there, reflected from three sides, I was baldly exposed. For the first time in weeks I scrutinized my body from head to toe.

True, I hadn't gained weight. But the subtle rounding of my body was shocking evidence that *something* was happening. I could see my sharp hipbones, but there was that firm little belly suspended between. Turning sideways revealed a thickened midriff and full, if pendulous, breasts. My heart was skipping beats, making me breathless as I considered the reason why.

Could I still be pregnant? I wondered incredulously.

No, impossible! At my age? I was nearly half a century old, my reproduction system was a wreck.

And yet something was altering my body.

I pulled on my gown, walked out of the bathroom, through the bedroom and down the stairs. Icy sweat dampened my nightgown. In the den I lay down on the couch in a curl of limbs, shivering.

When David came downstairs, I was asleep. He was full of concern and questions, as well as a reminder of our flight to Austin this afternoon. Evading him, I went back upstairs to bed, uncaring of whatever plans he'd made for us.

At ten I awakened again, and it was a flash flood roaring out of the deep of night. I was pregnant.

Standing in the shower under icy needles of water cleared my head somewhat. I could be jumping to conclusions; goodness yes, wasn't David always on my case for taking those flying leaps from suspicion to fact without a qualm?

Never mind that I'm right most of the time, this is one conclusion that's going to be checked out, I thought grimly. All my pregnancies had been difficult, and I'd been a young woman then. Wrapping myself in a towel, I dug out my old address book, and the number of Dr. Wagner's clinic.

He had long since retired, but a new member of the staff would be glad to see me—say three o'clock Friday?

"A week from now? I'd be a basket case by then," I snapped. "Today, and as early as possible. It's an emergency."

I supposed I sounded desperate enough; if I arrived in the next half hour, they would manage to work me in before noon.

"I'll be there in fifteen minutes," I said.

"Just go with the nurse and we'll take a look-see," the youthful doctor said with a cheery smile . . . smirk? I followed the nurse's broad, white-clad hips, undressed when she said so, put on the inadequate paper gown she handed me and got up on the table. She left the room and I studied the gleaming instruments on the table. I felt so *abandoned*. And cold—damn but it was cold in this twentieth-century torture chamber.

"Alrighty!" the doctor said, opening the door. "Let's see what we've got here."

"What we've got here is a middle-aged woman who's freezing her ass off, Doctor," I snapped, something I wouldn't have dared do ten years ago. But this gangly, red-headed oaf annoyed me.

He chuckled. "Yes, well, just put your feet in the stirrups. . . ."

God, I hated the indignity of this wide open position. Feet in stirrups, sheet covering my belly and knees, I watched the shaggy male head disappear between my legs, felt the probe of icy steel and rubber-gloved fingers, wondered, as I'd always done, just what the hell a man thinks of while he's doing this.

I squirmed, and squirmed again. His fingers were rough and they hurt, goddamn it! "No, no, you're not hurting, just get through with it, will you?" I snarled at the eyes which popped up between my knees. "Do you think it's possible that in another century or so your profession will have developed a more humane method of examining a woman?" I asked, remembering my painless, much more dignified examination in another doctor's office.

Eons later, the nurse said, "You may get dressed now," and handed me a tissue. My vagina dripped K-Y Jelly, and one tissue cannot cope with the mess, yet that's all they ever give you. Muttering opinions of this and various other things, I grabbed a handful and cleaned myself, then got dressed and followed her to the inner sanctum.

For the second time this summer I sat in a doctor's office and listened to him turn my life upside down.

There was no longer a shred of doubt. I was still very much pregnant.

Chapter 21

The doctor said he wasn't concerned about this pregnancy.

I looked at this blind masculinity with fury. It didn't help that I was old enough to be his mother. "Of course you're not concerned. You're not having this baby, I am. And *I'm* concerned, you idiot! I suggest you call Dr. Wagner and confer with him about my pregnancies, at least request my past records."

"But you said you hadn't been here before, Mrs. Bently," he protested, rightfully, I conceded.

"My name is Roseanna Bently Tait. I've been Dr. Wagner's patient for years. Check with him. I'll call you in a day or so and then we'll see."

Rising, I stalked out of his office. "Smug little bastard," I muttered as I strode past the nurse.

Inside I was shaking, stumbling along in a daze, unable to cope with this mass of contradictions named Roseanna Tait.

I didn't want this baby! I wanted it with a passion!

I was horrified. I was elated.

The complications! Oh, God, the *complications*! My head reeled when I thought of all this pregnancy entailed.

Although concerned about myself, I was even more concerned about those who loved me. With stiletto ferocity, questions kept stabbing me. What would Lexi say? How would our friends react? And most important of all, how would David take it? He would be the father of another man's son! I ran a stop sign on that one.

In private, I cried, I prayed, I cried some more.

In public, even for an audience of one, I smiled and coped as I'd always done.

I told no one, not even Viveca, the only one likely to take it calmly and commiserate with me. And, God, did I need commiseration!

And I wasn't speaking to God.

Day rolled into night, night into day, and I rode my emotional roller coaster by hanging on with tooth and nail. At night I felt smothered, as though a great weight was pressing me into a darkness too terrifying to examine. I wept, for Nathaniel, for David, for myself, and this incredible web in which we'd become entangled.

Contrarily, when I imagined holding Nathaniel's daughter in my arms, my heart sang in notes far above my mental turmoil.

But imagining the look on David's face when I told him I was pregnant transformed it into such an *appalling* thing!

The shock of it kept leaping out and attacking me when I least expected it.

I am pregnant.

The fact gained substance until it was seemingly a single-minded entity that would insinuate itself into the most common of thoughts. I think I'll work at the gift shop today *and I am pregnant.*

David wants me to meet him at Tony's for dinner with Tweedledee and this dress has a stain on it, dammit, *and I am pregnant.*

Finally I could contain it no longer. "Viv, help!" I said, half laughing, half crying, when I dropped by her house a week or so later. "I'm sorry I've been such a witch lately, I really am, but I just—" Gulping a breath, I blurted, "Viv, I'm pregnant! I'm going to have Nathaniel's baby, in early January or thereabouts."

The words were visible slaps on her whitening face, and for a moment we were two frightened women faced with something too big for us to handle. "But I thought it wasn't possible here, I thought you were . . . well, that you couldn't!"

"I know, I know. I thought so, too. But it's confirmed, Viv," I said tiredly. "And I don't know what to do about it."

"Oh damn, Rosie! I don't know how much more of this I can take! I've felt like I've been squatting on the edge of a live volcano all summer, and now this?"

"Well, I don't know how much more I can take, either, Viv. Son of a *bitch*! I'm so screwed up I can't see straight!"

"Well, you are that," she drawled.

I stared at her, at the twitch of mouth and slant of eyes, and the laughter came, shattering walls, cleansing foul little clots of self-pity and bitterness, weaving us into a warm embrace that empowered as well as comforted.

"So. Whatcha gonna do, darlin'?" she asked, bringing me rather abruptly back to my earth.

"Tell David, of course."

"Tell him what?"

Impaled upon that question, I lost my breath to its painful simplicity. The easy way out, of course, would be to let him think it was his baby. And weakling that I am, it was tempting, I admitted to Viveca. "I'm so scared, Viv, so damned scared! I feel like a knocked-up teenager! Stupid, huh?"

"How about just human? It's a two-pronged dilemma, seems to me: whether to have the baby, and then if you do, whether or not to tell David it isn't his. I'm here for you, Rosie, you know that. But this is one decision I refuse to take part in. You'll have to decide all by yourself."

"The first part is moot: of course I'm having this baby. But the second part. . . ." I squared my shoulders. "Well, that's an 'of course,' too, Viv," I said with steel-magnolia resolve.

My resolve weakened as I drove home. There was no hurry, I didn't have to do it tonight. . . . Coward! *Always do what's right, Roseanna, and you'll avoid hell's terrible torment.* More motherly advice. But wrong, I reflected. For surely this is a small taste of hell I'm experiencing right now. And what did I do to deserve it? I wasn't a bad person when I was alive, not really. . . .

When I was alive. The thought held me enrapt as I remembered an eternity ago, lying beside Nathaniel, cuddling into his hard, warm body, watching his face as he slept.

Have you been awake long, love? Yes, I've been watching you sleep, do you mind? No, darling, I do that quite often.

Ragged echoes of words from a sweet, haunting long ago, another lifetime ago, on another world. The pain swelled into a torrent of seething need and funneled into a wild shout of his name that beat against my lips.

Breathing hard, I concentrated on driving. Memories of Mother sprang to mind: the eternal discord between us, her anxiety-tinged love for David, the pride she took in Lexi. Recalling the last time I saw her alive could still make my heart ache. She was ancient, but not from the passage of time. A stroke had robbed my mother of all her elegant, natural dignity. She had lingered for weeks, kept alive by those monstrous, life-forcing machines. I hated them with a scalding virulence; how could you call this living! She didn't speak or eat or smile or love. She simply existed.

Now and then her eyes would open and fasten on me like leeches, wanting something, always wanting something, which I of course could not give her. But that was the functioning extent of the shrunken thing lying there in her stark white bed. That's what she was, a *thing,* and even the doctor admitted she would never be more than this. Her death, when it finally came, was a razor-edged blessing.

And the very same thing could happen to me.

I shivered, recalling the doctor's warning when my blood pressure sky-rocketed during my last weeks of pregnancy.

But I hadn't died, I reminded myself sharply, I hadn't been felled like a strong tree by the axe-blade of a stroke. I'd had my baby then and I would have this one now. With or without David.

And very likely without, I allowed myself to admit. That stony Tait pride would never tolerate a wifely affair, much less the fact that I was carrying another man's child.

Although it was not yet five o'clock, David's car was in the garage. My nerves tightened. What was he doing home this early?

Mims met me at the kitchen door. "The mister came in around three. He's in a mood," she warned. "Nearly bit my head off when I said we were out of ice. Icemaker's broke," she added succinctly, and hurried out the door to her own car.

Silence, thick and heavy, settled around me. As I approached David's study, apprehension knotted my stomach. God, I dreaded confronting him! Knowing he was in a foul mood certainly didn't help. I felt brittle as glass and nearly as breakable. But it had to be done. Shoulders back, chin up, a reasonable facsimile of courageous woman, I tapped on the door and entered his private domain.

David was sitting in his swivel chair, his feet propped up on his desk and his hands folded behind his neck. An open bottle of Scotch stood on his desk. The only light was a small, gooseneck lamp. Its radiance gleamed on his smooth hair, but left his face in shadow.

"I hate to interrupt, but I need to talk to you," I began.

"Good timing, Roseanna," he cut in. "Really good timing." His laugh was ugly, grating. "Given half a chance, you could screw up a two-car funeral with that sense of timing."

"I—I don't understand," I said nervously.

"Yes, you do." Very slowly his hands left his neck to refill the glass sitting beside a photograph of Lexi and me taken years ago, when she was little and I was a wide-eyed innocent. "But *I* don't understand," he said bitterly. "I don't understand a goddamned thing."

Baffled, I watched him dispatch the whiskey in one

hard swallow. "Look, if this isn't a good time, if you'd rather I wait—"

A fist slammed down on the desk. "I'd *rather* you get out of here, Roseanna. Just get out of here and leave me the fucking hell alone!" Straightening, a simple act that revealed his struggle to retain his habitual control, he splashed more liquor into his glass. "But there's nothing to be gained by delaying the inevitable, is there? So, who is he, Roseanna? Whose little bastard are you carrying? Anyone I know?"

His words, combined with the impact of tortured brown eyes blazing into mine, threw me into stammering confusion. "No, no one you know, but how do you, I mean—"

"How do I know it's not mine? Because it can't be mine," he intoned. "Because I've had a vasectomy, Roseanna."

Shocked beyond expression, I stood frozen as his words rolled over me, flattening me, leaving me scalded with disbelief, and then, even worse, far, far worse, with belief.

"You did that? You did that to me?" The next question almost gagged me. "When?"

"Right after we buried Davey," he said flatly.

"Oh God, you couldn't," I said, clutching my arms as I tried to grasp the enormity of his betrayal. "You couldn't do something like that!" But he had, and to know that he was capable of such cruelty overwhelmed me. "All those years I wanted another child, tried to give you another child, *ached* to give you, and you. . . ." I couldn't finish.

"Goddamn it, don't you look at me like that! *I'm* the wronged one here, I'm the one who's hurting! I've done nothing to you!"

"Oh, but you did, you did," I whispered, holding myself with a little, rocking sway. "Why, David, *why*? Why on earth would you do such a terrible thing?"

"What I did is not the issue here!"

"Oh yes it is. For now, it is. I asked you why."

His face came into the light, his features sharpened as if by knifepoint. His voice had the timbre of ground glass as he lashed out at me. "Because I had to, dammit! For my own self-preservation, if nothing else! We'd buried three babies, and yet there you were, fresh from that last funeral, babbling about how we'd have another one—"

"For you, not for me! I'd have done anything to wipe that dreadful look from your eyes, even risk another pregnancy!"

"My son barely cold in his grave—all my dreams, all my plans, my hopes for the future, shoveled into that hole with him!" he exploded. "I was half crazy with grief and pain, out of my head with the hurt, and you thought putting me through that hell again would solve our problems? Christ! I couldn't take that risk, I knew how persuasive you could be!"

"You had a vasectomy because you were afraid I would persuade you to. . . ." I shook my head to clear it. "To what, David?"

"To trust you with another baby."

I felt as if he'd stabbed me. "Trust me? *Trust me?*" My voice rose despite my efforts. "Good, God, David, listen to yourself! Our son's death wasn't due to neglect, it was respiratory malfunction, you know that!"

"A perfectly healthy baby died for no apparent cause, that's what I know!"

He drew himself up, visibly fighting to keep his composure. So important to him, I thought, fighting a similar battle.

Blinking at tears, I said dully, "And you blame me for that. All these years you've made me the scapegoat for your disappointment, made me carry the guilt, as if I *let* it happen, as if I just stood there and watched him die." My hands clenched into nail-clawing fists. "Well, no more, David. No more guilt, no more wondering what I could have done differently. This twisted reasoning is your problem, not mine, not any longer."

"My, aren't we getting assertive!" With a short, hard laugh, he wheeled from me, and lurched sideways.

I caught his arm. "Are you drunk?"

"God, I wish I was." Jerking free, he dragged a hand across his face. "Let's get back to the subject, shall we?

Which is *this* baby, and what you're going to do about it."

"How did you know I was pregnant?" I asked quietly.

"Old Dr. Wagner called my office this afternoon. Seems your devoted doctor is worried that you're not taking your condition seriously enough."

Sighing, I sank down on the leather couch. "David, I'm sorry you had to hear it that way. Believe me, I didn't intend this."

"I'm sure you didn't. But as I told Wagner, there's no problem, because you will abort the little bastard. Of course I didn't use that particular phrase, but still, let's call a spade a spade."

"And let's call a toad a toad!" I jumped to my feet on my hiss of outrage. "If you think I'm aborting this baby, you're dead wrong, David!"

"I don't think, I know."

"No! No, I want this baby." I swept out my hands in appeal. "It wasn't the way you think, David, not just an affair, this was different, totally outside the norm! If you knew what really happened, if you understood the—"

"I understand perfectly! My wife was out whoring around and got caught." He dragged in a breath. "And now you expect me to raise the result of your deception? You tear my heart out and I'm to go right on *living*? What the hell do you think I am, a robot? No feelings, no pride, just . . . I'm a man, goddamn it!"

He stopped, obviously at a loss, and hating it. He looked old, suddenly, and my heart wrenched. Moving with care, he sat down behind his desk. "But I'm a man who can compromise."

"Compromise?" I wet my lips. "What do you mean?"

"You get rid of the baby; we go on as before."

"W-what?" I croaked, wondering if I'd heard him correctly over my thudding heartbeat. "We go on as *before*?"

"Yes." He refilled his glass. "No divorce. I know you're surprised, certainly I have ample grounds, but—"

"But you can't afford a scandal," I said on a note of discovery. "If this got out you'd be a laughingstock, wouldn't you, David? Certainly not someone to be taken seriously by the local 'good ole boys.'"

His mouth twisted. "You find that funny?"

"No," I said, sighing, "I don't find any of this funny. I apologize for what I've done to you, I really do, even though I think you bear a share of the blame. I was starving for affection—"

"I'm not interested in hearing why, or how, or when and where!" He inhaled, and moderated his tone to brusque reason. "I need a wife, so we'll stay together. However, I will move into my own suite, which will give us both some breathing space. After you . . . after this is over, nothing more will be said about it, either inside or outside this house. We'll simply forget it and go on with our lives."

Now beyond mere astonishment, I stared at him.

He swiveled in his chair, presenting me with his rigid back. "My continued tolerance is contingent upon two absolute conditions: you will never see the man again or ever mention his name to me; and you *will* get rid of his baby. That's all I have to say on the subject."

"Well, it's not all I have to say," I snapped, then shrank back as he shot to his feet with ferocious speed.

"For God's sake, Roseanna, how much more of this do you think I can take!" he grated.

"David, please, I can feel your pain. I know you're hurting. So am I. But we can't just leave it like this."

"The hell we can't!" Swinging past me, he strode from the room and slammed the door so hard a picture fell off the wall.

I suppose David slept at his club that night. At any rate, he didn't return after he tore out of the house. I cried myself to sleep and woke up at dawn feeling completely drained of energy. Finding myself alone when I came downstairs was a welcome respite from combat. Regardless of what he thought, or perhaps just hoped, nothing was settled between us.

I fixed the icemaker by unsticking its little metal arm, and wondered why no one else ever thinks of doing that.

Apparently I made coffee, for I was sitting at the

kitchen table with a steaming cup in hand. I felt suspended, distanced from the normality of routine.
Thoughts swirled around my mind like rabid bats, mad-
deningly persistent. To stay sane, I walled them off and
went upstairs to work on my manuscript.

Viveca came in around four. I poured us cups of incredibly strong coffee and joined her at the kitchen table.

"So what's happened?" old X-ray eyes asked.

I gave her a verbatim account of my confrontation
with David. She looked appalled, then confused, then
furious as she chose which side to take.

"That lowdown bastard! What does he think you are,
some kind of doormat for him to wipe his holier-than-
thou feet on!" she exploded. "I assume you told him to
go screw himself?"

"He slammed out before I got a chance to tell him
much of anything," I said wryly. "But he'll probably be
home tonight, so. . . ." I shrugged, knowing I wasn't
fooling anyone, not even myself. Just contemplating another hateful scene with David made writhing snakes of
my nerves.

"Oh, Rosie." Viveca squeezed my hands. "As much
as I'd like to drown you in my wisdom, this is another
one of those times you'll have to go it alone. But you
can do it, honey. Just stay cool. And remember, love,
I'm here if you need me." Rising, she glanced at her
watch. "Well, I have to run, got a counseling session
tonight. Doesn't that sound impressive?" she asked
lightly.

In recent weeks, Viveca's analyst, delighted by her
recovery from what he termed over-forty-divorce
trauma, had enlisted her help in establishing a therapy
center for emotionally traumatized women. "Women in
shock," he called them. According to the good doctor,
knowing firsthand the formless fears and anxieties which
afflicted a woman after a traumatic experience of any
kind was a valuable tool in helping her regain control of
her life.

Although Viveca downgraded her talents, she was secretly proud of her efforts, and I was proud of her for trying, whether or not she succeeded.

"It doesn't just sound impressive, it is impressive," I stated. "You are doubtless a genius."

"I am doubtless not. I'm simply a woman who can now say to other women, 'Listen, you are *not* stupid, you are *not* tomorrow's garbage, by God, *you* are *you*.' Remember that, Rosie," she commanded. "By God, you are *you*."

"By God, I am I," I said obediently. "Now if we could only figure out what this me is! See you later, love."

"Later." She hugged me fiercely. "Call me if you need me?"

"Don't I always?" Laughing, I waved her on her way, then collapsed in a puddle of tears.

When I'd dried out, I went outside to the deck to sit and think, something I always do better when looking at nature. That David blamed me for our baby's death wasn't all that surprising; in my secret heart I'd always known he'd held me accountable even though he never said so. Maybe I even accepted the guilt, I reflected. Maybe that's why I'd hung on so long, even after our union had become a mockery of the lovely thing it once had been.

But a practical mockery, I thought with strengthening irony. David still considered me useful in some ways.

I heard his car drive in. The snakes were back in my stomach, alive and writhing. I glanced toward the heavens.

"By God, I am *I*, and don't You forget it!" I muttered to whatever lay behind that bright blue sky. Then I went inside to finish this charade once and for all.

I watched him walk into the den, so familiar in his well-tailored three-piece suit, barbered and tonsured to perfection. And yet, such a stranger, I thought sadly. A stranger I had once loved and who had loved me. My throat tightened until I had to force words through it.

"We need to talk," I said before he could escape to his study. "Sit down, please."

'Roseanna, I just came in, for God's sake. I'm hot and tired and in no mood to talk."

"Just sit down and let's get this over with, please? Or stand if you want, it won't take long. I'll keep it simple."

He set down his briefcase, then stood waiting with exaggerated patience.

I drew a steadying breath. "It's over, David. We can't continue with this mockery of a marriage any longer."

"This mockery of a marriage has served its purpose for years; I see no reason why it can't continue doing so," he said arrogantly, and, I sensed, a little nervously, too.

"It doesn't serve *my* purpose. It never has, not really. I tried, I truly did, David. Because I loved you I hung in there, even after it died between us," I said, grimacing. "But that's not important. Who hurt who, who's right and who's wrong, none of that's important anymore. Because I'm through trying. I want a divorce."

"No. That's my last word on it, Roseanna."

Just that flat declaration.

"Then let me put it this way. You can either give me a divorce, or read all about *my* suit in the newspaper, complete with details. I don't want to do that, I'd rather keep this cordial. But I—David, you don't want me, let me go!" I cried, breaking down despite my resolve. "And let me go in peace!"

"I can't let you go, I. . . ." David savaged his face, tried a laugh. "Christ, Roseanna, I've been married to you for so long I don't know how *not* to be married to you!"

I didn't respond.

"Look, let's try being sensible? You know you can't have this baby."

"I know nothing of the sort. And God willing, I will have this child, David."

"That's just plain stupid! Having a child at your age is not only dangerous, it's ridiculous. Have you given that any thought at all?" he asked incredulously. "For God's sake, you're old enough to be its grandmother! And if you'd look at life realistically instead of romanticizing everything, you'd realize that, even if you did by some miracle bear another child, your life would be a nightmare. Because when push comes to shove, you're hopelessly outgunned, Roseanna. You can't do it. You know that and I know that. There's no way you can even hope to make it without me."

"The hell I can't! I've got money, money I've saved and some from Mother's estate, and if that isn't enough I can earn more! I don't want your help, your money, *or* your advice!" I calmed myself, grabbed for some steel-magnolia courage. "Now try taking my advice for a change and contact your lawyer. Because I'm seeing mine tomorrow. So I think you'd better pack up and leave. We are through. Finished, David. Kaput. At least I am."

"Shut up." he said, his face mottling. "Just shut your mouth and keep it shut! I won't take this from you, goddamn it!"

He stepped closer. Knees trembling, I held my ground.

"It's settled, David. I don't care what you say or do, I'm through—Oh!" My statement ended in a sharp cry as his hand slashed my cheek.

The scene became surrealistic. Stumbling backwards, I grabbed the arm of a chair to stop my fall. My hip hit the end table and a lamp overturned and crashed to the floor, bringing down a large flower arrangement with it. Both the ceramic lamp base and Mother's lusterware vase shattered. The sound seemed to ring on and on in my ears.

"Roseanna, oh my God, my God." Slowly David lowered his hand and looked at it, then at me, and the hand I flung to my cheek.

Our breathing was harsh in the tranquil room, as if battling for a dwindling air supply. Shocked at how ugly this had turned, we stared at each other over the ruins of our marriage, our love, our friendship.

My eyes were running, my nose was running, my cheek flaming from his furious blow. Trying desperately to regain my dignity, I stood up, head held high and painfully stiff.

"Get out, please," I said, dead level.

His mouth worked, but no words came. Turning on

his heel, he walked out of our house, and I closed the door behind him with quiet, bleak finality.

The next day David left for good. To my amazement, it was not an acrimonious parting; indeed, it was all done in a smashingly civilized manner. Regardless of his other faults, David was not a violent man. My swollen cheek obviously pained him.

"I'm sorry for that," he said tersely. "I don't know what came over me." He took my hands. "Roseanna, we've acted in such haste. Maybe we ought to give ourselves some time to think about this. Do we really want to call it quits after all these years? Are our problems so insurmountable?"

"I don't know, are they?" I said quietly. "It's me and my baby, David. Or it's nothing at all."

He released my hands. "Dammit, you know I can't deal with that. Raise another man's child? No." He shook his head. "No."

"I raised another woman's child," I reminded him.

"That was an entirely different situation, you know that."

"Yes, I do know that. So." I gave a graceful little shrug. "End of discussion."

"So it seems. Well, I'll be in touch." His mouth twisted in that familiar way. "Or, rather, your lawyer will be in touch with mine, I should say. Good-bye, Roseanna, take care."

And I said, "Yes, I will. Good-bye, David."

He raised his hand before backing from the drive, and I waved back. Had there ever, in all of recorded history, been a more pleasantly conducted parting?

I closed the door and leaned against its cool, solid surface. He was gone and he wouldn't be back, ever. The thought splintered something deep inside me.

During the following week I felt locked in a frozen inner landscape too fragile to dare probe its icy recesses. My first hurdle was Lexi, and I dreaded talking to her.

But I needn't have fretted, I thought ironically. David had already explained things to her. My heart clenched like a fist as I looked into her lovely face. Naturally she was hurt and bewildered. She was also filled to over-flowing with righteous outrage. I winced, dreading the inevitable explosion.

Accusations and questions began spewing from her pretty mouth before I'd even sat down. How could I do this to David? To her, to our friends, our family? How was she going to explain my behavior to her fiancé? And to her fiancé's *family,* for God's sake!

"What on earth will they think of us! His mother's so aristocratic, such a *lady*! When she hears about this . . . I can't believe you'd shame us like this, Mother! I just can not believe it!" she raged, quietly, for I'd arranged to meet her in a restaurant. "That you'd behave like a—a common slut is beyond comprehension!"

"Lexi, that's enough," I said, suddenly fed up with being pummeled. "I have never in my life behaved like a common anything. This was not an ordinary affair. I loved the man. I still do."

"You're not thinking of marrying him!"

"No, sweetie, I'm not thinking of remarriage. I just want to be left alone, to raise my baby and try to find some small measure of contentment."

"I can't believe that you'd even *consider* having this baby. It's beyond comprehension!" she said, looking as incredulous as she sounded. "That you could do this to us, that you could hurt Daddy so! Don't we mean anything to you? Or at least me—have you stopped loving me, too?"

"Of course I haven't stopped loving you. Dammit, Lexi, I'm hurting, too. This hasn't been easy for me, either, you know!"

I subsided as I looked into her wounded dark eyes. She would never forgive me for hurting her father, or for humiliating him, whatever. "I'm sorry, darling, but I can't undo what's been done. As much as I love you—and I do love you—I can't change any of it."

"Yes, you can," she leaned close to say. "You can get rid of that man's baby! Or not," she amended swiftly as I shook my head. "I mean, if abortion is against your beliefs, then okay, we can handle that. You can go away somewhere, have the baby and put it up for adoption without anyone being the wiser. Daddy would accept that."

"No, love," I said, gently, for she looked so stricken.

"Then we're back to the other. There's simply no other choice," she said firmly. "Good God, Mother, even to think of having a baby at your age is ludicrous! And dangerous—isn't it dangerous? Of course it is. And then to insist on a divorce, right when Daddy's getting ready to run for mayor? No. You just can't do that. And you can*not* have this baby!"

"I'm sorry, darling, but I can. And I am. Please believe me when I say this is not some vile conspiracy to sabotage your father's political career," I said, bleak-humored. "So. Am I still involved in your wedding?"

"No! No, I . . . I'm sorry, Mother, but I just can't cope with this. There's Daddy to consider, and anyway Clark thinks perhaps we should just have a simple wedding performed in the judge's chambers, avoid the hassle of a big affair. Neither of us really has the time to spare, we're both so busy."

"Oh, shit, Lexi, you don't have to make excuses. We're two adults here. Live your life as you please, sweetheart," I said wearily. "All I want is for you to be happy."

Later that week, wearing a simple black suit and wraparound sunglasses, I met with David's attorney. We hammered out an agreement—my house, furniture, and car; his stocks, bonds, and investments.

That evening I took a walk, down the winding paths I'd strolled so often with Carasel. My chest hurt as memories assaulted me.

I thought of David and the good years.

I recalled the times Lexi and I had walked this path and the talks we'd had, the dreams, fears, and hopes we shared.

In endless succession the years unrolled in my mind. Oblivious to dampness, I sat down on a mossy log and cried.

So simply does a marriage end.

Chapter 22

November drizzled out with a series of gray, rainy days embellished by chilling winds. I was housebound, orders of my new doctor, a bright, sensitive woman who monitored my pregnancy with weekly visits and curtailed most of my activities. I couldn't drive, I couldn't do housework (not a great loss, but still), I couldn't stand on my feet for any length of time.

So I sat at my computer and wrote, hour after hour, a fictitious tale of nonfiction that acted as a cathartic on my depressed system. For a little while, at least, I transcended time, space, and pain.

Mims the maid, eyebrows atilt, nasal twang intensified, was a daily now. I still did not much like her and she still intimidated me, but circumstance had forced us into a relationship of sorts.

She had left me some homemade vegetable soup, which I dutifully ate. Then I showered. Then, hopeful and yearning, I padded to the closet, my arm extended, fingers reaching to check the door to my Paradise Lost. Just rough plaster under my fingertips. I swore, a potent mix of outrage and naked plea, both futile.

Jerking a nightgown over my head, I crawled into bed and pulled up the covers, an action that should and please-God-would, precede deep, obliterating slumber.

It's after midnight and I'm wide awake. Despite my almost ravening desire for peace of mind, my brain still runs its ceaseless treadmill.

This big house is empty except for me. I'm not afraid, just miserably tired and restive. And lonely. Oh God, am I lonely! A bone-deep loneliness that will not be appeased by those whose lives brush mine. Lexi still has her cinnamon stick as a companion. David is living in one of those snazzy high-rises near the park, a much-sought-after man-about-town, according to our local society columnist. I, of course, have ceased existing. Ex-wives aren't much sought after.

Lexi has aligned herself with her father, none too surprising since she's always been "Daddy's girl." She's decided to join his firm, which I suspect pleases David to no end.

Leaning my head back against the pillow, I submit to the pincers of pain, familiar and apparently eternal, that sting my eyes with tears. Does it ever gentle? I wonder. Will it, God forbid, always be this sharp and hurting?

And, when you turn out the light, are you so damned *alone*? I have to bite my tongue to keep from asking Viveca to stay with me. That would be selfish, I remind myself. She is so involved in this group-therapy thing. I think she's actually found some inner peace. Lucky her.

The rain has started again. Lying here staring at the ceiling, so pregnant my stomach creates a miniature alp beneath the comforter, it's very hard to keep from wallowing in the primal ooze of self-pity. It's such a deliciously intimate foe, one that will snuggle up and comfort when nothing else can.

I wait impatiently for sleep, for when I sleep, we are together again. I run across a flower-strewn meadow with a little dog racing joyously ahead. Her furious yelping alerts the cottage to my arrival, and my love rushes out to meet us.

"Nathaniel!" My voice rings across the hills. Then I am caught up in strong arms and held against his chest and I am young again—young and alive, all golden in the sunlight!

Then we are in his bed, in the soft grass, or the warm waters of a moonlit lake, and that sweet, hot flood of ecstasy sends us soaring higher and higher. For the moment the gnawing loneliness, the eternal chill, the aching pain are driven out, and the void filled with the warmth of ten thousand suns. I know joy again, the honeyed taste of happiness. I am blissfully content. . . .

And then I waken with a convulsive start that disintegrates into a wail of loss renewed, again and again and again.

This house is so quiet. Except for my clock—oh, that clock won't stop, it won't cease ticking away the minutes, it won't respect this hot anguish suddenly tearing at my guts—*not that goddamned alarm clock*! "Nathaniel!" I scream aloud, bringing it up from the depths like a clot of blood. Oh, God, I miss him! Oh, God, I need him! And God, I hate that fucking clock, this fucking house, my fucking weakness—my whole fucking world!

Shaken by the raw outburst of fury, I make a deliberate attempt to return to my habitual level of dull acceptance, willing away frustration until the lovely opiate of apathy comes stealing in.

Loneliness and guilt. You mustn't forget the guilt, Roseanna, I taunt my wretched self. What you've done to David is shameful. A swift shake of head rejects that; I feel no shame for loving Nathaniel. But I'd hurt someone who didn't deserve it. What was David's crime? Not loving me? "Not much of a crime, Rosie," I mutter with a clawing sigh.

Having lost my sense of humor, I've also lost my lifeline in a sea that promises only to get a whole lot rougher before the storm is done.

And here I am, crying again.

December whirled in, cold, but still without a frost. On an overcast Saturday morning I walked out to the deck to feed the birds, or maybe just to feel the wind on my hot face.

I was tired—well, I'm always tired—but more so than usual. I had stayed up until three A.M. finishing a detailed outline to send to my agent, who was going to be surprised as hell at the kind of book I was now writing.

"Roseanna, what the devil are you doing out here? And barefoot! You'll catch cold. Why are you barefoot?"

Viveca's scolding voice made me jump. "Oh, hi, Viv. Uh, I'm barefoot because . . . well, my feet, you know. Shoes are so uncomfortable."

"Have you been taking your pills?" Viveca pounced.

"Yes I have!" I replied furiously. Damn everyone and their round, oval, square, oblong, multicolored pills!

Her face softened. "All right, love, all right. Come inside, have a cup of tea with me? It's colder'n hell outside."

"Hell is hot, Viv," I informed her with a toss of head.

She patted my immense belly as I passed her. I remember Liz's belly, the proud bow of a great ocean liner. In comparison, I am only a small tugboat, but a fat, waddling slug of a tugboat, lying low in the water and barely afloat.

Liz, I thought wistfully. How had she fared when the babies came home? They must be wonderfully active by now, maybe even crawling. And maybe right this minute, Nathaniel is sitting on that new but soiled couch holding the infant who bears my name.

So far away. The immensity of that distance crushes me each time I think of it.

"Well, scratch another teaspoon," Viveca said cheerily.

"What?" I asked, even as I looked down at the spoon I held. It was now a neat letter U.

Taking the mutilated spoon from my nervous fingers, Viveca continued in that same terminally cheerful vein, "What's the latest report from the doctor?"

"The same. Still undecided as to a Caesarean or not."

"Want to decorate the house today?" she suggested, taking the steaming teapot from Mims. "It's nearly Christmas, you know."

"No."

"Okeydokey."

"Oh, for God's sake, Viv, cut the cornball stuff?"

"Begging your pardon, Miss Scarlett," she said, bowing. "When are you going to visit your hairdresser for a color job? All that gray hair doesn't help your morale, or your appearance. In fact, it looks awful. Makes you look ten years older."

"Thank you, Viv. I feel so much better now."

We laughed, but mine was lame. Viveca was wearing a rich cream-colored sweater with one of those heavy cowl necklines, and a rust and blue plaid skirt. She looked so slim and stylish, I felt like a watermelon on a skateboard, with about the same sure balance.

Tormenting myself, I glanced at my reflection in Mother's little gold-framed oval mirror. Lord, I look awful, I thought. making a gargoyle face. My hair is pulled back into a ponytail that leaks straggly wisps around my ears. Doubtless I resemble a slattern in this tent of a maternity frock. I haven't any shape anymore, I'm just a pity-filled blob on spindly legs.

"Shit!" I muttered disgustedly.

"Where's your hairbrush? I'm going to do something with that hair," Viveca promptly responded.

"The fuckin' hairbrush is in the fuckin' bathroom!"

Viveca's eyebrows shot up.

I glared at her. "Why is it that everyone else in the world can fling that word about with abandon, yet when I try it I get shocked looks and raised eyebrows?"

"Because you're our sweet little Rosie, that's why," she crooned. "It's like discovering mud at the bottom of a bowl of tapioca. Mims, would you get the hairbrush, please?"

"I'm sorry. I'm acting like a spoiled brat," I admitted as Viveca unloosed the rubber band around my ponytail.

"Acting like a woman who's been pregnant since the second day of Creation," she crisply corrected. "You have a perfect right to be cranky." Taking the brush Mims had fetched, she began pulling it through my hair in long, gentle strokes. "I know you're miserable, darling. But don't you feel any joy or anticipation about this baby?"

"Oh, Viv," I said, tears spurting. "I do, of course I do! At least I should, because I do want it, but I . . . I can't feel joy anymore, you know? I'm *joyless,* Viv! Incapable of it."

"Maybe if we started preparing a nursery—"

"No! Call me superstitious, but I—I can't prepare another nursery." I grimaced. "Which makes me awful, I suppose. Or stupid, as David is fond of saying. Am I, Viv? Even the doctor says I'm taking a dangerous risk having this baby. A baby I'll likely have to raise alone."

"Well, that part's stupid," she snapped. "What am I, chopped liver? Dammit, I'm helping you raise this baby, Roseanna! I'm going to be godmother and auntie and anything else she needs! And screw David, okay? With a power saw, preferably. You're not stupid, honey," she said, quietening. "You're terribly unhappy, full of rage and grief. It's a wonder you don't split wide open with all you're carrying inside you . . . no pun intended."

I giggled, a foreign sound coming from my lips. She grinned and began giving me all the latest really wild gossip, half of which she made up on the spot, I suspected, but I rewarded her efforts with laughter now and then. I love her so, this soft-eyed friend. We are so close that she knows my feelings as surely as she knows her own. How wonderful it is to have someone who senses the exact second your mind has left this world and gone seeking among uncharted stars!

"Where's the outline and chapters you want mailed?" she asked. "How many now, twenty? Terrific! Don't let me forget to take them with me. Now pack your things, you're spending Christmas at my house. At least I have a wreath on the door."

"Okay, I will. And we'll watch Rudolph and the Grinch and—oh, God!" I gasped and grabbed my belly. "Oh Viv, oh Mims! Look, it's started! My water's broken!"

"No," Viveca said in a strange, tight voice. "That's not amniotic fluid. Get an ambulance, Mims, and hurry!"

My world is drifting shadows and iron chains tethering me to the tiny space I occupy. I float in and out of awareness, snatched to the top of my dark, turbulent sea by bits and pieces of conversation, by voices unknown and vaguely known, by pain that lances or slithers or knifes in and out of me. A vast exhaustion has sapped the marrow of my bones and I lie weightless. Perhaps that is why I'm tethered.

There is an explosion of voices, fingers moving over me, doing intimate things without my permission. A soft whimper halts the voices, and someone says my name sharply.

"Roseanna?"

"It hurts," I accuse. Who said my name? I recognize the voice, yet I don't. It is strained and so very weary. My nostrils are pinched together and there is pain there, yet I am aware, somewhere, that no one pinches me, that there are tubes coming from them, slender white worms someone is adjusting.

Where am I? And why am I in this place where sound echoes ringingly, on and on until my ears hurt? I would open my eyes and see, but there are weights on my eyelids.

The weights are monstrously heavy, but I raise them, only to be stabbed with hideously bright lights.

Terror zeros in. They do not want me to see where they have taken me! "I'm sorry, I'm sorry!" I wail. "David, don't! It was my baby, too, David!"

Someone shushes me. Furiously I struggle against the chains binding my arms. "I will not stay here—I am going to the meadow!" I tell them.

"Roseanna, lie still, dear," that oddly raw voice commands.

"I will go . . . to the meadow!" I insist, a thick, slurred sound that scrapes my throat. Carasel is digging at the base of the boulder, and I know her plans. She will dig her way to me.

She'll get all dirty and David will notice! "Wait, Carasel, I'm coming!" I tell her. But she doesn't hear me.

My struggles increase. I am wild to get free and go to her! For where she is, Nathaniel will be. But the bonds are so strong and hands restrain me. "Please, oh please! Please let me go to her!" I plead frantically.

"Jesus Christ," I hear a masculine voice mumble. David's? Of course. I had forgotten I had a David. But wait a minute, I *didn't* have David, not anymore. So who was it?

"Roseanna, lie still, love. You must rest awhile first, don't you see? Just rest awhile first." Viveca's voice. Ragged; she is crying. But if she's here, then I am safe.

I am hurting so, everywhere, hurting. "It hurts, Viv. I hurt." Simultaneous with my complaint comes the sharp prick of a needle, and my doctor's taut voice.

"You had a Cesarean, Roseanna. It will stop hurting in just a minute."

The word echoes through my mind and tumbrels crash into place. Nathaniel's daughter has been born! But why are all the voices so strained and weary? "The baby!"

"No, no, your daughter is fine, sweetie. A trifle small, but beautiful and perfect."

"My daughter!" My glad cry breaks into her soothing monotone.

"Yes, a daughter. You have a daughter, Roseanna."

A man's voice again . . . there's something wrong with David being here, something wrong with his voice, too, but it's too elusive for my befogged mind. The mists are rolling over my sea now, long mares' tails stretching out in foaming loveliness, sparkling in the sunshine.

I float, drifting, soaring, feeling the brilliant bits of light kaleidoscoping as I pass through them. Nathaniel's eyes gleam in the moonlight, catching and holding the silvery rays until they sparkle deep in the green depths. Part of him sleeps. But part of him joins me with a glad cry as we meet.

"Our daughter," he echoes.

"Yes, my love, we have a fine daughter!" I delightedly assure him. He scoops up Carasel and stands still, his head cocked as though listening. I see the smile curving his mouth.

"She's a beautiful baby, my darling," I whisper. "Perfectly formed, the doctor says. Her name is Bethany Rose, for your mother and for mine."

Then he's gone, and I'm so terribly alone.

"Shh, sleep, Roseanna. You have a daughter and all is well," David repeats in that haunting voice. I feel the wrongness again, but I cannot hold onto it, or put it into words. Even as I grope for it, gossamer clouds drift between the words and myself, and I must be going now.

"Good-bye, David, I must go now." Joyously I leave this battered body and wing out across the star spangled sky, searching through the infinite realms which spin out in a dazzling ribbon of beauty. Time passes; I can see it. And then there is not time, only universes of astounding beauty.

Illusionary planets, insubstantial as clouds, bear the weight of my temporal feet as I search each one for the sweetest illusion of all, the meadow.

And there it is and there he is and there they are! With a joyous cry I descend like a bird, my bare feet on soft grass not even bent by their touch, my heart captured and held in the beauty of his emerald eyes.

But why is he crying?

The wind keened softly through the grove and rippled the greening meadow grasses. The rains had come, and in every crevice and nook, wherever the sun reached down to warm and nurture, flowers bloomed. Everywhere birds sang in a frenzy of mating, and the sun licked gently at the mantle of snow shrouding the mountain peaks. It was springtime in the meadow, and a singing glory to the soul.

The small party moved slowly through the soft, lush grass; three men, one woman, and an excited little dog who raced ahead with eager barkings, returning to the tall young man for a quick caress on her silky gray head before setting off again.

"Carasel knows the way!" Nathaniel said. Michael laughed and clasped his arm.

I hovered over them, yearning to be a physical part of this, knowing instinctively that I could not.

The ancient gray boulder glistened in the early morning sunlight. The party approached it in single file, and stood awkwardly for a moment, their heads tilted in expectant pose as they waited. The smaller man examined the fraying ropes that suspended a large bronze bell. When he jerked the ropes, it sent a clamorous peal across the verdant lea.

"Good grief, Matt!" Liz protested, clapping her hands

across her ears. When the noise stopped, she squatted at the base of the boulder where a single blue columbine swayed like a dancer on its tall, graceful stem. Numerous other buds were still tightly closed, and only this one had unfurled its satiny petals. "So lovely," she murmured.

Nathaniel knelt beside her and touched a fragile petal with a hint of reverence. "Yes, it is lovely. I remember one time. . . ." He stood up in a swift, uncoiling motion and stared unseeing around the meadow. "We'll have to replace that rope soon," he said evenly. "It's pretty weather-beaten."

Michael was opening the bottle of champagne he carried. He dredged four glasses from a shopping bag and filled them with the sparkling liquid. The glasses were long-stemmed, tulip-shaped. Holding them high, they stood in a semicircle. As the older man began to speak, the little dog laid down in a hauntingly familiar spot of grass and closed her eyes. The small, clipped ears cocked at mention of beloved names.

"We drink to Roseanna, whose spirit is with us even now. Her voice rides the wind and I can feel her sweet presence like a warmth upon my heart.

"We drink to Nathaniel, who keeps her memory alive because it brings him joy, not sorrow.

"And last but foremost, we drink to the child who now unites them regardless of where they dwell. We drink to my brother's daughter and his beloved wife, who came to him in a dream last night to share with us this blessed news. We do not doubt that, for love has no limits, knows no boundaries." Michael's voice softened to infinite tenderness. "And we drink to the day when they will return to us. May God give it to us soon."

The crystal glasses shattered on the gray boulder. Flowing down the stone flanks like a silvery river, the shards fell in a glittering mound around the blue columbine.

I drifted in and out of conscious time. Some part of me was aware that my body was growing stronger. My mind, mired in its drugged depths, began to surface for longer and longer periods of time, until one morning I opened my eyes and remained anchored in reality.

It was raining outside my window, but the watery light still hurt my eyes. Snatches of recall, like nightmarish film clips, moved in rapid sequence across the screen of my mind.

Gentling images followed, of Viveca, constantly Viveca, of my doctor, so kind and caring . . . and David? *Had* he been here?

A nurse interrupted my perplexed reverie with seemingly heartfelt pleasure that I could scowl at her. She removed the IV from my arm. I flexed the stiffened muscle, welcoming the pain that excused the tears leaking from my eyes. I had not seen my baby and I ached to do so, a physical ache that manifested in my throbbing breasts. I knew I could not nurse her, that my mother's milk was being chemically dried up. But I still *needed*.

The nurse cranked up the bed until I was sitting in a most uncomfortable but upright position. Soon, she promised, we would be on our feet, taking a few steps. "We, huh!" I muttered, gasping at the pain that movement engendered.

"Good morning, Roseanna!" Viveca, resplendent in suede and leather, materialized beside my bed, a nosegay of huge purple violets in hand. "Welcome back to the land of the living," she said gruffly, kissing my cheek. "How are you feeling, love?"

"Good morning, Viv. What pretty flowers." I licked my dry lips. "I don't know how I feel. I don't even know what day it is. Have you seen the baby?"

"It's Friday, darling. And of course I've seen the baby. She's gorgeous. Fabulous, even! The violets are from her father. Well, in a way they are. I just felt the urge to get them."

I held them to my nose, feeling my throat thickening at the evocative perfume. "Her father and I thank you. I can't wait to see her, later this afternoon, the nurse said. Oh, Viv, her name—have I already told them the baby's name?"

"Yes. Bethany Rose Viveca Bently Knight. I had to repeat it several times; no one believed you when you blurted out that long moniker! It's a beautiful name," Viveca said, smiling.

"I think so. Was David here?" I asked abruptly.

"No. I called, but it seems both he and Lexi were out of town."

I lay back and closed my leaking eyes. "Well, I didn't expect him to come. After all, I dealt him a pretty nasty blow. And Lexi has to stand by her daddy."

Viveca shrugged. "I guess. But we don't need them, babe. We have dear Colin."

My eyes flew open. "Dear Colin? Your ex-boyfriend?"

"My ex-lover," she corrected crisply. "I'm far too mature to have boyfriends. But yes, he stayed with me when you. . . . Oh, Rosie, it was awful, just awful!" she burst out. "There was so much blood and you were unconscious and whiter than any sheet and then emergency surgery and Code Blues and God knows what-all!" She gulped a breath. "And I was all alone and so afraid and everytime I turned around you were either going into cardiac arrest or had already gone. . . . God!" she shuddered.

I forced a grin. "So you called dear Colin."

"Yes. Yes, I . . . ." She cleared her throat, her voice easing. "Well, I was scared peeless, Roseanna. I needed *someone*. Someone just to hold my hand and tell me you were going to be all right. And that's just what he did. Amazing, huh! Would you like to try some of this juice now?"

"Amazing, all right." I took the glass with my achy hand, slopping juice on the sheet. "Sorry," I said rather grimly.

"It's okay. Want me to hold it and you sip from the straw?"

How gentle she was! "I don't want any right now." I gazed at her measuringly, and then I said with soft surety, "I was there again, Viv. In the meadow, I mean. They were all gathered by the boulder, Nathaniel, Michael, Matt and Liz, all there. And Carasel was there, sleeping in the circle. They drank to the baby, and smashed their glasses on the stone."

I felt her stiffen, and my words came faster, building a fortress of fact. "Viv, listen to me, please. It was *real*, honey. That glorious moment I said good-bye and left the hospital room to wing off among the stars was as real as if I'd packed a bag and boarded a plane. I was *there*. I even touched Nathaniel's face. But he didn't see me. None of them saw me, not even Carasel. But I *was* there."

I lifted my chin in defiance of whatever Viveca was thinking.

"I did not imagine it, or dream it. I remember distinctly the fresh, clean scent of springtime. Oh, Viv, I listened to their conversation, I watched them drink their toasts to my baby and me, and smash their glasses on the boulder. And I know, I *know* without a shred of doubt, that there's a mound of crystal shards at the base of that stone, just as I know that among those shards grows a wild blue columbine."

"How would Nathaniel know he even *had* a child?"

Her voice was neutral. Nevertheless, I bit my lip as I formed a reply.

"Apparently I told him. In a dream, Michael said. I admit I don't remember that, but I . . . look, he knows, okay? In some lovely, mysterious way, Nathaniel knows he has a daughter. Maybe it was only a coincidence that he chose that precise day to come to the meadow and drink to his child, I don't know. But it isn't important how, it matters only that he knew. And that I joined him at that priceless moment. Dear God, if only I could have physically touched him, let him know I was there!" I drew a shuddery breath and cleared my throat. "It happened, Viveca. It did happen."

She smoothed my hair, speaking quietly, indulgently. "If you say so, love, if you say so."

I watched her face close out my words. "Viv, I find it curious that you can take all this—all that's happened, in stride. Yet you buck at accepting the idea that I might have gone there, that some way, I left this world and went back there, in spirit," I said softly.

"It's just that, I don't know about spiritual things," she replied, equally soft. "The other part of it, I saw with my own eyes, but this. . . . I don't know, Rosie, this whole thing has been so weird, who am I to say it couldn't happen?" she admitted tiredly. "So many strange things, why not one more? Here, drink your juice now. Colin will be here in a little while. Can you imagine? He's become the protector of helpless women."

"Then he'd better look elsewhere," I said, taking the juice.

"Right you are." She laughed and stuck my violets in a waterglass. "Because I'm moving in with you, Rose-anna."

"Oh, thank God!"

"And between us we'll make . . . one whole woman, I guess."

"One and a half," I corrected. "Don't forget Bethany Rose Viveca Bently Knight." I lifted the juice, tears streaming down my face again. "Here's to us, honey! Oh, Lord, do you think I will *ever* stop this blasted crying?"

Chapter 23

$\mathcal{V}$iveca had brought me a soft, silken nightgown the color of alpine anemones. After helping me into it, she brushed my hair and tied it back with a lavender ribbon. This bit of feminine cosseting felt incredibly good.

Then she left, because they were bringing me my baby, and I wanted to savor in private my first meeting with Bethany Rose Knight.

She was a pink, pretty baby, her skin devoid of the trauma marks of natural delivery. Carefully I searched the little face for traces of Nathaniel, but there were no distinguishing characteristics. It was just an infant's sweet, innocent face.

Her lashes were dark crescent fans on her cheeks. She stirred, and her eyes opened, that dark, unsettled, newborn blue. She was so tiny! She opened her mouth with such a wail, I startled at this astounding volume of noise from one so small. I poked the rubber nipple in the general vicinity of her mouth, laughing as she grabbed it with most indelicate gusto.

I was utterly entranced. When I touched one miniature fist, equally miniature fingers wrapped around it in a snug grip. I laid my face in her cornsilk hair and inhaled the precious, indescribable scent of a baby. Eyes closed in bliss, she suckled like a little pig, making marvelous smacking noises.

I loved her. It was a physical beating to feel such love! My tears wet her hair. The morning sun haloed her face, turning her skin to tawny gold under the disguising new-born pink.

Nathaniel's skin.

"Oh, baby, baby, he would have been so proud of you, so proud!" I whispered with heart-wrenching fierceness.

Ignoring my surgical discomfort, I cuddled her on my shoulder in time-honored fashion, patting her back, feeling the seductive warmth of her against my breasts as I listened to the sounds beyond our room. The corridor was alive with voices, with cries, soft shushings and feminine laughter; with deep, husky murmurs of men who were now, by choice or not, fathers.

It was very quiet in my room. Bethany Rose obligingly gave forth an audible burp, and a long, satisfied sigh. I closed my eyes and held my baby, letting the peace of this lovely moment wash away the pain.

When I came home with my baby, Viveca had obligingly provided a crib and a small layette. I immediately in-stalled a monitoring system that covered the entire house. We could hear every breath Bethany drew. I would not lose another baby, I told Viveca with fero-cious determination.

After we'd finished decorating the large, airy nursery with enough whimsical furnishings to satisfy both our maternal hearts, we turned to redoing the house. I chose what to keep and what to discard from my home; she did the same with hers.

Those were busy, wonderfully exhausting weeks. But when we were through and a workable routine was es-tablished, I found myself struggling to define my iden-tity. It was hard enough just drawing all the pieces of Roseanna together. Discarding the pieces that were no longer valid was even more difficult.

One intractable piece was the apparently indelible image of "Roseanna, wife of David." Try as I might, I couldn't dislodge it from its twenty-five-year niche.

I had not seen David since the divorce. Perhaps that's why my mind persisted in preserving useless scraps of the past regardless of my wishes. Despite all that had passed between us, I still lacked what I called, for want of a better word, a sense of closure.

Viveca, mind-reader extraordinaire, interrupted my melancholy reverie with a crisp suggestion one misty April morning. I was sitting on the deck holding the baby when she snuck up and caught me in my blue funk.

"Since we're going out to lunch today, I think a look through your wardrobe is in order," she said, taking Bethany.

"Thanks, honey, but I really don't care to go out."

"Did I ask if you cared to go out?" she retorted. "Now hold the door for me and come on upstairs. I like the color of your hair, by the way. You look like a teen-ager again."

"Sure I do," I grunted, for my ego was the size of a peanut. But I opened the door, and followed her upstairs.

After putting Bethany in her crib, we went to my closet. Nothing fit me. "Nothing decent, anyway," I said. "The baby, you know. I've still got this stomach and these chunky thighs."

"The baby is four months old, Roseanna. But you're right, we're both out of shape. I'll take care of that soon enough."

"How?" I asked warily. I loath dieting.

She smiled. "Worse than a diet, honey. We're joining an exercise spa. And then we'll hire us a personal trainer. Meantime, we'll find something loose. Yes, this shift will do."

"That's a pre-maternity shift, Viv, and if you think I'm. . . . Oh, shit. All right, give me the ugly thing."

"It's not ugly, it's a lovely shade of griege," she countered. "Now, let's get to work on the rest of you."

So we did, laboring long and hard to produce a so-so image. The shift wasn't ugly, indeed it was quite smart. Also nondescript. I'd fade into the wallpaper if I wasn't careful.

Viveca had made reservations at one of the restaurants David and I had often patronized. Still, it never entered my mind that I might encounter him. Head high, ego bolstered by Viveca's assurance that I was still worth a second look, I stepped smartly into the restaurant, at which point my assurance sloughed off in palm-dampening layers

David was just rising from his table, and I nearly walked into him. Handsome, impeccably groomed, right down to the paisley silk square decorating the pocket of his custom-tailored suit, he stepped back with an sharp, indrawn breath.

He recovered quicky, smiled at me, greeted Viveca.

She returned his greeting and kept on following the hostess. I, however, was nailed to the floor by surprise.

"Well, David, my goodness, what a surprise!"

His tone superbly wry, he lifted an eyebrow. "Why? We live in the same town, so we're bound to meet now and then."

I gave him one of those vague smiles that cover anything. When he turned and introduced the lovely young woman who shared his table, it was a jolt, one I felt to the tips of my toes.

For an instant, a scalding flash of bitterness, anger, jealousy, resentment, and God knows what else wiped out my ability to think. When I regained my wits, I gave her a reasonably nice greeting as I sought to place her. She was young: mid-twenties, I calculated. She had finely chiseled features, and skin as smooth as antique ivory silk.

Swallowing, I watched the scarlet-nailed hand she laid on his arm, blatantly possessive as her eyes coolly met mine. The message was clear, sent and received—and she was just one step away from being physically assaulted. For there was triumph in her tawny cat's eyes, subtle, but recognizable to any woman with an ounce of intuition.

Sensing I had somehow been humiliated and wishing to minimize the feeling, I steadfastly contained the question clawing at my throat. What did it matter how long he'd known this woman?

It mattered.

Because I suddenly remembered where I'd seen her before. She had been a law clerk in his firm. Two, maybe three years ago. Had they been involved even then?

In that hot, suspended moment, David gave me a slanting glance and smiled. It was the wrench needed to destroy the image of Roseanna, wife of David. For a dreadful instant, I thought it would destroy Roseanna as well.

Feeling dowdy and matronly and perhaps even pathetic, I smiled with all the grace I could muster.

But then grace fled and in came spite, and I slanted my eyes right back at him and drawled, "I see you're still collecting trophies, David. Of course, this one won't gather dust in a glass case," I murmured, chuckling. "Well, so nice to meet you, Miss, ah, Barbie, was it? Oh, Camille. Of course. David. . . ." With a negligible wave, I sauntered on to my own table, cursing that sonofabitch David with satisfying venom.

"Did you know about that woman, Viv?" I asked when I joined her at the table.

"I suspected, but. . . ." She lifted an elegant shoulder. "Didn't you, Roseanna?"

"No, of course I didn't! Why didn't you say something, why didn't. . . ." My protests died as her level gaze impacted mine.

I lowered my head. "Yes, I guess I did suspect. Or at least wonder. I guess I just didn't want to know." My mouth twisted. "Shit, no guessing about it. I didn't want to know, period."

"Well, who does?" she tossed off. She grinned. "I sure did like your parting shot, honey."

"Yeah, me, too," I said, laughing. But the tears were just below the surface, simmering like froth on my anger. "When I think of the time I've spent wallowing in guilt because of what I did to him, feeling lower than low, eating *dirt*, blast it!" I burst out in fierce, low tones that seethed with resentment. "And all the while he was. . . ."

Fearing I would choke on the words, I left them unsaid and gave myself a hard mental shake. "But that's history now. God, I feel like a beer barrel in this dress. Let's just have a quick salad, Viv? Then we'll have time to stop by that friggin' spa you mentioned this morning."

"Ah!" Viveca lifted her waterglass. "Here's to moti-
vation, Rosie. You never know where you'll find it!"

Don't think, just don't think, just live, just do, just *be*.

Today I'm slim and trim, today my book was sold for
an astonishing sum, today the baby crawled, today I
changed a flat tire, today I showed Bethany my trea-
sured pictures and she said "Da Da." All the good
todays added to the bad ones make up another year,
and you've gotten through it just fine.

Remember Viveca's smile as she says, "Oh, Rosie, it's
so good to see you laughing again," and remember,
above all, to laugh.

"Happy birthday, sweetie!" I said to my precocious,
gifted impossibly brilliant one-year-old. With great dar-
ing, she stepped into the six inches separating us, flung
her arms around my knees, and crowed at the feat.

When those green eyes look up into mine, an old
knife turns in my heart. Like spring leaves in sunlight,
darkly lashed and glowing, they are beautiful eyes. But
then, she is a beautiful child. Her hair is a red-gold mass
of curls around her sculpted head, shining in the afternoon sun. She grins at me, and the knife turns again.
The dimple in her cheek is not my flirtatious little dimple. It is long and deep, and compels a touching fingertip.

"Poppysicle, Mama?" she wheedles. Like her father,
she can charm a bird down from a tree. But I am
mother first, and charmed woman second. No popsicle.

April drifted in on a wave of seductive, wisteria-scented
warmth. I would have liked to have slept through the
second anniversary of my meeting Nathaniel, but I
awoke early and lay listening, hearing only the whirring
of my overhead fan. I got up and stood on my balcony.
It was dawn, a lovely pink and lilac dawn, radiant with
spring-song. The evocative essence of this season made
me ache deep inside.

I brought Bethany into my bed, which I'd discovered
to be a delightful way to begin the day. I told her all
about meeting her daddy and how at first I'd thought I

was crazy or dreaming, for how often does a woman fall into Paradise for no reason at all?

"Had I been a more saintly person, perhaps, but your mother is no saint," I confessed, and she laughed and plopped down on my stomach with blithe disregard for the condition of her diaper.

"Roseanna? Don't forget, workout at nine-thirty," Viveca called.

Muttering under my breath, I took off Bethany's damp clothing. I loathed aerobics and working out despite the undeniable fact that forced exercise had worked wonders on my figure. But our trainer hadn't been so bad. A muscular male with a short, blond ponytail, he reminded me of Colin the Hunk in many ways.

Colin, bless his hunky heart, was now in Tibet or Peru or somewhere like that, seeking proof of his existence with all a young man's passion. Oddly enough, I missed him. At least for a little while he'd filled the part, however haphazardly, of a male role model for Bethany to cut her teeth on.

I stripped off her shirt and denuded myself of my dampened nightgown. We went into the closet and I showed her the place, holding her little fingers on the wall while I told her that her daddy was so near, just a breath away. And I told him we loved him. Did he hear?

"Daddy!" she said.

Dammit it, did he hear?

There were violets on my dresser. Lowering my head, I sniffed their faint, fresh scent and was instantly catapulted back in time. . . .

Viveca's light knock put an end to my retreat from a rather frenetic reality. "I brought you some herbal tea, to mellow you out a bit," she said, nose wrinkling in response to my scowl. "Do you like the violets? They're blooming all around that old tree stump."

"I like the violets. And you."

Her eyes softened. "You were remembering, weren't you? Strangley enough, so was I. I woke up this morning thinking of that little grove and the water we drank from the spring. It was the damnedest thing, Rosie, but I could recall exactly how that water tasted, sweet and icy and flavored with mint, remember?"

"Oh, yes, I remember," I said, grateful that time had given me the gift of remembering without copious tears. Not only was my anguish muted, but Nathaniel was very close to me. I had a distinct sense of his presence, as though he was standing just outside my range of vision and if I but turned swiftly enough, I would see him there beside me. The times when these moments of sentience occurred and I actually did whirl around were painful, but a kind of sweet anticipation softened that pain. Next time, I would be swift enough. Next time, he would be there.

That this was a childish game, I accepted; that he would never be there, I did not and would not accept. I'd play this game for the rest of my life if I had to.

"We leave for the airport in about fifteen minutes," Viveca warned.

"All right, I'll be ready," I replied with martyred reluctance. Another ongoing game I played was that of An Independent Woman of Means. My book had made it to the *New York Times* bestseller list and stayed there for twelve weeks; I had done radio and television talk shows with astounding success; locally, I was, as Viveca put it, bloody well famous.

I was about to become even more famous, if I survived it, by appearing on Donahue's talk show. We were going to New York for a week, Viveca, Bethany, Mims, and I and a ton of luggage. My agent and publicist had set up all sorts of entertaining things for me to do.

We flew first class, of course. Independent Women of Means do that. When we were finally in the air, Bethany promptly climbed onto my lap, thus ensuring that I would arrive in travel-wrinkled attire.

Viveca moved over beside me, Mimosa in hand, eyes sparkling with pleasure. "Oh, Rosie, this has all been so exciting—and now New York! Limo service, the Waldorf hotel, shopping in legendary stores and eating in fabulous restaurants! Now aren't you glad you published Nathaniel's story?" she crowed.

"It's had its pros and cons," I said frankly. "But okay, you're right, it has been exciting and I'm glad we're going to New York."

"Me, too. Sometimes I wonder, what would have happened if you'd never started writing in the first place?"

I stared out the window into billowing clouds. "Maybe in some other world, I never did," I said softly, recalling Nathaniel's theory on parallel worlds. "Maybe in some other world, I haven't changed at all. Maybe I was too afraid."

My arms tightened around my sleeping toddler. "God, that's sad, Viv. That is so damned *sad.*"

It's like in your audience," Hazel cut in. "Everybody's
agreed, she's been exiled, and all that can go wrong is
in to New York."

"Mr. Tree somewhere I wonder what would have happened to which I never dared write in the first place."

he sighed, and the shadow fell. "Follow me, you're
maybe in some other world I never saw." I said softly,
reading. "When darkness we parallel codes. Maybe,
in some other world I think, I know, I thought it all. I knew I
was in earnest." ...

My arms reached around the sleeping contours
and there is a joy. There is no loneliness."

Chapter 24

New Year's Day began with a hangover. Viveca had one, too. Since 'eighty-five had been kind to us, we had toasted, with some very fine champagne, both the old year's departure and the new year's entrance.

Despite my headache, I had to smile when my bleary gaze lit on the small, personal Christmas tree Bethany and I had placed in front of the balcony door. It was decorated with anything that caught a little girl's fancy, tinfoil, cookie cutters, shiny bows, tiny plastic dinosaurs in gaudy colors. The holidays were such bittersweet magic, I thought wistfully; our house aglow with the lights and music of Christmas, an enormous fir that seemed to float on a raft of gaily wrapped gifts, good friends dropping in for eggnog and good wishes.

"Merry Christmas!" they wished us, and it was. A family of three, we had gone to the mall to have our pictures made with Santa. We even made Mother's cinnamon lace cookies and Viveca's special banana-nut bread. Most important of all, though, we'd had a little girl whose wide green eyes shone with the wonder of the season.

"First her birthday and then Santa Claus—how can one little person hold all that!" I'd caroled, laughing with Viveca as we'd borne the exhausted, but still protesting child off to bed. . . .

Urging my reluctant body to leave the comfort of my own bed, I made an experimental move to the side, and eventually swung my feet to the floor. "Coffee!" I cried piteously, sniffing the air for that lifesaving aroma. A futile quest; evidently Viveca wasn't up yet.

Stumbling to the closet for a robe, I gave the wall my usual quick check along with the usual brief, breath-holding offering of hope. Hope, I thought sadly, that became more fragile with each passing day. I hurried on to Bethany's room, who had now begun clamoring for attention. "Little icepicks in Mommy's head, Bethany," I explained when she persisted in making inordinate amounts of noise.

She was hungry, she had to potty, she wanted *out* of her frigging crib. Although she didn't actually say "frigging," her tone implied it. At two years old, my precocious child had an equally precocious temper. Just last night she became so enraged at a doll whose head persisted in falling off that she had banged it on the floor with a furious, "Shit, shit, shit, baby!" I was appalled even though I had nearly choked on a laugh. What would her father have said about that?

"Bad, bad mommy," I had flogged myself as I fled to my bedroom to give in to some vastly inappropriate mirth.

"Well, light of my life, maybe he wouldn't be so hot at fatherhood, either: You ever think of that, huh?" I growled, lifting her out of the crib and kissing all over her face just like I used to do with her father. "But I hope with all my heart that someday you'll have a chance to find out, baby," I added fiercely, and danced her to the bathroom, headache and all.

Mims arrived around noon, leaving Viveca and me free to compose ourselves enough to attend an "open house" in River Oaks later that evening. I dressed with care, for I knew David would be there, and I had a score to settle.

My hair, grown long again, was the soft, glowing, red-gold hue I intended to take to my grave. Plastic surgery on my eyelids for improved vision purposes had restored my wide-eyed, innocent look. After I had done all I could possibly do with what I had, I presented myself to Viveca for inspection. I wore a fitted red silk cocktail suit, red hose and red spike-heeled pumps; my hair in a chignon, adorned with a black silk rose.

"Smashing," she decided. "Except for the hair, much too tidy . . . there!"

Glancing in the mirror, I frowned at the flushed little face now framed with wispy tendrils. "But now it's messy."

"True. And sexy. Trust me, you'll have more fun."

"So I'll trust, what do I know?" I said tiredly.

Still, it was a nice way to spend time, eating and drinking and talking with friends, eyeing your ex-husband's new wife and hoping your casual greeting had rung true.

His nubile law clerk had apparently been found lacking, for this was a different woman, a soft-faced brunette. She was attractive. Oh hell, she was gorgeous, was what she *was*. I wondered if she loved him. I hoped so.

A little surprised at feeling so charitable toward him, I watched her give him a quick kiss before they parted to circulate through the crowded room. Catching his eye, I nodded and began my own circulatory route towards the buffet table.

David caught up with me and put a detaining hand on my arm.

"You're looking very good, Roseanna. I've never seen you wear anything quite so . . . red."

I thanked him with a sparkling smile.

Casually he drew me into an alcove that offered a measure of privacy. "A celebrity now, hmm? Rich and famous," he said, shaking his head. "I admit that surprised me."

"I don't know why, I told you I could make it alone. Actually, it isn't at all unusual for a woman to bloom after she's . . . free." I smiled again, dazzlingly. "You're looking good, too, David, and your young wife is beautiful."

"She's not all that young, she's twenty-six. You make it sound illegal," he said with a wry twist of mouth.

She was twenty-six and gorgeous; I was fifty and hanging on with both hands. Dammit, it *should* be illegal!

When he laughed, I saw my flash of outrage through his eyes. "What are you laughing at?" I snapped.

He laughed again, a soft sound that remembered. "Oh, Roseanna, my incorrigible Roseanna!"

So I laughed too, and patted his hand. "To the bitter end, David, to the bitter end."

"Amen," he said wryly. "Any regrets, Roseanna?"

"Yeah, a few. I should have been more assertive, forced a few issues into the open before they calcified. I should also have called you dickhead more often. I think it was good for you, like letting the air out of an overstuffed balloon," I added, slanting him a glance.

He grunted. "If you're referring to my ego, you did a good job on that, believe me." His taut features eased. "And if I remember correctly, you were quite good at pricking my balloon, too. But you're right about one thing; we should have brought things out in the open, communicated better—"

"Talked about our feelings, all that emotional crap."

He made a face. "Yeah, that, too. Anyway, I'm sorry if I acted like a jerk at times."

"*If* you acted like a jerk?" I riposted, but I had to lower my lashes against the prick of tears. I had needed an apology of some kind—of any kind, I admitted—from him. "I, too, am sorry, for whatever pain I caused you," I continued on a softer note. "I never deliberately tried to hurt you. Things just happened, that's all." In control again, I looked up at him. "I'm so glad we could talk like this, David. I don't know about you, but for me, it's healed a few old wounds."

"I'm glad, too." He caught my arm again. "But don't rush off so fast, I've a few questions that need to be asked and answered while we're healing old wounds."

"Ask away," I invited, freeing my arm. "What do you want to know about him?"

"Who he was, for starters. Where you met him and when. And why he never showed up after I left. I expected you to marry him—I mean, knowing you, how could I expect otherwise? But you didn't," he said, his gaze quizzical. "In fact, you've never been seen with him in public. In private, either, as far as I know. Why not?

Why aren't you together? If you went so far as to bear his child, then you must have loved him."

Not bothering to hide my surprise, I replied slowly, "Thank you, David, that's a very nice thing to say. I did love him. I *do* love him. I always will. But circumstances keep us apart."

"What circumstances?" His eyes narrowed. "Is he married?"

"No, of course not. He's . . . just different."

"Different?" His eyebrows collided. "You mean he's gay?"

"Oh, goodness no, most definitely not gay," I said, feeling a sly tickle of enjoyment undercutting my sobriety. "He's just . . . well, actually, he's an extraterrestrial," I confided.

After an exceedingly sharp glance, David snorted and shook his head. "You almost had me there! But you know what's even worse? I think *you* almost believe that, Roseanna. I'd nearly forgotten how your mind works, the tortuous, labyrinthine pathways it travels to reach its exiguous conclusions!"

"Well, la-di-da, David," I drawled. "All those big words—jeez, how can I possibly parry such a thrust? Still, you do have a point; I couldn't follow your dogmatic, linear form of logic if I wanted to, which I don't. It's just too safe, too predictable. Boring, if you want to be truthful. There's no magic in your way of thinking, no mystical awe and wonderment, no fabulous surprises. Just A leads to B leads to C leads to D. There's heaven above and hell below, and in between there's this meaningless little puff of life on an obscure little planet. And beyond? The *void*," I said in a creepy whisper.

Laughing at his pained expression, I placed a fingertip to his chin. "Well, I'm here to tell you right now, that's bullshit, babe. There are marvels out there, wonders and magic and things undreamed of! Good grief, didn't you read my book?"

"No. I did try, but. . . ." Another shake of head rejected any possibility of comprehending Roseanna's convoluted thinking.

"Oh, shit. There are my tender little feelings, hurt

again. Well, if you're really interested in how Bethany came to be and why I'm still alone and what possessed me to betray you for another man, read my book," I said, coldly serious. "Not the one coming out this fall: the one I wrote right after our divorce. You might just benefit from it, who knows!"

After a moment, he shrugged, his finely chiseled mouth stretching into a smile. "I'll give it another try. So, you're still waiting for this . . . alien to return to you," he said, relaxing into jocularity.

"I live for the day," I said simply.

A sticky web of silence fell over us.

Then he burst out, "Christ, Roseanna, sometimes I wonder what the hell you expect from me!"

The bitterness in his voice disturbed me. I looked away. "It's not important what I expect of you, or even that you believe me, not anymore." Freeing myself of the ghost of whatever emotion he had evoked in me, I said waggishly, "But if I ever turn up missing, you'll know where I went!"

He frowned, eyeing me as if reluctant to confront my sparkling amusement. Baffled brown eyes betrayed his growing sense of strangeness with something once so familiar as to be mundane.

"Do you plan to go somewhere?"

"Not right now, but who knows what the morrow brings?" I said lightly. "David, I know it ended badly between us, but I still have some good memories. Do you?"

"Yes. And some bad ones, too."

"Well, me, too," I blazed up. "In fact, every time I look at you I see twenty-five years of my life just frittered away!"

He leaned closer. "Was it frittered?"

My mouth worked as I stared at him, at his hard, drawn features, the intense dark eyes from which all light had fled. Was he asking for validation, from *me*? Did he think I had forgotten his own enormous betrayal of trust?

Rock-steady, I held his gaze, my mouth curving in

sudden, startling awareness; the greasy shadow of that particular memory no longer stained my heart.

I really am free! I thought exultantly. At last—at long last!—I had reached that marvelous point of maturity where compassion and forgiveness feel so much better than bitterness and spite.

"Better for the complexion, too, I bet," I muttered, mystifying him no end. "But to answer your question, no, it wasn't frittered. Well, some of it was." I tilted my head and laughed, feeling stronger, more powerful, taller, even. "But all things considered, I'm glad we met, glad we loved and married," I said sincerely. "I'm also glad *I'm* not your young wife."

"Another pinprick!" His laugh was devoid of humor. "Before you go, I do have one more question. Why, Roseanna? Why did you leave me? Why did you destroy it all? Was it so damn bad?"

Sensitive to the edge in his voice, I shook my head in rueful admission. "Yes, it was. And the reason I left you is really quite simple: you didn't love me like I deserve to be loved."

"Oh, for. . . . Will I ever understand you?" he exclaimed, exasperated again.

"I doubt it." I laughed and touched his hand. "We're not only total opposites, our minds are positively alien to each other! Well." I looked up at him, my smile gentle. "It was good seeing you again. Good-bye, David. Take care."

"Good-bye, Roseanna. You take care, too," he said.

But I was already walking away.

Spring was so lovely it hurt. The breeze coming in my open window was beautifully warm and fresh, smelling of earth, of rain, of life renewed. Unable to resist its siren's song, I opened the door and stepped out onto the balcony.

This slender area overlooks the dense, fragrant garden that is my backyard, and the woods just beyond the fence. The peach tree David had planted seven years ago had climbed to the second story. Its limbs, studded with exquisite pink blossoms, were just within touching

distance. I looked down upon blooming azaleas and ca-
mellias, my gaze traveling slowly up and over the fence
to the woods where entire saplings were engulfed in
yellow jasmine, and newly leaved trees were misty,
watercolor green. Such beauty gentled the soul even
while it stroked memories that were better left alone.

Feeling weak and still a little achy, I came back inside.
I could hear Bethany's chatter interspersed with
Viveca's gorgeous laugh. We were going to the zoo today. One was as excited as the other about this long-
delayed expedition. Delayed because I'd had the flu for
two solid weeks and didn't feel up to an excursion. So
I'd been brave and unselfish and told them to go without me.

But they had elected to wait until I could go too.

I began making the bed, my movements slow and
awkward with this inner lassitude. I wasn't happy, I
wasn't unhappy, I just *was.* I had forgotten how it felt to
skim the earth on winged feet. Yet sometimes my feet
remembered. I'd forgotten how it felt to wake in the
morning and taste the wine of anticipation fizzing
through my veins. But some mornings, when I first
opened my eyes, still hovering on the cusp of sleep, I
felt it like a faint wisp of remembered perfume.

And then it would all disappear in a numbing rush of
reality.

As my gaze lit upon the small vase of violets Viveca
had picked for me, my mind flashed back to a hot summer day when I had lain in the grass and watched a
beloved young man strew these blossoms all over my
naked body. Did that sound even remotely possible?
What followed afterwards was as implausible as fly-me-
to-the-moon.

Of its own accord, my hand delved into the night-
table drawer and took out solid proof that it did happen.
The photographs spilling over the bed were enchantment captured on film. A picture of Nathaniel in the
meadow one lovely summer evening; the wind ruffles his
hair and he is laughing at Carasel's attempts to bring
down a tormenting butterfly.

Liz, monstrously pregnant, that glorious smile enveloping her face and those dimples outshining the sun; Matt, my gentle leprechaun. Snaps of the colony; the lake; the bronze bell Nathaniel had installed for me. *Three rings, followed by a ten-second pause, and I'll know it's you, Roseanna.*

Nathaniel again, head cocked, eyebrow arched, an irrepressible grin, quite likely hectoring Liz, who is only a soft, green blur at the edge of the picture. Nathaniel's cottage . . . me picking tomatoes . . . him lying on the couch with my beloved Carasel on his chest. . . . All so dear, so poignantly remembered.

Here is a picture of Roseanna, so young and radiant she tears my heart, laughing at the beloved photographer as she coquettishly lifts her skirt above a shapely knee.

And here is Roseanna, crying again, I thought derisively, blotting tears. I wish I could say that this, too, had changed, but I still bawl like a baby given the slightest opportunity.

But my cherished pictures were fading, getting brittle as ancient sepias, and I was losing my faith in miracles. I swept the pictures back into the drawer and laid down again.

The inner glow given by this lovely morning vanished and I felt wretched all of a sudden. Then the door burst open and Bethany Rose Viveca Bently Knight came barreling in.

Green eyes framed by lacy dark lashes twinkled up at me, an eyebrow slanted with her impatient question. "You ready to go to the zoo, Mommy?"

Oh my love, my beautiful child. Bits and pieces of Nathaniel in that determined chin, the arch of eyebrows and darting dimples. I squeezed her until she squealed.

"Not yet, sweetie, but soon, soon."

Viveca came in with a breakfast tray. A little silver schnauzer dogged her every step. She had summarily decided we needed a dog in our manless house, and while Silver was something of a comfort, I couldn't warm up to him. He was haughty and proud and wouldn't chase a butterfly if his life depended on it.

"How are you feeling?" Viveca asked briskly.

"Better. Bethany, stop bouncing on the bed!" Frowning at my child's wild gymnastics, I threatened, "I mean it, if you don't stop at once, you're in big trouble, young lady!"

She stopped, and eyed me with lively interest. "Are you gonna tear my little butt up?" she asked with a winsome smile.

I stared at Viveca, who stared at me with the same open-mouth question: Where did she learn *that*?

"Mims!" Viveca said.

"Of course. Well, I'll speak to her. Who was that on the phone a little while ago?" I asked, scowling as Bethany began jumping again. She was such an *active* little thing!

Viveca's arm made a graceful loop and nabbed her in midair. "Telephone solicitor. Here, your pills and your juice."

"Viv, you're babying me," I charged, but my voice was colorless.

"I am not. Drink it all." *And sit up straight and stop looking like a whipped puppy,* her eyes pleaded.

"Well, all right, Madame Dictator! How much longer do I have to take these bitching pills?"

"Until your bitching blood pressure settles down. By the way, I took us off that idiotic ballet committee . . . told Countess Blanche and Princess Leona they could get off their bony asses and do a little work for a change."

"Viv, did you really say that?"

"Certainly I did. Whose pictures do you see in the paper every year? Not *ours* . . . the rest of that juice, if you please?"

I began to laugh. "Viv, you are fucking well amazing!"

"Ah, that's more like my Rosie. Once you start spouting obscenities, I know you're all right. Now you get dressed while I fix breakfast. Bethany, come out, come out, wherever you are!"

Smiling, I watched her unearth the little girl from her hideaway beneath my dressing table. Viveca was still lusty, waggish, witty, and vivacious, but time had mellowed her sharp tongue, if not her penchant for bawdy language. She was wearing one of those floaty caftans in misty shades of lavender. Without a shred of makeup, she was so lovely she pleasured the eyes.

Down the hall a telephone rang. I plugged mine in and took the call. "It's my agent," I told Viveca, not bothering to cover the receiver. "Harassing me again, no doubt." I listened, enjoying his chuckle, and then his words, which made me shout, "What? You're kidding! Who? Oh jeez, no, I can't! I mean, how can I? I'm a mother!"

"What?" hissed Viveca. "What? What?"

"Change that to 'who' and you'd sound like an owl," I told her, and heard Goodsen chuckle again. "That movie option on my book—it's a go! Hollywood, too, and I'm invited to visit the set! Oh, and guess who's playing me?" I named a famous actress who slightly, very very slightly, resembles me. "Yes. Gorgeous Goldie! Can you believe it!" I chortled, our voices colliding as she squealed her excitement. Returning my attention to Goodsen, I thanked him for his call and said I'd think about Hollywood.

Viveca danced around me. "Well? What do you think? How do you feel about seeing your name up there on that big screen? Frigging fabulous, right?"

To be truthful, the prospect of seeing my name "up there on that big screen" gave me a glow equal to the kick of a magnum of champagne. "I'll believe it when I see it," I said, falling back on Mother's method of insurance against the fall of too-high hopes.

Viveca snorted her opinion of this, and soon we were deep in discussion, considering the projected movie from every angle. It was an extremely satisfying interlude. Except to Bethany.

"Skip the bath," Viveca advised, corraling the toddler before she made it out the door. "Just throw something on and let's get moving. Bethany will explode if we don't head for the zoo soon."

"Yes, all right, I won't be long."

I watched her sweep out of the room with the lovely imperiousness that had conquered so much fear and pain. We had come such a long way together that she seemed merely an extension of myself at times. I had expected to grow old with David, I had wanted to grow old with Nathaniel; I would quite likely grow old with Viveca.

Well, that wasn't such a wretched fate.

I had given Lexi the wedding ring that belonged to David's grandmother. Lexi was his only surviving link, and someday, through her children, the Tait line would go on.

I wore Nathaniel's ring, and someday it would belong to his daughter, and in a roundabout fashion his line would also go on.

I felt incredibly wise and incredibly ancient and so weary I could cry.

And in the long run whether I laughed or cried or even ceased to be didn't matter very damn much, I thought moodily, because it would all go on.

And if it didn't, if I ever found out God screwed me on this, there would be a reckoning!

Chuckling at this absurd threat, the incorrigible Roseanna took off her beruffled white gown, arriving naked and shivering in the black confines of her closet. The light dispelled the darkness, but not the chill. It must be fifty degrees in here, I thought, vaguely puzzled.

The aromatic scent of cedar was very strong. I reminded myself to leave the closet door open to air it out.

Taking down a pair of jeans, I glanced at the shadowy space between my shelf and the closet wall. The pale glimmer of white plaster could easily be discerned. I paid no attention to my hand reaching out to touch the wall. By now the gesture had become as automatic as brushing my teeth.

The carpet snagged my attention. Besides the fact that it needed vacuuming, it was badly in need of replacement. But I had become careful with money. Someday Bethany would be entering college and it was up to me to see that the funds were there when. . . .

My mind went completely blank. As acutely real as an electrical shock, I felt the tingle running down my outstretched arm. A bath in fire, an icy shock of glacial waters, a gentle rocking as the earth slowed beneath my bare feet.

My fingers were not touching the rough white plaster of a wall.

My fingers were touching nothing . . . *nothing*!

The world literally rocked.

Unable to breathe, I stood stock-still, too stunned to dare move a muscle. Nearly three years ago to this day I had stood in this exact spot and watched my fingers go through the seemingly solid molecules of a wall.

I had been naked then, and a little gray schnauzer had pushed between my ankles.

I was naked now, and a little silver schnauzer pushed between my ankles.

Trembling, I stared at my outstretched arm. With an inner ear, I heard the sigh of a soft wind rippling through a distant meadow. My own heartbeats throbbed in my ears like drumming hooves, growing louder and louder, and still I heard the wind.

Unbelieving, afraid to hope lest disappointment destroy me, I moved my hand up and down . . . a nonexistent wall!

Silver growled deeply.

"Oh God, *oh, dear God*!" I whispered, shaking all over in the rapturous rush of excitement that came with belief. The door to Nathaniel's world was open again!

I froze, a conflicted shudder clawing at me as my new reality and its heart-jolting implications struck home. Thoughts raced across my mind like scudding clouds, thoughts of Nathaniel and Carasel, Liz and Matt and the babies; thoughts of David and Lexi, of fond friends and good neighbors, this beloved house and the roses I'd just planted; of my movie, my new book, the public and private uproar that would result should I suddenly vanish from the face of the earth; a crazy-quilt of thoughts that threatened to smother the rekindled flame of joy and anticipation.

But only for an instant.

Then I threw back my head with a mighty shout, calling Viveca! Bethany! screaming their names at the top of my voice, yelling like a banshee until I heard my dear friend's footsteps pounding up the stairs!

Another wave of chill air washed over me and I shivered, but I laughed, too, for I knew from whence it came. Grabbing up my discarded gown, I clutched it to my breasts with one hand, while my other hand remained outstretched, fingers spread, holding onto a miracle with bone-aching intensity.

Tears spilled all over my laughter as Viveca burst into the closet with Bethany splayed across her chest. Startled questions filled the air, but I could only laugh and cry in joyous abandon.

Stilling, Viveca stared at me, at my arm, at my face again, her questions answered before I even spoke.

"Viv, you are my soul-sister," I reminded her softly.

She caught her breath at the enormity of what I was asking. Then her lovely amber eyes began to sparkle.

"Yes! Oh God, yes!" she responded fully, knowing, even as I did, that our lives had suddenly, irrevocably, radically changed.

I looked at Nathaniel's daughter and the words burst free. "Your daddy, Bethany! You're going to see your daddy!"

"Daddy!" came her gleeful shout. Viveca laughed and Silver barked and Bethany sang, "Daddy, Daddy, Daddy!"

The air stirred again, cold, crisp, invigorating, beckoning to me, whispering to me, calling softly, seductively. *Come home, Roseanna, come home to love.*

Epilogue

𝒯he ancient gray boulder glistened with blue-white points of light under an alien moon in a star-spangled sky. In its hulking shelter, the circle of grass gleamed with frozen dew. Shards of crystal glittered with pristine fire in the moonlight, mounded around the base of a wild columbine now a dry rattle of blackened leaves. Frost rimed the stalks and edged the leaves until the plant glowed unearthly in the dazzling light.

The lambent silence was suddenly shattered by the sounds of feminine laughter and a child's amazed voice. Beside the boulder, suspended on a wooden mount, a shining brass bell began to sway, its pendulum striking softly, slowly at first. Then it gathered strength and poured its great basso voice into the sleeping stillness.

They heard it in the meadow, down the valley, by the lakeside. The deafening, brassy sound of a bell rolled across the moonlit land like a shock wave of joy, rousing the night and frightening the tiny creatures who made their homes in the shadowed grove. Again and yet again, its voice rode the frosty air, a bold, metallic, impassioned song that startled a heart and stopped the breaths of those who knew its meaning.

Three times it pealed, then stopped for ten seconds. Three times it tolled its triumph over the little hill and down the mowed strip of meadow now brown and sere and dead in the light of a cold white moon. The coded message reached inside a small, darkened cottage like insistent fingers, rousing, stirring, exhilarating. At the foot of a bed, a small dog lifted its head, then sprang to its feet with a canine cry of recognition and hurled itself at the door.

Behind it, a tall, dark-haired man struggled to simultaneously pull on a pair of faded jeans and cram bare feet into suede boots. Laughing, his green eyes alight and suspiciously damp, he cussed a jammed zipper, grappled with an inside-out sweater, raked shaking fingers through his rumpled hair. The truck keys—where the hell were the truck keys?

The last notes of the big bronze bell died away, leaving the meadow lying hushed and still. It lasted for only a quivering breath of time. Then the commanding peals rang out again, calling to the meadow, to the lakeshore, to the small cottage now ablaze with lights, heralding the arrival of one who had come again.